A LITTLE BIT BIT PSYCHO

J.L. STRANGE

This book is dedicated to my family and everyone else who has supported me on this journey. Thank you & much love!

CHAPTER ONE

Worcester, Massachusetts

Is this what it feels like to die?

It's dark wherever I am. The darkest of voids, and I'm nothing. There's no white light waiting. No tunnel. No long-dead relatives offering a guiding hand to eternity.

I never expected to be aware of my own death. That the brain keeps working even after the heart stops beating. It shouldn't be like this. Except—

Ba-dump…ba-dump…ba-dump…ba-dump…

There's a perfectly timed rhythm. The slow and steady drumbeat of life. Mine? It must be, right? Maybe I'm not dead after all.

But if I'm alive, then why can't I feel anything? Why can't I see?

Somewhere in the middle of my darkness, a disembodied voice appears. Gibberish at first, but unmistakably human. I struggle to hear individual words. The voice is female. There's been a horrific car crash on I-290. Three fatalities. A lone survivor clings to life at Worcester Memorial's trauma center.

"…and police say that speed was a factor."

Who is she? This smug bitch, full of feigned compassion—her act is too exaggerated to be real. Everything about the sound of her voice bothers me. Yet she's the one thing linking me to the real world. Hearing a voice should be cause for celebration. It means I'm alive. Why am I so irritated? I sift through a confused mess of thoughts, searching for one that makes sense. This woman and her accident are not important, but the hospital she mentioned is. A familiar place, close to home. In the same city we work. Adam has performed many surgeries there.

That's right…Adam. My husband. My supposed savior. The surgery. Where the hell is he?

I try to open my eyes, but I'm greeted with more darkness. With nothingness. The woman has changed topics. A strike. Grocery store workers. Wait a minute—this is a news program. How could I not have realized sooner? Someone must have turned on a television. Now that I know, her voice sounds too loud and grating. It puts me on edge. Again, I focus on opening my eyes. Again, darkness.

What if this really is a nightmare? I scream, hoping to attract attention, but no sound comes out, no matter how hard I try. Surely someone must be near. They have to notice me. They have to notice that I am *here*. The television watcher, perhaps. Someone. Anyone?

Help me!

Panic clouds my thoughts so quickly, I don't know what is real. The only constant is desperation. Disconnected thoughts. The overwhelming feeling that everything is just beyond my reach. That, if I'm running, no matter how fast or how far I go, I'll never arrive at my destination.

I force myself to calm down. Imagine taking deep breaths, even if I can't feel them. Thinking clearly is necessary for survival. I need to keep calm and really think about my situation. I remember being prepped for surgery. Adam. Recovery room…the surgery. Of course. How could I have forgotten? It's coming back to me. Piece by piece. If I'm having conscious thoughts, then the surgery must have been successful.

Except something nags at me. A single, intrusive thought. When did Adam install a television in the recovery room?

Details. They're important. Adam hates television. He thinks because he doesn't watch, nobody else will miss it. The reason I don't remember him installing one, is because he didn't. It's the first solid clue that something might not be right. That I'm not where I should be. Or am I? Am I just overreacting? Maybe one of our staff brought the television. Maybe I'm just being paranoid.

It's disturbing, but I fight back panic and try to focus on the positive. I'm alive. I'm having conscious thoughts. And if Adam is correct, my other senses should come back soon. He said it will take time to wake up and function like normal. That everything would come back piecemeal. Like a huge power grid coming online. I can't do anything until that happens.

If it happens. What if years go by and I remain in this state? It is one of the risks with this surgery. Being trapped in limbo. Alive, but not living. I've read stories about such phenomenon. Coma patients who survive months, even years, hearing doctors and loved ones carry on conversations around them while they are unable to communicate back. What if that's my fate? What if I never wake up again?

Stop it.

Those thoughts are not worth entertaining. I shouldn't torture myself. I can at least hear again, therefore I should be thankful. My brain is functioning. That means we succeeded. Still, I can't *feel* anything.

Patience, Katherine.

That's what Adam would say. He would say I should have trusted him from the beginning. Patience, patience, patience. It has been a recurring theme during our quest to remove me from the shackles of a body that insists on quitting—on failing. Katherine Powers is not a failure. She doesn't quit. Only Adam has the technology to make that a reality, and from my dark, numb, frustrating mind cage, it seems he has succeeded.

See, Adam? I can be calm and rational, even when I don't know what the fuck is going on.

The swishing of air pushed aside forcefully, followed by a hollow click and a thud, interrupts my musing. A door opening or closing? The thumping rhythm of footsteps and slight squeak of rubber-soled shoes on commercial vinyl flooring. Rustling cloth and the muffled sigh of air being squeezed out of a reluctant foam seat cushion. Amazing what the ears can hear without other senses to distract. Is it Adam? I have no way to tell unless he speaks. I want to think that after seventeen years of marriage I'm more than just a patient, that, despite our differences, he at least wants to fucking talk to me.

Great. Now I've killed my good mood.

Nothing left but a thin veil of irritation. Then…humming. Light and breathy. Female. Fine, so it isn't Adam. It must be Chloe. She's the one he assigned to watch over me and care for me. We'd both chosen her. Petite. Pretty girl. Blunt, but agreeable most of the time.

Efficient and thorough in everything she does. And she doesn't ask questions she shouldn't be asking. She is, quite possibly, the world's best nurse. Even if I don't trust her.

"How we doin' today, Dove?"

Not Chloe. Who, then? Did Adam hire another? This voice is much richer than Chloe's. Lyrical. Vibrant. With the trace of an accent. Jamaican? Some other Caribbean island? I can't be sure.

"I got the feelin' we'll be seein' those eyes, wide awake and ready to go, any day now." She starts humming again. A tune I don't recognize. "Any day now."

That irritation lingers. Claws at my consciousness. What happened to Chloe? We had both agreed she would be best for the job. So, who is this strange woman? And why is she here when Chloe is a perfectly good, perfectly competent nurse? Maybe she cracked? Or betrayed us? With the kind of work we do, maybe it became too much.

"I'll be back to check on you later."

At least someone is talking to me. Someone is taking care of me. That's all that matters, isn't it? This woman, whoever she is, has Adam's trust. So, I should have trust too. Trust that he knows what he is doing.

Patience, Katherine…

***

It's difficult to track days with any sort of certainty. My mind drifts in and out of consciousness, and when I become aware again, there's no real way of knowing how long I've been out. My Jamaican friend visits regularly, and the sound of her voice provides some comfort. Besides the television, which isn't always on, she is my only consistent tie to reality. A tangible link to the world outside my mind. I've kept a tally. Eighteen visits. Even if I don't know how much time has passed between each one, I know it's eighteen more than my husband has made. And the longer this goes on, the more I realize one of my earlier presumptions must be accurate. I'm not in our private facility. This must be a hospital.

His absence is troubling, but there's nothing I can do about it.

Today, for the first time, a tingling sensation appears. A faint itch left unscratched. I try to stretch my consciousness outward, to figure out where that feeling is coming from, to reign it in and gain control of it. Perhaps, if I concentrate hard enough, I'll even be able to move my limbs. Whatever this is, it's only the beginning of something. A spark, maybe, but it's a *feeling* nonetheless.

When the door opens again, I'm already expecting chatter from my attentive nurse.

"Still no change, huh. So, Doctor Rose, be straight with me. Do you think there's any chance the patient will recover?" A male voice. Stern and hard. Impersonal. Is he talking about me? "I believe we have a positive identity, and I need to know as much information as possible before I notify the family."

Notify the family…what? He must be joking. Yet it's enough to elicit a mental pause, the kind that might accompany a chill of unease. Because this man sounds like a cop. A cop is not good news.

"Well, to be honest, I don't know what will happen when the patient regains consciousness. If that even happens. There are signs surgery was performed, but right now we have no way of knowing what exactly was done or how extensive it was. We might never know. Fortunately, there is definite brain activity present and a strong, steady heartbeat. We will try to get answers, but my number one concern is the patient's recovery. And that will take as long as it takes."

"I understand. Of course." The gruff voice is followed by a frustrated grunt. "Well, I'll come up with something to tell the family, I suppose."

Their conversation ends abruptly, followed by the echoing of footsteps as they leave the room. And I am once again alone, with only my mind to keep me occupied.

New people. Possibly police. Something has gone terribly wrong. Adam wouldn't suddenly hire all new staff or abandon me, unless…What if the lab had been raided? Adam might be dead. Maybe he's been arrested. Or he could be in hiding. What about everyone else? Our core staff, like Chloe or Thiago? While the conversation I just witnessed was rather short on details, there is no indication they have anyone in custody. So, it's well within the realm of possibility that Adam and the others are okay. I can only hope.

The tingling, itching sensation grows stronger. Maybe it's in response to my distress. Maybe it's a sign I'm finally becoming one with this body.

CHAPTER TWO

One year, three months earlier

Why did my husband suddenly look so old? Maybe it was too much time spent burning both ends, between his work as a surgeon, his private practice, and countless hours of research. Being twenty years my senior, it made sense, but why hadn't I noticed before? Nothing new happened to spark the observation. We were alone in his office, viewing the results of an MRI. Something we'd done many times. But I couldn't get the thought out of my head. I let it distract me from the images on his oversized computer monitor, because that was something I wasn't ready to face. The results from my own MRI.

"Cancer. To be specific, two rather significant-sized tumors in the gastric wall, along with a much smaller metastatic tumor in the esophagus. Meaning its spread, of course." Deep lines on his forehead, crow's feet, undereye bags, gray hair. I focused on those, not the subtly condescending tone when he addressed me. In the past, my normal reaction would have been to pretend I didn't notice, to not let it bother me, but now I felt myself growing tense. Irritated. Maybe something inside of me had finally snapped.

"Of *course*."

Jackass.

I had enough medical training to know what metastatic meant. That he felt the need to qualify it with an explanation…no, it wasn't worth getting worked up. I wasn't even close to angry, just on edge.

The severity of my illness had come on suddenly and with unexpected ferocity. It started with some nausea, fatigue, aches and pains that came and went. I'd ignored them and done what I'd always done in life. Loss of appetite? Sucked it up and dealt with it. Random bruises I didn't remember getting? Maybe it was stress, or because I hadn't been sleeping well. The problem with being a medical professional was sometimes you tended to dismiss your own symptoms as no big deal, when you should have known better.

Now there was no ignoring it. In the span of a couple of months I'd gone from minor discomfort to constant pain, to being unable to eat, to complete weakness.

"But there is good news. It hasn't spread to your brain." Adam was the consummate professional—his smile a façade that approximated friendliness, but also lacked intimacy or true affection. He held my hand in a limp grip. He was right there next to me, but not really with me. Those pictures foretold my death—his wife's death—and he couldn't even muster a dribble of concern.

"Well, isn't that fucking wonderful. I'll be fully cognizant while I'm on my deathbed." He didn't so much as flinch at the irritability in my tone. I was, after all, entitled, wasn't I? The cancer was in my throat, my stomach, my liver—most of my internal organs had been affected. I had trouble eating. Swallowing was torturous. Keeping food down, damn near impossible. I'd already lost ten pounds. The goddamned tumor diet. I'd be dead in a matter of months, not years. Radiation or chemo would only prolong the inevitable. Surgery to remove the tumors was useless.

So, excuse me if I'm a little upset.

Still, Adam was so calm and self-assured. He believed he could do something.

"I have no idea the window of time we're talking about here. It could be weeks, months, or even a year." Instead of comforting me, his tone remained as clinical and matter-of-fact as the florescent lights that illuminated my fate were harsh and unforgiving. "I'm afraid your prognosis for survival is not good."

There was no such thing as mood lighting for being told I was going to die. No serenade. No sonnets written in my name. Only the glimmer of hope in my husband's eyes, masked as reassurance. He barely concealed his excitement over trying to solve a medical impossibility.

"I'm going to leave this decision in your court. I can refer you to an excellent oncologist, of course. I know two personally, and both are well-respected in their field. I fear, at this advanced stage, there is very little they can do for you. But there is an alternative."

He paused, and I waited, already anticipating what was coming.

"I can fix this. Everything we've been working toward—the technology is there. I can save you."

"You mean like Emily. She might as well be a fucking zombie. You would really do that to me?" To be more accurate, he wanted me to volunteer myself to become his lab rat. Emily had been the first transplant. Only a partial success. Her body was mostly functioning, but one side often froze, leaving her with an arm and a leg that hung limp and dragged behind her. And her speech…yeesh. What a hot mess. She mostly drooled and moaned. These were but a few of her many issues.

Despite this, Adam kept her alive and doted on her. And he wanted to do that to me. No, he wanted me to *let* him do that to me. I couldn't stand his cold, patronizing manner with me *now*. I couldn't imagine having to put up with it for the rest of my life, unable to communicate with him or leave when I'd had enough.

"I know what went wrong with Emily. We'll fix it with you. It'll be different." He didn't say as much, but he was pleading with me to trust him. Sixteen years of marriage and I knew that tone. But the question was, did I trust him? Did I want to? It could very easily be me foaming at the mouth and dragging my limbs someday. "I've been working non-stop to streamline the procedure and ensure that we've reduced all chance for error. What happened with Emily will not happen to you."

I could only hope. It could also be me dying. It *would* be me dying.

In the end, did I have a choice?

"But it wouldn't be *me*. Supposing everything works and then what? You'd have a complete stranger lying next to you." It was a silly hang up. A superficial one. A body was a body, wasn't it? You could change an infinite number of things on the outside, but the inside was what truly counted. My mind would always be mine. At least, that was what I tried to convince myself.

He planted a kiss on my forehead. His lips were moist, like he'd just licked them, and my skin felt tacky after he'd moved away. "You could never be a stranger to me. I'd always know it was you, no matter what you looked like on the outside."

How could he be so sure? Maybe that confidence could be infectious. I wanted it to be.

"We'll find one that you're happy with. We'll be meticulous about it. Make sure it's the right one."

How absurd. My laugh came out in an unattractive snort. "You make it sound like we're shopping for a new car or a set of furniture."

"It's far more important than that."

I forced my body to relax with a heavy breath and closed my eyes for a moment. Was I really that important to him? Adam had never been overly affectionate in our relationship, but then again, neither had I. That was how we functioned. A simple partnership. Still, stuffing away my emotions where they couldn't hurt me had become so normal I didn't realize I was doing it. Until now.

He's more excited about the prospect of cutting me open than worried about my well-being.

That was my first thought. Immediately followed by the realization that it was simply how Adam showed he cared about me. Wasn't it?

When I opened my eyes again, he was no longer watching me. His attention was back on the computer screen. And the pictures of my wonderfully pure brain. Still untouched by the ravages of the horrific disease. Our window of time was extremely limited. A tumor could begin its growth at any time, marring any chance of a future. My future.

"How will we find one?" I asked, but I already knew the answer.

"Katherine, they'll come to us. I've already set up a new sleep trial. Offering $6500 to qualifying participants. That is, after all, what our organization is known for. Sleep research and such." He patted my hand. "And of course, it's time to branch out. Thiago has the scanner up and running. The ambulance will provide another outlet for finding test subjects."

"There's no guarantee we'll find anything of value that way. It's sort of like fishing, you know. We have no control of what ends up on that hook. It could be a marvelous, powerful fish. It could be one riddled with parasites. It could even be nothing more than a clump of seaweed."

Adam looked back at me, silent. His expression illuminated with hope. "But it is, nonetheless, a chance. And I feel, with every ounce of my being, that we will find what we need. I'm sure of it."

I only wished I had his confidence. Medical advancement often far outweighed right or wrong, but when I allowed myself to think about what we were *really* doing, I had a tough time wrapping my head around it. There was a difference between using unsuspecting patients to gather raw medical data and sacrificing their lives.

"Isn't there another way?" I asked.

"How else do you expect to find a host?" His tone changed from incredulous to mocking. "What, do you expect people to line up and offer their bodies to you? You can't allow yourself to get too sentimental in this line of work, Katherine. I thought you were better than this."

There was no point arguing. His attitude had shut down the possibility of discussion. Instead, I stowed the reservations away. Locked them inside me. He was right. Saving my life would require sacrificing another. Finding a coma patient and a family who was willing to donate the body as he had with Emily was a once-in-a-lifetime chance. I didn't have a lifetime to wait for another. If I wanted to live, I had to put it out of my mind.

CHAPTER THREE

This body is a virtual prison. Infinite days and nights in solitary confinement, with only my sense of hearing connecting me to the real world. I've progressed to the point of experiencing physical sensations, but not fast enough. Tingling turns to heat. Then cold. And itching. The goddamned itching that can never be scratched to relief, and all I can do is just *exist* and endure every conscious second. My body is a machine where the settings are going haywire — maybe there's a short circuit lurking somewhere deep within. A misfire. More than one.

I try to focus my energy, channel it into each limb and identify where that energy is going. If I can imagine it, I can do it. Is this an arm? A foot? And then I start to notice light and dark from beneath my closed eyelids and it almost makes me giddy. Little by little. Day by day. Exactly how Adam said it would be. It almost makes me forget that I'm not where I'm supposed to be. That something has happened, and Adam isn't here for me.

But then her voice cuts through the comfortable silence of my room. My womb. Where I await rebirth. Her voice — an unwelcome intrusion and one that thrusts my existence into uncertainty.

"Oh my god." It's little more than a hoarse whisper and a squeak, but there's something familiar. Something bone-chillingly familiar about that voice.

"As I explained, we don't know precisely what happened, but it does appear surgery was performed on the head." It's a man's voice. I think it's the same doctor who's visited before, but I can't be one hundred percent sure. "That said, all the testing we've performed indicates considerable brain wave activity and he's got strong, healthy vital signs. We won't know the extent of the damage, or what kind of mental state he'll have when he wakes. But he could come out of the coma at any time."

He?

He, he, motherfucking *he*. A single pronoun, but the wrong one. Is this a joke? Is this really happening? I've had extremely vivid, lucid dreams before. I remember one from right before the surgery, where I dreamt of plums that grew in great clusters from vines along the ground. I woke up remembering having eaten one, and the taste and texture of the sweet, soft flesh as I sank my teeth into it. Completely absurd when I think about it. Yet it had been so vivid. So real. It had taken several moments to realize that it was, in fact, a dream. Is this such a moment?

But that voice…I know it and I know why it's familiar. I remember. And I know this isn't a dream.

"Well, I'll leave you with him. If you have any questions or concerns, Zoe will be able to help."

"Mama, he got to come back to you." That voice I recognize as my nurse. Zoe. "Some things are just meant to be, and *he* wouldn't have sent him back to you if he didn't mean for you to be together."

My respect for her drops a notch. The kind, motherly woman who comes in and talks to me daily. The only one who talks to me, like she knows I can hear. And now she's spewing nonsense about God? And fate? No god would allow *this*.

"I didn't think I'd ever see him again."

"And yet here he is, right before your eyes." The shuffling scrape of a chair being dragged across the floor is grating to my over-sensitive ears. "Here. Sit with him awhile. Talk to him. The doctor says he might still be in there, you just gotta bring him back. Like tossin' him a life raft, you know?"

"What…what do I say?"

"Just tell him about your life, what you been up to while he was gone. I'll leave you two alone."

Please, no.

This can't be right. It can't be what I think it is. He wouldn't do this to me. He couldn't. How could a husband even entertain the idea of doing such a thing to his wife? Maybe my mind is playing tricks. It must be. Why would Adam choose *him*? The one I wished we'd abandoned. I had a bad feeling about him the moment we picked him up.

There's an extended moment of silence after the door closes. I listen to her sniveling and sniffing, unable to do anything to stop it.

"Sean." It's the only thing she can get out before breaking down again. Hiccupping and crying. More wet sniffling. My mind tries to fill in the blanks of a face I can't quite remember — I'd only seen her in person the one time — and the result is a generic woman, devoid of recognizable features other than puffy, bloodshot eyes and running makeup.

"Baby, it's Theresa. I'm so glad…so glad they finally found you. I thought I'd been going crazy. That night…"

She trails off, and I think again to that night. To the uneasiness I'd had. But this…this body was only supposed to be the last test subject. Before the real show began. So why am I inside of *him*? What happened to Louise? What happened to the one I'd chosen?

"You know, I'm clean now." A choked-up laugh. "Almost six months. I haven't touched anything, not even a drop of alcohol."

I can't listen to her. Don't want to. That means facing a reality I'm not ready for. The worst part is, I can't get away from it. Away from her. Away from this life.

***

Theresa talks to me every day. Poor scared Theresa who's worked so hard to get her life back on track since her husband disappeared.

There's something uncomfortable about having a stranger pour her heart out to me as though I'm someone she knows. In a way, I feel sorry for her. She didn't ask for any of this, and Adam severely underestimated the fortitude of a drug addict in the middle of the lowest point of her life. She hasn't given up on Sean. Has instead used his disappearance as motivation to fix her life. She's been vigilant. Attended meetings. Found Jesus. Maybe answers really could be found in church, she'd said, but it didn't explain the horrors her one true love had endured.

She keeps using words like that, the entire fucking time. *My soulmate. Meant to be. One true love.*

But it's through Theresa's incessant babble I learn bits and pieces about how I was found. Adam and his entire staff have vanished. They left behind the bodies of all our test subjects. Headshots. How fitting for a man who spent his life's work studying the brain, to literally spread their brains across floors and walls, heads blown apart like battered piñatas. I had been the only survivor.

What Theresa can't give me are answers to the real questions.

What exactly had his angle been, putting me into *this* body?

Had something gone wrong with the other?

Was it out of spite?

What *had* happened?

Theresa rests her head, weighted and warm, on top of my chest. Her voice is muffled as she speaks. It has the nasally, congested sound of someone who's been crying.

"When are we ever going to catch a break?" She caresses the skin on my arm. "Why can't we just be happy?"

I am an intruder. An unwelcome voyeur in a private moment that doesn't belong to me. It's awkward and uncomfortable, and I can't get away from it.

"Although"—she clears her throat—"my church group…they've set up a fundraiser online. To help with the hospital bills. So you don't need to worry about money. You don't need to worry about anything. Just wake up and get better, okay?"

Swirling light and shadows dance beneath my closed eyelids. I am progressing. Each day a new sensation. At this rate, it will likely be a matter of days until I can move. Maybe even speak. And then what?

What am I going to do? There won't be many options, at least not at first. If I'm on my own, with no money, no home, nobody else to take me in, then there isn't much else I can do other than masquerade as this man. If the choice is between living on the streets or having a roof over my head, maybe the choice is obvious. Even so, it'll be temporary. I'll find a way out of it. I've always been resourceful. Able to adapt. But this? This pushes the limits of everything I've ever known.

All at once the magnitude of what Adam has done becomes an unbearable weight. He hasn't saved my life. He's imprisoned me. Because of that, I'll be leaving this hospital with a strange woman who thinks I'm her husband. I'll go to an unfamiliar house and immerse myself into a life that is not my own. And I'm stunned to realize that I will do it, if I have to. I will go through the motions. Pretend. Maybe feign memory loss. Because, the reality is, I need to find Adam and in my current state, I need Theresa, too.

CHAPTER FOUR

Past

We received a surprising number of applicants for the sleep study. Almost two hundred. Offering a substantial sum had brought some of the most desperate, destitute people out of the woodwork. Most of them we were able to rule out with a single interview. These were the dregs of society. Lured in by the promise of quick cash.

And then there were the ones too risky to keep on. They had family nearby who would miss them. A spouse. Children. A few of them would become patients, for legitimacy. They would go back out into the world and talk about how they'd been helped by the great Dr. Powers, spreading the word about the medical miracles we performed in our state-of-the-art clinic.

A balancing act.

We narrowed the keepers down to two or three candidates. Healthy young women. No close ties in the area. Potential transplants, I preferred to call them. Something other than human sacrifices.

"Louise Rodriguez?" I stood in the doorway to the waiting room, clipboard in hand, wearing a lab coat. The girl was slightly overweight, with glasses and shoulder-length brown hair. She was forgettable to look at, but that was the least of my worries.

"Yes?" She glanced up from her phone.

"Come this way." I smiled and held the door open while she hurriedly turned off the phone and shoved it in her pocket. I noted the slight hunch in her posture, the downcast eyes, the sprinkling of acne on her chin. She was, according to the paperwork she'd filled out, twenty-two. "My name is Katherine Powers. I assist my husband, Adam, with his research here. I'll be guiding you through most of the testing procedures. If you have any questions, feel free to ask."

Louise nodded.

I opened the door to one of the exam rooms and gestured for her to step inside. She sat on the exam table, while I sat opposite her in the chair and opened the laptop waiting on the counter. We'd already created a file for Louise from the original application she'd submitted. From her chart, I found the questionnaire she'd filled out in the waiting room and transcribed her answers into the computer version.

"Now, it says here you're originally from Arizona?"

"Yes, Ma'am. From right outside Phoenix."

"What brought you out to Massachusetts?"

"I'm going to school."

"I see." But why go to college all the way out here when she lived on the other side of the country? Surely there were other schools geographically closer. I searched for a tie. Relatives, family friends, boyfriend or girlfriend. "Any relatives out here?"

"No."

"Close friends? Roommates?" When she didn't answer right away, I offered a smile. Not a very chatty individual. A textbook example of a loner. "People in the area who we could contact in case of an emergency. Not that there would ever be one, but it's standard procedure to ask. We prefer to keep a phone number on file."

"Oh. Well, no, not really. I kind of keep to myself. I guess you could have my parents' phone number in Arizona just in case."

"That would be fine, Dear." I typed in the digits as she recited them. "So first I'm going to give you a brief rundown of how this all works. Essentially, it's a one-month study. You will be staying in the facility here. We'll start with a series of thorough tests to get a picture of your overall health. And after that, we would begin the sleep studies. Any questions so far?"

She shook her head.

Louise was the last candidate in a handful of young women who had made it past the initial screenings and into this final interview. She would undergo complete body scans, blood tests, stress tests, pretty much everything under the sun, and then Adam would make the final decision as to whether her body would be able to withstand the procedure. We also needed to confidently rule out any possibility of disease. After all, it would be pointless to trade one damaged body for another.

We scheduled a date for the studies to begin, a month or so out. Then Adam decided he needed one more test run. One more guinea pig.

But the sleep study wasn't the only way to find test subjects.

We had a way to listen in and intercept 9-1-1 calls. And an ambulance Adam had purchased at an auction two years prior.

It was late in the day, and Adam and I entered the large garage attached to the facility. He opened the back doors to the ambulance, climbed inside, then held out a hand to help me in.

"This is a little too risky don't you think?" I seated myself on the small bench situated along one side. Adam and I had rehashed this conversation several times since Thiago first demonstrated the scanner. I questioned the morality. Adam countered with logic. Each time we talked in circles, never really arriving at a common ground. Sampling volunteer patients at the clinic wasn't any better, but an ambulance was out in the open instead of behind closed doors.

"Think of the big picture," Adam said. He sat opposite me, on the gurney. "If we're selective, it's a little like harvesting society's unwanted. These are the people hospitals don't want to treat anyway. Maybe they don't have health insurance, or the money to pay for services. Or maybe the staff will patch them up, but they'll be back in a few months and worse off, because they never really learn."

Thiago appeared in the open doorway with his laptop and a small briefcase. He was yet another person caught in my husband's snare. A Brazilian immigrant with a brilliant mind for technology, who'd somehow ended up under Adam's employment, taking care of all the so-called dirty work.

"But what if we get caught?" I leaned back while Thiago climbed inside and began setting up.

"We will not get caught," Thiago said in his heavily accented English. There was no emotion in his voice—just a simple statement. He set up his laptop on the small fold-out table next to me and removed a Bluetooth headset. Not one of those little earpieces, but something you might see a call-center worker, or a teenager playing videogames, wearing. "If we restrict our response to calls coming from specific neighborhoods."

"There's very little risk when you know what to look for. We'll take care of the details, Katherine." Adam didn't say it, but he may as well have concluded his sentence with *so you just sit there and be quiet.*

I bit my lip, irritated that I'd been shut down yet again, but Adam had already implied he wasn't open to any further discussion on the topic. I wasn't in the mood to argue anyway. There was a dull, throbbing ache in my abdomen. An acidic burning in my chest and throat. I distracted myself with Thiago's laptop screen. On it was a map of Worcester.

"I set it up so that when 9-1-1 calls are dialed from certain GPS locations, they are automatically diverted to me as the designated hub." Thiago tapped the screen. A handful of neighborhoods were highlighted, while the rest of the city map was grayed out. "I can switch this on or off at will, of course. Only when we're actively searching for subjects."

"Shall we give it a try?" Adam looked at me. Waiting. When I didn't respond, he opened a compartment that contained folded uniforms. He handed one to me and one to Thiago. "We'll need to look the part when the time comes."

I shrugged. "Of course." He had uniforms and shoes sized for the three of us, ready and waiting. Which meant this was expected of me. What else was I supposed to say? I turned away from both of them and changed, and by the time I'd finished and turned to face them, both Adam and Thiago had changed as well.

Thiago held out the headset. When I didn't immediately take it, he mimicked the motion of slipping it onto his head. "You put it on just like a pair of headphones."

As if I can't figure out how to put a headset on by myself.

I snatched it from him. No, it wasn't the device I had reservations about. It was participating in something I wasn't one hundred percent on board with. "You want me to play the operator."

"We talked about this," Adam said. "You're best suited to the job. Poised, professional, and calm. Your voice, I mean."

We'd talked about it *once*, but I never agreed to do it. Out of the three of us, I probably *was* the best choice, but that didn't mean I thought it was a good idea. But I'd been outvoted. "Fine."

I knew enough about 9-1-1 calls to fake it, and Adam provided a script for the basics. When the first call came, I stowed all my reservations away. I didn't think about how we were playing with another person's life. I didn't think about right or wrong. I shut off the tap to my emotions and became the woman who didn't feel.

"9-1-1, what is your emergency?"

On the other end, a female sobbed. "I can't wake him up…Sean? *Sean?*"

"Is he breathing?"

"I don't know…yeah, I think…he's moaning, but I can't wake him up."

"Can you tell me what happened?"

"He took something…he just…*Sean?*"

Thiago pinpointed the GPS location of the call and programmed it into the ambulance's navigation system. He climbed into the driver's seat and started the engine.

"Stay on the line, okay? There's an ambulance on the way to you now."

The woman on the other end sobbed and babbled incoherently. The ambulance raced through the streets, lights blazing, into a derelict neighborhood and to the shitty, run-down triple decker we were looking for. It was pale yellow with an array of satellite dishes stuck to the side.

We pulled in the driveway and immediately a woman came running out the front door, down the walkway. She was young, maybe early to mid-thirties, but rail thin. Dark circles under her eyes. Stringy, limp blonde hair. Maybe she'd been quite pretty when she was younger, but now she showed the characteristics of a longtime drug addict or alcoholic. Prematurely aged. Unhealthy. Disgusting.

She was sniveling and snotty and hysterical, clutching at Adam's arm.

"He's upstairs, hurry!"

Thiago and I carried the stretcher and the medical bag, then we followed this woman up two flights of stairs that smelled vaguely of cat piss. Nausea tickled the back of my throat and I swallowed it back.

The inside of their apartment was no better. Unkempt. Mismatched furniture. A generally unpleasant smell that was a combination of things, not the least of which was the overflowing ashtray on the coffee table. How did people live this way? How did they get to this point?

Sean, the victim, was on the bed. He was unconscious. Convulsing. Vomit on his chin and puddled next to him on the bed. He'd pissed his pants.

The woman hovered close behind us, wailing. "Is he going to be okay? Is he going to make it?"

I turned and rested an arm on her shoulder. "Everything is going to be fine. Just stand back and we'll take care of him, okay?"

"Yeah?" The tears followed, and her expression crumpled into a tangled mess of lines and wet, splotchy skin.

"What's your name, Dear?"

"T-T-Theresa." Her pupils were dilated, far beyond what was normal. Maybe she was on something, too. That was good.

I patted her on the shoulder. "It's okay, Theresa. He's going to be fine. We'll take care of him."

"Can I...can I come along?"

"Of course." I smiled. Offered another reassuring pat of the shoulder. She was shivering, but I didn't think it was from being cold.

Adam and Thiago carried Sean on the stretcher, down the flights of stairs, outside, then into the back of the ambulance. Theresa sat next to him, clutching his hand. Somewhere along the way we'd have to slip her something. To put her out. Adam kept syringes of ketamine on hand for such an occasion. We'd have to time it right. Before she realized we weren't headed for the hospital. That meant soon. The potential for side effects included hallucination. When she was found, she'd be taken to the hospital. They'd test her for substances. She'd be an unreliable witness.

I sat next to her and glanced out the ambulance's back window. A couple of curious bystanders stood on the sidewalk. Not ideal, but we didn't stick around long. They'd lose interest once we were gone.

It was late and dark, and we knew how to disappear if need be. As if on cue, Theresa slumped forward, eyes fluttering, jaw slack.

"I never would've pegged you as a risk-taker." Adam deposited the spent syringe into the sharps container. Theresa had fallen against the side of the gurney, so her face rested on the patient's arm. Boyfriend? Husband? He wore a wedding band, but her leg obscured the view of her hand. She probably wore a matching one as well.

"I was worried she would cause a scene if I refused her. This was the lesser of two evils."

"Mm." There wasn't agreement or disagreement with what I'd said. Only polite acknowledgement.

The ambulance sped through the streets, Thiago driving, while Adam and I sat in silence. Sean was still unconscious, but stable. Most importantly, still alive. It was a shame, really. A waste of a human life. This one was handsome, boyish and innocent-looking. High cheekbones, full lips, shoulder-length brown hair. He was a little scruffy and unkempt. Average height—maybe a couple of inches shy of six feet—and a slim build. Yes, a waste. How did one go so wrong in life?

I switched my attention to the unconscious woman leaning against him. Questioned my judgement. "Do you think she'll be an issue?"

Adam was expressionless. "No. This dosage should cause confusion and vivid hallucinations when she comes to. She won't have a coherent story to give."

I should have been reassured by his words, but I wasn't. Something clutched tight within me. An uneasy, restless feeling I couldn't shake.

What if somebody believes her?

Theresa would have been able recognize and identify all three of us. Even drugged as she was, even with an outlandish and unbelievable-sounding story, it was dangerous.

Then, there was the man, Sean, to contend with. If she was concerned enough to call 9-1-1, surely Theresa would miss him.

"He would've died, Katherine. A couple minutes longer and that life would have been extinguished. It was that close. At least this way, it won't be a complete waste. He'll be able to provide a valuable service to us and our research."

I nodded, although I didn't agree. It felt wrong, what we were doing. It was something I struggled with constantly. Right versus wrong. Where did the lines blur? I knew at that point, however, I was complicit in everything Adam had done. Everything that stretched across the ethical borders of medicine and scientific research. I was not merely a passenger. I was a participant. Others would not understand.

While at times I had doubts, I also knew deep in my heart that there was a greater good. Not only to save my life, but to change the future of medical technology. How we perceived death. And life.

As Adam would say to me often, death did not have to be permanent. I wasn't sure I believed him, but I wanted to.

CHAPTER FIVE

Present

I'm alone in the room when light and shadow coalesce into a mass of blurry shapes, one indistinguishable from the other. It takes a few moments to register what is happening. I've opened my eyes. I am seeing.

I strain to focus. To turn those blurry shapes into actual objects. I am so concentrated on this task, I don't hear the door at first, until the footsteps follow after.

"Oh, dear lord, there he is." Zoe. She's a shadow above me. Little more than a dark shape amongst a field of light. "Welcome back to the world, Sunshine."

What follows is a flurry of activity I'm not prepared for. Bright lights white out my newfound vision in a blinding blur. Then the questions. Do I feel this? Can I see that. *Can you speak? Can you nod your head? Blink if you understand me.* I've fallen into the middle of a vast swirling whirlpool and I'm trying desperately not to be pulled under.

Help me...

An anguished, low groan fills my ears. Is there another patient in this room with me? Whoever it is, he sounds miserable. Maybe he's dying. Except, in the entire time since I woke up, there hasn't been a single reference to another person staying in this room with me. And that voice I just heard was too loud to be coming from the other side of the room. Which means...

Of course, I already know the situation. I've already figured it out. I fucking know what Adam has done. But that knowledge doesn't prepare me for this voice coming out of my own throat. It isn't overly deep, but it is decidedly male. Unrecognizable. This is not me. Maybe I won't be able to do this after all.

"Easy now." Zoe's voice is soothing, or trying to be. "I know it must be confusing for you, but everything's gonna be okay. You're in the hospital. You're safe. Shhh."

Her face comes into focus briefly—the first tangible thing I can see. She is younger than I pictured, thinner, her hair kept in a close, short cut. Smooth dark skin. Caring in her eyes. But she doesn't understand.

She doesn't understand.

Nobody would.

What the fuck was Adam thinking? What has he done to me? How dare he put me in this situation. How dare he take away my ability to choose for myself. I am better off dead than being trapped in this body. He acted like it would all be the same and brushed off any reservations I had. He's wrong.

Why on earth would I ever think it was a good idea to allow Adam to cut my brain out and stuff it into another body? Even female, it would have been a stranger's body.

"That's it, that's it." She caresses my hair.

Because you were desperate, Katherine. You were dying.

I agreed to let him operate because I didn't want to die. It was torturous having a strong mind locked inside a failing body. Bleeding from every orifice. Wasting away. The pain had been unbearable. I'd seen hope in what he was promising and chosen not to worry about the consequences.

Adam and I never really got into the psychology of becoming someone else. There is no real preparation for what I might face. No plan for how to cope when I see a new face in the mirror. Or hear a strange voice and have to reconcile it as my own. As far as Adam was concerned, these are not issues. He saw bodies as little more than a physical shell. A vessel for the mind. But here, in this moment, realization hits hard. The body matters. It is part of our identity, part of who we are.

And I most definitely am not prepared to be a man.

***

The despair doesn't really go away—it lingers beneath the surface. Waiting. Like a thief hiding in the shadows. Doctors and nurses are constantly at my side. Constantly checking on me, now that they know I am awake. A fucking revolving door of people asking me how I am doing. If I can speak. Do I understand the things they're asking? *Nod yes or shake your head for no.*

I don't dare open my mouth or try to utter a word. I won't give them the satisfaction, although when I'm alone, I practice moving my lips. When I'm ready to hear it again, I add my voice.

25

"Help me…"

"…Help me…"

"…Help…"

"…Me."

"So, you *can* talk."

A voice startles me, but it takes considerable effort to turn my head and meet the man's gaze. Tall and lean. Dark skin. Bald head. Impeccably dressed. He's wearing cologne—a bit too much, and it makes my eyes water. This is the owner of the cop voice I heard before I completely awakened.

I offer a shrug. "A…little."

He nods. Doesn't seem like a very expressive guy. Not a shred of emotion on that face. I relax into my pillow, exhausted from the minimal movement I've already performed. Wary of appearing too able in front of him or anyone else for that matter, because you never know.

"I was wondering if you'd be willing to answer a few questions." Then, as if he's forgotten his manners, he reaches into his coat pocket and pulls out a badge. FBI. "My name is Agent Gordon Nelson. I'm working on a case involving the man who abducted you. Since you were the only survivor at the Powers Institute, I'm looking for anything you might remember. Anything at all could help. We're just trying to piece it all together."

"I don't…know." And honestly, it's doubtful Sean would know or remember anything. He was unconscious when we picked him up. Adam administered drugs once he was stabilized from the overdose, so he never would've woken up. It's not like I'm lying.

"That's okay, that's okay. How about the last thing you *do* remember? Can you take me back to that night?" His words are coated with a thinly veiled impatience.

So, I find myself thinking, what *would* Sean have remembered? I close my eyes for a moment and picture the scene Adam, Thiago, and I walked in on that night. I open my eyes again. "I remember…sitting on my own bed." I swallow. My god, I'll never get used to hearing this voice come from my mouth.

Focus, Katherine.

Theresa had revealed Sean's habit of drinking large quantities of booze and snorting Adderall during one of her many visits to me. How she'd been afraid to nag him for it, that he'd get mad, even though she knew it was bad for him. She blamed herself for what happened.

I recall the scene we walked into, with Sean convulsing on the bed. What would he have been feeling? Would he have remembered anything coherent? "Then I felt funny. Sick. And my heart…was racing. I remember panicking, and then I blacked out." I meet his eyes. "That's the last thing I remember. Before waking up here."

He studies me for a moment. Does he know I'm lying? I suspect he does, at least on a subconscious level. Maybe that is warped by the knowledge I recently came out of a coma. I'll have to be better, though. Whatever it takes to be convincing. This man, this FBI agent, can be a valuable source of information for me. I need to know what he knows about Adam. But I also need to proceed with caution, because I don't know how I am going to approach that yet. Because this man can also be the end of me.

A subject change is in order. "Is he dead? The man who took me?"

The agent's eyes dart to meet mine, then quickly back to his notebook. Is he surprised? Why wouldn't a victim want to know if their captor is dead or not? For a couple of seconds, I regret asking, that maybe somehow I've said the wrong thing, but if he was bothered, or suspicious, the moment has already passed and the cop mask is back. "No. Not that I'm aware. But we need to find him. Before more people are harmed."

What do they think Adam is, a deranged serial killer? Maybe in a way he is. To an outsider it must appear that way. Six bodies left behind. Nobody knows if there are more or how much he's done that they haven't found. I need to be careful how I react, and how I talk about Adam. Sean wouldn't have any affection or sympathy toward him. He would have a completely different point of view. Of a monster that took advantage of a tragic situation. Of losing months of his life.

My survival depends on my ability to blend in. To become this man—Sean. "I'm sorry…my memory…I just don't remember much."

Better to play it safe. Err on the side of dumb. A cop out, I know, but my gut is telling me to play it close to the vest with this one. The last thing I need is an FBI agent sticking to me when I don't even know how I'm going to find Adam.

Agent Nelson nods, stoic. "It's okay." He reaches into his pocket and pulls out a business card. When I don't make a move to take it from him, he sets it on the table next to my bed. "If anything does come to you, no matter how small it might seem, please give me a call. Anything at all." He hesitates before making any move to leave. There's a folded piece of paper in his hand. "Before I forget, there is something else."

With a shaking arm, I take it from him. Sweat coats my face and neck from the exertion. Fuck, such a basic movement. I still have so far to go. Still need to regain my strength.

"That was found tucked in your hand. Mean anything?"

That's Adam's messy scrawl on the paper. I'd recognize it anywhere.

Fly free, my bird.

That stupid fucking man. He thinks he set me free?

Or is he taunting me?

"No. I have no idea what it is." I let the paper fall from my hand. I should be on the verge of losing control. I should want to throw or hit something. But I don't. The anger I *should* have is absent, and I don't know whether to be thankful or disturbed by it. This note was meant for Katherine, not Sean, and I can't let him notice it has any significance. I can only hope Sean's face hasn't betrayed any of this. I need to hold the cards. I need to be the one in control.

Agent Nelson scrambles to pick the paper up from the floor. "Sorry."

"Well, it was worth a shot in the dark." He almost smiles. "Thank you for your time, Sean. I'm sure we'll be chatting again."

After he leaves, I am filled with an unusual calm. Survival mode at its strongest. I will have to push through the unpleasantness as best as I can. I will set aside any personal hang-ups or reservations. Becoming Sean will be an enormous challenge, but honestly, what choice do I have? Adapt or die. That's what it boils down to. If I want to find Adam and confront him for what he did, I must accept the fate I've been given.

***

"How are you feeling?" Theresa. Sean's wife. She's petting my arm, my hair, the side of my jaw. Her eyes, which I now see with clarity, are a warm, honeyed brown, and swim in a seemingly bottomless well of emotion. Understandably, she spends a lot of time crying. It's annoying. I force myself not to shrink away from her, but inside I am consumed by the realization that I don't want her touching me. I can't stand it. Each swipe of her fingertips across my skin elicits gooseflesh. I resist the urge to move away.

"Not like myself." It isn't a lie, but it also isn't enough to keep her hands off me. How long will I be able to endure this?

"I know." More petting and stroking. Dear god, will she ever stop? "The doctor said if you keep working hard with the physical therapist, you'll be able to come home in a couple weeks."

Ah yes, physical therapy. Torturous sessions I endure every day while I learn how to walk and feed myself and use the toilet. That alone had been a shocker. The first time I went to urinate on my own…I knew what I was going to find, but it didn't prepare me for living it. Not when you're a woman, when you've always been a woman, and suddenly you're standing at the toilet holding your own cock in your hand. It's a jarring experience, to say the least. I ended up sitting on the toilet seat instead, partly out of habit.

Most of the time I can push thoughts of what I am out of my head. I can pretend that none of this bothers me. Not when I am faced with *that*.

But every time I start to lose my grip, I force myself to remember. There's an end goal. Find Adam. Confront him. Make him pay. There's no good reason why I should be the only one suffering. He created this situation. Thrust me into this man's body and simply vanished to live his life without me. Well, if he thinks that's going to fly, he has another thing coming.

"I can't wait to have you home." *So we can move on with our lives,* is what she doesn't say, though I can read between the lines. Theresa is crying again. Always fucking crying. "It's going to be different this time. I promise."

She has no idea how different. Her eyes seem to plead with me. *Don't you want this too? Please tell me that you want this too.* Yet I can't muster the strength to comfort her, to reassure her that everything is going to be okay, or that she is going to get the happily ever after she so desperately clings to. Maybe I should. Maybe I should pretend for her benefit as well as mine. After all, if I'm going to masquerade as Sean, I need to make some effort. But this sniveling, weak person in front of me…I can't.

"I'm sorry…I'm just not feeling myself right now. It's going to take some time." I turn away from her, but not before seeing the flicker of hurt flash across her expression. She doesn't understand. She sees her husband's body, his face, his clear blue eyes but none of the things she'd fallen in love with are there. The bond is gone. Every time she interacts with him—with me—I know she is searching for signs of it. And I'm not giving it to her.

"I know, Baby. But you'll get there. I know it." I wonder how long she will hold on. How long will she cling to her memories? "And then everything's going to be fine. Better than fine."

CHAPTER SIX

Past

I watched him often. That man, the pinnacle of my husband's years of research. Sean had been a happy accident. We'd salvaged his wasted body on the cusp of death and Adam restored him to complete health. A virtual success. He'd been kept in a sort of suspended animation the entire time. Alive but not alive. On hold. Ready. Adam said maybe he'd find a donor brain, give the surgery one last trial before mine. To work out the bugs. I didn't think about where that brain might come from.

"Hello, Sleeping Beauty," I said to him. His skin tone had evened out to a healthy glow since we'd brought him here. Most of the chemicals he used to pump into his body had been leached out. We'd purified him. His heart still beat. Blood still flowed through his body. Machines kept him asleep with his lungs taking steady, shallow breaths.

Adam came up behind me and rested his hand on my shoulder. "It's remarkable, isn't it? He's done much better than I ever could have dreamed. It'll be a shame to put him to waste."

"That night, it was too close. We could have lost everything. I think after...after the final procedure—" I still couldn't say *my* procedure. "I think it really should be the last one."

The man's wife—her name was Theresa, I'd nearly forgotten—she'd been all over the news in the days after he disappeared. A pale, jittery, tear-stained wreck of a woman. She reminded me of an animal that had been abused or neglected. Small and frightened. She'd also elicited a fair amount of sympathy from the public. The woman who woke up next to a restaurant dumpster to find her husband had vanished into the night.

The news media milked the story for all it was worth. The phantom ambulance that rode off into the night and disappeared.

Was this the work of some new breed of serial killer? Would there be a sudden rush of ambulance-related disappearances? There'd been a news clip played over and over, a manufactured mini-panic, with the kind of slanted interviews that made you believe this incident was something everyone was concerned about.

You should be concerned, too.

But one stuck in my head. An older woman was interviewed, probably in her late sixties or early seventies. *"I'm scared to call 9-1-1 now. What if I just disappear?"* she'd said. It seemed absurd when I first watched it, but the more I thought about it, the more unsettled I became. We'd created this. What we were doing had real world ramifications. I wasn't comfortable with it, but I'd spent so long suppressing those feelings, it shocked me when regret set in. Even Adam had enough sense to realize the news coverage could be bad for us.

We'd have to shelve the ambulance indefinitely.

"Mmm, I suppose retirement will be on the cards." His tone suggested otherwise—that, no matter what I wanted, his work would go on. Even if he stopped temporarily. "We've narrowed your choices down to three. Have you decided?"

There were three women we'd selected from the interviews. All were well over ten years younger than me; in a couple of instances, over twenty years. Practically children. It seemed a little odd. Adam said that young was better, that the bodies would heal faster. They'd be less apt to reject a new organ. Blood types all matched mine. But did age really matter? Despite his youthful appearance, Sleeping Beauty had to be pushing forty at least. Maybe older. He nearly was my age, and he was doing well.

What would his reaction be to my choice? Chelsea was average all over, unremarkable, and Louise was the least attractive of all of them. But it was obvious he'd entertained fantasies about the blonde one—Deanna. His gaze lingered on her longer than the others. He hadn't even bothered to conceal it. It wasn't like we were selecting formal attire, where looks were the only deciding factor. It wasn't about what he wanted. I was the one that would be living with this decision.

"Louise."

Go ahead, Adam, make an issue out of it.

His fingers tightened on my shoulder for a moment and he struggled to control a breath out. "Well, then. Louise it will be." He kissed my temple and made a half-assed attempt to massage my shoulders before he let go of me.

I'd gotten to him. After seventeen years, I knew this man inside and out. Was that disappointment? I hoped so.

***

The original plan had been to keep Louise and let the other two go after their sleep study, but the line between success and fatal error was so fine and easily crossed that we decided to recruit all three women. Just in case something went wrong. And then I found out Adam had selected two additional women without telling me. *Alternate test subjects* he called them. A total of five. Five women to keep quiet and compliant—a tall order even in our high-tech facility. He'd made his own plans without consulting me, again.

And I was furious.

"I thought we weren't taking any more. It's too dangerous." Tracking data and monitoring patients in a full sleep study was time consuming with our limited staff. More people meant more things that could go wrong. All it took was one suspicious person for everything to unravel. And we couldn't keep them locked in their rooms twenty-four hours a day. What was he thinking?

The stress was getting to me. I felt lightheaded. Sweat coated my face and neck. I tried to clear the growing irritation in my throat, but it triggered a coughing fit instead. It tasted metallic. Blood. I'd coughed up blood this time. I pressed a handkerchief to my mouth and spit into it.

He rubbed my back until the fit subsided. "I've decided to implant another. Before I do your surgery. I need to make certain everything is perfect."

Did he change his mind about using Sleeping Beauty for the last test subject before me? Or was this in addition to the ex-drug addict? While his words masqueraded as love and concern, it likely had more to do with his desire for perfection. It had become an obsession to him.

"I get that. But the more people we involve, the more people that go missing…the more chances someone will catch on. And then there will be no experiments. No surgery. All of this will be wasted, and you'll be sitting in a jail cell while I'm rotting in a fucking coffin, six feet under."

"Calm down, Katherine—"

"Don't tell me to calm down. You are putting all of us at risk, involving more and more people, instead of only what is needed."

"I know what I'm doing. You're just going to have to trust me. I've taken all the necessary precautions." Something changed in his demeanor. A darkening of the eyes and a hardening of the expression. The underlying message was clear. *You dare to question me?*

The retort fizzled and died in my mouth. We stared at each other, two stubborn souls butting heads, but my will to fight was quickly evaporating. Was it even worth the effort? He'd already made up his mind.

When another one of my disgusting, bloody coughing fits took over, he softened his tone. "Look, I understand your concerns. I do. But we're running out of time. There are still a couple of bugs to work out, and I want to make sure I can do this right." He paused to caress my cheek, seemingly oblivious to the bloody rag I clutched. "I only have one chance to get it right with you."

Even so, more people meant more chance of getting caught.

Should I stop this somehow? Force Adam to end all these experiments before any others were sacrificed?

Perhaps I should've let them go, like someone busting into a kennel, unlocking all the animal cages, and yelling, *run free, all of you.* But people had stories to tell, didn't they? If I'd let them go, I'd be right next to Adam on his sinking ship. Guilty as he was. And I'd deserve whatever I got.

But you could die with a clear conscience.

Clearer. There was probably nothing I could've done to atone for my part in his work.

Besides, what other choice do I have?

It was weird how self-preservation warped the mind. How it made you consider things you normally wouldn't. Because Adam was right. We were at the critical point where failure was no longer an option. My prognosis for survival in my current state was not good. The cancer had been aggressive in its pursuit to destroy my body. Yet still, miraculously, there was no sign it had migrated to my brain.

"If eating is going to continue to be an issue for you, I think it's best we start administering intravenous nutrition on a regular basis. Having your body nutrient-depleted doesn't help our cause." His decision to change the subject wasn't surprising. Whenever he saw I wasn't going to back down, or that I was getting heated, he tended to avoid prolonging any conflict. "I'll have Chloe set you up with an IV this afternoon."

And I didn't have the energy to argue. "Mm hmm."

What else could I do?

Eating had become impossible, and I was already losing weight rapidly. It wouldn't be long before I became a skeletal ghost of a person. Malnourished and pale, with gaunt features and sunken eyes. We were running out of time.

"I'd like to show you something, if you don't mind." Adam nodded toward the door, and I slid off the exam table to follow him. We walked down the hallway, past the other exam rooms, back near the animal lab and Thiago's office, and stopped in front of a door. Adam produced a key from the pocket of his lab coat, attached to a bright orange, rubber-coated coil—it resembled a section of cord from an old telephone formed into a loop—and unlocked the door. He gestured for me to follow him inside. "I had Thiago set it up this week. What do you think?"

What do I think? As if you care what I think.

It was a room completely out of place in a medical facility. One that tried to masquerade as home. As comfort. There was a bed with a thick floral comforter and multiple pillows. Matching curtains. A plush area rug. Everything was in completely color-coordinated shades of blue. The room had obviously been designed with care and an eye for detail.

In front of the window, a heavy wooden desk and a chair faced the view. Not that there was anything to see other than a row of manicured hedges and the parking lot. The desk had a small vase with blue-tinted hydrangeas in the corner. Against the wall furthest from me stood bookcases, and each shelf displayed the colorful spines of dozens of books. Above that, spaced evenly on the walls, were framed prints of impressionist paintings — Monet's *Water Lilies* series. I stood in the doorway, taking all of it in, with a heavy, sinking feeling.

This room was for me. Adam planned to keep me here. What exactly was I supposed to say about that?

"I'm not asking you to move in to the facility," he said, pre-empting my response. He was right about the asking part. There hadn't been any *asking* whatsoever. "You should think of it more as a convenience. As your treatment becomes more complicated, and as your illness progresses, it would be beneficial for you to have a place to rest. While you're here."

The room was far too stocked and decorated to simply be a place to rest while I was here.

"It's lovely."

"It is, isn't it? Look, I know your habit of not listening to medical advice and pushing yourself too hard when you should be resting instead of working far too well. This is here for convenience. Because when your body begins to decline further — and believe me it will happen — you will be grateful to have a comfortable place to rest. While still allowing you to be close to the action."

"How very thoughtful of you." I didn't believe what I was saying and it showed in my tone. Was I being irrational? Overly sensitive? Maybe being sick had lowered my tolerance for nearly everything. He was right at least on some level. I did enjoy being close to the action. What I liked even more was being included in his plans as the partner he always claimed I was.

CHAPTER SEVEN

Present

It has been two weeks since I woke, and I've progressed fast enough that I've been moved to a rehabilitation facility. Round the clock care and scheduled therapy sessions—both physical and mental—means little time to myself. I don't know if this is a good thing or not.

"That's it, Sean, you got it." Rachel, the physical therapist, beams up at me as I pedal the stationary bike, her eyes wide and eager. She's nodding. She's annoying. "Just a little bit longer. You're doing amazing!"

I grunt in response. Sweat pours out of every pore in my skin and my body is drenched. The muscles in my legs scream with each turn of the pedals. My heart pounds. The bike is on the lowest resistance setting, and I've only been riding for five minutes, but this is my first time on it. And the bike is a step up from walking. It's progress.

"That's good, Sean!"

Two weeks, and I still can't get used to being called Sean. I have to remind myself that people are talking to me. Pay extra attention. Always be aware. That is almost as exhausting as the physical therapy.

Sean's legs—my legs—begin to feel rubbery, the quadriceps and hamstrings to the point where they just can't push anymore, and I stop pedaling. Winded and feeling dizzy, I close my eyes and try to steady myself. "I...can't..."

Rachel is quickly at my side, placing one hand on my back and the other on my arm. "It's okay, it's okay. You're doing awesome."

I don't feel awesome, but I am alive.

Rachel helps me back to my room, allowing me to walk, unaided, but stays uncomfortably close behind. Hovering like an overprotective mother. I hate it. I keep reminding myself this is temporary. The annoyance of near-constant interference from other people will only last as long as I am here, and if I can just progress a little faster then I'll be free sooner.

It's already late, and I endure a bland chicken and pasta dish with a small bowl of salad for dinner before the security lights dim for the evening. An aide stops by to clear my tray and offers to help me wash up and change, but in the nights since I've been here, they've learned not to push it. When I'm finally alone for the night and in my bed, I toss and turn, restless and unable to shut off my mind. I have this fear, this constant lurking fear, that if I fall into a deep sleep, I'll never wake up again. Every time I start to doze, it feels like I'm falling and I startle back to being fully awake. Will I ever adjust to this new reality? There are far too many things to process. Far too many thoughts to navigate if I ever have any hope of living a normal life. Who am I kidding? I will never live a normal life.

I've been given a second chance, but it will be an isolated one. There are so few people who know what happened to me, people who know the truth, and yet I don't know if I'll ever see any of them again. Which means no matter what I do, or who I become, I'll be living a lie.

Fuck you, Adam.

I trusted him. I hadn't asked for specifics, because I trusted that when I woke up in my new body that he'd be by my side. That we'd be safely in our new home.

I'd obviously been foolish to believe in him.

My brain gets stuck on the same endless loop of questions. Why had Adam put me in this male body? Why did he leave me behind? Where is he?

I am going to find him, no matter the cost, but first I need to make this body stronger.

I sit up in bed. Dim nightlights cast a yellowish glow onto everything. This place reminds me of the room Adam created for me when I was sick. A hospital room masquerading as something more homelike and personal, but it doesn't feel like home.

Getting out of this place will be my first priority. Away from prying eyes, the poking and prodding, the constant stream of questioning. If ever there is a time to keep a cool head, it's now.

Survival depends on my ability to adapt. Even if that means going home with Theresa. Even if that means pretending I'm someone I'm not. It will only be temporary. I keep telling myself that, over and over. Pretending to be Sean poses problems, but it is temporary. It is necessary. It is survival of the fittest, and I am going to win that race. Even if winning means eventually sacrificing my life in the end. But first things first. My physical state is not where it should be. Not yet.

I peel the blankets back and swing my legs over the side of the bed. If I stop moving for too long, maybe this body won't work anymore. If I fall asleep, maybe I'll fall asleep for good. Logical me knows it's an irrational fear, that if it was going to happen, it already would have, but the anxiety is still there. Always lurking. Waiting.

The bare toes of Sean's foot sweep across the cool floor, and I feel the resulting shiver. Maybe someday it will be *my* foot. Not his. Not some suit of living meat I've been stuffed into. I rest both feet on the floor for a few more moments before standing. The muscles in these legs are still sore. Our muscles? It helps to imagine Sean and I coexisting together. As one. Two parts of the same machine.

The doctors who have taken over my care since Adam abandoned me wouldn't know about a transplant. A whole-body transplant isn't something the medical community would suspect, and I'm not about to volunteer that information. It would be an invitation for more scrutiny. Maybe a one-way ticket to the nuthouse.

I stretch my arms toward the ceiling, then relax. Repeat. I do a series of squats. March in place. Jumping jacks. My heart pounds, and I am lightheaded and dizzy. Sweat coats my upper body. They are the minor discomforts of a body finding its way again, not symptoms of illness. I am alive.

This is my routine every night. I am building my strength. While it's frustrating and tiring, and at times boring, I also know it is necessary. And there has been a vast improvement since I've woken. I can do all those exercises without difficulty now.

I'm undoing months of being a vegetable. If only Rachel knew I'm conducting my own exercise sessions at night. When I should be resting.

I can't help it. The drive to get out is one of the few things that keeps me motivated. Staying physical helps ease the mental. Knowing that I could be dead, instead of living and breathing and feeling everything, is constantly in the back of my mind. I'd been sick. In a body full of symptoms that would never go away. This is a new chance. A new life. I repeat that over and over until I believe it.

Still, there are little things.

Even with the focus on my physical therapy, walking is not the fluid, precision motion I remember it being. I have a bit of a limp. A laziness to my step. It isn't constant, but it seems like my muscles get stiff and suddenly want to stop working. Persistence. Patience. I pace back and forth across the room, thinking. I will do whatever it takes to get out of here. To get stronger.

But that goal is constantly under attack by my own self-doubt. No, my complete lack of self. Who am I supposed to be?

Who am I?

Despite the stiffness, I make Sean's legs take me to the bathroom. Under those harsh lights, I force myself to look in the mirror. How am I ever going to get used to this? Any confidence I started to build crumbles away. It's a shock every time. No matter how many times I look at that face.

This is not me.

This is a completely new identity.

I run my fingers along the side of my jaw. Feel the weight of them through the thick, coarse hairs of the beard. The roughness of those hairs prickle against my fingertips. And yet, even as I feel these things, even as I know they are happening, there is nothing more than a stranger standing in front of me mimicking these motions.

That's not me.

That's *not* me.

Not. Me.

This is the scenario I feared most when Adam first talked about transplantation so many years ago. Because identity is woven heavily into facial recognition. If I look at a photo album of my life it won't match who I am now. If I look at a photo album of Sean's there will be no memories attached.

I close my eyes.

Stop it, Katherine.

There is no room for sentimentality or hurt feelings on this journey. Survival hinges on my ability to accept what has been dealt to me, to adapt to it, and move on. The stranger in the mirror will be my ally. Like it or not. Survival of the fittest.

Sean, you and I will have to work together.

***

There is a whole process involved with preparing to leave rehab. Physically, I have progressed rapidly. This body was already in good health. Despite the substance abuse issues when we first picked him up in the ambulance, Sean had been an active, outdoorsy type of individual. Once the toxins were leached out, his body recovered quickly. After waking from the coma two months ago, it's simply been a matter of muscles growing accustomed to moving again. What was at first a grueling battle to keep this body upright and moving is now all about improving on that progress.

But mentally? How am I doing mentally?

There has been surprisingly little focus on that aspect of my recovery. Once the trauma counselor was satisfied I didn't have memories of my time in Adam's facility, or of the kidnapping, they let it go. I've been left to my own devices, to work it all out in my own mind. Then, out of the blue, I'm scheduled to meet with a therapist.

We meet in a small, brightly lit room with two couches, a chair, and a series of generic still-life paintings on the walls. She's young, probably under thirty, and dressed in a charcoal-colored pants suit.

"Nice to meet you Sean, my name is Sarah." She smiles pleasantly, and when I don't offer any more than a nod in acknowledgement, continues her introduction, unfazed. "I hear you're recovering quite well. The doctors say you've progressed rapidly. You'll be ready to go home soon."

"That is the goal."

"The reason I'm here is to talk with you a little bit, make sure you're ready to re-enter the world. I know with coma patients it can be hard to cope with the lost time. You were with your family one minute, and then suddenly you wake up and time has passed. In your case, months. Even if you don't remember the trauma itself, it can be difficult. You must be eager to get back to your wife."

"I don't remember my wife." Possibly the most honest thing I've said since waking.

She flinches. It's subtle—not quite startled, but more of a muscle spasm. She doesn't say anything at first. Just blinks rapidly a few times.

Something caught in your eye, Sarah?

It's probably the last thing she expects. "You don't...remember your wife?"

"That's what I said. I don't remember her, or my life before the kidnapping. It's basically this big black hole of nothing in my past when I look at her."

"How did she react when you told her this?"

"I didn't."

"You didn't tell her?"

"Why would I?"

"Well...because she's your wife."

"If your husband came to you and said he didn't remember you, and therefore had no feelings for you, wouldn't you be upset? I was trying to avoid unnecessary issues." I lean back in the chair and study her. There's something therapeutic about the revelation Sean doesn't remember his past life. And something amusing about watching this counselor scramble around for answers as she tries to figure out how to react.

She must have decided—she's frowning. "Well, I suppose your trauma could have caused amnesia. You really don't remember anything at all?"

"I remember waking up in my hospital room." I crack my knuckles. "Before that, a big, black nothing."

"No memories at all?"

"Nope."

"Not even your childhood?"

I shake my head. "I believe that's what nothing implies."

She's writing furiously on her notepad.

"You know, I heard the doctors talking before I fully woke up. They think I was given some sort of brain surgery after I was taken. Do you suppose they could have removed part of my brain? Or somehow damaged it?"

"I...I'm not sure that's...I mean, I doubt they removed any of your brain. Damage is possible, I suppose, if they were in there..." Judging by the way she stumbles over her words, it is obvious the possibility of surgery or brain damage hasn't been on her radar.

"I think I might have someone else's memories." I gauge her expression. Feel a strong sense of satisfaction when it registers more surprise. "I might actually be another person."

"I...really? Are you being serious right now?"

I nod.

"Who do you think you might be? Whose memories do you have, if not Sean's?"

"It's a little unclear." I'm not sure why it pops into my head, but suddenly I'm gripped in the middle of an intense, violent fantasy. One where I watch her life slowly grow dim and fade away until nothing is left behind. In it, I reach out and crush her windpipe with the brute strength of my bare hands. Soft flesh. Bones that will put up a fight, at first...

Wait. Where is this coming from?

"...and it is very possible that the trauma was so great, you have blocked it out, as a way to cope." She rests her notebook on her lap, calm and collected once again. Whatever surprise I elicited is gone. The professional is back. "I would recommend regular therapy sessions to help you work through some of these feelings you're having. Even after you leave this facility. Eventually those memories will resurface, and you can continue the healing process. It will not be an easy road, but with some perseverance, I believe you can make a full recovery."

"Well. Whatever you think is best." There's no way in hell I am going to continue therapy of any kind after I leave here. The sooner I put all this behind me the better.

CHAPTER EIGHT

Past

Looking back, my life had a black cloud that started following me long before my illness manifested itself. Long before my own husband began making plans to cut me open. Maybe happiness was not meant to be.

Our first and only attempt at creating a family was doomed from the start. I'd had a rough pregnancy, almost like my body was punishing me for daring to think having a child might be a good idea. At thirty-one weeks, the doctors said I wouldn't be able to sustain the pregnancy much longer. My blood pressure was dangerously high and they couldn't get it under control. They put me on bed rest for the rest of the pregnancy.

Charlotte was born a month and a half premature only a year after Adam and I were married. Our daughter. She'd been tiny. Fit in the palm of your hand. Not much over two pounds and spent almost the entire first month of her life in the hospital. Why did this happen to me? To her? It wasn't fair. How were we supposed to form a bond with the walls of an incubator as a barrier between us? The pain, the feeling of absolute failure. I carried them with me until the weight was too much to bear. Maybe I didn't try hard enough. Maybe I didn't do enough. So I shut them off. All of my emotions.

Perhaps it would've been best if she had not survived, because years of suffering and heartbreak followed. And many, many more stays in the hospital.

She had a rare heart defect, the kind that led doctors to tell you *your daughter isn't going to make it to adulthood.* Followed by *you'll be lucky to get a few good years with her.* She'd been a pale, quiet, sickly child that I wasn't emotionally capable of dealing with.

Strange, yes, that I would put it that way. *Dealing with her.* I did love her. Very much so. Yet I spent every day wondering if tomorrow would be the day it finally happened, when her little heart stopped beating, and I couldn't bear it. It tore me apart inside, and instead of loving and comforting her as a good mother should have done, I admired her from a somewhat distant place. Physically by her side but not really there. Not allowing myself to grow too attached. Bracing myself for the inevitable.

Adam, on the other hand, doted on her. For a man who was sparse in his affection, he spent it all in one place. He bought her everything she wanted and then some. There were zoo trips and movies in between doctor visits and hospital stays. Cakes and cookies when they thought I wasn't looking. I hated to admit it, but Adam helped her live the life she deserved to live and he was the only one who did.

It would be the one regret I held.

At twelve years of age, when it seemed her heart had begun to give up the fight, it took all the courage I could muster to go to her side in that hospital room. I remembered thinking, this was the first time I'd ever forced myself to look at her. To really look at her. She was so small, so frail. She appeared so much younger than twelve, yet at the same time there was this ageless, much more mature, almost haunted demeanor. She was a child who was fully aware of her own mortality. She knew she was going to die and she'd already made peace with it.

Her skin and her lips had a blue pallor. She studied me, calm. Too reserved for a child.

"Where's Daddy?"

I stroked her hair. "He's got a few things to finish up at work first and he'll be by later." I cleared my throat. What was wrong with me that I didn't know how to act around my own daughter? "I thought…I thought maybe we could spend some time together."

"It's okay, Mommy. You don't have to." My god, the way she studied me—that look. It was pure Adam, right down to the slight tilt of the brow, the cold, calculating stare. The downward slope at the corners of her mouth that made her appear angry even when she wasn't. Well, that she'd gotten from me. I'd had more people tell me to smile or cheer up in my lifetime than I could count. Funny how complete strangers felt the need to offer unsolicited comments and advice about your mental wellbeing.

"I know you're busy." The way she said it was so matter-of-fact. What sorts of things did Adam say to her when I wasn't around? He'd been making excuses for me her entire life.

I forced a smile. It probably looked every bit as strained as it felt. "Nonsense. I just happen to have the day off today, and we haven't always had the chance to spend time together. Not like you and Dad…" Yet again I found myself fumbling for words in front of my own child. Truth be told, she made me uncomfortable. Closeness to people in general made me uncomfortable. Even my own flesh and blood. And it was my fault. I created this gap between us. Wholly my fault. This tiny, frail child in front of me knew it too. There was no fooling her.

She didn't return my smile. Instead she shrugged. Rested her head against the pillow. "It's fine."

"Do you want to play a game? Or maybe I can see if we can put a movie on. Would you like to watch a movie?"

She shrugged again. "If you want."

But it shouldn't have been about what I wanted. She was humoring me. Just saying what she thought I wanted to hear. It hit me at that moment, like a punch to the gut, how much I'd failed as a parent. Maybe even as a human being. My own daughter may as well have been a stranger's child.

It was too late. I would be powerless to repair this relationship.

Then, the widest of smiles lit up her face and it was like she was seeing right through me. I hadn't even heard the door open.

"Daddy!"

"Hi, Pumpkin." He perched by her side and hugged her tight. Ruffled her hair. All this before he even acknowledged me. "Katherine." He placed an obligatory kiss on the side of my temple.

It was weird how, at that moment, ghosts of things I'd once dreamed about flashed before my eyes. As a child, I'd imagined what my adult life would be like. There'd never been a husband or children, the fairytale so many young girls fantasized about. Maybe I wasn't normal in that respect, but I'd never wanted to be a mother. I'd never longed for that close-knit bond between all of us, the kind that could never be broken. Things had somehow evolved in that way. I should have done more. Instead of scoffing at other people's unrealistic expectations. In this reality, I had done nothing to create a happy family life. You couldn't break what had never existed in the first place.

I realized all of that too late. I soaked in it as I watched my husband and daughter interact and their inseparable bond. A bond I had no part of. A relationship I existed in only on the periphery. I might as well have been invisible in that moment. My attempts to connect were too little too late and only the result of my guilt. All those years I'd gone through the motions, did the things I needed to do without truly being present. Yes, I'd been physically there for every birthday and for every milestone, but had I really *been* there?

This weird, isolated feeling that weighed on me was my own creation. I tried to join in, but it felt hollow and empty and half-assed.

We lost her three days later.

When that terrible, horrible day I had dreaded for so long came, everything I'd kept pent up for the twelve years she clung to life, unleashed in a fury of tears and screaming.

"Katherine! Get a hold of yourself. She's gone." Adam kept me in a death grip. Tears flowing.

"Why won't they let me see her?" Me, screaming. Hysterical. The one and only time in my life I ever lost control. "Why won't they let me see her?"

"Calm down. It doesn't matter anymore. It doesn't matter." Then he was hysterical too, crying, clinging to me, but leading me out of the building instead of to her side.

I never got that moment.

I never got that closure.

I carry her death with me and the weight of a hundred worlds on my shoulders.

CHAPTER NINE

Present

The one thing that has been glaringly absent since I woke as Sean is his family. It has only been Theresa. Day in and day out, just her coming to visit. Doesn't he have parents? Siblings? I can't ask. If I'm supposed to be Sean, that wouldn't be the kind of question I'd ask, would it? So, in my head, I draw my own conclusions. They're estranged, perhaps. Or dead. Maybe he's an only child. In any case, it doesn't matter, because less family is a good thing for me. It means less people to act in front of. It means less people I'll need to disappear from when the time comes.

"Ready?" Theresa takes my hand, and she looks at me expectantly. "Are sure you don't want—"

"No." They want to wheel me out to the car in a wheelchair, but I insist on walking. What the hell is this incessant need to be so overcautious, so overprotective? Is it for show? It's not like I can't walk. After all, I've been practicing for a couple of months now. I had to prove I can do it to be released, for fuck's sake. There's no need for a wheelchair.

As it is, we are forced to leave through a back door. Away from the prying eyes of the media. I hadn't realized while I was inside the rehab's walls, but they caught wind of my story and have made numerous attempts at gaining entry to speak with me. Thankfully, the police presence kept them away from me. Although, judging from Theresa's haggard appearance, it wouldn't be surprising if they've gotten to her. She mentions nothing about it and I don't ask.

It's a hot, humid summer day when I'm led out to the passenger seat of an older model Honda Accord. Silver with a dark gray interior. Four doors.

My first taste of freedom.

I'm slick with sweat almost immediately, but I don't care. Minor discomfort in the grand scheme of things. I sink into the passenger seat. The car is stifling and reeks of stale cigarette smoke. Theresa hits the air conditioner the moment she starts up the car, but I roll the window down instead, wanting to feel wind against my skin, not the same machine-manufactured air that I've been trapped inside the past few months.

"Baby, it's hot. Wouldn't you be more comfortable—"

"I don't care. I want them open."

"Oh…okay." She looks at me, startled, but rolls her window down as well. Shuts off the air. She really is damaged. A complete mess. Too eager to please. She will do anything I ask, no matter how unreasonable, because she doesn't want to lose what she thinks she has. This will be useful.

I turn away to conceal my smirk. Close my eyes and enjoy the sensation of the hot wind soaking into my skin. It's like someone blowing a hair dryer or an electric heater at me full blast—completely hot and uncomfortable, but I don't care. This is what freedom tastes like. What it smells like. What it feels like. To be outside the confines of that rehab center is priceless.

It isn't long before we pull up in front of a dilapidated, shitty triple decker. I remember it from that night. The night with the ambulance. Quite possibly the night that led to Adam's downfall. The end of his little experiment. The beginning of my new life. I shiver at the thought, even though sweat pours off me in streams and rivers. My t-shirt is soaked and sticks to my skin. How in the hell am I going to survive this?

Playing house?

Playing husband?

What if she wants…sex? Or intimacy in general?

Ha! No. There will need to be ground rules. Compromise. I will put up with this little charade for the time being, but there are limits. Definite limits. And the sooner I set them the better.

I open the car door and climb out. Theresa is immediately by my side, trying to help. I swat her hand away, irritated. "I can do it myself."

I cast a sidelong glance at her. Gauge her reaction. As expected, she looks stung, but forces herself into recovery. "Of course you can, Baby."

What kind of person had Sean been? What kind of husband? And how long before his complete lack of affection pushes Theresa to her breaking point? I follow her into the house, up two flights of stairs. Inside their stuffy apartment. My stuffy apartment. The last time I was here Sean had been lying on the bed soaking in his own bodily fluids. Come to think of it, Theresa had been crying then, too. Will I make her cry again?

Will this stuffy, shitty little apartment become my tomb?

"You can lie down if you'd like."

I don't bother hiding the irritation in my tone or on my face. "Why would I? I've been lying down for months." What I do want is a shower. To be alone, if only for a brief few moments. I find my way to the bedroom. Theresa starts to follow me, then seems to think better of it. I close the door, not wanting her to catch me trying to figure out which dresser holds Sean's clothes, and which one holds hers. I choose the one to my right and am relieved to see men's clothing. I open and close drawers until I've selected underwear, shorts and a t-shirt.

I'm about to leave to find the bathroom when…who is Theresa talking to?

I press my ear to the door.

"Yeah, Sean came home today."

She sniffs. There's no other voice that I can discern. She must be on the phone.

"Yeah…no. I don't know. It's fine." She sniffles again and mumbles something inaudible. "I guess."

"He's just been…different since they found him."

"I don't know. Sometimes he looks at me, and it's like he's a complete stranger. Like he's looking right through me." She clears her throat, then suddenly her tone becomes more decisive. "I know, I know. He's been through something traumatic, and he's going to need some time." Then in a softer, more timid voice. "I just worry that he won't love me anymore."

I don't want to hear it. I push the door open and, with clothes tucked under my arm, go down the tiny hallway until I find the bathroom. I lock the door behind me. The water is a welcome feeling on my naked skin. It isn't quite the shock anymore, considering all the time I've forced myself to get used to looking at my new, naked self. But there's still something completely surreal as I examine the hard, angular planes of this body. No curves, no breasts, no natural swell of the hips. Sean has no fat on his body, either. He isn't muscular or particularly defined, but slim.

Is the brain blind to gender? If I didn't have memories of being a woman, of growing up and going through puberty, of periods and sex and pregnancy, would any of this be easier? I'm not so sure. And I'm not sure if I will ever get completely used to it. I might be able get used to seeing a man's face in the mirror, but I'm still a woman inside. That isn't going away. It will probably never go away. The question is, can I really do this?

Or am I doomed to continue life in the grips of this inner turmoil? A constant battle between playing a role and being myself. Because on one hand, I know adapting is surviving. But what is the cost? And am I willing to pay it?

I dress myself and go to the living room. It's clean compared to the night I was last here. No trace of an ashtray, a dirty dish, or even an empty wrapper. Has Theresa really turned over a new leaf? Or is this simply in honor of Sean's homecoming? She meets my eyes as I enter the room, and while every instinct is telling me to go sit in the recliner, away from her touch, I force myself to sit next to her on the sofa.

"Things are…confusing." I'm not lying. She would have no idea what I'm really referring to. That could be why Theresa won't hold my gaze. "I'm sorry. I think it's going to take a while to get back…my memory…whatever they did to me, it messed up my memories. Messed them up pretty bad."

I allow her to touch the scar that runs along the edge of my hairline. I've examined it closely in the mirror many times—it's angry and ugly, and certainly not Adam's best. The bastard. Hack job stitch work. A scar to rival that of Frankenstein's monster.

"How bad?" She seems fascinated by the scar.

"Well, honestly, I don't have any clear memories at all."

She pulls her hand away and lets it drop in her lap. "I…I see."

"And I know it's probably not what you want to hear, but I can't just go back to *us*, because I don't really even know what that is right now. I want to prepare you for the possibility that I might never be the same man you married. Right now, I don't know what's going to happen."

I think, maybe, this sliver of honesty is doing her a kindness. Ripping the bandage off in one swift motion rather than easing it away. Her eyes tear up again, but she forces a smile and pats my knee. "It's okay. I'm just glad you're alive, and you're here. Whatever happens next is what's meant to happen."

It goes better than I thought it would, though I suspect she will probably cry herself to sleep. Still, I've set the parameters. Given her a reason for my distance. It's the most I can offer. Adam has always told me how ruthless I can be. How disconnected from other's feelings sometimes. He's obviously wrong.

CHAPTER TEN

Past

I assisted on the surgery that created Emily. Just like I had with many of Adam's pet projects. But Emily was different. She was special. She was the result of two imperfect halves — one teen girl who was clinically brain dead and another whose body had failed her. Adam said the host body was in optimal condition. It belonged to a teen runaway who'd suffered a traumatic brain injury with no hope of recovery. The donor brain came from the pediatric cancer center. Adam's friend had introduced him to both girls' families and somehow convinced them to donate their daughters to science. I doubted they understood the complete ramifications of what they were agreeing to. But Adam was charming when he wanted to be.

The key was to keep both the brain and the body alive and thriving until the time was right. And it was during this pre-op time period, before we could even declare success or failure, that Adam started calling his creation Emily. Maybe naming her provided some mystical good vibe to get the surgery right. Or the motivation.

The girl's body lay on the operating table, her body still near frozen. A temperature control unit kept her in the right state — another of Adam's inventions. It was to be a delicate, precise procedure. A procedure with no room for error. Adam had practiced on monkeys. Out of a half-dozen there'd been a single success. It had died within a couple of months, but for a brief time it had been awake and aware. At least as far as we could tell. When I expressed the idea that we might not be ready to move on to human subjects, he countered that the only way to know if it would be successful was to try.

Emily was in what Adam dubbed *true sleep*. Maybe he thought he was being clever coming up with an alternate name for it. Something less clinical. As if any of that mattered. As if it made the procedure more palatable. It was still a very deep, very cold, medically induced coma.

Since it was a complex procedure that involved removing the entire top half of the skull, the surgery needed to be performed while the patient was in a vertical position. So, the operating table was adjusted until Emily was sitting, with tight straps securing her in place at the shoulders, waist, and legs. Lastly, a bizarre-looking metal apparatus, which attached to her jaw and cheekbones with clamps, would hold her head still while the operation was underway.

"Katherine, scrub down."

I nodded and went to the sink. Soaped up my forearms and hands, and ran them under the water. Chloe came over and patted them dry then helped me into gloves. I took my spot beside Adam, waiting for his instructions.

Adam caressed the top of her bald head. I was the one who'd shaved off all that pretty dark hair. Left it in clumps on the floor and watched in amusement as Chloe rushed in to hurriedly sweep it away.

He applied antiseptic to the skin all around her scalp. My emotions crossed between fascination and revulsion. There was something odd and unnerving about the attention he paid to her. Something bordering on affection, but I couldn't tell if it was some attachment to the girl or simply that she was his first human subject.

"Do you remember what we rehearsed?" He looked at her with such tenderness, and yet with me, his wife, it was all business.

"I do."

"The life support apparatus must be activated the instant the brain stem is separated from the spinal cord. You have mere fractions of a second, no room for error—"

"Yes," I snapped. There he went, talking down to me again. How much more of this could I possibly put up with? "We've gone over this so many times. I could do it in my sleep."

He stopped, went rigid, and the tips of his ears turned red. "I'm being completely serious."

"As am I."

"If you're not up to it, I could have Chloe assist instead."

"Why do you have so little faith in me?"

"It's not a lack of faith. I'm sorry. I've just got so much invested in this and only one chance to get it right."

It was an empty apology, one that chafed right under the skin, but I relented anyway, scolding myself for being too sensitive. Maybe we were both on edge. Maybe I was just so eager to have him recognize me for what I could do, what the two of us could accomplish together, that anything less seemed hurtful. Like an attack on my character. But Adam wasn't like that. He wasn't malicious. He was extremely selective in the praise he doled out.

I would have to work harder.

"I'm completely focused and ready. Let's do this."

Adam offered a curt nod. I could see him mentally preparing himself, could almost sense the butterflies that must have been fluttering around in his gut. Then he picked up the bone saw and brought it to her temple.

It took a while to do a complete, clean cut and Adam was taking his time. When he was finished, he set the top half of her skull on the surgical tray. I readied the clamps. Chloe wheeled the holding tank with the replacement brain inside. There were similar tiny electrode clamps attached to the nerve endings and a larger one to the medulla. These, in turn, were hooked to a computer. We were a team. The three of us. And Adam was the star. The only one capable of the intricate microsurgery necessary to attach nerves and ensure their proper function.

Once the delicate operation was finished, the exposed brain would be covered with a protective wrapping while the swelling went down and until Adam was able to determine that every connection was in its proper place. Electrodes kept a constant current travelling between the brain and its host body. There would be no way to know if they were communicating successfully until the patient regained consciousness. Bringing her to consciousness would have to wait until everything was properly healed. Which would take considerable time.

If that time ever came.

***

Almost a month had gone by before Emily showed signs she might be on the cusp of waking. It was a little sooner than Adam had hoped, but we were cautiously optimistic. There had been consistent brain activity. Twitching of the limbs, eye movement beneath the closed lids. A whole host of other so-called signs. Excitement and anticipation built among our small team. Had Adam really accomplished what no other doctor or scientist thought possible? Had we done it?

Between Adam, Chloe, Thiago, and me, someone was with her at all hours around the clock. Watching for the slightest change in her condition. It just happened to be Adam who was by her side when she first opened her eyes. He'd called us all in, excited to share the news. She didn't fully wake, but it would be soon.

I was already in a good mood that day, feeling light, cheerful, and optimistic, and I thought I'd do something nice. For all of us. I'd ordered food from an upscale restaurant in downtown Worcester — Level 22 was the name of the place — and they packed up an exquisite three-course meal for me, even though takeout or catering wasn't a normal service they provided. A little monetary persuasion was all it had taken.

With Chloe and Thiago's help, I transformed our facility's cafeteria into a beautiful dining area. Burgundy silk-blend tablecloths, white placemats, candles, fine china, crystal wine goblets, and Adam's family heirloom silver flatware.

We arranged the food on a table against the far wall. Pan seared scallops, roasted potato with chives, salad, stuffed lobster, and asparagus with a balsamic sauce drizzled on top. We put baskets of fresh baked bread on the table. Plates with little pats of butter. A small pitcher of garlic infused olive oil. Two bottles of champagne in a bucket of ice. No one spoke as we set it all up, but nervous energy buzzed about the room and the entire building. The excitement and anticipation of what was to come.

She was on the cusp of waking. Which meant Adam's years and years of research and trial and error would finally be realized. Everything we'd all worked for. The secrecy, the sleepless nights, the constant monitoring. She'd opened her eyes, only briefly, but it was cause for celebration. It meant the rest would follow soon.

I straightened the chairs one last time. "I'm going to get Adam," I said. He'd see how supportive I was. Maybe we bickered from time to time, and our relationship had cooled, and maybe I just hadn't shown him enough how much our work meant to me. How much it meant to all of us. He'd once said I wasn't enough of a team player. That I was too cynical. This celebratory feast was going to prove that he was wrong.

I ventured down the hallway to Emily's room. Adam sat by her bedside, typing on the laptop he used for recording data and notes.

"How is she?" I lingered in the doorway, hands clasped loosely on my stomach.

He burst with excited energy, almost giddy with joy, something I hadn't seen in a long time.

"She's vocalized off and on for the past hour. And her eyes have opened a couple times."

I went to his side and squeezed his shoulder, silently noting the stiffness in his movement as he reached out and put an arm around me. Had I become so undesirable? Sure, I'd aged, but it was minimal as far as such things went, and I hadn't been one of those women who'd put on a ton of weight. Was he having an affair? He hadn't touched me in ages. At least not in any way related to affection. Not since Charlotte had died, two years ago.

I didn't want to think about it, so I put it out of my mind.

"That's great news." I meant it, of course.

"It's better than great." The tightness in his voice further indicated I was an unwelcome intrusion on this moment. It had ceased to be a team effort and was now Adam's creation. His time in the spotlight.

"How about a break to celebrate? We've got the cafeteria set up with dinner and champagne."

He didn't bother looking up at me. "Not now, Katherine."

"But—"

"I can't leave her side now. What if she wakes while I'm gone? We can celebrate when she's awake and I know everything is okay."

"But we've got the food all set up. Can't you just take a break for twenty minutes?"

"Save me a plate." He focused back on the computer screen, and with one response I'd been shut down.

Maybe I should've anticipated his response. I'd been so fixated on planning and setting everything up, that I expected him to be grateful. It had been foolish, wishful thinking. But I put so much effort into it. I thought of everything, and now he was just brushing me off. I should have exploded on him. Ripped him to the tiniest of shreds. He would have deserved every biting word.

But I didn't.

"Well. I'll leave you to your...*watching*." Without bothering to conceal the venom in my tone or to stick around and see if it had any effect on him, I turned and left the room.

Thiago was coming up the hallway toward me and must have gauged something unpleasant in my expression. He offered a sympathetic smile and a friendly wink. None of which I was in the mood to entertain, although it paused my sour mood. "Katherine. Are we ready to celebrate?"

"I lost my fucking appetite."

Before I could brush past him, he grabbed my arm. "Then perhaps you'll join me for a drink? I think we both need a break from these walls."

A drink sounded like just what I needed. Only one or two to take the edge off. Maybe it would dislodge some of the pent-up frustration and I'd end up having a good cry. So I nodded, grabbed my coat and bag from the office, and followed him outside without a word. Funny how Thiago knew the right time to say and do things. I'd never appreciated it enough.

Outside, it was a crisp fall evening. Already getting dark. The kind of night that I truly loved. Would've soaked it in had circumstances been different. I climbed into the passenger seat of Thiago's pickup truck and put on my seatbelt.

Thiago stayed silent as he slid into the driver's side and started up the truck. Maybe he sensed my mood was off. Was he going to let me vent at my own pace or pry for answers?

"I'm not sure how much more of this I can take, Tee." I looked out the window rather than at him.

"You should not let it bother you," he said softly. "Dr. Adam gets himself so wrapped up in his projects he doesn't see anything else."

I snorted. "He hasn't seen *me* in a good many years."

"That isn't true." He probably didn't believe that any more than I did, but effort counted for something.

"I fantasize about leaving. All the time. But where would I go? What would I do with my life?"

"You could, if you wanted."

I laughed. "No. No I couldn't. I'm far too tangled in his web to get free. I know too much. I've helped him do all these...awful things. He would never let me go." I paused and considered it, a little stunned I'd said it out loud to someone. The desire to leave my marriage, to abandon our life, had been one of my deepest, darkest secrets. One I'd never dared to entertain for more than a few fleeting seconds in a moment of frustration. But it was little more than a fantasy and probably safer for me to stay. I wouldn't escape alive. "Or he would let me go, and then send you after me with a bullet."

"Then that makes two of us who are caught in his web." He stared at the road in front of him, before offering a brief glance in my direction. "Although, if he ever ordered me to kill you, I wouldn't do it."

I wanted to believe him. That maybe I'd found a comrade, at least one light spot in the darkness that had slowly enveloped my life. But could I? Could I truly believe it? My trust was not easily given, and even Thiago, who gave the illusion he'd bend over backwards to help me—what did I really know about him?

"You know what?" Screw Adam. I shouldn't have let him get to me. I shouldn't have let him ruin what I'd created."

"What?"

"I think I am hungry after all. Let's go back and eat, shall we?"

Thiago laughed. "Whatever the lady wants."

CHAPTER ELEVEN

Present

It's a little after midnight and I'm still wide awake. Sleep doesn't come to me easily, but then again it never really has. I've always had trouble turning my mind off. This night is no different, except for the restlessness, which is so pronounced that leaving the house seems the only way to remedy it.

I wait until Theresa is asleep before leaving. Since I've already elected to sleep on the living room sofa, rather than in the bedroom with her, it's only a matter of being quiet. Does Sean have a vehicle of his own? There's only Theresa's Honda as far as I can tell. He does, at least, have a license. Theresa handed me his wallet earlier. There's a smiling Sean. Slightly less bearded. Tanned. Shoulder-length hair with streaks of blond that many women pay big bucks to duplicate in the salon — he resembles an aged surfer boy, the kind of man who flees responsibility and spends weekends getting high and drinking cheap beer. All this I get from a single driver's license photo. That and a birthdate. October 15th. Sean is 41.

I slide Theresa's keyring off the hook in the hallway and slip out the door, locking it behind me. She won't hear me leave over the sound of the air conditioner, will she? I don't care.

A rush of adrenaline hits the minute I sink into the driver's seat and turn the key in the ignition. I've been restless, needing freedom. Needing this. And I know exactly where I'm heading — it's instinct really. A few exits down the interstate and soon I'm following a familiar network of winding roads to the quiet residential neighborhood I once called home.

Are the FBI or the police watching the house? I coast to a stop at the curb and shut the lights off. Then the engine. I sit there, silent and still, watching and listening. The buzzing and chirping of insects and frogs fill the night air. A light breeze lilts through the open car windows like a lover's caress. So different from the dump I am staying in now.

We had it made, Adam and me. A big house. Lakefront property in a quiet, secluded neighborhood.

The house is dark now. Empty. Probably completely combed through, but what if Adam has left something behind? I need to know. Anything that might be a clue to his whereabouts. I know where he stashes things. I know the combination to the wall safe.

I pause and rest my fingers on the car door handle, indecisive. I know the security code to get into the house, too. Unless Adam has changed it. But he hasn't changed it in the ten plus years we lived in that house. Why would he do it now?

I glance over my shoulder. There's nobody that I can see, but that doesn't mean somebody isn't watching. In a neighborhood such as this, if people see a strange car hanging around, they're more apt to call the police than anything. Even in the middle of the night when most people are sleeping. Especially in the middle of the night. And now, in this body, I don't belong here. I have no excuse.

I have to operate under the assumption that I'm being watched. No, I'll come back another night. Maybe park at the public beach a couple of streets over and hoof it. Trek through the woods, if necessary. Blend in and be inconspicuous. Not here like this.

But I need to get inside that house.

***

It's almost two by the time I pull into the driveway at Sean's house. I refuse to call it my house. It doesn't feel like my home. I'm all about compromise and survival, but it's merely an acting job. I don't feel any of it.

There's a light on in the apartment. I haven't left any lights on. Which means my trip hasn't gone unnoticed.

She's sitting in the recliner in the living room, her legs tucked to the side. Eyes red.

"Where did you go?"

"I couldn't sleep."

"So, you just…" She seems to choke on her words. "You took off, in the middle of the night? Without telling me? The doctor said…you shouldn't drive yet. That your mind could still be foggy. Your reaction time might be off."

"My mind is completely fine." It comes out sounding harsh. Maybe a bit defiant.

Question my mental state, will you?

"And there was hardly anybody on the road." When this doesn't satisfy her, I try a different tack. "I feel confined, Theresa. Trapped. I've been lying in a bed for fucking months, with people monitoring every move I make. Do you know what it's like to have someone bathe you and wipe your fucking ass and rush to help you every time you so much as dare to blink? Do you have any fucking idea what that's like?"

My god, she's cowering. A sniveling animal. Without even realizing it, I've raised my voice, and this male voice has power. It's the kind of voice people listen to without accusing it of being hysterical. Or shrill. Or overreacting.

"No," she whispers.

I smile, because it's a victory. I'm not feeling happy or reassured. But I am winning. "That's right, you don't. I was sitting on that couch and it felt like the walls were closing in on me, and the air was smothering. Suffocating. I needed to leave. I needed freedom."

"But I was worried…"

She doesn't have much fight. She doesn't want conflict, and she most definitely isn't used to standing up for herself. What kind of relationship did they have? Was Sean abusive? Did he cut her down? Or is she simply a docile, obedient wife who will do anything to keep her husband? How curious. "Well, next time I'll leave a note."

Maybe it's selfish. If it had been me, if I was Theresa, and my husband was the one leaving in the middle of the night, I'd be angry too. So maybe, just maybe, I have the tiniest sliver of sympathy for her. Or I can at least understand where she's coming from. But that's as far as it goes. The fact is, I'm not Sean. I don't want to be Sean. And I most certainly don't owe this woman anything, least of all an explanation.

But then...my existence depends on her right now, doesn't it? Sean doesn't have a job to go back to. I need her. That kills me. To get what I want, I need to rely on this strange woman. At least for now. What a fucked-up predicament Adam has put me in.

CHAPTER TWELVE

Past

It was obvious very early on in her recovery that something had gone wrong with Emily. She responded to some stimuli. She could see, hear, and feel and we were reasonably sure she could smell. But intelligence, understanding, connecting the dots of basic logic— these were things that she was lacking.

"Darling, over here." Adam rang the tiny bell next to her ear. It dangled from a blue ribbon, which he pinched between his thumb and forefinger. Her body twitched, a recurring neurological tic that hinted toward a deeper issue within the nervous system. All of her movements had a slight jerkiness. There was no fluidity when she finally did turn her head toward the sound. A continuous string of drool dripped from the corner of her mouth and ran down the side of her chin. "Bell. That's a bell. Can you say bell?"

She tilted her head, seemingly fascinated by the sound, then reached out and snatched it from Adam's hand. She immediately shoved it into her mouth.

"No!" Adam scolded. "Spit it out." He held out his outstretched palm in front of her face and she sniffed it. An overflowing fountain of drool poured from her mouth as she chewed on the bell. "That's not food. Spit it out."

As far as I could tell, he may as well have been talking to a wall. There was nothing to indicate she understood what he was saying to her. Just the crunch of her teeth on the tiny metal bell. Adam shined a flashlight in her eyes. It was sufficient distraction for him to grab hold of the end of the ribbon and pull the bell out of her mouth.

"Something obviously went wrong," I said from behind them, right out of Emily's line of vision, watching all of it transpire.

"Not now, Katherine." Adam didn't bother trying to conceal the annoyance in his voice. "We've still got many tests to run. It's only been a couple weeks since she's woken."

"Maybe it's you who needs to wake up. She's not going to get any better than this. And *this* is no better than an infant."

"I said, *not now*." It was a warning. A dare, perhaps, to push the issue any further.

"I never said *this* wasn't a miraculous thing." I waved my hand at Emily. She was staring at me now, watching every word fly out of my mouth. "The fact that she's breathing and upright is something nobody else has ever accomplished. You are light years ahead of the medical community. Obviously. I'm just suggesting that trying to teach her things probably isn't going to have the results you want. Maybe you shouldn't waste your time."

"Nothing about this is a waste of time," he snapped. Something resembling a growl gurgled out of Emily's throat. Adam petted her nearly hairless head to calm her. There was about an inch worth of growth. Soft fuzz, like a little duckling.

"I feel like you have more expectations for it than is reasonable."

He was making a significant effort to keep his temper under control. "Her, Katherine. I have high expectations for *her* because *she* is important. *She* is priceless. Nobody has done what we have done with even a fraction of this success. My god, you of all people should understand this."

I didn't like the tone he was taking with me and fired back. "I get all that. I just think that you should lower your expectations. She clearly doesn't have the mental capacity."

"That child is the single most important living piece of medical science on this planet. Don't you understand what we've done?"

"I do. I understand it very well. But you've got blinders on. You're trying to squeeze water from dry sand."

Before Adam could respond, Emily let out a howl and charged me. She latched on and knocked me flat on my back, fingers digging into my flesh, teeth buried in my neck. She growled like an attack dog. Pain radiated from the bite, down my neck, into my shoulder. I fought to push her off. To dislodge her teeth from my neck. She hadn't broken the skin yet, but she was biting hard, and it was only a matter of time before she drew blood.

"Get this fucking *thing* off me!"

It all happened in a matter of seconds, but Adam stood there, watching. Maybe it was only a delayed reaction. Or indecision. Shock. Only when I started hitting her head did Adam spur into action. He came around her from behind, placed a hand on either side of her face, and gently tugged her back. Then he whispered soothing words in her ear.

"It's all right, Darling. Shhh. It's all right."

He wasn't soothing me, the one getting attacked, but the monster latched onto my flesh. And yet, even though he wasn't whispering to me—even though my own husband lacked the capacity to care for me, and instead chose to coddle this creature—I closed my eyes and listened to his voice. I let my body go limp. It was like letting myself drown. I floated in the darkness. Sinking. Slowly. The pain receded. The voices and snarling were mere echoes. Drifting further away.

I think I left my body for a time and was simply a consciousness floating. Nothing but a detached piece of myself. Maybe I didn't care anymore. Something inside of me had snapped and this was the last straw.

Still sinking.

"Katherine?" The voice was so far away. Not Adam. "Kat?" Chloe. The only one who ever shortened my name. I'd told her I didn't like it when we first met, but she'd ignored that and continued to call me Kat. Which after a while, kind of grew on me. I never admitted that out loud. "Let's go get you cleaned up, 'kay? You got a little bit of blood on you. Can you sit?"

Then Thiago was at my side, an arm around me, lifting me to my feet. I recognized his scent before anything. He always wore this cologne, or maybe it was deodorant, but it was so muted you could hardly smell it.

Chloe held one arm, Thiago the other, and somehow, I walked. Stuck in a fog and barely breathing. Sunken in a dark pit I didn't want to crawl out of. Why should I? What exactly was waiting for me on the surface? We floated down the hallway. I knew where we were headed. Chloe's little exam room. They might as well have been leading me to my death.

"That sick fucker," Chloe muttered under her breath. At least, that was what I thought she'd said. Maybe I'd imagined it. Maybe I'd been the one who said it.

They coaxed me into a chair, even though I didn't remember sitting. Chloe popped open the latches on the first aid kit and laid it on the table next to me. Rummaged through it and pulled out a couple of packets of gauze. "Antiseptic please?" She held an outstretched hand toward Thiago. When he made no move to get it, Chloe gestured impatiently toward the cabinet to her right. "Top shelf."

Thiago opened the cabinet and found a bottle of antiseptic. Chloe took it from him, saturated one of the gauze pads, and began to clean the wound on my neck. I barely felt the stinging or the coolness.

"My god, she really did a number." Chloe frowned. With a firm grip, she tilted my head at an angle. "There's going to be bruising. A lot of it. Jesus, how long was this going on before we got there?"

I couldn't find the voice to answer her. Just shook my head. Blinked away the tears as I started to return to my body and emotions appeared. Unwanted emotions. Something I never dared show anyone, not even Adam. That arrogant asshole. I choked back the tears.

Not now, Katherine. Not here in front of them.

It was not the time to be weak. They were both looking at me with pity, probably seeing a weak woman. A woman who stayed, despite the fact that her husband was a cold heartless bastard.

Why did I stay?

Why the fuck did I stay?

Chloe finished cleaning the wound. She covered the entire area with a fresh bandage and applied tape along the edges. I imagined invisible hands filling the cracks of my façade at the same time. Patching the holes. Repairing the thin shell that covered my existence.

"It wasn't your fault." Chloe's voice was soft and soothing. She threw away the wrappers from the gauze and packed up the unused supplies. "You do realize that, right?"

"I should've just walked away." It almost sounded like I was listening to someone else talk rather than my own voice. "Besides, I had no idea she was dangerous."

"It doesn't matter. My god, it was like he didn't even care that she was attacking you." It felt odd to witness someone so vehemently upset on my behalf. Chloe had always seemed so even. So subdued. Subservient.

It was the first time I'd ever seen her disapprove of or even disagree with anything that Adam said or did. She'd always gone along with what he wanted like a devoted employee.

Both Chloe and Thiago had swooped in for the rescue this time. Maybe it was pity. Maybe it was remorse for turning a blind eye other times they could've intervened.

"I'll be fine." I stood, forcing myself to be steady. Eager to be away from their prying eyes. "I'll just need to remember to stay away from that...*thing* he insists on keeping alive."

It might have been my imagination, but I noticed a slight twitch in Thiago's expression. A crack in the impenetrable. So fast, if I had blinked one more time I might have missed it. What was that about?

"I'll check on your wound tomorrow and change the bandages. Please let me at least do that." Chloe squeezed my shoulder.

"It's fine." The situation caused embarrassment on a level I'd never experienced. Usually, if Adam did something or said something, I could brush it off, unnoticed. Pretend. Not here. Not now. It was obvious he had put this creature above even me, his own wife. Maybe it was time to remove myself from the project. Put my foot down. Refuse to be involved with the entire project and let him come crawling to *me* for help. "I'll be fine. Thank you. Both of you."

CHAPTER THIRTEEN

Present

One. Zero. One. Nine. Seven. Two. That sequence of numbers might as well be etched into my brain. I don't have to think about it. Once I hit enter and the green light comes on, signaling the alarm has been disarmed, I twist the knob on the back door and push it open. Careful not to catch the bolt on the strike plate, I quietly shut the door behind me.

The air inside the house has a stale, dead quality to it. Faintly musty or moldy, the smell of damp laundry left in a pile instead of hung to dry. Like the humidity has started to breed toxic life into the walls. The carpets, too. It's unpleasant and unlived in. The smell of a house left to decay. Or maybe a life left to decay.

Our life.

Isn't that what Adam has done? Left our future together in a rotting tangled mess? There is no future together. He has abandoned me. True he's given me a body, but it isn't the right one. It isn't the one I chose. It isn't even the right fucking sex. And then he disappeared.

Every *man* for himself.

Adam covered his own ass while leaving me in a strange body, where I have to pretend my life is something it isn't, and I can't even do that right. I can't pretend. This whole situation is more complicated than I first thought and I loathe him for it. No, Adam will pay. If it really is every man for himself, then I will be the one to come out on top.

I creep up the dark staircase to the second floor. Past Charlotte's bedroom, left exactly as it has been since the day of her death. At the end of the hall is the master bedroom. I still remember every step, every creak, even in the darkness. Even in this body. Some things you never forget.

Everything is untouched, left undisturbed. For months, probably. I sit on the edge of the bed. Yet the strange thing is I feel detached from this house. It's familiar, but I don't really care about it. When did that happen? I used to love this house.

I sit for a few moments longer. Maybe this isn't home anymore either. Maybe I have no home.

At least it's quiet. I'm alone, with my thoughts. I click on the tiny flashlight I have stuffed in my pocket, get up from the bed, and start opening drawers. He's left all the clothes. I pull them out, piece by piece, and toss them onto the bed. Nothing hidden in the drawers. After that, I move on to the safe. Eight. Five. Seven. Zero. Click.

I open the door. Inside, there are two envelopes. One fat, one thin. My jewelry, our stock certificates, Adam's rare coin collection — they're all gone. Our passports are gone. I open the thicker of the two envelopes. It's cash. All hundreds. Easily ten grand, but I'm not going to count it. Has he left it for me? Just in case I'm resourceful enough to enter our old home and look for him. Why else would that be in there? I tuck the money back inside and open the other envelope. This one holds a folded-up piece of paper.

My hands shake as I open it.

In Adam's scrawling penmanship:

K,

If you are reading this, obviously our little endeavor was a success. I'm sure you will be angry. I'm sure you will have questions. And I would advise you to let it go. This is an opportunity for growth. A new beginning.

Your life is a gift. Enjoy it. Until we meet in the afterlife.

Yours,

A.

That solidifies in my mind, without question, Adam has abandoned me on purpose. He has no intention of ever finding me. He doesn't want me to find him. I crumple the note and whip it across the room. Sure, I suspected…but this is proof. Irrefutable proof. And ironically, I don't care. I don't feel anything. Why is that? Shouldn't I be angry? Shouldn't I want to destroy every trace of him and our lives together inside this house? I tuck the envelope inside the waistband of my shorts, pick up the nearest thing—a small abstract glass sculpture we purchased on our trip to Paris—and hurl it against the far wall. A fountain of glass shards sprays back at me.

Years worth of possessions—my collection of glassware, the Hummel figurines Adam's grandparents had left to us, framed photos—I don't stop until I smash all of them. Useless things. Reminders of a life I once had. And now? What do I have? The life of a former drug addict. A man's body that I don't want. A man with a fucking wife. This is unacceptable. He will not get away with this.

I exit the bedroom. Destroying everything in there was somewhat satisfying, but as I walk through the house, toward the back door, I'm completely calm and levelheaded. There's no adrenaline rush. It's surprising, but maybe I'm better off. It's easier to keep a clear head when you're not overloaded with emotion.

I slip out the back door, reset the alarm, and stride across the backyard. What am I going to do? Adam has been several steps ahead of me. Of course he isn't going to leave anything behind to help me find him. I need to be more resourceful. People don't simply disappear. I've been married to the man for almost eighteen years, for fuck's sake. There's no way he remembered to cover everything.

Think, think, think Katherine.

I'm so deep in thought, I don't register the twig snapping or the crunch in the underbrush off to my left until I'm confronted.

"Stop right there, hands where I can see them. Police." The faceless voice comes from the darkness, but the minute the flashlight shines in my eyes, I freeze and hold my hands up. He approaches, his flashlight trained on me, over-bright and still focused on my face. Probably on purpose. Probably to confuse me. Or to intimidate me. Maybe both. He assesses me for a long while. "Mind telling me what you're doing here?"

"My dog got loose." The lie falls out before I even realize I'm doing it. "I've been walking around for almost two hours trying to find him."

The cop stares at me a moment before responding. "You do realize this is private property."

"Yes, and I apologize. I'm parked over by the boat landing. We were walking one of the trails, and there was a squirrel or something that got his attention. He got away from me."

Again with the staring. The light is still focused right in my eyes. Part of me wants to lash out with a snarky comment, but if there's a time to exercise self-control, it's now.

"What kind of dog?"

"Yellow lab. His name is Chester. Friendly, dumb as a box of rocks. But he's a runner."

"And you always take him for walks this late at night?"

"I couldn't sleep."

"The park closes at 9:00, you know." He's a persistent motherfucker, quick with his tongue, but I'm going to win this battle.

"I wasn't aware."

"There are signs."

"I didn't see them. I apologize."

He pauses again. "May I see some ID?"

I'm not going to let this bastard intimidate me. "Of course. My wallet's back in the car." If I was wearing a woman's skin instead of Sean's, I have the feeling he wouldn't have been asking me for ID either. He would give me a stern warning and send me on my way. Then again, most trouble with authorities can be avoided by simply showing polite respect instead of being contentious. Good behavior is gender blind. So is getting pegged as a troublemaker. I don't need that.

"Well, then. Let me give you a ride."

He leads me back to the cruiser parked by the curb and opens the rear door. I slide into the seat and let out a slow, calming breath. I can't tell if the cop is buying anything I've told him, but I know I have to ride it out. Acting nervous will arouse his suspicion even more. I will keep playing it cool. Pretend I'm just some guy with dumb luck. The cop pulls into the parking lot a couple of streets over, next to Theresa's little Honda.

He gets out and opens the rear door of the cruiser to let me out.

I nod and smile pleasantly. Act exactly as I would have in my old body, but his expression remains stoic. Act natural is my plan.

Forget that I've been stupid and careless. Forget about the cash that I shoved down my pants and has since slid into my underwear. Just make this police officer believe I'm some poor sucker who's been out walking his dog and lost him.

I left Sean's wallet in the center console. I purposely take my time going through it and pull out Sean's license, then hand it to the cop.

"You're quite a ways from home." In other words, I don't belong here. It's suspicious that I'm in this neighborhood to begin with, let alone at night. I knew this was a risk. I knew it would be an issue if I came back. He holds the license out to me and I take it.

"Like I said, I couldn't sleep. I didn't want to wake my wife, so I took the dog and we just left. I used to work as a landscaper in this area, and I discovered the trail then. I figured I'd take a quick walk and then I'd go home." It's a story that makes sense. Theresa told me that Sean was a landscaper. There's no way to prove he didn't work here at one time without going door to door and asking every resident. Even then, these people wouldn't necessarily even know what the workers look like.

"I see. Well, you best be on your way. The park is closed."

"Thank you, Officer. I'm sorry if I've caused any trouble. But if you don't mind, I want to take one more sweep along these streets to see if I can find Chester. My wife would be pretty pissed if she found out the dog was missing. I promise I'll be quick about it."

He seems to consider this before offering a curt nod, and soon I'm back behind the wheel of the car, windows rolled down. Driving at fifteen miles an hour and whistling for a dog that doesn't exist while the cop follows close behind me. I clutch the steering wheel tight, and finally, once we reach the stop sign at the end of the street, I turn left, and he goes right. I can breathe again.

By the time I reach Sean's home, it's about three o'clock and I'm exhausted. There's no sign that Theresa has woken and realized I left. At least she isn't waiting up for me this time. I kick off my shoes, stretch out on the couch, and pull the thin blanket over me. The envelope of money Adam left behind is now tucked beneath the sofa cushions. I'll find a better hiding place tomorrow when Theresa is at work.

I've been stupid. Impatient. Careless. Thankfully this time it has worked it in my favor. But next time, I'll have to be more careful. I can't afford any more stupid mistakes.

CHAPTER FOURTEEN

Past

I had this wooden jewelry box. It resembled a small treasure chest with thick bands of iron around the edges and an elaborate forest scene carved into the top and sides. I'd purchased it from an old woodcarver in a small village in the German countryside during one of our European excursions. It was a beautiful piece of craftsmanship. One of a kind, no doubt.

And it held an impressive collection of expensive, unworn jewelry.

That was Adam's thing. A symbol of his contrition. Although, to me it never really felt sincere. When he knew I was mad, or a line had been crossed, he simply opened his wallet. Each piece of gold, every diamond added fuel to the quiet rage building inside of me. How a person could think that something so shallow, so callous would be enough to make up for such a complete and utter lack of respect for another human being was beyond me.

His most recent donation to the graveyard of unused jewelry was a bracelet. It was a chain of gold filigree flowers with diamonds at the center of each. I knew the instant I saw it that I'd never wear it. It was gaudy and pretentious, and it symbolized everything I loathed about my marriage.

In the past, I would have accepted it with a forced smile and a peck on the cheek. It wasn't worth a fight. It wasn't worth the effort to get angry. There was something different this time. A line crossed that hadn't been before. The final straw.

"It's one of a kind," he said when he presented it to me. He held the open box in front of my face. Close enough that I could read *with love, Adam* engraved along the inside. His smile was all self-satisfaction and cluelessness. That this piece of jewelry was exactly the bandage to fix everything. What kind of reaction he was expecting? Especially considering this latest transgression. As Chloe had warned, there was an impressive amount of bruising. Dark purple and red, yellow around the edges. A Rorschach ink blot on the side of my neck with scabbed-over bite marks. "Beautiful, isn't it? I think it suits you."

It suits me?

"I'm not sure what gave you that idea. It'll look lovely locked away in my jewelry box with all the others." I followed up with a death glare. "Just put it over there."

He had the nerve to look surprised. "You don't like it?"

"Did you actually think this would make everything all right?"

"Katherine, you've always deserved the best. I merely wanted to show you how important you are to me."

"Don't give me that." I pointed a finger at him. Anger clouded my vision. "You stood by while that creature *you created* attacked me—"

"She didn't mean anything by it. She seems to be very protective of me, and she knew I was upset and she perceived you as a threat."

"You stood there and watched her attack me and you did nothing. Did you honestly think a fucking piece of jewelry would fix that? How can you be so clueless?"

Adam took a step back, straightened his posture, and his smile melted away. There was an extended pause where he just stood, frozen, lips pressed tightly together. I rarely raised my voice. He obviously didn't know how to react to that.

"I'm truly sorry, Katherine. I don't know what more you want me to do." For an apology, it didn't sound very sincere.

"I want you to keep that fucking pet thing of yours on a leash as long as you insist on keeping it alive."

"She's made so many breakthroughs. Made so much progress." He set the bracelet on the dresser and grasped both my upper arms. Forced me to face him. "You are a part of this, Katherine. Don't you see? I want you there. I want you to witness all of it. I want you to continue to be a part of it."

It was when he said things like this, when he pleaded with me, that I started to doubt my anger. Something swooped in to diffuse it. Those little threads of attention contained nothing more than a vague hint of respect, but respect was something I craved far more than jewelry or money or material things. I clung to those threads. Because deep down I really did want to be part of it. I wanted to have done something, though. Not to be a convenient side piece. I wanted what anyone in my position would have wanted — to be recognized for my role. For my accomplishments. Because as much as he loathed to admit it, Adam's little side projects would not have been possible without me. Or Chloe and Thiago.

In the end, would anybody really pat me on the back and say, *hey Katherine, you sure do know how to reel them in, don't you*? No, they wouldn't. Collecting specimens was hardly a talent. It wasn't something worthy of recognition. But getting in there and helping with one of the transplants was another story altogether. Controlling another human life in the palm of my hand. Connecting the electrodes too soon or too late and that life could be extinguished in mere seconds. Getting it at the right time? It was an indescribable feeling. A feeling of power.

But it was so rare that Adam recognized my role. He seemed to see me as interchangeable with Chloe. He'd taught us both from the ground up but I was his wife.

Would I ever have my day?

"Don't you understand, Katherine? I need you, by my side. Your role is vital in all of this." He was luring me back under his spell. I was losing the battle. It always happened. Every time.

Could this have been why I was stuck? Was I so weak that a few well-placed words kept me from trying to leave his trap?

"You're stronger than anyone I know," he whispered, and I closed my eyes.

But I didn't feel strong. I didn't even feel human. I was the hollow shell of a woman, taking up space in a world I felt I didn't belong in.

CHAPTER FIFTEEN

Present

I wake to the sound of Theresa rushing about the kitchen. Cabinet doors banging shut. The smell of coffee. I get up to use the bathroom, pretending not to notice that she's watching every move. I'm exhausted and want nothing more than to go back and lie down, but I feel obligated—like I should go and sit with her. So I steer myself into the kitchen, grab a mug, and pour some coffee. Cream, no sugar.

"Good morning," I say.

"Morning." She eyes me suspiciously as I sit at the table.

What the hell is her problem now? "What?"

"Since when do you like coffee?"

What ungodly kind of person doesn't drink coffee in the morning?

"I must have changed my mind."

She watches me take a sip, kind of like a deer frozen in the glare of headlights, before she finally shakes her head and sits across from me. We've had our talk about my supposed lack of memory, yes, but I can tell each little difference noticed between me and the Sean she knew eats at her. It chips away that positive exterior. It will continue to chip away at her. She pretends she's happy that Sean is okay and back in her life. But it won't last. There will be a breaking point, and it will probably be big.

"I guess I'm just not used to the changes in you. Even the way you talk is...different." She punctuates this observation with a nervous-sounding laugh and a swipe of her fingers through her hair.

Instead of acknowledging her, I down the rest of my coffee. "Do we have a computer?"

"Uh...yeah. Your laptop is in the bedroom closet." Along with her disappointment that I've redirected the conversation.

"Does it require a password to get into?"

Another look. The crease between her eyes and on her forehead becomes more pronounced. I'm getting under her skin. "My date of birth."

I wait for her to provide the date.

Why is she looking at me like this?

I squeeze my fingers in fists to avoid slapping myself on the forehead. Sean would have known this information. A spouse forgetting the other spouse's birthday is high up the list of offenses one should never commit.

"April zero three." Are those the beginnings of tears? "Capital on the A."

"Thank you."

She nods, fighting emotion, before smoothing that façade back into place. "Anytime." She pauses to drink her coffee, then clears her throat. "Well, I should probably get going. I told my boss I'd be in a half hour early today."

I smile at her. In many ways she's not different from what I had once been. Trying desperately to stuff away her emotions and hurt feelings like they don't matter. Like it's no big deal. Trying not to inconvenience the other person with such a display of human weakness. "Have a good day, Theresa."

Except, I have been better at it than she is.

***

After Theresa leaves for work, I stash the money inside a sock in Sean's underwear drawer with another sock wrapped around it. Then I find the laptop in the closet and bring it to the living room table. An idea has come to me. Lingers in the back of my mind. Can I find anything about Adam's whereabouts through his email accounts? Our old bank accounts? There has to be some clue, something he's overlooked or neglected to cover up.

I start with our bank account. It immediately asks me to verify a whole host of personal information because I'm logging in from a different computer, but once I've answered the questions, I find that Adam hasn't bothered changing any of the passwords. There also hasn't been any recent activity. Nothing in the last six months. He's vanished off the face of the earth.

Both of us have.

But prior to that, there were some interesting transactions. Large sums of money wired to another account. Via Western Union. Had he been sending it to himself? Yes, he had to be. Adam wouldn't give money away. Especially not in such high amounts. I log out of the bank account. Maybe his email will contain more info.

Adam never acknowledged whether he noticed it or not, but I spent considerable time snooping through his emails when we were married. I know all his passwords. They're variations of the same thing and always something painfully obvious. At least to me. He has the bad habit of hiding things from me. I despise lying. I despise cheating. Ironic that I've had my own fair share of secrets.

Hello…

He hasn't changed his email password, either. And if he hasn't changed any of his other habits, then there should also be an unnamed folder. Meant to be inconspicuous. It's where he keeps all the things he doesn't want anyone else to read. Why he keeps them and doesn't delete them, I have no idea.

I find the folder. Now if it had been me, and I wanted to hide things from my significant other, I would have created an entirely different email. Under an entirely different name. But not Adam. Perhaps he's cocky? Or he's so smart he lacks common sense? Maybe he thinks I won't notice.

He already suspected I would search for him.

Most of the stuff I've already read has been deleted. But there is an interesting series of emails. From the bank. Confirming the transactions from the bank account. Thing is, it doesn't really tell me much. It gives me a name, but not a full account number. Email receipts from the wire transfer company. Sending x amount of dollars to one Alexander Simmons. There's no way I can check the new account or get any details about this Alexander Simmons. This *has* to be the alias Adam is using. But how can I prove it? What the hell am I supposed to do? I slam my fist against the coffee table, and almost knock it over in my effort to get up from the couch. I pace, heart racing, muscles tense. There *has* to be a way. I'm not watching where I'm going, and my shin catches the leg of a small side table. Frustrated, I kick it over, sending a cup full of pens and a notebook scattering across the floor. It's about that time I notice someone shouting. Pounding on the door. How long has that been going on?

I pick up the pens, the cup, the paper and set the table right. I use that time to compose myself, before going to the door.

Dammit!

My gut rockets up my throat. It's that FBI agent I met at the hospital. Neilson? Nelson? What the hell is he doing here? He's dressed in an expensive-looking black suit and crisp white shirt, completely neat and wrinkle free. Odd that someone can look so put together when it's hotter than the pits of hell outside.

"Sean? Agent Nelson. We spoke in the hospital." He offers a hand and I shake it. "Nice to see you up and looking well. May I have a few moments of your time?"

"Of course. Please come in." I hold the door open and gesture inside. Stuff away my nerves. Has he been watching me? Have they been monitoring Adam's email and bank accounts? Have they somehow traced activity back to me? My mind races with all the possibilities. "I apologize, I'm afraid the house is a little untidy at the moment. Have a seat."

"No apology necessary." He sits in the recliner, and I shove the blanket aside and sit on the couch. I cross my legs, on instinct really, as I always have.

Sean probably doesn't sit this way, does he?

I don't care.

"What can I do for you today, Agent Nelson?"

"Well, I got an interesting phone call this morning, Sean."

He doesn't elaborate, and I wonder if it's to make me squirm. To trick me into spilling my guts. I can't let that happen. He doesn't know who he's dealing with.

I rest my hands in my lap and smile, knowing full well what that phone call had likely been about. At the same time, I'm kicking myself for not being more careful in the first place. Why didn't I consider this possibility? That they're keeping tabs on me? Maybe they think Adam will come back for me. Or maybe they think I'll remember more. "Is that so?"

"It seems you lost your dog in the same town, the same exact neighborhood, that your former captor lived in. In fact, you were found by an officer coming from the man's own backyard. Mind telling me a little bit about it?"

I should have expected that the police would alert Mr. FBI to my whereabouts the other night. I've been careless. Cocky. Stupid. And here I was logging into all of Adam's accounts, probably putting a giant target right on my back.

"There's not much to say. I was out for a late-night walk." Had I still been female, I might be able to charm my way through this, but judging by his expression, it's obvious Sean won't have that same effect.

"Kind of a coincidence, don't you think? I wondered if maybe you remembered something."

"I'm not sure."

"Did you ever find your dog?"

"I might have…fibbed a little about that."

"Mm hmm."

While we converse, or rather, while he has me in his crosshairs, another idea inserts itself in my brain. I want to be able to use him to find information about Adam, don't I? This is the perfect opportunity. "It's kind of hard to explain, because I'm not sure if what I'm experiencing are actual memories or dreams. But I think I remember hearing things while I was in the coma."

"Go on." I have him interested. He's pretending not to be, but I can see it in his eyes.

"Things have been coming to me. Bits and pieces of conversation, but they're out of context and, quite frankly, don't make a lot of sense. I kept hearing about this house on Shady Elm Lane. On the lake. He—this man—kept saying how it would be tough to leave it behind."

"So, you decided to go visit."

"I couldn't sleep. I kept thinking about it, you know? Was it real? And then I went, and I saw the house, and the name Powers on the sign, and I thought maybe…maybe there was something."

He doesn't allow much in the way of facial expressions, but I catch a minute raise of the brows.

"It really was his house, huh?" It's apparent either he knows nothing about Adam's whereabouts or he's got no intention of telling me.

"Yes."

"Then maybe…some of the other stuff is also real. There was a name tossed around. Between that doctor and a woman. Alexander…" I trail off, pretending to try to remember, even though the name might as well be engraved in my brain. Because suddenly giving him this information doesn't sound like such a good idea. "It began with an S, I think? Alexander…something. They were going to transfer some money to an account with this name, but the way they talked about it made me think maybe this was an alias. Or maybe someone he was working with. It all seems so fuzzy, but do you think that's possible?"

"At this point, anything is possible." He pulls out a notebook while I'm talking and writes furiously. "Alexander, you said?"

I nod. "Yes. I'm sure of it."

"You don't remember a last name?"

I shake my head.

"And what made you think this was an alias?" His writing hand stops flying across the paper, but it hovers right above the page, waiting.

I frown. "I can't be sure. I mean, it's only a hunch. He—the doctor—he kept saying *everything will be in place soon*. And he was reassuring her. The woman. He told her, *everything is going to be fine*. That they'd have to leave the house behind, but they'd have money." I pause. "Of course, I only caught pieces of conversation. And I tended to just drift out of awareness without realizing it was happening. I mean, I don't think it was even full consciousness, because I couldn't open my eyes or move. It was more like I was caught in darkness, drifting…"

Agent Nelson continues to jot down notes. If he comes back, I will need to tread carefully. Give him too much information, and he might discover Adam and detain him before I even get the chance. He also isn't going to share details of any findings with me. But maybe I can coax him into sharing just enough that I can figure things out on my own. What a confusing predicament.

"Do you think he and his wife took off somewhere? That they went into hiding?"

Agent Nelson glances up from his notebook. "Mrs. Powers didn't go anywhere with him."

"I…I see." *Mrs. Powers didn't go anywhere with him.* What did that even mean? Did Adam leave my body behind? When Agent Nelson doesn't elaborate further, I find myself filling the space. "I'm sorry, I don't know if any of this is helpful or not. I know it doesn't make much sense. At least, it doesn't to me."

Agent Nelson stops writing again and while he doesn't lift his head, he does meet my eyes. "Well, I'll be honest, Sean — I'm not sure how any of this stuff fits together yet, and it's not a lot to go on. That said, every little piece of information helps." He stands and tucks the notebook inside his coat pocket. "Thank you for your time. I've got to be going."

I rise and follow him to the door. "I'll definitely contact you if I remember anything new."

"Thank you, Sean. I appreciate it. Keep in touch."

After I lock the door behind him, my heart pounds, and I try to calm my nerves. What have I been thinking? That an FBI agent is going to help me find Adam? Yeah fucking right. What I've done is keep myself on his radar. I might not have volunteered a whole lot of information, but what I have provided is hope. The sliver of a chance that I might at some point remember something useful. I smell the desperation all over him. Sense it behind every word that comes out of his mouth. And desperation does funny things to people. It makes them take risks. Cling to hope, even if it's only present in the smallest shreds.

It is time to hang back and assess my situation. My brain doesn't always function as clearly and precisely as it had prior to my surgery. I'm not as on top of my game as I had once been. I've never been prone to impulsive behavior. I've always carefully thought out and plotted my way through everything. Has the operation impacted that somehow? Has it somehow made me reckless? Unable to think properly?

The fact that I'm sitting here, aware and conflicted about it, gives me hope. If I can make myself focus. If I can come up with a concrete plan, rather than floundering from one thing to the next, indecisive. Changing my direction. So, I do what has always calmed me and cleared my head. The one thing that reminds me I'm in complete control.

I clean.

Maybe it's conditioned behavior. I'd find myself doing it often when Adam and I were married, especially if I was feeling depressed or hopeless.

He didn't listen to me. He never listened to me.

I might not be able to control this weird turn my life has taken, but I can scour away every bit of dirt, dust, and grime. I can make this place feel more like somewhere I want to live. Somewhere more comfortable.

I scrub every floor, dust all surfaces, and clean the toilet, shower, refrigerator. What they don't have in the apartment is a washer and dryer, and I desperately want to clean the linens and clothes. I'll ask Theresa about that. Maybe there is a laundromat nearby. I'm not overly familiar with this part of Worcester or any of the surrounding neighborhoods. Without a car of my own, my ability to explore is somewhat limited. And I sure as hell won't be lugging a laundry bag or basket onto one of the city transit buses.

***

By the time Theresa returns home from work, my mood has improved. She pauses in the doorway, sniffing, a frown forming.

"Is that bleach?"

"Yes." And it's preferable to the smoke smell that had been soaked into literally everything. Theresa hasn't lit a cigarette in my presence, so maybe she quit — or it had been Sean. Either way it's a smell I can't tolerate. I've even gone as far as washing the walls and ceilings, and all the yellow-brown residue. I don't tear my eyes from the newspaper I'm reading. Earlier, I had ventured out for a quick walk, down the street to the small convenience store and used the last bill from Sean's wallet to buy another can of coffee and a paper. "I did some cleaning."

There's that deer-in-the-headlights look again. Apparently, Sean had not been the housekeeping type. The picture in my head of this man's behavior, of their relationship dynamic, is much clearer.

"I see that."

I set the newspaper on the coffee table. "Is there a washer and dryer in this building?"

"Uh…there are a couple sets in the basement."

"I'd like to wash the linens and curtains. The blankets too."

She's got the funny, confused expression of someone who's just walked into a neighbor's house by mistake.

"What? What's wrong?"

What exactly did Sean do? By her look, I suspect it wasn't laundry or cleaning or anything remotely domestic. Even Adam would throw a load or two in to help. He wouldn't have folded them, but he did wash and dry. I spent many of our early years together making damn sure he knew how to do these things. That they were a shared responsibility. I wasn't a maid. Even during later years, when we had a cleaning lady who came by once a week, I still needed that control.

"I can run to the bank and get a couple rolls of quarters. Tomorrow morning. I…uh, don't have to be at work until noon."

"Well, then. Tomorrow morning it is." I'm just going to continue pretending there's nothing wrong here. "There's a fresh pot of coffee. Would you like some?"

"Sure, thank you." Again, that uncertainty creeps into her voice.

"Please, sit. You must be tired. I'll go get you a cup." I get up and head toward the kitchen. "How do you take it?"

"Cream and sugar."

I feel her watching me, all the way into the kitchen. If I'm going to be the master of my own destiny, that means being who I am meant to be. That means showing Theresa who the new Sean is at every opportunity. Showing her who is boss. And the fact that she's so clearly uncomfortable with these changes is exhilarating. It's validation. I've lost everything but a chance at life. I'm not going to lose myself too.

I pour a cup and take my time stirring in cream and sugar, then bring it to the living room and set it on the coffee table. I've startled

Theresa, who is examining the newly cleaned living room in apparent awe.

"Oh, thanks."

I sit on the opposite end of the couch. Her vision drops to my crossed legs, then back to my face.

"So, how was work today?"

She sips her coffee. "Fine."

I lean my arm against the back of the couch and tilt my head, so it rests in my hand. "It looks like you've got something on your mind."

She shakes her head and sets the coffee cup on the table. "I guess I just can't get over the changes in you. You're so different."

I stare at her. "Different good or different bad?"

She clears her throat. "I'm not sure yet. I probably just need to get used to it." I thought she might choose to leave it alone but I'm surprised when she continues. "You were gone for more than six months, you know? I didn't think I'd ever see you again. I kept most of your belongings, although I sold your truck back to Billy." She pauses, seeming embarrassed. "You know, since it still had the landscaping business logo on it. Speaking of Billy. He, uh, called earlier today. He and Pam invited us over for a cookout. It's tonight. If you want to go."

"I could use a change of scenery. A cookout sounds fantastic."

"Uh…okay. I'll call them and let them know we're coming." She drinks more of her coffee, then stops when she notices me watching her.

"What's wrong?"

She has this startled, uneasy look about her. "Nothing in particular. Although, this coffee is very good."

"Why, thank you. It wasn't my best. But it was the best I could do, considering there wasn't much selection at the convenience store." When she doesn't respond with anything other than a forced smile, I stand. "Well. I've been busy today and I could really use a shower and a shave."

I clear the fog from the bathroom mirror. Shaving. I haven't really thought about it, or the mechanics of shaving one's face. It can't be much different from legs or armpits or bikini area.

Ha ha ha.

Although, Sean could use a little grooming in *that* department as well. No. *I* could use the grooming. I catch myself doing that often. Separating my consciousness from Sean's body, as if we are somehow two different entities. At this point that isn't possible. Perhaps I'm still doing it because I haven't fully accepted my fate.

But a beard? It's yet another thing that's tough to wrap my head around. Still, the thick coarse hairs covering my face now make me look unkempt and wild. Borderline homeless. I don't like it.

There's shaving cream and those garbage-quality disposable razors under the sink. Also a pair of scissors. No electric clippers. None of it is ideal, and I don't know if I'm going about it the right way, but after years of living with a man I've picked up a few things. I start trimming with the scissors. Then lather up with shaving cream. By the time I'm completely clean shaven, I've cut myself three times. They're shallow cuts, but they bleed like a sonofabitch.

I stop the flow with little wads of toilet paper and clean up the fallen hair. I've made the decision to continue this charade, and I need to own it. But this whole scenario has its problems. My personality in Sean's body doesn't mesh. It isn't expected. I see it every time Theresa looks at me. Which means other people will likely look at me the same way. And because I've been enjoying Theresa's discomfort, I've now put myself in the situation where I'll have to socialize with more people they know.

***

We drive the couple of miles to this Billy's house in relative silence. Theresa keeps glancing at me. She nearly passed out earlier when she saw I shaved the beard. I don't acknowledge it. Don't acknowledge her. I'm asserting my personality at every opportunity. Reminding her how much I'm unlike the husband she remembers.

We end up in a seemingly typical middle-class neighborhood. Modest houses with neat yards. Nothing spectacular, but certainly not the urban dump we came from. Theresa guides the car into the driveway of a small ranch-style home.

The man I presume to be Billy greets us at the door. He's older, graying, and with the weathered skin of someone who spends a significant amount of time outside in the sun. His face brightens, and an impressive array of wrinkles frames his almost too-wide smile.

"Hey, there he is." He thrusts out his hand to me and when I extend my own hand to shake it, he pulls me into a sort of half-hug. Pats my back. A friendly display of male affection that I force myself to go along with, because, while I don't know this man from a hole in the wall, Sean apparently did. "Good to see you alive and kickin', Kid."

"Thank you."

A flash of uncertainty crosses his expression. It's fleeting, but I pick up on it. He makes eye contact with Theresa, then covers it with a smile. Maybe she warned him Sean isn't himself?

"Well, c'mon in, you two. Food's already on the grill."

Again, I am faced with the consequences of an impulsive decision that I'm not ready to own. Socializing with people who know Sean and Theresa as a couple. A man that Sean worked for. I don't want to be here.

Billy yanks the cap off a beer and hands the bottle to me. I've never been a beer girl, never cared for the taste, but I know a thing or two about sucking it up and eating or drinking things I don't like to be polite. I accept the bottle from him and nod thanks as I take a sip. It has a bitter, yeasty flavor, and I choke it down. Theresa goes off to sit with Billy's wife, leaving the two of us and an awkward lack of conversation.

"You know Theresa's glad to have you back. She had a rough time for a while there."

I don't know what to say to that. It almost sounds like it's leading into a lecture, or he's preparing to pump me for information.

"She says you lost your memory. How bad is it?"

"Everything." There's no point sugarcoating it. The little I know about Billy, he seems like a straightforward kind of guy.

"The doctors think it'll come back to you?"

I didn't come here for the third degree, even though I should have expected it. Can he see how irritated I am? I'm fighting the dirty look I want to hurl back at him. "The doctors don't even know exactly what happened to me."

"Shit." He downs the rest of his beer.

"Yeah."

"I don't mean to pry," he says, then pauses. Of course he means to pry. People don't say things like that unless they're trying to minimize their own bad manners or behavior. He knows exactly what he's doing. "But I was wonderin' what your intentions are with Theresa if, say, you don't get your memory back."

"I hadn't thought that far ahead." I fix him in a cold stare, daring him to defy me. "I would hope that my memories would return. If not, we may end up going our separate ways. Or we may build a new relationship. I simply do not know how I will feel."

"I can't even imagine what you must be goin' through."

No, you can't.

"I just worry about that girl. She been through a lot, and I love her like my own daughter. I don't wanna see her broken again."

His thinly veiled threat sits about as well as rancid food in the gut. He thinks he can intimidate me?

"Well. I will try not to break her." The acid in my voice is so blatant, I don't know how he could possibly miss it. But he doesn't react. I'd love nothing more than to wipe that smug look off his face. Had he always talked like this to Sean?

We stare each other down for a few moments, a silent battle. Finally, he nods and looks away. Maybe I've won for now, but I doubt I've seen the last of Billy.

CHAPTER SIXTEEN

Past

Sometimes my daily walks were the only thing that kept me sane. There was a small park near Adam's facility. It wasn't anything special. Just a paved walkway looping through a tiny patch of woods and immaculately kept lawns. During the middle of the day, it was filled with people on lunch breaks and mothers with young children. At night, the inhabitants were much shadier.

Still, it got me out of those walls for a time. Offered a brief distraction during my long work days. Once Emily was "born", we spent much less time at our own home. Adam worked tirelessly, and I was expected to follow suit. He was obsessed with every bit of progress, like a parent, eagerly awaiting each milestone. Except with Emily, the milestones were few and far between, and Adam's excitement was little more than a grasp at something that wasn't there.

On a crisp November morning, I came back from my walk to observe Adam's latest round of tests on Emily. Adam was in one of the exam rooms with her. She sat on the floor because she couldn't seem to understand the concept of a chair or how it worked no matter how many times it was demonstrated to her.

I opened the door quietly and slipped inside where I was supposed to be recording results on the laptop. It sat on the counter at the far end of the room. I wasn't ready to trust he'd keep her from attacking me, although Adam assured me it would never happen again.

He offered a brief, stiff nod of acknowledgement when I entered the room. I was late, and he was annoyed, but rather than agitate Emily, he brushed it aside. Still, he couldn't conceal it completely. He never could.

I took my place on the stool by the counter and powered up the laptop.

Adam sat on the floor across from Emily. He had a deck of cards in his hands. Not playing cards, but large flashcards with colored shapes and numbers on them.

Why does he insist on wasting his time with this?

He laid out three cards side by side. They each had a circle in the center of a white background. One blue, one yellow, and one red.

"Emily? Look at the cards." Adam tried to direct her attention toward the cards, but her unfocused gaze wandered the room. He tapped the floor. "Em! Right here. Do you see?"

I began to type:

Subject does not respond to her name. Does not demonstrate any definitive understanding of words and concepts. Three flash cards have been presented…

Adam tapped the floor right next to the cards. "Emily, focus!"

I'd hesitate to say she looked at the floor where he'd tapped. It was more like her head turned in that direction in a kind of lopsided, swaying motion. Her tongue lolled out of the corner of her mouth.

Hearing is strong, as she responds to sound…

"Can you show me the blue one? Come on Sweetheart, which one is the blue one?"

A lost cause if there ever was one, but I'd learned my lesson with regards to voicing my opinion. My only hope was that sooner or later he'd realize how useless this one was, learn from it, and move on to the next.

Emily swept a hand across the floor, disturbing all three cards in the process. Perhaps by chance, she crumpled the blue card in her fist, which she'd grabbed along with the yellow. The yellow one slipped out of her grasp and fluttered to the floor. The blue one, still crumpled in her fist, was promptly shoved in her mouth.

"That's right! That's right Emily, the blue one." The excitement in his voice was palpable. And as I sat there typing notes on what was happening, it occurred to me how easy it was for differing perspectives to form based upon one's perception of a situation. I saw how deeply Adam wanted to believe that this creature could perform basic tasks. Yes, she'd grabbed the card he pointed out, but was it really on purpose? From Adam's perspective, yes, she had, because that's what he wanted to believe. From mine, it was a random act. A happy accident. Pure dumb luck.

Emily mouthed the card until it was completely soaked and some of the blue ink mixed with her saliva and ran down her chin. She was, as I had previously said to Adam, no better than an infant. Little more than a collection of primal urges and impulses. Instincts. And this was where our beliefs parted. He thought, much like an infant, that Emily would grow and continue to make progress. I, on the other hand, saw something irreparable. A defect. Something had gone wrong, whether it was prior to the surgery, or during, or even while in recovery.

I suspected it was some sort of brain damage that occurred before she was implanted into the host body. It could have been something as simple as the brain went without oxygen for too long between harvesting and the stabilization period that immediately followed. Or sometime during the incubation period, which was where he kept the few live, intact brains that he'd harvested.

But Adam didn't want to see it.

The more I watched him with her, the more irritated I became. I couldn't quite place what bothered me. Surely it wasn't jealousy. It couldn't have been bad feelings that he was paying attention to this damaged child rather than me. Not possible.

No, it was something else. This obsession—it was unlike anything I'd ever seen with any of his other projects. It was hyper-focused. Like a matter of life or death. Like he was throwing all his faith into this one thing and it couldn't fail or it would destroy him.

"Maybe she's had enough for today."

Or maybe *I* had.

Adam startled, as if he'd forgotten I was there. Emily growled when she heard my voice. Adam reached out and stroked her arm to calm her, but she sounded like a guard dog preparing to defend its property. Ready to attack.

"I'd like to spend a little more time with her, but if you could just go compile today's notes and make sure the log is organized, that would be helpful. I don't want her to get any more riled up than she already is."

I shrugged, to show it didn't make a difference one way or another, even though I was feeling the sting of yet another dismissal. He wanted me to compile notes, did he? Well, I'd just have to be very honest and detailed about what I'd observed. Brutally honest.

CHAPTER SEVENTEEN

Present

Insomnia has plagued me off and on for most of my adult life. Over the years, I've tried every trick and tip available. Eventually I accepted that a full night of uninterrupted sleep isn't in the cards for me and I've learned to appreciate those rare occasions when it does happen. It's been worse since the operation, post coma, with the difference being now I don't bother fighting it. Sometimes your only choice is to give in when the mind won't shut off.

So, I pull out the laptop and type in a search for newspaper articles and news clips about the raid on Adam's lab. I've avoided it until now. There wouldn't be anything available to help me find him, so I'd written it off as a useless waste of energy. Still, I'm curious. About what happened. About what people perceive happened. And maybe even a little bit about what people think of me. Is Katherine Powers considered as much of a monster as her husband? I shouldn't care. Whatever was displayed in the media is only part of the truth. They'll never know the real work that went on or the motivations behind everything.

I am rewarded with a seemingly endless stream of material. Article after article. Dr. Death, they called him at first. Then Dr. Frankenstein once they'd conducted their investigation of the facility and the so-called atrocities they'd found. Atrocities. That's how the news media painted his experiments.

I click on one of the articles. It's all so predictable. One big clichéd innuendo after another. Frankenstein is the obvious go-to name and they try to be clever in their portrayal of Adam as a mad scientist. Just because body parts have been found. Organs he harvested, kept in jars. It isn't like he was sewing dead bodies together and bringing them to life, so their stupid plays on words aren't even accurate.

I stop reading. Eight victims? Surely that's wrong. Unless Adam has offed some of the help. Maybe Chloe, or that lab assistant, Michael. Still, something made my skin crawl. Call it a sixth sense. I have the feeling I know who that eighth person was.

I hesitate before entering another search. My own name, a beacon. The question is, do I really want to see what that beacon shines its light on? If Adam was so willing to stick my brain into a man, rather than the woman I'd chosen, then god only knows what he did with my body. *Mrs. Powers didn't go anywhere with him.* No, *Mrs. Powers* didn't get a say in much of anything, let alone *going* with him.

I figure knowing is better than not knowing and, kind of like ripping a bandage off in a single, quick motion, I enter the search and brace myself for the results. It's every bit as bad as I feared.

Well, at least they won't be looking for me. In the eyes of the law, I am no longer complicit with any of Adam's schemes. I'm not a fugitive. It's still no solace for finding out your husband stuffed your body in a freezer and left it there. I don't know what alternative I'd been expecting, but it stings nonetheless.

A funeral? Really Katherine?

It's not like I'm dead. No, but I expected him to treat my body with a bit more respect.

I read through dozens more articles. Force myself through them. They all spent considerable time painting the picture of a disturbed man. A monster. The type of person who has no regard for human life. What they don't have is the motive behind it all, so everything he did is out of context. When he fled, Adam took all his records. Paper records. Hard drives. The computers that he left behind were destroyed beyond salvation. There was no data to be found.

And that triggers a memory. Something that makes me believe he'd been plotting this for quite some time.

Thiago, moving boxes of equipment out of the lab in the middle of the night. More memories surface of how I'd been kept far enough out of the loop that I didn't know when or where we would make the move. How Adam sidestepped the subject any time I asked for specifics. I never pressed the issue but looking back, there had been signs. All these little things add up. If you are paying attention, which, at the time, I wasn't.

Thiago. Why didn't I think of him sooner? Maybe the obvious answer to *where's Adam* has been in front of me all along. Even if Thiago has followed him into hiding, there's a chance he might answer my call. In the months leading up to my surgery, Thiago and I bonded. He was loyal to Adam, but it had seemed more duty-based. Job loyalty. What you had to do to survive. But he and I had real conversations. He consoled me. Just how far did that job loyalty stretch? Did he take off with Adam? I wonder…

No matter how I roll it over in my brain, I can't imagine Thiago being okay with Adam sticking me in this body. Did he try to talk him out of it? He'd never been afraid to contradict Adam. In fact, in the last couple of months leading up to my operation, I overheard both him and Chloe arguing for things on my behalf on more than one occasion.

And always with the same result — *I know what's best for my wife.*

What if Thiago didn't follow Adam into hiding? Maybe I can contact him. It's possible he knows something, has some clue to Adam's whereabouts. The question is, where do his loyalties lie? He's always looked after me, always come to my defense. If I seek him out now, and he allows me to contact him, then what? Will he give me the information I need? My gut tells me it's a risk worth taking.

But some caution is necessary. Especially if he's on the FBI's radar. So even if he hasn't followed Adam, they might still be watching him. Monitoring his phone calls and his comings and goings. I wonder if they're also watching mine.

I remember the money I stashed in Sean's underwear drawer. I could go buy a cell phone. One of those prepaid ones you pick up at a Walmart or some other store and you don't need to attach a real name or other personal information to it. Thiago and I once had a conversation about the necessity of covering one's tracks, of staying invisible, especially if you thought there was any chance you were being watched.

It's worth a shot. I know Thiago's number by heart. Both cell and his family's painting business. Sure, he might have changed them, but it's something to go on, isn't it? I also know where he lives. It isn't too far from where I am now.

Now that the idea to contact him has inserted itself into my thoughts, I'm obsessed with it. He might be my only hope.

***

The next morning, after Theresa leaves for work, I walk the couple of miles to a Walmart and buy a phone. I'll probably have to hide it from Theresa, at least for now. She doesn't know I have money and I'm not about to clue her in.

I stow the packaging at the bottom of the trash barrel — even go as far as digging through the existing trash and covering it over. As

I sit on the couch and activate the phone, it occurs to me I'm behaving exactly like a cheating spouse. Hiding evidence of my indiscretions. That could be a way to get out of this sham of a marriage.

*Sorry Theresa, I've found some*body *new.*

Once I find Adam, none of that will matter anyway. I spend a long time holding the phone in my shaking hand, staring at the keypad on the screen. Unable to bring myself to enter the numbers. Do I do it or not? Will he even believe it's me?

If I do, will he tell Adam? Will he tell Adam that I've contacted him?

I have to risk it. My gut instinct is that he won't. I always had the sense his loyalty swayed more in my direction than Adam's. That perhaps he even fancied me a bit. I have to hope. Make a leap of faith. Because it's better than waiting here. I dial his business number and let my finger hover over the call button.

If I call his business and he's being watched, at least I can play it off as someone looking to have work done. The cell phone won't be traceable to Katherine Powers or Sean Malone. But what am I going to say to him?

Before I can fixate on it any longer, I press the green call button and my stomach churns as I listen to it dial.

"Three Brothers Painting." It's a woman.

"Hi. I was recently speaking with a man named Thiago about getting an estimate and I was wondering if he was available? I had a couple more questions."

"Thiago stepped out of the office, but he should be back later this afternoon. I could take a message and have him get back to you when he returns?" She has a heavy accent, and I wonder for a moment if this is the sister he sometimes mentioned. Or maybe his wife. He never talked about being married, but Thiago never spent much time talking about himself or his family. Only bits of information mentioned in passing. Anything is possible.

At least he hasn't fled. And it's entirely possible nobody knows his connection to Adam and me.

"That would be wonderful. Could you tell him that it's Sean and Katherine Simmons calling regarding a renovation job?"

"Oh, sure. Of course."

"He should know what this is regarding." I can only hope he'd figure out the call came from me. Thiago is sharp. I've used both my names. He'll know it's me. I recite my new number.

"Okay. I will let him know you called." I can almost hear the wheels turning, like she's trying to figure out if she should pass along the message or not.

***

My weak attempt at keeping my mind occupied while I wait for Thiago to call back consists of reading more internet articles about Adam.

If he calls back.

He will.

When the phone rings I nearly jump out of my skin. The number that shows up on the screen is Thiago's personal cell.

"Hello?" My mouth is dry. My heart pounds.

There's a pause on the other end of the line. I can hear him breathing. "Katherine?"

I let out a slow breath, but it does nothing to relieve the jittery, nervous feeling inside. This is the first thing resembling excitement, or maybe even relief, I've felt since I woke in this body.

"Is it you?"

"Mm." I don't often allow myself to succumb to emotion, and don't seem to have a large range of them as Sean, but the tears immediately well up. It's so good to hear a familiar voice.

"Are you…well?" Is that a hint of disbelief? I can't tell if he's unhappy to hear from me or just surprised.

No. That isn't quite it. He's never heard this voice. He's trying to reconcile the Katherine he knows with the male voice that he's hearing.

I laughed. It was bitter and ironic and maybe even a little angry. The closest I can get to feeling without really feeling. "What the fuck do you think?"

"I'm so sorry…I didn't realize what he was doing until it was too late." He pauses, his voice hushed, but clearly sounding torn. "That arrogant…" He doesn't finish the thought, just leaves it hanging there as an insult. There's a fierceness to his tone, enough that I almost believe the sincerity. "If I could have done anything to stop him, I would have. You have to know that."

"Well, to be perfectly honest I don't know that, Thiago." I push the anger from my voice, but the icy tone is unmistakable. Nobody had done anything to stop Adam. Not Thiago, not Chloe. They didn't stop it. I repeat this in my head until it sticks. Any excitement about hearing a familiar voice fizzles out.

There's an extended pause on the other end. He starts to say something, but it comes out as a grunt and a huff of breath before he finally speaks again. "How…how are you adjusting?"

"I'm still trying to wrap my head around the fact that I have a cock. And a fucking *wife* who probably wonders why I have no desire to fuck *her*."

"You have a right to be angry."

"I'd rather be dead."

"You don't mean that."

"I mean everything I say. You know that better than anybody. Thiago, he needs to pay for this. He needs to pay for what he did to me."

"I know."

"Will you help me?"

"It's not safe right now…maybe you're better off living where you are. Count your blessings that terrible man is out of your life." That sounds an awful lot like giving up to me. I'm not giving up.

"Will you fucking help me?"

"Katherine…"

"Oh, haven't you heard? It's *Sean* now."

"It's too risky. The feds are watching. I'm not even sure we could get to him."

"They don't know where he is. One of them was sniffing around me for information."

"I see."

"But *you* know where he is." He falls silent on the other end, but I know what his answer is. He knows where Adam went. No…wait. Of course he knows where Adam is. He helped move supplies there, didn't he? "Please, Thiago. I'm begging you."

He sighs, but I sense, even without seeing his expression, that he's relenting. "Let me think about how to approach this. Until then, please lay low…and take care of yourself."

"Thiago…"

"I'll figure out what to do and get back to you, okay?"

"Fine."

I hang up with mixed thoughts, shut the phone off, and shove it in my pocket. I still don't know how much involvement Thiago had in what happened to me. For all I know, he was right there beside Adam helping him. But what if he wasn't? I needed to hear a familiar voice, though, and it felt good. I have to believe Thiago will help me. He seemed hesitant. But maybe that hesitancy has to do with protecting me rather than Adam. I will have to convince him it's in my best interests. And that it's also in his best interests.

Thiago might be my only hope in finding Adam.

CHAPTER EIGHTEEN

Past

A crash came from the lab where we kept the animals. Did one of them escape from its cage? It happened from time to time. Somebody didn't latch a door properly, and the next thing you knew, there was a panicked rat running around, knocking things off the table or counter.

The room was dim, with nothing but the nighttime security lights illuminating it with an eerie glow that left the rows between the cages draped in shadows. I nearly flicked on the light switch but something told me to stop.

The sounds coming from the corner drove the cold needles of dread deeper into my bones. Lapping and lip smacking, with loud open-mouthed chewing. It sounded like a large animal feeding. I should've gone to get help, but instead my feet cemented in place. For an eternity, I stood in the open doorway, cursing at myself for not doing something.

Something brushed across my upper arm and I jumped, nearly crashing into the nearby shelf unit, but catching myself just in time. Thiago. It was only Thiago.

"What is it, Katherine?"

I pressed a hand to my chest and willed myself to calm down. With a gulp of air, I caught my breath and was able to find my voice. "I think…I think one of the animals got loose from its cage," I whispered.

Thiago gave my shoulder a reassuring squeeze. "We'll have to catch it. Make sure it doesn't get out."

We slipped inside the room and quietly closed the door behind us. Thiago held a finger up in front of his lips. He was frowning. No doubt he heard the same thing as I did.

I don't remember having any pigs on the animal lab roster.

That was the first thing the sound brought to mind. Visiting my uncle's farm as a child, and the fat hogs feeding on the scraps of vegetables he used to get from one of the local grocery stores. The produce that was too old to sell to customers but still edible. They'd set it aside for my uncle to feed his animals and in return he'd sell them fresh pork for a lower cost. And judging from the happy grunts as they gobbled it up, it was a good setup. Even though the pigs were eating their way to their death.

The grunts and the wet chewing continued.

Thiago stepped around me, still frowning, and thrust an outstretched arm in front of me, indicating that he was going to go first.

"Shouldn't we turn the lights on?"

Thiago shook his head. "We do not want to startle it."

I nodded. There were two rows of cages in the middle of the room, spaced about three feet apart, and cages along the far right and back walls. The sound seemed to be coming from the back corner. We crept on quiet, careful footsteps toward the back of the room. I couldn't cast away the bad feeling.

Then Thiago froze. His face turned ashen.

"What's wr—" The words dried in my throat almost instantly. Not a pig. Emily. Crouched, squatting in the corner between two open cages. Blood everywhere. Her face and hands coated. It puddled all over the floor in a great crimson pool. She clutched a half-eaten rat in a tight fist. Its entrails dangled from the still-twitching body. Pieces of meat with fur still attached poked out of the corners of her mouth. And she was chewing.

Loud, wet, open-mouthed chewing.

"Oh my god." I gagged, then shoved a hand over my mouth to stifle it. So far, she hadn't noticed us. She was too focused on the rat. Or rats, plural. As I edged my way around Thiago, I noticed a second carcass on the floor, behind her outstretched leg. It was completely torn apart, almost unidentifiable, with a splintered bone standing upright from the gaping hole in its side.

I turned away from the scene and bumped into Thiago. He was shaking. Looking shocked. The man who hardly seemed rattled by anything was most definitely rattled. He backed up a step. Maybe it was involuntary.

"We need to get Dr. Adam," he finally whispered.

No sooner did the words come out than Emily's attention jerked up at both of us. Her low purring growl morphed into an earsplitting shriek. She started to get up, wobbly and slow like a toddler.

"Katherine, run. I'll be right behind you."

Shock turned to adrenaline.

I whipped around and booked it for the door with Thiago right at my heels. Once she was on her feet, Emily was faster than I thought she'd be. We crossed the threshold and she was already only a few feet behind, hampered only by the leg that didn't seem to function quite right. She caught Thiago before we could close the door and grasped onto him. Thiago was taken by surprise, but he recovered in an instant and flipped her onto the floor. Pinned her down. She was a writhing and thrashing wild animal, but Thiago held her in place.

He angled his head toward me, sweat pouring from exertion. "Get Dr. Adam. Now."

I broke into a jog down the hall and, as I turned the corner, almost collided with Adam, who was running toward us.

"What's going on?" His voice was raised, his face flushed, clothes disheveled. I'd assumed he left, but he must have fallen asleep in his office.

"Your fucking creature broke into the animal lab. Apparently, she has a taste for rodent."

"What the hell are you talking about?" But before I could explain, he pushed past me, toward the animal lab. He grabbed Thiago by the back of the shirt and yanked him off the writhing, screeching Emily with a ferocity that was uncharacteristic for Adam. "Get off her! What the hell is going on here?"

And again, Adam abandoned all reason. He knelt beside Emily. Caressed her hair. "Shhh, Sweetheart. It's okay now." She calmed slightly—as in, she wasn't shrieking as loud. Then the shrieks turned to moans. It was tough to tell if she was responding to him or simply getting tired. One eye was a little out of sync with the other, which seemed much worse than usual in her agitated state. "That's it, that's it. Ahh, poor baby. Look at you."

When she finally calmed down, Adam pulled her to a sitting position, then scooped her into his arms and lifted her up. "Let's go make it better." Without so much as a second glance in my direction, he started down the hallway away from us. Then called over his shoulder, "Thiago, get someone in here to clean up that mess. Or clean it up yourself. I really don't care."

I crouched on the floor next to Thiago, who sat with his knees pulled to his chest and his head clutched in his hands.

"Tee, are you okay?" I squeezed his shoulder. I'd never seen him this distressed before.

"There is so much wrong with this, you cannot even comprehend." His eyes were bloodshot and watery, as if he were holding back tears. He did not elaborate on his cryptic answer. Only stared at me long enough that I was able to soak in his pain, the hollow despair of his expression. For the first time in my life, I felt the intense desire to help, to take away that pain. I understood that something far greater than this incident was lurking inside him. Some deep, dark secret perhaps. A pain unmatched, yet not unlike my own that I kept locked away from the prying eyes of those nearest me. There was a spark of a connection there. Not sexual chemistry or attraction. More like a mutual understanding of the souls. I needed to know what it was and absorb it as my own. Maybe it would swallow me whole and send me into a swirling, endless whirlpool. Maybe I'd never escape unscathed.

As fast as the moment took hold of me it evaporated, and Thiago pulled away. He made a concerted effort to reign in his emotions. We weren't so different, Thiago and me.

He tilted his head back. Punched the wall. Then swore under his breath, followed by something else in Portuguese, something that sounded of frustration, before getting to his feet. He offered a hand to pull me up but wouldn't look me in the eye anymore. Whatever moment we shared had passed and we both resumed our stoic façades. I noted the red on his knuckles as his hand slipped away from mine. It would bruise. He'd hit the wall rather hard.

"What can I do to help?"

"There is nothing you can do to help." There was blood on his shirt and streaked on his arms from his struggle with Emily. "Why don't you go home, Katherine. Get some sleep. It's late."

And as Adam had done so many times, he brushed me aside. I might have been sick, but I wasn't a complete invalid, incapable of doing anything. "I'm not just going to fucking go home. I wouldn't be able to sleep anyway." I marched down the hall to the supply closet, yanked it open, and pulled out the cleaning cart. Gloves. Trash bags. I slammed these on top of the cart and wheeled it past Thiago and into the animal lab. "Let's clean up this fucking mess.

***

"Katherine, put it in the bag," Thiago said from beside me.

I had zoned out and was holding the bloody, gory rat carcass in front of me. Clumps of blood, now dark and syrupy-looking, made a slow-motion drop to the floor. I shook away the cobwebs in my brain and dropped the rat into the opened trash bag.

"You did not need to stay and do this."

"It's the middle of the night, Tee. We're not calling cleaning staff now. Can you imagine trying to explain that? Adam's little pet decided to have a snack?"

Was that the hint of a smile?

"I was going to take care of it myself."

I shrugged. "It'll go faster if I help."

"Not if you keep staring off into space."

I wanted to ask him more about earlier, about how deeply he seemed to have been affected by Emily, but I decided against it. We didn't have that type of relationship where one shared intimate secrets. We couldn't exactly be considered friends. In a way, we were merely victims of the same circumstance. Two people stuck in the same nightmare. That was our common bond.

"Katherine, you're spacing out again."

I'd been wiping the same puddle of blood in a circular motion without cleaning off the rag, which did little more than push it into a pink, foamy, swirling shape. I plunged the rag in the water bucket, rinsed it off, and squeezed out the excess before wiping at the blood again. Midway through, Thiago got up and changed the water.

"What do you suppose it will take to get him to understand this one is a lost cause?" I wasn't necessarily looking for an answer. I already knew what it was.

"He's too committed to her." Thiago deposited his rag into the trash and pulled out another one. Most of the blood was off the floor. Only some pinkish foam remained. "He's too committed to seeing her succeed. I don't believe he will give up until he gets the results he wants to see."

And that was what made me furious. That he was so fixated on this idealistic result, he couldn't see reality. Maybe he would never see reality. How could he call himself a true man of science and medicine if he couldn't at least set aside emotional attachment? "But what happens when that result never comes? Isn't it up to us to make him face the truth?"

Again, one of those odd, cryptic smiles transformed his face. "Dr. Adam does not look at what he does not want to see. He will only face his own reality."

"Ah. So, in other words, you think there is nothing you or I could say or do to make this right." I dropped the rag I was holding into the trash and peeled off the gloves. There wasn't a trace of blood left on the floor that I could see. We'd go over it with a mop and bleach solution as a precaution.

"Nothing we could *say* to be sure." Something in the way he said it implied there was more to be read into his answer. An additional meaning. He didn't say anything more, but I suspected what he might have meant. That something could probably be *done* instead. Did that something mean Emily? Could she be taken care of in such a way that Adam wouldn't know what had happened? How he would react if he showed up in the morning to find her cold and stiff, locked into whatever pose her body arranged itself in death. The thought filled me with an almost giddy excitement. Something I knew was wrong to even think about. Something I knew was completely messed up.

Thiago's gaze found mine. "Katherine? Whatever you are thinking about, perhaps it is best to really *think* about it first."

"It's not a crime to think." Although, it quite possibly made me a monster.

"No." He shook his head. "Not a crime."

I patted him on the shoulder. "Then let me at least hold onto the fantasy for a while. I need some light at the end of the tunnel. A pot of gold at the end of the rainbow." I yawned. It was well past midnight. "I think maybe I *will* go home and try to get some sleep. You should go home and sleep too."

He nodded.

Did he feel the same way? Or was he going along with what I was saying just to make me happy? Thiago was hard to read. I couldn't tell if he was on anyone's side or just out for himself, but maybe it wasn't smart for me to confide in him too much. For all I knew, he was running back to Adam and giving word for word recaps of our conversations. And I sure as hell didn't need that.

CHAPTER NINETEEN

Present

I find Theresa and Sean's photo albums on the kitchen table the same day I discover a half-empty bottle of vodka under the sink. I didn't hear her get up or leave for work or even sit in the kitchen to drown her sorrows. It's cheap vodka, too. Some plastic bottle crap with a handle.

Our Wedding is printed on the top book. Is she trying to jog my memories? Or wallowing in her own? Maybe a little bit of both.

I open the cover and feel a pang of…something, as I look through the photos inside. Regret? Jealousy? They'd been a happy, close couple. On their wedding day, at least. It's an extremely generic-looking ceremony, obviously done on a budget, and yet they were smiling and touching and kissing in every photo. Having fun.

I think back to my own wedding. The lavish affair it had been. The formal photos with strained, forced expressions. We spent so much time posing them, and the photographer had taken hundreds. After the ceremony, Adam spent the rest of the day socializing with people he didn't even like rather than staying by my side. It irked me for appearances' sake only. I wanted nothing more than to slip away into a hot bath. In hindsight, our marriage was not the fairytale we presented it to be.

Sitting here, staring at Sean's happy memories, I'm having a sudden moment of clarity. Adam and I spent a significant portion of our relationship creating an illusion. The perfect house. The trips to Europe. Our own business. All of it just as posed as our wedding photos. And as I look back now, I don't have any feelings of fondness for my marriage. His actions have soured any love I might've still harbored, but if I'm being completely honest, much of the romance had fizzled by the time he slipped that ring on my finger. The rest of our time together was a mix of duty, doing what we were supposed to do as husband and wife and maintaining the illusion for the world.

But here, in these photos, genuine smiles. Sean was always touching her, grabbing her, kissing her in every fucking picture. No wonder she is so needy for his attention.

What a peculiar display of excess weddings are. Pointless, really, when all one needs is the piece of paper for legal reasons. Then again, I've never been one for sentimentality. Yet these two appear genuinely happy.

I close it and look through the other book. They are older photos. Sean's childhood, by the looks of it. He'd been a scrawny, smiling kid.

Theresa enters the room, looking disheveled and recently rolled out of bed. It's almost noon.

I shoot her a pointed look. "Rough night?"

She tenses. Shrugs. Then the tears come again.

"You know, a hangover is the body's cry for help when you've overdone it."

"It was one time. One slip-up in over six months."

"I'm not judging you, Theresa." I gesture for her to sit down. I'm feeling unusually charitable. Maybe it's that I'd finally found an in, that I know Thiago is the key to getting me to Adam. "Why don't you tell me what's on your mind?"

"I don't know which is worse. Having you here, like this, or not knowing where you are and if you're still alive. It's kind of…tearing me apart inside."

"Go on."

"I see…I see the man I fell in love with, but it's like you're a shell. It's like you're completely vacant, like you've got no feelings, and sometimes when you look at me, it's frightening. And I know, logically, that you've been through this trauma, that your memories aren't there, but I'm having a hard time separating the past from now. It was almost better thinking you were dead, because this is torture."

She looks at me, stunned, as if she can't believe these words came out of her mouth. I want to feel sorry for her. I want to feel bad. But I don't feel anything toward her. And why should I?

"I'm sorry you feel this way, Theresa."

"Don't say that!" she hisses. "You're not sorry. It's like you're dead inside. The way you talk, the way you look at me, it fucking creeps me out. It's like you're a complete stranger."

"I'm sorry."

She slams her fist on the table. "No, you're not! You're not fucking sorry. I can hear it in your tone. It's like you're mocking me."

"What do you want from me, Theresa?"

"I don't know." She's crying again. Shaking her head. "I don't know."

While watching her cry, a thought occurs to me. What if Sean's body still has some attachment to her? Like an impression or an imprint left behind. Something that happens on a cellular level, where maybe traces of his connection to her have lingered. That's the only explanation for the feelings of uncertainty I have. The second guessing. Am I truly feeling sorry for her or is it because I'm inhabiting her husband's body? I stare at her for a while, wondering what to do.

"Maybe we should go away somewhere. Take a little trip." It's out of my mouth before I can think about what I'm saying. And once something like that is out, there's no taking it back.

She doesn't respond, but the tears have slowed.

"It's possible it could trigger my memory." Which is complete bullshit. "Or maybe the change of scenery would give us the opportunity to get to know each other again."

"When?"

"How about next week? Or the week after? Let's see what we can put together, and maybe you can take some time off from work."

"Okay. I'll see if I can get someone to cover for me." She's calm. Amazing how one impulsive suggestion has completely taken the fight out of her. It's softened her expression. All the hard lines and creases of anger have smoothed and faded. I've given her hope. She clears her throat. "I…uh, I guess I better get ready for work."

I press my lips into a half-smile and nod as she gets up to leave room.

She's gone. I can breathe.

There's a knot between my shoulders that won't go away. It's deep and throbbing, and I stretch my arms above my head for relief. There's nothing satisfying about this impulsive decision. I don't feel good knowing that I've made her happy. I also don't feel guilty that I've given her hope where there isn't any. But wouldn't this make sense? If I really was a husband trying to reconnect with his wife, wouldn't a weekend getaway be a logical choice?

A change of scenery could be beneficial. Besides keeping up appearances with Theresa, it would buy more time if Thiago takes forever deciding whether to help me or not. I can't move out on my own, even with the cash Adam left behind. I like to think it won't take any longer than a few weeks or a couple of months to find him, but what if it *does* take longer? What if the FBI truly are watching all of us? If *Sean* suddenly leaves his wife, or starts behaving oddly, they might watch closer. These are all things I need to consider. It's time to keep a cool head.

CHAPTER TWENTY

Past

Emily had to be sedated to perform an MRI and a CT scan just so she'd hold still. She lay motionless on the table, her eyes open but heavy-lidded and her jaw slack. The side of her mouth was wet. She was in a weird half-conscious state, sedated enough that she almost seemed human. Just human enough that it elicited feelings for her. She appeared to be the young, innocent teenage girl that perhaps she had once been.

Who had she been? Both inside and out? One had to wonder if her mental state was the result of damage or if, instead, it was the result of emotional trauma. What if the owner of the brain hadn't been consulted or agreed to this surgery? I highly doubted Adam had asked. He wasn't accustomed to getting his test subjects that way. He never asked. Maybe waking up in unfamiliar skin had been too much. Maybe Emily wasn't damaged. She'd simply fallen over the deep, dark abyss into total madness.

The table slid into the MRI machine. It wouldn't find anything useful. I kept that thought to myself, but my gut feeling was it would be a futile effort. Nothing I could have said would change Adam's mind, though. He was singular in his mission to fix Emily. To make her a whole human being again. Even if deep down she didn't want that.

Adam had to have been cooking something up. He hadn't scanned her brain since shortly after the transplant, so he was searching for something new. Something beyond a normal exam. At the time, there'd been no visible damage. All nerves had been attached properly. Basically, we had no explanation for what might have gone wrong. At least, nothing obvious.

Until now.

He zoomed in to one of the scans and tapped on the screen with his pen. A couple of small, dark spots that didn't belong. Shadows where there should have been none. I knew what it meant even before he said it.

"As I suspected, we're seeing some small, isolated patches of tissue damage. I'm not sure if this is the result of the host body rejecting the brain or if the cell death had begun prior to transplant and it's simply spread."

It wasn't surprising. Her behavior, her lack of progress, it had been obvious something was going wrong.

"I'm planning another surgery for Emily." And finally, there was an explanation for the scans. He paused and looked at both Chloe and I. Thiago was notably absent. And neither one of us responded, we only waited for him to finish his spiel. "In all the testing that's been done since she's woken, I've been unable to determine where exactly we may have gone wrong." He glanced at me. It was fleeting, but enough to raise my hackles. As though he'd insinuated I was somehow the reason things went wrong. "That being said, I do see signs the capability for speech is still there. There is still hope for progress."

He tapped the screen with the scan images. "There's no sign of physical abnormalities in the frontal lobe. She does attempt to form words, but they get stuck. Kind of like a vinyl record when it hits a scratch and skips."

Chloe looked at me, her disbelief apparent. I didn't blame her for being skeptical. It was something I shared. As much as I hated to admit it, Chloe and I shared many opinions. It was weird to think we might have things in common. But I still didn't think she was someone I could trust.

Adam was seeing something that didn't exist. Helping her form speech was one thing, but there didn't appear to be any actual thought going on inside Emily's head. You could fiddle with the brain's speech mechanism all you wanted, but without the intelligence to drive that speech, it was useless.

Chloe chose her words carefully. She always did. Perhaps that was why Adam liked her so much. "So, you think you can get her unstuck somehow?"

"It's certainly worth trying, isn't it?" Adam was a child just about to open his last present on Christmas morning.

I answered before Chloe could. "Well, I don't think she could possibly get any worse than she already is." I heard Chloe snort lightly under her breath. It had been discreet, and Adam probably hadn't even noticed.

"Thanks for the vote of confidence, Katherine." His expression darkened.

"I'm not doubting your abilities. If you feel there's a chance you could improve her…condition, then I'm all for it." I wasn't going to let him intimidate me. Or belittle me. Just because he insisted on pursuing this delusion, didn't mean I had to feel bad about not sharing his enthusiasm.

Chloe seemed to sense the spark of electricity between us. The friction. A potential explosion if the two of us butted heads. She'd already proved herself to be a master at diffusing Adam's lit fuse. "What would this surgery entail?"

That was all it took to break the spell. To neutralize the potential bomb. She knew both of our personalities too well.

"A precisely placed electrode, along with the corresponding neurostimulator. The intent is to trigger activity and hopefully speech. To open the lines of communication between thought and speech, if you will."

"So, a little like the device used to help Parkinson's or epilepsy patients." Chloe sounded genuinely interested now.

Deep brain stimulation. Adam had performed this procedure numerous times, and I'd assisted on many of them. There had been a night-and-day difference for many, one that had a profound effect on lessening symptoms and drastically cut down the medication the patient needed to use. The result had been amazing.

Adam nodded. "Based on the same technology, yes. But the device we'll be using has been enhanced with a state-of-the-art nano-chip. It is still in development at this stage, but preliminary results have been promising."

So much for being a partner in his research. Yet another thing Adam had decided to keep from me. He'd said nothing about including implant technology. That he hadn't even mentioned it as a possible direction was yet another needle sliding beneath my skin. I had a collection of them already. A regular pincushion.

"I don't understand. How would it work?" Chloe sounded uneasy, or at least uncertain.

"Well, first off, instead of needing to be placed in a precise location as with the traditional device, this one will be inserted into the brain stem. It utilizes adaptive technology. In other words, it will be able to send signals to the appropriate regions of the brain to bring about the desired effect. We would have the capability of adjusting the frequency via computer. So, once it is implanted, there will be no need to reopen the surgical site or implant a new one."

"Wow, that's…that's amazing." Chloe stumbled over her words, like she couldn't decide how to react. We made brief eye contact. Was that concern? Surprise? Adam obviously hadn't shared any of this with her either.

Emily began to stir. She writhed like a helpless infant, her eyes half-opened and not focused on anything. She was moaning. I had doubts that surgery would improve her condition. But I would go along with it like everything else that Adam did. I would help. While I was a skeptic, there was a part of me that wondered if maybe he was on to something. That maybe I wasn't giving credit where it was due. What if I was being stubborn and contrary because I didn't want Adam to be right?

Things had been tepid between us for some time. There was only the thinnest illusion of a happy marriage, when in reality, we merely tolerated each other. People who didn't know us well were fooled by the façade. Those who spent the most time with us, however, had to have noticed.

Chloe tilted her head slightly. Her expression indistinguishable between interested or just humoring him. "When?"

Leave it to Chloe to keep him engaged.

"I'm performing the surgery sometime early next week. There are a few supplies I'm waiting to receive and a little more preparation that needs to be done, but other than that, I'd say as soon as possible."

***

Unlike a traditional surgery of this type, Emily didn't have to be awake. Since placement was a fixed location and everything else could be tweaked after, it wasn't necessary to use the patient's conscious state to adjust settings. And with behavior as unpredictable as Emily's, it was simply a safer option to have her asleep.

The headgear used to hold her in place was similar to that from the original operation. Shining metal. Attached to her cheeks and the sides of her head. Screwed in so it didn't move. For now, she was in a seated position, but once the surgery began, she would be tilted forward, almost suspended in place, so the back of her head was exposed. Only a small patch of hair needed to be shaved. A bald spot right where her head met her neck. You could see the shiny, raised scar from the original surgery right below her hairline. A reminder.

This time it would be a minimally invasive brain surgery. Simple. In and out.

Adam moved so he was directly in her line of vision, and he mimicked talking using both hands like puppets. "Can you say *hi*, Emily?" She was still awake, but heavily sedated, and her eyelids hung on the verge of closing. Her attention was focused on him, but it was difficult to discern exactly how much she understood. In other words, no different than any other time he had tested her. When she didn't respond with so much as a sound, he tried a different approach. "Can you hum? Like this? Hmmm. Hmmm. Hmmm."

She opened her mouth. "Ah. Uh. Uh. Uh." It came out in a weird monotone staccato.

Adam's expression brightened. "That's right, Em. You almost have it. Hmmm. Hmmm." He pinched his fingers in front of his mouth. "We keep our mouth closed to hum. Hmmm."

"Ah." She snapped her jaws shut, but her lips were still open, baring her teeth. Her chin was sopping wet. "Nnn. Nn." Then she opened her mouth again. "Nngaah. Ah. Uh."

"Good job." He patted her arm, then reached down and squeezed her hand. He turned to me. "I think we can get started now."

***

The entire procedure went smoothly, without any physical complications. Emily was alive. Alert. Or, as alert as she could be. She was wheeled into the recovery room and, once she began thrashing around uncontrollably, sedated again so she wouldn't hurt herself or anyone else.

"So, how does all of this work?" My question seemed to catch Adam off guard, because his mouth hung open and he looked ready to go on the defensive. Anticipating an argument? But I wanted answers, and to know how it worked, so I kept myself calm when I talked. "What I mean, is how do you make the adjustments? You made it sound like there are different settings, or different options rather than just the strength of the frequency. Are we talking a closed loop system? I don't see magnets as being accurate enough to create the type of outcomes you seem to be alluding to. Likewise, monitoring cardiac activity. So, the system must be able to automatically adjust changes in brainwaves? Is it by preprogrammed therapy? Do you use a wireless device?"

"It responds to the brainwaves only. I can leave it at a preprogrammed setting or adjust it remotely." His answer sounded scripted.

"Yes, but how does it work? What's the scope of this technology? The range? You're telling me nothing—"

"Not right now," he said. "It just works, and someday, when I have the time, I will show you all of it, I promise. Just not now."

Then, before I could rebut, he up and left the room. Leaving me to simmer in unreleased frustration and anger. To be shut down just so…why hadn't I persisted more forcefully? I should have followed him down the hall and demanded answers until he had no choice but to give in.

It wouldn't have turned out that way even if I tried, would it?

No, he still would've found a way to shut me down.

And all I could do was wonder. What possibilities were there with this procedure? In a healthy brain, they seemed endless. In a damaged one such as Emily's, there was only so much. There was far more to this device than Adam was divulging.

All these questions, thoughts, the distrust. A realization wormed its way beneath my skin. An infection that bothered, not in a painful way but annoying. Adam didn't see me as any kind of equal. He never had. I was little more than a glorified assistant. Worthy of getting information only when Adam felt like sharing. Kept in the dark when he didn't. And for years, I'd just let it happen.

I was getting tired of the brush-off.

CHAPTER TWENTY-ONE

We decide on the Cape. Maybe spend a few days at the beach now that the worst of tourist season is over. The Sunrise Motel. It's an Americana relic from the mid-twentieth century with an oversized neon sign out in front of a single-floor, pastel-colored building. The lot has only one other car parked in it and borders so close to the beach, that sand coats the spaces along the far end. Although it's late September, the weather is still warm, the sun bright, the sky a brilliant, clear blue. It's the kind of day that makes you happy to be alive. Maybe I can forget what I've become.

Theresa is quiet most of the ride. Maybe I feel bad for her and what she's lost with her husband. Or I've simply given in without having any feeling involved. It's difficult to sort through my own thoughts sometimes. I've never in my life been impulsive, but this trip has been. Why did I ever think this would be a good idea?

I don't owe this woman anything.

Add that to the growing list of impulsive things I've done and regretted since waking in this body.

We check in and park in front of room ten, which is at the very end of the building. I carry our bags while Theresa unlocks the door. It's on the small side, with one queen bed, a dresser, and clean, but outdated, décor. Katherine Powers would've rented a little cottage on Martha's Vineyard, not this type of place. Still, there's something quaint and pleasing about it. It isn't terrible. I can live with this and try to enjoy it.

Theresa is quiet and subdued. She's been acting that way since the day I found the liquor bottle. It stayed under the sink where she left it, and still half full, so whatever demons she's been working through, she's kept them under wraps. Mostly. She's sitting on the edge of the bed, fidgeting with the phone in her hands and staring at the floor. But now she keeps glancing at me, chewing on her lower lip, and I *know* she wants to say something, so I just stare back and silently dare her to spill whatever is weighing on her mind.

"Where did you get the money for this?" She doesn't make eye contact for more than a second or two.

So this is the source of her mood. How quickly I've forgotten the nuances of married life. Like when unexpected money suddenly appears or disappears. I haven't, for obvious reasons, told her about the money Adam left behind.

"I helped a new acquaintance on a couple small jobs. He runs a painting business."

She eyes me suspiciously. "Oh. You…never mentioned anything."

I shrug. "I figured I'd see if anything more would come from it first."

"I see." She squeezes out a smile but her demeanor indicates she's not satisfied with my answer.

She's choosing not to pursue it, rather than creating an argument. Theresa does that a lot. I haven't missed those subtle cues, though. Which aren't that subtle, but men often miss them, don't they? At least, Adam always did. When you're female, you know how the female mind tends to work. Not always, of course. It isn't as though being female means being part of a collective, singular way of thinking. But there are some tendencies we share. Ideas about how woman are supposed to act and react in certain situations that are so deeply ingrained, we don't even question them. We just accept them as normal. Women are supposed to be people pleasers. Nurturers. We're the glue that holds a family together—somehow responsible for our spouse's and our children's well-being and happiness, even if it means sacrificing our own wants and needs. Theresa's the type of woman who chooses her battles carefully, because she doesn't like conflict.

Her smile looks forced. She gets up from the bed and crosses the room to where her suitcase rests by the door. "Well, whatever. We're here, we might as well enjoy it."

I settle onto the edge of the bed and zone out while Theresa starts unpacking. How much longer should I wait for Thiago to take me to Adam? He's stalling, no doubt about it. I'm nearing the end of my rope. Playing house with Theresa is getting old, and it's getting harder and harder for me to conceal. What's going to happen if I snap?

Theresa sits next to me. Her hands are folded on her lap. And she also isn't saying anything, so I find myself searching for a way to fill the space.

"You know, I read some news articles about the person who kidnapped me. They said he experimented on his own wife. Then he discarded her butchered body in an old chest freezer. Just left it as a rotting pile of old meat. What kind of person would do such a terrible thing? Can you even imagine?"

"No, I can't. That's…that's horrible." The hard crease of a frown rests right between her eyes. "I…I tried to avoid most of the news articles. It was too terrible to imagine what might have happened there. And this monster…" She bunches her hand into a fist. "When I saw his picture on the news, I recognized him from that night. He walked right into our home and took you."

So, she does have memories from that night. My instincts had been correct. Adam insisted she was too far gone to have any coherent recollection. He was obviously wrong. Or maybe he didn't care. That cocky bastard.

"And that…that vile woman who was with him. She tried to pretend she was comforting me, but I know now, she was only trying to distract me. To keep me from interfering."

Vile? That seems like a bit of an overreaction. "Maybe that woman was just as much of a victim as you were. Maybe she'd been brainwashed into believing what she was doing was the right thing."

The foul look she gives me implies that couldn't be further from the truth. "That woman knew exactly what she was doing. She was pure evil. They all were."

Funny how perception can be so drastically different from one person to the next. Evil. Ha. If she only knew I'm the same woman she's talking about.

"Well, I guess it doesn't really matter," she says after an extended silence. "You're back and you're alive. That's what's most important."

Theresa and I lock eyes and the entire time I'm painfully aware of how uncomfortable this moment has become. I freeze, unable to pull myself away from her gaze. Knowing what is coming next and feeling powerless to stop it. She caresses my cheek, letting her fingertips drag lightly along the side of my jaw until her thumb reaches my chin. She rests it there and leans in to press her lips to mine. I'm too dumbfounded to do anything other than kiss her back. At least at first. I close my eyes and try to remember the last time I felt anything resembling desire or wanting to be touched by another human being. I've shut myself off from feeling anything for so long. And now, it seems impossible. I break away from her kiss and open my eyes.

She rests a hand on my leg. Slowly slides it up the inside of my thigh, then stops right where the leg meets the groin and squeezes. I catch her by the wrist before she goes any further. I'm not ready to explore my sexuality as a male. My mood has soured considerably thanks to that conversation, and a sort of heavy, black cloud fills my head.

"Not now. I think…I need to get cleaned up first." Maybe giving her hope that something will happen between us is not the brightest thing. I only know I need to get away from her. To be by myself for a little while, and hopefully this feeling in my head will go away. This darkness.

She nods and withdraws her hand. I get up from the bed without looking at her and go into the bathroom.

For such a small room, there's a decent-sized bathtub, and the thought of soaking there, alone, is suddenly appealing. Maybe it will clear the fog.

Maybe it will make me feel like a human being again.

For now, it's an escape. I close the door behind me anyway.

CHAPTER TWENTY-TWO

Past

I didn't think it was possible. I'd assumed there were no thoughts going through her brain. There'd been nothing indicating any level of intelligence resembling a human being. Until I stumbled across Adam having another one of his sessions with Emily. And I heard it.

"Da…dee."

Of all the words she could have learned, why on earth did it have to be that one. The only person who should've been allowed to call Adam "Daddy" was our daughter, and she was dead. Anger welled up in the pit of my stomach. That creature. She was only half human. That was the most I would give her. Fucking *half*. And that was being generous.

Then Adam, completely ignorant of my seething rage, looked up at me with tear-filled eyes. "She spoke. Did you hear that? She spoke."

His emotional display was jarring. More evidence that he was detached from reality. That maybe his experiments had become his children. That *she* had somehow replaced our daughter in his heart.

How could he have forgotten Charlotte? Why would he allow this creature to affect him in such a way?

She didn't show anything resembling affection. It was likely she wouldn't progress beyond speaking single words, and it was probably because she imitated what Adam was trying to teach her rather than thinking of them on her own.

Had Adam wanted her to call him Daddy?

"I did. I heard it." I folded my arms. "Impressive."

My tone was frosty. Borderline hostile.

But Adam didn't notice. He was far too caught up in his own excitement. "Isn't it?" He faced Emily again, with eyes wide and an encouraging smile. She was babbling, a string of *da-dee*'s, sounding like an infant. "Emily, sweetheart. Can you say muh-mee?"

Oh, please god, no. Don't involve me in this.

I tensed. There was no way I was playing mother to that thing. And maybe it was instinct, something primal, because the moment her attention was trained on me, she hissed, like an angry cat. Almost like she sensed my disgust. Like the feeling was mutual. If such a thing could have feelings.

My mere presence riled her up.

Adam grasped both her arms firmly. "Easy, now." She struggled against his grip. Strained to get at me. The hiss turned to a growl. She practically foamed at the mouth. Adam wrapped both arms around her, but she thrashed out of his arms and charged me. Except she was off balance and smacked headlong into the sharp corner of a cabinet. A gash split down the center of her forehead and soon her entire face was covered in blood.

Emily shrieked. The howls of pain were deafening, yet she still clawed at the floor trying to get to me. Thick, foamy drool sprayed from the corners of her mouth and ran down her chin. It landed in little splats on the floor.

Adam pulled a syringe from his coat pocket and plunged it into her neck. She whimpered and cried out, but within seconds she'd stopped struggling, and Adam cradled her in his arms.

"Now look what you've done to yourself." She'd clawed at the cut on her face too. Blood smeared all over her fingertips like crimson finger paint. Adam held one of her bloodied hands in his and kissed it. Like a father comforting a child.

Is this what he thinks of her? That she's his child?

The more I watched him with her, the more the nausea tickled at the back of my throat. Emily had almost completely quieted, except for a few stray whimpers. Adam still held her and rocked her, and he was humming. A violent shiver passed through her body followed by a puddle of urine that spread on the floor beneath her. Adam seemed oblivious to that too. "Shhh," he whispered. "It's all better now."

He looked at me. "You know, you shouldn't get her worked up like this."

Right, because I'm the problem.

Because it was perfectly normal for her to fly into a rage every time I encountered her. "I didn't do anything other than enter the room and stand here. She's the one who's overreacting." I leaned into the door frame. "Why do you bother keeping her alive?"

"So she doesn't deserve to live just because you don't think she's making enough progress? If we treated every minute medical advance like that we'd never get anywhere. She is a living being. And no matter how small her strides have been, she still has value from a scientific standpoint. She's not a complete failure, you know."

That didn't change the fact her existence felt wrong to me. It made me uneasy. "If I end up like that, you better put a fucking bullet in my brain."

"You won't." He caressed her hair. "Would you get me something to disinfect this and some gauze? I need to clean her wound. Then I'll have Chloe stitch it up."

I rummaged through the cabinet. Emily appeared calm, but even sedated, she tensed and moaned as I approached to hand Adam the gauze and alcohol pads.

"Perhaps it's best if you leave, Katherine. I'm not sure what's come over her."

I cast a glance over my shoulder. Adam still hummed to her. I recognized the tune — *Hey Jude* — even though it was slightly off key. And it pissed me off. He coddled her and comforted her, but if I raised even the slightest concern for my own safety, he dismissed it. Like it was nothing. Like I was crazy. I left without saying a word. Disgusted. Anger drove my feet away from the room and down the hallway. The walls blurred, pain pulsed behind my eyes, and I couldn't catch my breath. I snatched a breath in and sobbed it back out.

I'm fucking crying. Me. What the hell?

I swiped at my eyes. Anger. Revulsion. Maybe some lingering feelings about my daughter's death. Things I'd repressed. God, I hoped nobody was around. I didn't want anyone to see the cracks in my armor. Time to find a place to hide and collect myself. To smooth over those cracks. To push all the emotions elicited by that thing back down where they belonged.

"Katherine?"

Fuck. Thiago. Why did he always seem to find me at my most vulnerable? "Not now Tee." I brushed past him, so he wouldn't see my face, but our eyes met. And I knew it was too late.

He caught me by the arm. "Come with me."

I didn't want to go anywhere with him. I didn't want to see or talk to anyone. Yet, I found myself following anyway. He led me straight to his office — Adam had given it to him shortly after we'd purchased the building, although I didn't know how much Thiago used it

He flicked on the lights, closed the door behind us, and pulled a chair out for me. I didn't *want* to be around anyone, so why had I followed him? He gestured for me to sit. I sat. Did I look like as much of a mess as I felt? Thiago went to the cabinet on the far wall, opened it, and pulled out a bottle of Jack Daniels. I wiped my eyes and smoothed my hair with my hands. Thiago didn't strike me as the type to keep booze in the office. Then again, there was probably a lot I didn't know about him. He unscrewed the cap and handed it to me.

I took it but didn't immediately drink.

He tilted his head slightly to the side and offered a sympathetic smile. "Sorry, I don't have any glasses. If it bothers you, I could run down to the cafeteria and get a cup."

I shrugged, brought the bottle to my lips, and took a healthy swig. My eyes watered a bit more — it'd been quite some time since I'd drunk straight hard liquor, and it was always a shock. I set the bottle on the desk and let out a heavy breath.

"Something has rattled the great, impenetrable Katherine Powers."

I snorted in response.

"Would you like to talk about it?"

I took another drink to chase away the uncomfortable, under-a-microscope feeling. I'd tried therapy years ago, but hated the intrusive questions. This was no better. "Not particularly."

Thiago studied me, then picked up the bottle, drank, and replaced it to its spot on the table. What exactly was his motive? Was it to comfort me, or pump me for information he could report to Adam? "Sometimes I think you hold too much inside. I realize we are not close friends by any stretch, but it does no good to isolate oneself from others."

"The only person I can fully *trust* is myself. This has been proven over and over." I downed another swallow of the whiskey. Heat crept up the sides of my neck and my cheeks. Hard liquor always went straight to my head, and with it, an uncomfortable heaviness that impaired my judgement a little too much. When I was younger, I drank my fair share. I'd gotten myself into a few tricky situations. That was why I usually didn't drink at all.

"You don't need to trust someone fully to ask for help."

Persistent little bastard.

I ground my fingers into my palm. Why the sudden interest in my mental well-being? Was he pumping me for information? "Who says I need help?"

"Who says I'm talking about you?"

I laughed. Maybe the liquor had relaxed me too much. "Fair enough."

"Something must have upset you."

"I'm not sure upset is the proper word for what I'm feeling." I leaned back in the chair and crossed my legs. Closed my eyes and saw Emily in Adam's arms.

"What is the proper word?"

I was lightheaded and warm. Relaxed. My inhibitions and sense of self-preservation dulled. "I think my husband may have gone off the proverbial deep end. I'm not sure I can support his research anymore."

It was the first time I'd expressed it out loud, although it had been festering inside for quite some time.

"Emily?"

"He has her calling him *Daddy*. Can you believe that?"

Something flickered in his expression. The briefest moment of painful emotion, which he quickly covered up with that blank façade. Perhaps Thiago and I weren't so different in how we dealt with things.

"That is certainly…unexpected."

"Is it? He's been overly attached to this experiment since the beginning. To a point that I'd consider it delusional. Every other failure has been exterminated mercilessly. Snuffed out and discarded like it meant nothing. What is the difference with this one?"

"I don't know. Could it be the significance of this one experiment? She was, after all, his first successful human transplant." A grasp at straws if anything. I truly felt, from deep within my gut, that Adam's obsession with dear Emily was an unhealthy infatuation rather than pride in his work.

"Successful? She's a drooling fucking zombie."

"Okay, fine. Maybe that's not the best word. But she is alive. Many functions are intact, even if they may be deeply flawed. She is a walking, breathing human being. Your husband took a brain from one human being and implanted it into a donor body. Even with all her…flaws, that is a remarkable feat. No other person in the world has done this. This technology he's discovered is unprecedented."

"I suppose." Was I overreacting? Because like it or not, Thiago did have a point. Emily's existence was pretty remarkable, considering she was the first human transplant. Maybe I'd allowed negative emotions about my marriage to taint my viewpoint on his achievement.

"He should at least be acknowledged for the momentous accomplishment he's made. That doesn't mean he hasn't lost traces of his sanity in the process."

"It may be a bit more than traces." I let out an exaggerated sigh. Calmed again. Settled into the heavy-headed, warm numbness of a slight buzz. It would be so easy to drink my troubles away. But they'd still be there when I came down, wouldn't they?

"Katherine, a bit of advice, if you will. You are free to disregard."

I shrugged, indicating he could continue if he really wanted. It didn't matter one way or another.

"Sometimes it is better to play along. Allow yourself to fly under the radar. There is a time and a place for rebellion. A time and a place to stand your ground. For now, I think perhaps it is best to give the appearance of support. You never know in what situation you might find yourself in the future or if it would be beneficial to have him on your side. Or when he might turn the tables on you."

Cryptic advice at best. Almost like he knew something and was holding back, but at the same time trying to steer me in a specific direction. Did Thiago have something planned, or was I being paranoid? I quickly disregarded that thought. I didn't know Thiago well enough to assume his motives.

Hadn't I already been doing that very same thing? Playing along. It was only recently I'd started to question him. I was responsible for the wedge that had grown between Adam and me. The frequent snipes. The disagreements. Being contrary *just because*. Although, perhaps Thiago had a point. That attitude didn't accomplish anything. It only caused friction.

"I'll take that into consideration."

"You should go home. Get some rest. You're looking a little pale."

I smirked. "Thanks so much, Doctor Tee."

He laughed. "I'm no doctor. Only a concerned friend."

CHAPTER TWENTY-THREE

The water in the tub is a little too hot to be comfortable, a temperature that instinct tells me to retreat from, but I ease my body in anyway. My skin turns red on contact. The pain is welcome. It connects me to this body. I like it.

I sink into the water and open my mind. What am I doing here? Why am I playing house with her? What do I really hope to accomplish with this trip? Will it change our *relationship* when we get home?

I'm not sure. About any of it.

The utility knife from my back pocket rests on the corner of the bathtub. I pick it up and click the blade open. It presses against the tip of my finger. With very little resistance, it punctures the skin and a bead of blood wells up. I set the blade back down and stick my finger in my mouth. It would be far too easy to rip the blade up each arm. To open an artery and drain every drop of life from this body. I know exactly where to cut to go down that route.

What do I have to live for?

It would reach the news. If Sean, the man who'd been kidnapped by a loon doctor and mysteriously reappeared, is found sitting in a bathtub full of his own blood, it will be a sad footnote to his story. One that will reach Adam. He'll know he's responsible.

Or will he?

Don't be weak, Katherine. It doesn't suit you. I can picture him saying that. And he would be right. Checking out isn't something that suits me at all. Suicide is a one-shot deal. I'll never get to see the look on Adam's face when I confront him. No, I need that moment. I need him to feel the pain he's caused and to not be able to run away from it. Maybe that is something worth living for.

Theresa will be the one broken. If she finds her husband's lifeless body in here, drained of blood, it will put her over the edge. I can't do that to her.

Wait, is this empathy? Or traces of leftover emotions, as if Sean's DNA somehow clings to it, even without his brain in control. It seems preposterous. I—Katherine—don't feel any attachment to Theresa. I don't have any feelings for her. I simply go along with some of the things she wants because I know it will benefit me. It will help me reach my goal.

I focus on that goal as the water cools to a more tolerable temperature. I lie here, getting drowsy and my limbs feel leaden.

The door creaks open and Theresa lets herself in.

She's wearing a robe. With a timid smile, she kneels beside the tub, rests an arm on the side, and skims her fingers over the top of the water. "We used to take baths together, when we first got married."

I understand what she's getting at. That this is another attempt to reconnect the current me with the past Sean.

Not happening.

"I know things have been hard for you. Adjusting." I feel her watching me, but I refuse to look over. "It's been hard for me too. But I think I've been selfish. Like, I haven't considered how any of this has affected you. I feel guilty about that. Really guilty." Dear god, she's fucking crying again. This woman leaks like a sieve. A never-ending fucking fountain of snot and tears. "I know you said you're not sure about our future, but I wanted you to know I'm here for you. I'll stay by your side no matter what. Even if you never remember a thing about our past, I don't care—"

She stops to collect herself. Has she been listening to those fucking church harpies she hangs out with? For better or for worse, till death do us part, and all that other bullshit? Pathetic. I reach out to rest my hand on the top of her head and slowly stroke her hair. It's an impulsive gesture. Her hair is smooth—thin and fine like a silken waterfall. She closes her eyes and presses her head into my hand. A cat starved for attention.

What has Sean ever done to deserve this devotion? Desperation rolls off her in great waves. She clings to memories of someone who no longer exists. She is willing to stick by someone who shows her no affection, who makes no promises of building a future together, and yet here she is. Waiting.

She shivers under my touch. "I know we can be happy," she whispers.

I stop stroking her hair, my palm resting on the back of her head. No, there will be no happiness. For any of us. This mission—and yes, that's what it is, a mission—is not likely to end well.

With a detached fascination, I watch Sean's hand as it tenses and grasps Theresa's hair into a tight fist. As it plunges her head under the water. As it holds her, almost effortlessly, while she struggles and flails about. The water around her head churns and bubbles violently. Some of it splashes out onto the floor.

There isn't, as I feared, any mystical attachment left in this body. Nothing to indicate traces of Sean still exist within these cells. No empathy for a former lover.

Right, Sean? You have no control over me or what I do.

If there had been, perhaps he wouldn't allow her head to stay under the water. Perhaps he wouldn't continue to hold her there, even after she stops struggling. That pretty, silken hair floats along the top of the water. Her body goes limp.

"Sean is dead," I whisper.

She's been stupid to put so much faith in him. In their relationship. Love is a farce, an imagined chemical reaction. My own so-called lover has thought nothing of turning my life completely upside down. He's thought nothing of leaving me to fend for myself. And that is a relationship with many years behind it.

That's what happens when the chemical reaction wears off. When this thing called love evaporates, leaving behind nothing but fading memories and lingering resentment. Perhaps Adam harbored a secret hatred toward me for years and I never even noticed.

Maybe it has been mutual.

I loosen my grasp on Theresa's head. It bobs to the surface and floats there. She's a stupid, weak girl. It makes me want to be angry.

It makes me want to hate her. Yet, despite this, I don't feel anything. No guilt, no remorse. Nothing. I lift her head and shove her roughly out of the tub. Her body hits the floor with a heavy thud and lands in a misshapen heap. I sink back into the water and try to relax, but now my muscles are stiff and tense.

I need to call Thiago to help clean up this mess.

But not yet.

I rest my head back against the tub and let my eyelids shut. Force myself into relaxation. Push the stress out of my body. I almost doze off, but Theresa has left the TV on in the other room. The news and the incessant chatter grates on me. I don't want to get up and shut it off, so I try to block it out.

At least I've settled one problem. I peer down at Theresa from the corner of my eye.

Maybe I should check her pulse.

She still isn't moving, and it's been a good ten minutes.

The water has cooled to tepid. My mood for a bath sours. I stand, pull the drain plug, and reach for the towel from the rack next to the door. Wrapping it around my waist, I step out of the tub and kneel next to Theresa. Her skin is cool to the touch but not yet cold. Bluish in tint. Her eyes are open—vacant as the glass eyes of a doll. Thin, white foam pokes out of the corners of her mouth. No life to be had there. The body truly is just a vessel, isn't it?

I leave the bathroom to get dressed. Maybe everything that makes us who we are truly is contained inside the brain. Theresa knew I'm not her husband. She might not have wanted to admit it to herself, but I think deep down a part of her recognized the truth. Probably saw through my bullshit lies. What was it that kept her from giving up?

Maybe it was hope. Tied into her attachment to his physical appearance. We know each other by sight, by sound, by scent, but there is one thing that truly controls it all. The brain. Male, female, old, young, it doesn't matter. It's the brain that determines who we are.

I pick up the remote control from the bureau and flick the TV off. I'm exhausted. I flop back onto the bed. Consider a nap.

No, it's best to call Thiago first. He's a couple of hours' drive away and will need time to make plans.

I fish my phone out of the pocket where I'd hidden it in my travel bag. Thiago's number is the only one saved in the contacts list. I haven't talked to him since the day I first contacted him. He hasn't bothered to contact me either, which makes me think he's trying to avoid the issue. To keep me from Adam. That isn't going to happen.

He picks up after the second ring. "Katherine? Is everything alright?"

"No. Not really."

"Are you hurt?" He sounds worried.

"No."

"What is it?" Worry is turning to panic. Even in this body, with this voice, he recognizes something is wrong but knows I've never been the type to ask for help.

"I've done something…and I don't know how to fix it."

On the other end, a moment of silence, although I can still hear him breathing. "What happened?"

"Will you come to me? Please?"

Another pause. "Katherine, what did you do? Are you okay? Was there an accident?"

"Just…I need your help."

There's an extended silence, punctuated by a heavy breath, signaling his resignation. "Where are you?"

I smile, give the address, and hang up.

I close my eyes and open them again seemingly moments later to loud knocking on the door. I go to the door and look through the peephole. Thiago. As I open the door to let him in, the setting sun glints off his car in the parking lot. If the sun is already setting, hours must have gone by, because the last thing I remembered was hanging up on Thiago.

"Thank god, I thought something had happened to you. I've been knocking for ten minutes now." He looks genuinely worried. His dark eyes are tired and ringed with red.

"I'm sorry, I fell asleep." I gesture for him to come inside and he does, moving cautiously, as if anticipating an attack. He doesn't say anything. Just nods and closes the door behind him. He investigates the room with his eyes. There's a second travel bag. Theresa's sandals placed neatly next to the bureau. Her pink sweatshirt draped over the back of the chair.

"You are not alone?"

"No." Does he think *Sean* fits into a size small women's sweatshirt? "Well, I wasn't."

Something flashes in his expression. Worry? Fear? Perhaps I've rendered him speechless, because now he's staring at me.

"What?"

"I'm sorry. I can't get used to the fact that it's *you*. I know logically what he did, and I sense that it's you from the way that you speak, and just because I'd always know it's you, no matter what." He pauses and almost looks like he might reach out and caress my cheek but thinks better of it.

"Try living it. Every time I look in a mirror, every time I use the bathroom or shower. Every time I speak." I fold my arms. "Why haven't you called?"

"It is better to lie low for a while."

"That's ridiculous. Do you know how ridiculous that is? Time is wasting. I feel him slipping further and further away from me with each passing minute."

"Let's talk about this. He needs to pay for what he has done to you. I swear it. But you shouldn't be making any rash decisions."

I laugh. "The time for talk has passed."

"What did you do?"

I meet his eyes. Stare him down. "Something that can't be *undone*."

I nod toward the bathroom. He stares at me a moment longer before making the cautious trek to the open bathroom door, where the light is still on. Where Theresa still rests. I don't follow him in. Just sit on the edge of the bed and wait.

There's a sharp intake of breath. "Jesus!" Thiago backs out of the bathroom, stumbles over his own feet, and nearly falls in the process. "Katherine, what have you done?"

"Please, Thiago. You've seen a dead body before." My mood is quickly progressing to irritable.

"What have you done?" he repeats.

"It's fairly obvious. I held her head under the water until she stopped moving. She was a needy, annoying, weak woman. I couldn't take it anymore." What about this does he not understand? My patience has worn to nothing. "I'm tired of this charade. I can't fucking do it anymore."

"Katherine, listen…" His voice softens.

"No. You listen, okay?" I stand, abruptly, and sweep everything off the top of the bureau in one sudden, violent motion. "I woke in a hospital bed with my brain sewed into a fucking man's body and the knowledge that my husband betrayed me and took off on his own. I cannot live out my life pretending to be some woman's husband and ignoring what he's done. I just can't do it. It's driving me fucking insane."

Thiago hisses through his teeth and makes a lowering motion with his hands.

Am I really being that loud? I snap my mouth shut.

"That's the last thing we need—for someone to file a noise complaint, or worse, hear what we're talking about," he says in a harsh whisper.

I force a calming breath. He's right. Thiago holds out his hands, looking both panicked and helpless at the same time. Maybe trying to diffuse the situation before I—in a fit, healthy, strong male body—go nuclear. "It's okay Katherine. I understand. What is it you want from me? Why did you call me?"

"I called you because I don't know what the fuck to do with *that*." I gesture toward the open bathroom door. Toward Theresa. "I can't just leave it here."

He frowns, pinching his lower lip between his thumb and forefinger, a nervous habit that for some reason brings me a sliver of comfort. "No, you can't leave her like that."

"We would need to get rid of it, then."

"Katherine, *she* was a human being. It is not wise to speak ill of the dead."

"*She* is no longer living, breathing, or thinking. All that's left is a body, which is a thing. Don't personify it."

He sighs, resigned. "We'll throw her in the ocean. Then, in the morning, you will call the police and tell them she went out for a late-night walk but when you woke up, she had never come home."

"Absolutely not. No police."

"It's the only way."

"No. It isn't."

He's beginning to lose patience. I see it in his posture. In the hard creases between his eyes and the deep frown lines. A fight for self-control. "It won't matter whether her body is found or whether she's missed by others those first few days when she doesn't show up for work or answer calls from her friends. If you, as her husband" — he holds up his fingers in pretend quotes when he says husband — "don't report her missing, they'll immediately wonder why. You'll be cast under suspicion. It will call unnecessary attention toward you."

"Why should I call the police? I'm not really her husband. I'm not planning on building a life as Sean Malone. I don't give a rat's ass if some cop thinks I'm guilty, or how any of this looks. I won't be sticking around for scrutiny."

"That is a dangerous attitude to have, Katherine."

"Why? You're supposed to be taking me to Adam so I can—"

"When the time is right." He points a finger at me. He hasn't given in to emotion, or impatience, but there's more force to his voice. More finality. "Until that time, you will go back to your home and lay low for a few days. And then I will contact you."

"I knew there was a reason I called you." It's a childish retort, but he's completely insane if he thinks I'm going to just sit around and wait. Of course, if I want his help, I'll have to play along for now. Make him believe I'm being cooperative. But that has a limit. "Fine. What do we do first?"

He studies me. Almost like he knows I've given in too easily. "We wait until later. I will go stake things out, find a boat. Make sure nobody's around. You bring her down to the beach. Then I will meet you at the end of the jetty, in a boat. After that, we drive out to an appropriate spot and drop her in."

He'd obviously done this sort of thing before. He'd chided me for calling Theresa's body *it*, but this was so detached, so matter of fact, so impersonal. Getting rid of her was simply a job to complete.

"How does one know if they've found an appropriate spot?" I was toying with him now.

"When we are far enough out that she won't be found." He pauses. "Or that we will not be seen dumping her over the side."

"You've thought this through."

"This is not the first time I have had to fix…a mistake." Thiago breaks eye contact, effectively shutting down the conversation with a single look.

Adam's mistakes? Thiago already admitted as much. It's like now that Adam's closet has been opened, the skeletons are just lining up to crawl out. And with them, maybe some of Thiago's. Because you have to wonder about a man who can be so calm and cavalier talking about disposing of bodies.

CHAPTER TWENTY-FOUR

All of Adam's recruits were placed into a deep slumber shortly after they were brought to the center. They were led to a room with a bed in it; stark white walls and tile floors, and virtually no decoration. Then laid on that single bed and told they would be given something to help them relax. To help them fall asleep. That everything would be fine and dandy and they'd have the best sleep of their lives. It would be over before they knew it. They were put to sleep, completely unaware of the fate that lay ahead. Unaware that they'd never wake again.

Except it didn't always work as planned.

Sometimes the drugs would fail. Sometimes machines would fail.

One insomnia-fueled night, I'd been working late. Organizing notes I'd taken during the previous day's labs. Proofreading them until my eyes crossed. It was something I did when I couldn't sleep, because if I couldn't sleep, then why not do something productive.

But I wasn't being productive anymore. I had let my thoughts drift and hadn't noticed until that stupid little cursor blinking back from the computer screen snapped me out of my stupor. It reminded me how little work I'd accomplished in the past twenty minutes.

Because there was something else locked in my mind. The conversation Thiago and I had about picking your battles and taking matters into your own hands. It was obvious he'd been cautioning me not to act on impulse. But if you thought about an action first, really considered the consequences, that couldn't be considered impulsive, could it?

The more I tried to process it, make sense of it, the more Emily's existence seemed wrong. Snuffing out that life would be such a simple thing. It required little more than slipping into the medical supply room. Unlocking the cabinets where Adam kept the controlled substances. Finding something that would bring a humane end to Adam's pet zombie girl. That was the closest equivalent to what she was. Still living. But barely.

While my brain considered the actions carefully, my body acted on them. My hand picked up my keys and my feet walked to the medical supply room. Once inside, I flicked the light on. Adam had entrusted me with the keys, though I didn't understand why. It seemed like lately there was very little he trusted me with. Maybe he'd simply forgotten about the keys. That was the more likely scenario.

But in that cabinet...so many substances that could do the trick. An extra dose that would be lethal. Was it wrong of me, what I was thinking of doing? Maybe it made me a monster. Maybe wanting her dead made me a terrible human being.

Who are you kidding, Katherine. You'd never actually do it.

That voice in my head was probably right. I could fantasize about it all I wanted, but I wouldn't follow through. Not to mention, Adam was far too fixated on *her*. He'd probably figure out I had something to do with it. And then where would I be?

The silence of the night and my collective thoughts were shattered by a scream.

Had someone left a television on? Not likely. It was well after midnight, and we didn't have many on site. Adam called them a distraction. Then who? Chloe and Thiago had gone home, and I was the only one on duty. Which only left one alternative.

One of the patients must have woken.

As if to confirm my assumption, a muffled moaning and whimpering came from the hallway. A shaky voice.

"H-hello? Is anybody there?" When there was no response, it became more insistent. "Hello? Please...somebody?"

I closed and locked the cabinet. Did a quick check to make sure there was no evidence I'd been there and exited the room.

"Somebody, please...help me."

The situation devolved rapidly. She went from pleading to screaming. Bloodcurdling, panicked screaming. Pounding on the door.

Something must have gone wrong, because they weren't supposed to wake. What if the others did too? Adam had assured me it wasn't possible, yet here I was, listening to one scream herself hoarse. I hurried toward the patient wing. Toward the noise.

I pulled the phone from my pocket, dialed Adam, and held it to my ear.

"Hello?" His voice was rough with sleep. Disoriented.

"One of them has woken."

"What?"

"Where are you?" I didn't bother concealing my impatience. "Because one of them has woken."

There was a pause on the other end as, no doubt, his mind caught up with what I was saying. "Are you sure?"

"She's screaming bloody murder and pounding on the door trying to get out. I'd say I'm *reasonably* sure."

"Which one?"

I stopped in front of the private room, the source of all the commotion.

Of course, it had to be this *one.*

"Louise."

"Okay. Fine, I'll be right there. Don't do anything yet."

"Shouldn't I try to calm her down?" I was used to damage control. To avoiding crisis. Getting in there and making them think you cared. At that, I was an expert.

"No. No, just leave her be. Call Thiago. He'll have to help me restrain her."

"But it's the middle of the night..." I gave up arguing. Why did I have to be the one to make all the phone calls? Why did I care? It was Adam's operation. I was only doing the courtesy of telling him something had gone wrong.

"Call him. I will be there shortly." Without waiting for a response, he hung up. For a fleeting moment, I thought about the strangeness of the situation. How my husband had been home, probably. Sleeping. While I was here at his place of business. How I hadn't even known precisely where he was. And how until I needed to find him, I hadn't really cared or thought about where he might be. Had we truly grown so far apart?

When did that happen?

My phone weighed me down like a brick in my hand. Useless. I should have done what Adam said and called Thiago right away.

Instead I stood outside Louise's room and listened. She'd grown hoarse. That would be my voice someday. I tried to picture that voice coming from my mouth. It was a slightly higher pitch than my own, maybe warmer in tone. Would that be something I could get used to? Would it sound different at all with my brain operating that body? Her screams mixed with loud sobbing and half-hearted pleas. She banged on the door.

"Somebody…"

I'm the only one who can hear you, Sweetie, was what I wanted to say. I nearly jumped out of my skin when the phone rang. Nausea tickled my throat. My mouth filled with saliva and I swallowed hard to combat the feeling.

Not fucking now.

I closed my eyes and pressed the phone to my ear.

"Katherine, what's going on?" Thiago. He always seemed to call at precisely the right time.

The nausea subsided, somewhat, although my skin felt clammy and uncomfortable. I walked a few paces from Louise's door before saying anything. It wasn't likely she would hear me, but for some reason I didn't want my voice to register in her mind. Not even a rational fear, but I didn't have time to analyze it. "Your timing is suspicious. What are you doing awake?"

"What are *you* doing awake?"

"One of the patients has awoken and is having a bit of a meltdown. Adam is on his way. He told me to call you."

"You're still at the facility? Why didn't you call me?" Quick to react, as always. I could never tell if he was teasing me, or being deliberately obtuse, or if it was a genuine query. Maybe reading people was not my strong suit.

I shrugged, even though he wasn't there to see it. "I suppose I was getting to it."

"Uh huh. Well, I'm pulling into the parking lot now."

That was fast. Too fast. "Tee, how did you know to call when you did?"

"I know a lot more and see a lot more than you could imagine." There he was being cryptic again. Thiago was resourceful, and I was aware that he kept tabs on things for the lab, in addition to all the little undesirable jobs Adam concocted for him. Had he been watching security cameras? Seen me prowling the halls and the supply room? Or Louise screaming? The building had an elaborate security system, and it had been designed and set up by Thiago. Adam had once boasted about it, but I hadn't paid much attention at the time.

Something about it clicked. How else would Thiago know when and where to show up?

I felt the tap on my shoulder and whipped around to face him.

"You should really be resting, Katherine. Your body is weak. And you look terrible."

"Thanks for the kind words. I'll rest plenty when I'm dead."

"You'll have a good many years before that happens. Decades, even. For now, your future host body is wearing herself out."

I shivered at the thought. I didn't like talking about my impending surgery. Or even thinking about it. The closer it grew, the more nervous I became.

"Tee, I have a bad feeling about all of this." How did I describe it? Almost a vibe I was getting. That I might not survive. What if Adam didn't have what it took to complete a successful transplant? I could end up like Emily. Maybe dying in this wrecked body was my true destiny. If such a thing existed.

"Good, you're here." Adam nodded at Thiago. Was I invisible? I was beginning to feel that way. He might as well have been looking through me. "Katherine, go get some rest. Thiago and I will take care of this."

I nodded and left them, even though I hated myself for listening to him. Hated myself for taking orders like some puppet. But as I walked down that hallway, a soreness right to my bones turned my body to lead. Little pinpricks of darkness danced in the periphery of my vision. Dizziness. Nausea. I closed my eyes for a moment, until the feeling passed. My physical state was getting worse not better. It was almost like I could feel the bad cells, like I was rotting from the inside out.

As much as I thought I'd be okay with dying, that I'd made peace with it, I wasn't ready. I wasn't okay with it either. The thought of dying, of ceasing to exist was a terrifying black void. A deep chasm. I clung to the edge, so I wouldn't fall, but those walls were crumbling.

Instead of going to my room, I headed back toward Louise's. The screaming had stopped. The crying and whimpering had stopped. Thiago and Adam perched on either side of her bed, and she was once again asleep.

"What happened? How did she wake?"

Adam checked the little rubber tubes and the clear plastic hose connected to the machine that administered the drugs to her system and didn't make eye contact with me.

"Well, it appears there was a blockage in one of the hoses. The machine automatically shuts off if there's any sort of malfunction. It's a safety precaution." He didn't elaborate, but Adam took such mishaps as failure and absorbed them as his own. It was etched in every line and crease on his face. That one, he hadn't anticipated.

"Are you still going to operate?" All the issues we'd run into hardly inspired confidence. I wasn't convinced it was safe, and the more things went wrong, the harder it was to accept the risk for myself.

"All will go as planned. This doesn't change anything."

There wasn't a trace of uncertainty in his words. Was it wrong to doubt him? Because I'd always been a firm believer in following what your gut knows to be true. And no matter how many reassuring words he spoke, my gut was telling a different story. Proceed with caution, it said.

CHAPTER TWENTY-FIVE

Theresa is a scrawny little thing and I'm easily able to hoist her stiff, angled body over my shoulder. Thiago ushers me out the door and over the sand dune. It's an overcast night with no moon showing and near impossible to see anything on the beach once we're past the reach of the motel lights.

"Thiago, am I suddenly going to hit water?"

"Relax, you need to let your eyes adjust. Just stay close to me."

"I'm not a cat."

A snort. "You do have the temperament of one."

We trudge through sand, and my calves and thighs burn from the exertion. It's uncomfortable, but I never would have been able to do this in my own body.

"She's light, but she's dead weight." I stop walking to shift Theresa from one shoulder to the other. Sweat coats my back and underarms from the exertion, and my muscles are stiff. The only upside is I've vaguely amused myself by calling her *she* rather than *it*. Staying put for a couple of minutes is as much to catch my breath as it is to ease my sore shoulder. It doesn't help that her body is in complete rigor mortis, so she doesn't flop around or have any sway.

"I'm not carrying her for you, if that's where you're headed with this."

"I wouldn't dream of asking you to."

"This isn't something you should be treating lightly. You've taken a human life. It's not something you just come back from. You need to own the responsibility." While he appears to be cautioning me, and his tone is very matter of fact, there's an underlying sadness to his words. Or maybe a hint of remorse. Thiago has always been a bit of a mystery to me. Words of deep wisdom carried out in a monotone, expressionless package.

"Thiago, how many mistakes have you cleaned up for my husband?"

"With Adam, I would hesitate to call them mistakes. More like problems. Or inconveniences."

"Then how many problems have you made go away?"

He's silent for a moment. "More than I'd care to admit."

That halts our conversation and we make it to the jetty in silence. The sea is calm, and the water reaches out and nips at the sand, then gently rolls back into itself. "If you stay in the center of the jetty, the rocks are pretty even. There's a boat moored just a ways down. I'll meet you in a bit."

Without saying anything further, he disappears into the darkness and I fumble my way over the jagged rocks toward the end of the jetty. I'm glad he doesn't see me nearly trip and faceplant. I squint, even though my eyes have acclimated to the darkness and squinting isn't going to help me see any better. It's nothing but a collection of shadows and blacker shadows, so I move at an extremely slow pace, with one foot feeling its way in front of the other. I use the sound of the water lapping at the rocks to counterbalance my movement. To help keep me in the middle.

I try to tap into the feeling of when I'd first awoken, when hearing was my only sense. I'm traveling through a dark void, where time doesn't exist, where it's just me and Theresa and the sound of the ocean waves.

The end comes up suddenly. I almost lose my footing and drop Theresa, but quickly regain my balance. I lay her down and sit at the end of the rocks. The wind is much stronger out this far than on the shore. It whips through my hair and clothing and over my bare skin, relentless.

Where's Thiago?

I have no idea how long he'll keep me waiting. The trek to the end of the jetty has taken a ridiculous amount of time and he's still not here. So now I wait. Me and poor, dead Theresa. Wait, wait, wait. Maybe he's tricked me. Decided helping me isn't worth the time or effort. Or perhaps he's run into some trouble getting a boat. What am I going to do if Thiago doesn't show up?

It's probably be wise to form a backup plan. There's no way I'm carrying Theresa back to the beach. I can roll her into the water from here and hope for the best. Return to my motel room and pretend nothing happened. Then what? Do I talk to the police like Thiago suggested? He has a point. A husband that goes on with his life, without a care for his missing wife is, indeed, suspicious. The less suspicion cast in my direction, the better. The less suspicion, the longer I last.

Dear god, what in the hell is taking him so long?

No sooner do I position Theresa, ready to push her in the water, than the sound of a boat engine appears. The noise is shrouded by the whipping wind, but unmistakable. It grows closer. A light flickers, accompanying the engine noise, and both grow more pronounced as they near the jetty. It must be Thiago. But what if it isn't? What if it's some random stranger, or the police? I tense as the boater cuts the engine, then shines the light at the end of the rocks.

It has to be Thiago.

"Took you long enough." I mean it in a lighthearted, joking manner, but I'm stressed and irritated so it comes out sounding snippy instead.

Thiago doesn't bother acknowledging the comment. He grunts and carefully climbs out of the boat. A delicate balancing act of holding the boat close to the rocks and trying not to fall in the water. "Can you bring her down here please?"

I scramble to my feet and hoist Theresa over my shoulder again.

"It might be easier if you sit on the edge and slide your way down. So you don't fall."

I obey without argument and slide down on my ass, struggling to keep myself upright on the jagged, angular rocks. Even though I feel kind of like a child doing it.

"I'm going to hold the boat steady, so you can toss her in."

"I don't know if I can." My muscles are screaming from the strain of lifting, carrying, and putting her down. Then picking her up again. Maybe I need to start lifting weights when this ordeal is over. Not that I know anything about doing that. I edge close, slide my foot until it hits the next rock below. This one is at a sharp slant. My legs shake, and my arms burn even more as I try to stay balanced.

"You're going to have to." When I respond with an irritated grunt, he adds, "I can't hold the boat steady for you much longer. The tide is starting to come in."

I take a deep breath, sweat coursing down my face, neck, and back from the exertion.

God this is fucking ridiculous.

With one final grunt, I drop Theresa's body into the boat, then lean back, panting, heart pounding, sweat pouring off me and drying to a sticky mess in the wind.

When I finally get myself under control, I step one foot in the boat and land flat on my ass as I pull the other one in. I grasp the sides of the boat as Thiago gets in after me, then uses the oar to push us away from the rocks. He starts up the engine again. Soon we're racing out into the blackness of the night. Another void. I've never liked the ocean. Never liked boats. There's something frightening about how helpless it makes me feel.

I want to ask Thiago how far we need to go but think better of it. He won't hear me over the roar of the engine or the wind anyway, so I grip tight on the metal edges of the boat and keep my eyes shut even tighter. Just willing myself to stay calm. Because to me, this boat seems no safer than a flimsy tin can.

After an agonizing amount of time, the boat slows, the engine falls to an idle, and then we're drifting in the waves. The warmth of Thiago's hand on my arm almost sends me flailing out of the boat in surprise.

"I think we've gone far enough."

He doesn't say any more, though I know what he means and that it's my responsibility to take care of it. I lean over and grasp Theresa under the armpits. She's a complete dead weight and I have a much more difficult time lifting her than before. I stand, like a baby learning to walk for the first time, my legs wobbly and the boat rocking with each movement.

In the end, it's rather anti-climactic for all the effort involved. Theresa drops in with a baritone-deep, plopping splash. She sinks in slow motion, hanging in suspense with her feet descending, weighted and pulling the rest of her body down, until only her face shows above the surface. I press my hand against her forehead, and a few bubbles escape from her nose and mouth until she is completely below the surface. Gone. Just like that.

Bye, Theresa.

We ride the boat back to shore and climb out. Thiago hands me a flashlight, then pulls a pair of gloves from his pocket, along with a small aerosol canister. He puts on the gloves and sprays all over the surface of the boat.

"Keep the light focused on it, please." He sounds gruff and irritated, not like Thiago.

"Sorry," I mumble, even though I'm more confused than sorry. Wouldn't it be better just to get the heck away from here? "What are you doing?"

"I want to be positive you didn't leave any evidence." He turns his back to me and finishes spraying before tucking the small cannister inside his coat pocket. Leave it to Thiago to have such a thing. When he sees I'm still watching, he finally offers an explanation. "This will dissolve any possible fingerprint residue left behind."

"Wouldn't the ocean water take care of that?"

"Would you prefer to explain to the police why your fingerprints are on this boat I'm about to sink?" He pushes it into the water and wades in behind it. When he's about waist deep, he flips the boat over and gives a powerful shove. It falls beneath the waves at an angle, not fully submerged, with the mooring rope trailing behind it like a snake gliding through the water. So much bigger, and yet it sinks in the same slow-motion way as Theresa.

"Why would they even suspect this boat was used to get rid of her? For all anyone knows, the rope broke and it sank on its own."

"Katherine, investigation of a suspicious death is going to include any and all possibilities. Even a boat that appears to have sunk *on its own*." He holds his fingers up in imaginary quotes and widens his eyes. I turn the flashlight off so I don't have to look at him. He doesn't appear to notice or care that I've shut it off. "Literally all it takes is for one person to see one of us leaving this beach. If you would prefer to chance getting caught, by all means, wade in and put your hands all over that boat. I won't be sticking around to bail you out then."

Thiago's attention to detail is a comfort, even if I don't want to admit it to him. And as we walk back through the sand toward the motel, I force myself to think about what I've done. Something I never imagined I'd do. Logically I know it's a line that should've never been crossed. Yet I have a difficult time finding any emotion to attach to it. What I find instead is a void inside of myself, darker and blacker than the night closing in around us.

"Are you okay?" Thiago, asking me if I am okay under such circumstances, is the epitome of absurd. "How are you feeling?"

"I'm not feeling…anything." And it's the truth.

CHAPTER TWENTY-SIX

Past

If I died, would I have regrets?

My body grew weaker with each day. There was an all-out war going on inside of me. Cells battling cells. Organs bombarded by constant attacks, their defenses weakened and falling apart. Maybe it was time to wave the white flag.

As my surgery grew nearer, I spent more and more time alone. Reflecting on the past and life in general. Thinking about dying. It occupied my consciousness during every waking moment. It wasn't an ambiguous *someday*. It was a more than certain *soon*. And then what?

What would be my legacy? There was nothing impressive about me or my past. No accomplishments to boast about. My life was like gold-plated jewelry—shiny and rich on the outside but dull and boring on the inside.

I was just another woman who'd given up her dreams to follow in the footsteps of a man. Never mind that I'd once aspired to be a neurosurgeon. Not unlike my husband. That was how we'd met. Adam had been a guest lecturer during my first year of med school. He'd offered a once-in-a-lifetime intern opportunity, and I jumped at the chance. Once there, he took a special interest in me. As an ambitious—and completely star struck—young woman, Adam's attention to me had been intoxicating. When that interest turned romantic, I didn't care that he was old enough to be my father. He was *The Adam Powers*, and I basked in the glory of being his chosen one. Ambition had fizzled out shortly after Adam and I were married. When I saw the true nature of his work, and his plans, I was already completely under his spell.

I might have been naïve and star-struck, but I was happy. I smiled in spite of myself at the feelings those memories evoked.

What had happened? How did my life become *this*?

The smile disintegrated along with any good feelings the memories left behind. Had Adam always been a self-serving monster and I'd just been unwilling to see it? Or had he grown into it with age? Perhaps the only thing that had changed was me.

Facing your own mortality had a funny way of changing your perspective.

My stupid, fucking white-walled, pretend bedroom would become my tomb.

"You need a break from these walls. I think maybe a day out would do you some good." Thiago stood in the door. He was dressed in charcoal-colored dress slacks and a pink, pinstriped, button down shirt. Shiny black shoes. Not the type of attire I'd ever seen him dressed in—in fact he'd been almost exclusively a jeans-and-t-shirt guy for as long as I'd known him. But it went well with his dark hair and tanned skin.

And I was immediately suspicious.

"I'm really not up for it." The thought of being seen like I was now, out in public, looking like something out of *Night of the Living Dead*—minus the gore—didn't sit well with me.

"Dr. Adam has approved. He agrees it would be good for you to have a change of scenery."

"I'm tired, Tee." I was unwilling to meet his gaze. Or that of pretty much anyone lately. Katherine Powers as the world knew her was already dead.

"Tired, yet I know you will not sleep. I would find you wandering these halls an hour from now, would I not?" He had me there. Maybe being tired was not such a good excuse. The man knew I didn't have a valid excuse, a fact that was more than evident by that smug smirk on his face. He knew he was winning this battle.

"*You* are a pain in the ass." Yet, deep inside, it felt good that someone was pushing so hard on my behalf. Even if I didn't entirely trust his motives, even if he was only feeling sorry for me, I knew this was an idea Thiago had concocted, not Adam. I groaned in an exaggerated way like a teenager being forced to do their chores. It transformed Thiago's smirk into a devilish grin. "Fine. You win. Where exactly are we going?"

"That is a surprise. But first, we will stop at your house for a change of clothes."

"Tee, I have plenty of clothes here."

"Ah, true, but for this you will need to dress up."

Why the fuss? Why was he so insistent? I couldn't remember the last time I'd dressed up or made any sort of effort with my appearance. Funny how an illness could change one's habits. Perfect, polished Katherine had died a slow death. She had a giant, walk-in closet full of designer clothes and shoes, but what was the point when you had nowhere to wear them?

***

In the end, I relented. Recognized that saying no was not going to be an option. We stopped at my house, which felt cold and empty and a little bit foreign after spending two months sleeping at Adam's facility. I sorted through item after item of clothing without enthusiasm. The me that had once been so concerned about fashion and appearances no longer existed.

I held a fitted cashmere sweater. Or rather, what was once fitted—with all the weight I'd lost in the past few months, it likely wasn't so fitted anymore. It was the palest of blues. The silky material practically slipped through my fingers. It would do. I didn't really care what I wore, but this sweater had always been one of my favorites. For all I knew, it would be the last time I'd ever get the opportunity to dress up. Adam never took me anywhere and Thiago was obviously taking me out because he pitied me. Not because he truly cared.

My god, when did it get like this for me?

The dark, cynical, *bad* feeling? Feeling sorry for myself. It lurked everywhere I looked now. Behind my reflection in the mirror. At night when I closed my eyes. I couldn't escape.

Snap out of it, Katherine.

I removed my t-shirt and slipped the sweater over my head. As I'd suspected, it was more tunic-sized than form fitting. Not the same as it once had been. Not the same as I had been. There was no way the sweater was going to work, because it meant finding pants to match. Pants that fit. What was the point?

Adam was going to fix all of this. At least, that's what he claimed. I wanted to believe it. Could I believe it?

If I could, then what was this dark feeling? Maybe it was some sort of sixth sense. An ominous premonition. What if I didn't survive the surgery? *Just trust me*, he'd said, over and over. How was I supposed to trust, when he hadn't done anything to earn it?

Emily.

She was the only tangible thing he had to show after years of research and experimentation. A fucking half-human—more monster than human—and *that* was what I had to look forward to? Maybe I was better off taking matters into my own hands. Leaving on my own terms, rather than being subjected to what Adam wanted. By going through with the surgery, wasn't I just going along with what he wanted? What about what *I* wanted?

Thiago knocked lightly on the open door.

"Katherine? Is everything all right?"

Mirrors didn't lie. There was no way this was going to work. Couldn't he see that? "This is a terrible idea, Tee. These clothes look ridiculous."

He cocked his head to the side. "Not ridiculous. Just not the same as you're used to."

"I don't think I have a belt that would be able to hold up any of the pants I own. It's useless."

He frowned and pressed his mouth tightly closed. Probably trying to find a delicate way around this predicament. Probably trying to spare my feelings. "Perhaps a dress would be a better option?"

"Or we could just not go anywhere."

"Katherine, I think you need to make an effort with this." He paused. "If not for you, then for me. Please."

It was hard to say no. I was fighting a losing battle. One where it probably took more energy to resist than to give in and go. I rolled my eyes and turned away from him. Opened the closet. Blinked away tears.

He didn't see that, did he?

I busied myself sliding the hanging garments along the wooden rod, one at a time. It didn't matter which one I selected. There were over a hundred dresses in the walk-in closet. Ranging from casual to formal, in a rainbow of colors. They blended together as an unimpressive lump of fabric.

Just pick one, Katherine. He's not going to let you off.

I squeezed my eyes shut and hurriedly swiped away the few stray tears that had leaked out. With my eyes still closed, I selected a button-down shirt dress. Black with a floral print. It was light and airy, a thin rayon-silk blend. It would still be ridiculously big on me, but a belt might make it somewhat less shapeless.

Belts. I had twenty of them hanging on little hooks against the back wall of the closet. A belt would be an easy way to end all of this. Strong and durable. It would hold my weight. If I timed it right, it would be too late by the time anyone found me. But not here, not now. Not with Thiago a mere few feet away. He'd stop it, and then what? He'd tell Adam, and I would be under constant surveillance. I'd be treated like a prisoner.

Who was I kidding? I was a prisoner already. A prisoner in my own body, unable to escape my reality. Not only a prisoner in my ailing, decrepit body, but under Adam's rule as well. He'd kept me under control. Gave me the illusion of freedom when he'd been watching my every move. And I had allowed it to happen.

I was wracked with a sudden, intense feeling of guilt. Where did that come from? How had I sunk so low that slipping a belt around my neck seemed like a plausible reality? Where I was headed, death didn't seem so bad. Nobody would really miss me. Sure, Adam would be a little upset he didn't get the opportunity to complete the surgery, but he'd get over it. He'd find another candidate and I would finally be allowed to be at rest.

"Tee, please leave the room so I can change."

He studied me for a moment. Had he somehow read my mind? I knew Thiago was perceptive, but mind reading was a stretch. That was just my guilt talking. Distorting my view.

Boy, I'm really in a fucked-up place right now.

"Of course," he said. "I'll be right outside if you need anything."

I pressed out a smile and offered a curt nod. "It'll just be a few moments."

I held the dress on a hanger in one hand and a thick black leather belt in the other. I could wash all the sins from my life in a single fleeting moment. No more guilt for following along with Adam's plans. No more wondering if I should have stopped him. No more internal debates about the merits of science versus moral right and wrong.

With this belt, I release thee from thy suffering.

I chuckled at the thought, even though it was morbid and so very wrong. I could control my own fate if I really wanted to. My terms. My life to have or to end. It was all so simple. It would also have to wait.

Not now. Not here. I needed to be alone, and I needed to be one hundred percent sure. For some strange reason, having that option open to me was a comfort. Knowing that I could if I wanted, that I could be in the driver's seat of this shitty ride anytime I chose, and nobody else would have to know or have the power to stop me.

I took off the sweater and my pants, then slipped the dress over my head. There was no need to unbutton. It flooded over my skeletal body like a drop-cloth covering old furniture. The belt, even at its tightest setting, fell below my waist, resting solidly on my hip bones. The me in the mirror looked much older than forty-five years of age. Skin with the pale, nearly translucent appearance of wet rice paper. Protruding bones. Dark rings beneath my eyes. Limp, dull hair. I was a walking corpse. Makeup wouldn't help this mess very much.

I selected a pair of low, black heels. Then went to the vanity and sat in front of that mirror. It had been a good long while since I'd made any kind of effort. How strange it felt. Pointless. Would that be what I looked like in my own coffin? Because it was a lot like putting makeup on a corpse.

It wasn't so long ago I'd taken great pride in my appearance. Maybe beautiful hadn't been the best word to describe me back then, but striking, yes. Able to command attention. Put together from top to bottom. Clothes, makeup, hair—they'd all been pristine, and I wouldn't have left the house without feeling they were. But now? There was no joy in the ritual. Yes, it had once been a ritual. One that made me feel satisfied and in control. Confident. None of that was left. Only a hollow, desolate feeling that had overtaken my entire existence.

I could only manage a fraction of what I'd once done. A little eye makeup. Some tinted lotion — foundation seemed too strong somehow. Lipstick. I was a dead person mimicking a living, breathing being. The illusion of effort. The illusion of caring. That was all I needed to concoct. To keep the prying eyes of concern far enough away that nobody would suspect.

Nobody knew I was rotting from the inside out. Not only because of the cancer. Everything was dying. Including my will to live.

I stood, with nothing more than a passing second glance in the mirror. Thiago was leaning against the wall in the hallway, texting. He looked up from his phone, startled, as if I'd sneaked up on him. I wondered if I could still put on a convincing act, even in this state. With each step, the energy inside me seemed to disintegrate a little more. Dropping like sand into the bottom of an hourglass.

"Ready?"

He seemed to recover quickly. Maybe my act was convincing enough after all. "Of course."

I didn't bother asking where we were going. Just sat, quiet, staring out the passenger window. I rested a hand on my belt. My security. Tried to ignore the throbbing pain in my belly. The tickle in my throat. Anti-nausea medication helped make trips like this possible. Painkillers kept the worst of it under control. All of it, just enough to be functional. To appear human. Trick the ones who paid attention the most.

Look at this world passing by, without a care.

Time didn't stop. It didn't matter if you were dying. The world would leave you behind and time would go on.

Our destination turned out to be the Worcester Art Museum. I'd been many times before. I was even a museum donor, one of those people who regularly donated large sums of money to the museum and in return, received the privilege of attending openings, private tours, and all the other perks that went along with it. Not that I'd taken advantage of them in a very long time.

We parked in the lot right off Salisbury street.

"I have the wheelchair in the back if you're feeling too weak," Thiago said. The way he suggested it led me to believe he already knew what my answer would be.

"Don't be ridiculous." The thought of someone I knew seeing me carted around in a wheelchair was unbearable at best. It would be bad enough having them see me like *this*. Thin, weak. Not the Katherine Powers everyone remembered.

"Very well." He helped me out of the truck and we went inside. To my surprise, the director, Siobhan met us near the entrance. I hadn't seen her in months—probably six or seven months at least. That was how long it had been since I'd attended anything at the museum.

"Katherine!" She leaned in and kissed me on both cheeks. It seemed Thiago had prearranged our visit. Had he also warned her about my physical state? She showed no sign of being shocked or bothered by what she saw. "So good to see you."

"Thank you, you also." I returned the kiss. Forced a smile. More energy burned that I couldn't afford to lose, but it kept up appearances and appearances were important. Sometimes they were all you had.

"This charming young man informed me that it's your birthday and inquired about a special tour." She winked—the knowing kind, the approving kind. Did she think Thiago was my lover? And my birthday…well, that accounted for Thiago's insistence that I go out today. How could I have forgotten?

"He is certainly one of a kind." More forced pleasantries. Draining my resources. Thiago seemed oblivious to the entire conversation.

"I'm sure he is." She laughed. "Well, as it happens, we have a new impressionist exhibition that just went up. It's not open to the public for another week, but I'd love to give you a private tour."

"That's exceedingly kind of you."

"Nonsense. You've been generous to our organization for many years. We miss your lovely face at our functions."

And probably my money.

"Well, thank you." It had been so long since I'd been in the position of these types of interactions. I'd once been the master of small talk and exchanging pleasantries and projecting the general air of giving a shit about other people and their lives. It usually came so naturally. Appearances. That was all it was about. Remove that person and replace her with another and repeat the process. None of it really mattered. "I appreciate your time."

My body felt like little more than a battered husk. Most of my energy was being used simply to stay upright and appear okay. All illusions.

My fingers brushed against the belt. Illusions. Thiago met my eye. Did he know what I was thinking? Impossible. Yet I detected something in his expression. Knowing, and perhaps with that, a trace of fear. Maybe I was not so adept at concealing my pain.

A wave of dizziness passed through my body. It was always accompanied by a cold, prickling sweat. I closed my eyes, willing it away. Without saying a word, Thiago was at my side, grasping my elbow to steady me.

Weak. Useless.

"Well, come, come. Both of you." She ushered us through a closed door, into the exhibition hall.

I was beginning to rethink wearing heels. Even low ones. The pain in my feet had become excruciating. It shot up my calves, and my already weakened legs began to shake. Thiago gripped my elbow tighter and leaned down to whisper, "Do you need to rest?"

"No." Perhaps being stubborn would be my downfall. I'd worked through pain before. Suffer in silence. Don't let them see you sweat. It was all part of maintaining appearances. Still, Thiago wouldn't let me go. I knew he wasn't buying my act. But I also knew he wouldn't dare defy me in front of another person. So, I leaned my weight into him. "I'm fine.

CHAPTER TWENTY-SEVEN

Present

"I'd…uh, I'd like to file a missing person's report. Is there an officer that can help me?" I clear my throat. If ever there's a time to muster some emotion, it would be now. It's about five a.m. I haven't slept more than a few fitful moments, and my eyes are bloodshot and stamped with dark crescents underneath. I must look the part of a distraught husband, don't I? Isn't that good enough?

A few moments later, the door opens, and a uniformed officer gestures for me to come inside. I follow him down a short hallway and into an office.

"Morning. I'm Officer Hennessey, what can I do for you today?"

"My wife is missing." I let my eyes get glossy with tears and sniffle. "She…she and I got into an argument last night and she said she was…" I sniffle again. "She said she was going out for a walk and she never came back."

Officer Hennessey scrawls notes. "What's your name?"

"Sean. Sean Malone."

"What's your wife's name?"

"Theresa. With a T-H."

"Do you have a physical description?"

"Petite, five-two, five-three. Blonde hair."

He's nodding. Writing. "Approximately when was the last time you saw her?"

"Maybe around ten last night? I wasn't looking at the clock, so I couldn't be sure. I just remember it being like eleven, eleven-thirty and she'd already been gone for a while and I was starting to get worried…so I went down to the beach to see if I could find her…I called her name, but she didn't answer, and—"

He holds up a hand. "You said you went down to the beach. Did you drive there?"

"No. No, we're staying at the Sunrise motel. We're just…We just came into town for a few days."

He signals for me to stop talking again. "Okay, that's fine. I'm just trying to get a time frame here. So, you were right next to the beach."

"Yes, Sir."

"Can you tell me anything else about when she went out? Did she have a phone or anything with her? Could she have called somebody to pick her up?"

"No. Her phone, her shoes, her purse—they're all back at the motel room. She was only wearing a robe. She'd just showered, and we were getting ready for bed—"

"It's not possible she called someone to pick her up?"

"Well, I suppose it's possible." I frown. "If she flagged someone down and asked to borrow a phone. But even if she was mad, I can't imagine her just taking off. Not dressed like that."

"Sometimes people do irrational things when they're upset."

I think of what I know about Theresa. She certainly was an emotional person. Needy. A little too eager to please. Irrational, I'm not so sure. "I don't know. I mean, she's an emotional person, but that doesn't sound like her." How much longer can I go on like this? I can't tell if I'm selling this or not. As long as I don't look guilty of anything.

"Well, I have some paperwork for you to fill out. Then we'll send an officer to investigate. It could be that she's waiting back at the motel for you right now."

"I hope you're right." But she won't be. How long will it be before she washes up somewhere? Thiago said this beach is known for its strong currents. I didn't ask him how he knows this. I have no idea. I know very little about Thiago or his background. I never asked questions. Can I really trust him? I hope so.

***

Once I'm back in the motel, I take Theresa's phone off the dresser and scroll through her contacts list. I add the landline for the apartment, Billy's number, as well as Theresa's cell into my own phone. Then I place a call to the empty apartment back in Worcester. Leave a message on the voicemail.

"Theresa, if you're there, please just pick up. I'm worried."

If the police ever do look at my call history, there'll be evidence. Then again, it will also show a call to Thiago. I'll have to explain him away as a family friend. Which, if anyone bothers to check with Sean's or Theresa's friends and relatives, nobody will know. Fuck. But I'm getting ahead of myself.

I've done everything I'm supposed to do. There's no body to find. At least not yet. Maybe I'll get lucky and the sharks and other sea life will get to her. An unidentifiable piece of flesh might wash up on the beach rather than a body. She'll be so badly mangled, nobody will know how she died.

With my luck, she's completely intact, washed up on the sandy shore waiting to be found. It's tough to say if they can prove foul play or not. She's drowned, but won't an autopsy reveal fresh water in her lungs? Or will it not? I can't be sure. My knowledge of forensic pathology is extremely limited.

Adam would often dissect failed experiments. Mostly monkeys and rats, but I rarely had the patience or the interest to sit through those sessions. I never paid attention to what he'd found. In fact, most of the time when he did want to discuss his findings, I tuned him out.

I remain in the motel room, which now holds a quiet, bad vibe. There's a negative energy seeping out of everything. I want to leave, but I told the cop I'm planning to stick around another day to see if Theresa shows up. So, I kick off my shoes and lie on the bed. Close my eyes. There's no way I'm going back home to sit there and pretend to be a grieving, worried husband. Finding Adam needs to happen sooner rather than later.

Something isn't right inside me. The dark thoughts I've been having are uncharacteristic, and I wonder if something has become a little bit scrambled in my brain. Maybe it's incompatible with the male hormones.

Preposterous, Katherine.

Hormones might affect the way we process thoughts, the way we react. They might even affect the way we perceive different situations. But structurally? The human brain is virtually genderless. It's just the different sections that tend to be used more by one sex than the other.

Could I simply be going through an adjustment period? Where my brain is rewiring itself? Or is it something much more sinister?

Maybe parts of my brain are degrading or dying. Maybe something hasn't been stitched quite right. The planets are not aligned in the right way. Maybe I'm simply a few bad decisions away from turning into Emily.

***

I'm standing at the end of a long hallway. White, clinical. It resembles Adam's facility, but not. One of the florescent lights flickers, repeatedly, like there's a loose connection or the bulb is going. It's buzzing, loudly, and the sound sends all the hairs on my body standing on end. Drives me crazy.

Toward the end of the hallway there's a step ladder. A-frame. One of those aluminum ones, maybe six feet tall, just set up and waiting. But waiting for what?

There's nothing above it. No crawlspace or vent—only the ceiling tiles. As I approach the ladder, two voices, muffled, carry on a conversation. Where is it coming from? I can't tell. But I feel strongly that I need to climb the ladder. A compulsion to do it.

And the voices. Is one of them Adam? Of course it is—how quickly I've grown accustomed to life without him. Who is he talking to? I stand on the fourth step of the ladder, one hand braced against the ceiling. It's warm to the touch, resembling the feel of human skin, like it's alive. Somehow, I know the answers will be through there. I press the tile with my palm, hard, and there's some resistance. It stretches upward, the ceiling tile not behaving in a way that ceiling tiles should, with the elastic, rubber quality of a thin, flexible membrane. It's then I realize…my hands, my arms—*I* am female.

What the hell is going on?

This is too weird. I climb onto the next step of the ladder and push with all my strength. The ceiling tile seems to have stretched to its farthest limit, because it's taut. Sweat trickles down the sides of my face. I fight like this for a while. Straining. Pushing. Then finally, I'm rewarded with a loud pop as my fist punches through. A gust of warm, faintly humid air rushes out of the hole I left behind.

"What do you think the side effects will be?" It's a female voice, and while I recognize it immediately, it takes a few moments to remember the name I'm looking for. *Chloe.*

"It's hard to say." Adam. "This is completely unprecedented."

"Don't you think she'll be angry?"

"I have no doubt she'll be furious." A pause. "But she'll have to get over it. This is history in the making. Nobody has ever done what we've done."

I jolt awake, my heart racing and my body sticky with sweat. It takes a minute to realize where I am and what happened. I'm still in the motel room. It was a dream. A very bizarre, nonsensical dream. But I heard Adam and Chloe talking. The conversation had been vivid. Did that dream also contain fragments of actual memory? Maybe I heard bits and pieces of conversation after the surgery, while I was still in a coma. Maybe I heard them plotting about me without even being aware or awake enough to know what was going on.

I need to get out of this motel room, away from this place. It's suffocating. Appearances are the least important thing on my mind.

***

Should I feel guilty? Remorseful? I think about everything as I drive back to Sean and Theresa's shitty little apartment. Their home. Now my home, and only my home. I don't really feel anything. In fact, the only thing I'm concerned about is finding Adam. Maybe that makes me a monster. I'm not so sure I care.

That dream, no matter how abstract it was, still rattles me. Maybe I have more memories trapped somewhere inside my own brain. Things I heard without realizing I was hearing them. Answers, perhaps. But how would I get to them? There's no way to force dreams or memories, at least not that I'm aware of.

I guide Theresa's car into its space in the parking lot behind the apartment building. Adam probably knows a way to coax memories from deep within the brain. I turn the car off. Grip the steering wheel tight. Why the fuck does it always come back to him? My thoughts. They always divert back. It's driving me insane.

Breathe, Katherine.

I close my eyes. Those negative thoughts have to be harnessed if I'm going to be successful in my pursuit. Maybe I should keep reminding myself of that. I can't afford the loss of self-control. Like Theresa. What happened hadn't been out of anger, it had been a compulsion. Almost like I couldn't help myself. Like an itch that needed to be scratched and that was the only way to make it go away.

I took a life.

While, logically, I know this is wrong—horrific, even—what's more surprising is my complete lack of feeling. No emotions. No remorse. Not even a sense of panic that I might get caught or sent to prison.

Nothing.

I've always been logical. Rational. More prone to reasoning my way through a difficult situation than getting emotional. But I've never strayed into violence or cruelty. Never harbored fantasies about hurting someone or ending a life. In fact, I can remember a time in my life when I would have found such a thing completely repulsive. So, what has happened? How have I crossed that line?

I climb the stairs to the apartment, unlock the door, and step inside. I don't belong here. Now that Theresa's gone, the feeling is even more pronounced. The empty apartment feels uncomfortable, its walls a fresh reminder of the sin I've just run from. Theresa is everywhere I look. There's no erasing her presence, even when I so desperately want to. Despite this, it isn't guilt that I'm feeling, but a mild, gnawing anxiety. Theresa will always be lurking, even if she's not alive anymore. If I'm being watched, then Theresa being gone will be likely to attract more scrutiny. My stupid, reckless impulse could end up being my downfall. And Adam would end up getting away with all of this.

If I let it. I should be far more disturbed about this turn my life has taken.

But I'm not.

CHAPTER TWENTY-EIGHT

Past

It was funny how, once an idea crept into your head, it was near impossible to remove. It was almost decision time. Adam claimed he was fully prepared for surgery, that within a few days, all systems would be go. I would be in a new body. But did I really want that?

Did I want the risks associated with it?

There was a tremendous amount of trust necessary. Trust that I didn't have. The most sobering realization of my adult life boiled down to one thing—I didn't trust my own husband. Maybe I never had to begin with. Surely that wasn't true? Had I been so blinded by landing the rich, well-respected doctor that I'd overlooked all his faults? Perhaps what I had done was to mistake admiration, maybe even a bit of infatuation, with love and trust.

I remembered back to my twenty-three-year-old self. Hair piled on top of my head in a loose bun. Makeup turned up a notch above my normal daytime palette. I'd just been offered an intern position, a one-of-a-kind opportunity to work under the incredible Dr. Powers. I was at the top of my class in med school, an extremely diligent hard worker, but once I'd begun working for Adam, it became obvious those weren't the only qualifications he was looking for. Young and inexperienced, I mistook his romantic interest as recognition for my achievements, when it could have easily been any attractive, aspiring doctor in a skirt. I happily set my sights on him as well. Made that extra effort with my appearance in the hopes that he would notice. It had worked. Surely this man would be the best thing for me. For my future.

Except, sometimes what you thought you wanted wasn't really what you wanted at all.

How naïve I'd been. How stupid.

Now I'm paying the price.

Maybe being stricken with this cancer was some sort of cosmic punishment for being vain and superficial.

My insurance was a leather belt and a bottle of sleeping pills, tucked away in the nightstand next to my bed. The backup plan. A plan that looked a little better every day. I didn't want to be like Emily. I also didn't want to feel anything anymore.

Sometimes, I didn't know where the pain ended or where it began.

What if I didn't wake up?

What if I did, and I couldn't function properly?

I lay on the bed, on my side, staring at the wall and those were the thoughts swirling around inside my head. A giant, violent storm. End it on my terms. Or take a gamble that Adam would get it right this time, and I'd have the opportunity to live a long life. Maybe. It all circled over and over.

"Kat? You need to eat something." Chloe hadn't bothered knocking. None of them did anymore.

I kept my back to her. There was no enjoyment in eating anymore, either. If you could even call it that. "Let's not pretend it's anything other than what it is."

"Fair enough. Do you want to try something soft again? We could make a smoothie. Or maybe some ice cream. Get some fat into you."

There was something I never thought I'd hear. *Get some fat into you.* Ha. I'd always watched what I ate, even though I never had an issue with my weight until this illness took over my life. Except instead of taking it off, now I had trouble keeping it on. "You and I both know it isn't going to happen. I can't even get *that* down."

"Well aren't you a bundle of positive energy this morning. Feeding tube it is." That was one thing I liked—well, maybe not liked, but *respected*—about Chloe. Her unwillingness to take any shit. Her uncanny ability to brush off my bad attitude without a second thought. Then dish it right back when I probably deserved it. "Would you prefer to walk to the exam room or shall I get a wheelchair?"

"I'll walk, thank you." I rolled onto my back. Winced against the pain in my side and my gut, then sat and swung my legs over the side of the bed.

"Just think. It'll all be better soon. You'll be like new again. No more pain, no more suffering."

Whether it was from a successful surgery or sudden death, either could be true. No more pain. I'd have given anything for that.

"It sounds too good to be true." I managed to get to my feet, with considerable effort. Chloe knew enough to stay put, to offer her assistance only if I asked for it. For that, I was grateful. I didn't want to spend what was potentially one of my last few days on this planet being treated like I couldn't do anything by myself. Sometimes that was as bad as the pain itself. Losing independence, when you still had a strong mind, was the worst kind of affliction. "Especially now that I'm almost there."

"You have nothing to worry about, you know. Adam will take excellent care of you. It's a second chance most people would never have." She said it like I should be thankful.

I left the room, without acknowledging her, and gripped the rail along the hallway wall for support. Somehow, it was feeling more and more like a prison sentence. If Adam successfully completed my surgery, I'd be under his watch potentially forever. Under his rule. I'd never be free.

I'd never get away from him.

Or this life that I'd grown to loathe. I closed my eyes and clamped my jaw shut to combat the latest wave of dizziness. My head rested on the wall, as my body had leaned me toward it against my will.

"Are you sure you're okay, Kat?" Chloe was at my side, but still not touching me.

I was weak from the effort. My limbs shook. No muscle strength, no energy to use them. I may as well have been an inanimate, shapeless pile of flesh and bones for all the good it did me.

"No, I'm not okay." I used to make such an effort to conceal my own pain, or discomfort, or displeasure that this admission felt wrong coming out of my mouth. "None of this is okay."

Chloe visibly struggled to conceal her surprise. Even the people around me weren't prepared for this new attitude, apparently. She reached for me, but I swatted her hand away. "What can I do? How can I make things better for you?"

"Just leave me. Leave me alone."

"Kat…"

"Give me a minute." Maybe I shouldn't have snapped at her, but the constant hovering grated on me. Admitting weakness didn't sit well. It never had. But when you didn't have the energy to pretend, not even mentally, sometimes you did what you had to do to stay upright. Or even conscious. I waited for the latest wave of dizziness to pass. The simple act of getting up from my bed and walking wasn't so simple anymore. How much more of this could I possibly be expected to take?

Chloe backed off. Stayed within reach without saying a word. She knew. She had to. Had to have sensed my turmoil. Everybody was used to ice-cold Katherine. They talked about me when I wasn't around, that I was this unfeeling ice queen. How Adam's staff must have been chattering now that this impenetrable fortress was crumbling. Perhaps they were even taking bets as to when I would fall.

"Kat?" There was a fair amount of hesitance in her voice. Whether she was afraid of me or hurting my feelings I couldn't be sure.

The haze of dizziness lingered long after my vision cleared. I was losing the battle. "This feeling…"

***

I woke back in my own room. IV hooked into its slow drip. There was more clarity to my vision now.

"We'll need to operate sooner rather than later." I hadn't even noticed Adam was in the room, but there he was, sitting right next to me. "I'm shooting for next week."

"I'm not ready."

"You have no options left. Your body isn't willing to hold on any longer."

172

Options? I had options. I could opt out at any time.

Who are you kidding, Katherine? You can't even find the energy to walk down the hallway, never mind attaching that belt to a sturdy object. Probably isn't long enough anyway.

"Have a little faith in me and what we're doing here." The ever-present *Doctor Adam*, talking down to me, twisting the situation to be about him and his work instead of me and my health. No reassurance. No sign of a loving spouse. "We'd have to do another scan to be sure, but I believe the mass in your abdomen has grown considerably."

I wouldn't need a scan to show what I'd already felt on my own. It was even difficult to get into a comfortable resting position. Almost like a foreign object had become lodged inside of me.

Adam pressed his fingers into my stomach. Felt around through the skin. Felt my protruding rib cage and the unnatural lump right below it. It was grotesque. I was grotesque. Maybe I was the monster.

"It has definitely gotten bigger."

I sucked in a sharp breath. The feeling his touch left behind lingered long after his fingers moved from my skin. Like I'd been bruised.

"Is that tender when I touch it?"

I nodded, wincing. There was no use trying to deny it.

"There's nothing I could do to relieve the pain. I suspect it's a solid mass and not only fluid buildup. Everything's inflamed. Bed rest is the best option at this point. And since the growth in your esophagus has obviously made eating virtually impossible, we will need to be more vigilant about feedings."

"What's the point? My body is shutting down. Everything hurts. Feeding only prolongs the inevitable." *I don't have any fight left*, was what I didn't say.

"No, it preserves the most important organ in your body. We need your brain intact, don't we?"

"Of course."

After he left, I felt the weight of everything piling on top of me. Locked in a room that was swallowing me whole. Stuck in a body headed straight for death. Maybe I wasn't thinking clearly. Rational

Katherine had shriveled into nothing. I opened the nightstand drawer. The pills were gone. The belt was gone. Empty.

He was, yet again, one step ahead of me.

CHAPTER TWENTY-NINE

Present

The call comes a week after *it* happened. Just when I've started to relax and think that maybe nobody is watching. Maybe Sean is not on law enforcement's radar. Maybe I can truly focus on getting to Adam without any distractions. But the inevitable happens. Theresa's body washes up on a beach, three miles away from where we'd been staying. She's found by a woman jogging the beach just after sunrise. I drive the two hours to make the positive identity, worrying only about the scrutiny I'll be facing. Still, I meet the cop at the hospital entrance and he leads me to the morgue.

"I wish there was a better way to do this. It's not going to be easy to see."

I offer a curt nod to the sympathetic-looking cop, who held the door for me.

Theresa is in a stainless-steel drawer. They remove the sheet from her head only — the rest of her body, they say, is in considerably worse shape. Despite the discolored flesh and the waxy film covering it and her eyes, there's no mistaking who it is.

Would you look at that, Sean?

I still test it, every now and then, if only to reassure myself that there are no traces of Sean inside. I turn away from Theresa, stifling a gag, and my eyes water too.

"I'm sorry, I can't…"

I don't say any more. They silently cover her up and tuck her away, out of sight.

"Can you confirm that it's her?"

I'm still queasy, trying to reign control over my own gag reflex, and I stuff my fist against my mouth. Since when do I have such a weak stomach? I've never had issues being around cadavers before. I've never been this bothered by the smell of death. Why now?

Guilt, maybe it's guilt.

I offer a quick, jittery nod in acknowledgement.

"I'm sorry for your loss."

I nod slowly again, my eyes still watering.

This is your crime staring you back in the face, Katherine.

Her body taunts me from across the room.

Look what you did. You're a sick, sick person.

"I know this may not seem like the best time, but we need you to come down to the station and make an official statement." The cop is older, white, and balding with a big bushy mustache that completely hides his upper lip. "It's standard procedure any time a death is involved. Accidental or not."

Accidental or not? What does he mean by that? I don't get a negative vibe, but it's still possible they suspect I have something to do with Theresa's death. Isn't the spouse usually the first suspect? But there's no indication her death is in any way suspicious. Something stirs deep within the pit of my stomach. Not precisely guilt or remorse. Maybe it's simply the fear of getting caught. Maybe I'm reading meaning into his words that aren't necessarily there.

I nod once again, eager to get out of this place. To get away from Theresa's taunting stare. Even though she's covered with a sheet and tucked back in her metal drawer once again, I picture those glassy eyes glaring back at me.

Put me in the ocean, will you? Thought you could just get rid of me?

There had been no thought put into it. It was just something that I'd done. "This…this won't take long will it? I'm not feeling so hot and…"

Before I can finish my sentence, the faint queasiness skyrockets into a dire need to vomit in mere seconds. I make it to the nearest trash can before emptying the contents of my stomach, while both the cop and the medical examiner look on silently. Maybe with a little sympathy mixed in. I've never had a weak stomach or been prone to nerves, but then again, nothing that has happened recently can be categorized as normal. I don't even know what my own normal behavior is anymore.

Embarrassed, I take the paper towel the medical examiner hands me and wipe my mouth, then clear my throat. "I'm sorry…It's just, this is all so overwhelming."

They both nod, still seeming more sympathetic than suspicious. I can't be sure. And I can't let my guard down.

***

I force myself to follow along, to go to the police station and talk to them. They lead me to a tiny interrogation room and set a foam cup of coffee in front of me — black and overly strong, and maybe a tad burnt, but I drink it anyway.

"So according to the missing person's report, you and Theresa got in some kind of fight. How about we start with that? Just so I can get a clear picture of what happened." Mustached cop is all business in here. "What was the fight about?"

"Money." More lies sliding from the tongue, adding to the intricate web I've already woven.

"You were fighting about money?"

"Yes. She…Theresa, asked where I'd gotten the money for the trip. And I told her I'd worked a couple small painting jobs with a new acquaintance. She got mad that I didn't tell her about any of it, even though I'd only kept it a secret, so I could surprise her with the trip."

My confession earns the briefest of smirks. Perhaps there's some sympathy to be had if I play my cards right. "Money's tight?"

I shrug. "Theresa is…*was* the only one with a job." I pause and take a deep breath. "Earlier this year I was kidnapped. You might have heard about it on the news. When they found me, I was in a coma. I've been in recovery since I woke up, and I hadn't been cleared to go back to regular work, but I just wanted to help *somehow*. She's done everything for so long, and now she's gone…" I force some emotion into my voice, and thank my lingering nausea for the tears that well up and spill over. This is excruciating. "I can't believe she's gone."

He looks about to say something, but instead his mouth is open, hanging in suspense. The cops obviously haven't put two and two together, that I am the famous sole survivor in one of the state's most bizarre, disturbing crime cases. I can only hope it will be enough to throw him off. Ease his suspicion.

177

He's tapping his pen on the table. It's annoying. Fucking annoying.

Please stop before I reach across and make *you stop.*

Excessive, machine-gun tapping. I stare at the offending noisemaker, willing it to stop moving. Have I derailed his interrogation? Hopefully my revelation has disrupted his plan of attack. That attack is designed with one purpose, and it isn't finding the truth. If I'm guilty of something, the right amount of pressure applied will yield a confession. But that's never going to happen.

Then, at last, his eyes widen and the pen tapping stops. Now he's pointing it at me and nodding his head at the same time. "I *thought* you seemed familiar."

"The media wouldn't leave us alone. *People* wouldn't leave us alone." I pause my counterattack. It's a slight fib. While there had been initially some interest when I'd first been found, I had still been in a coma at that point. I'd somehow successfully evaded the over-zealous paparazzi scene. "We just wanted to get away. From all of it. And put it behind us. Now this..."

"Mr. Malone, I'm truly sorry for all you've been through. You must understand, part of my job is to find out what happened. If there's any chance it was something other than an accident..."

"I didn't do this to my wife. You can't think that I'd do anything like this, when we were just getting our lives back." Shit. Protest too much and maybe I sound guilty. Stay too calm and maybe it's suspicious. How does one act when their spouse is found dead? I suppose there isn't a singular reaction. What if crying isn't a normal reaction for a man like Sean?

"Easy, Mr. Malone. I'm not accusing you. I'm just trying to get a clear picture of what happened. So, you two argued, and then what?"

"She stormed out of the motel room and said she needed to get some air." I shrug. "I thought I'd just let her cool off. Then it got to be an hour or so and she still hadn't come back, so I started to get worried. I walked down to the beach...walked the beach and called her name, but I couldn't find her. I don't know, I guess a part of me just assumed she would come back when she was ready, so I went to the motel room to wait. But around five in the morning she still wasn't back, so that's when I went to the police station."

The story is etched into my brain now. It might as well have been real.

He's nodding. Still taking notes. "Okay, okay. Well, Mr. Malone, I think that's all we need for now. I realize this has been a rough all-around day for you. We'll be in contact if we need anything further, but I think this is pretty straightforward."

I keep my expression stony. Maybe just a notch above emotional breakdown—that constant threat of boiling over one gets after something traumatic happens. The kind where people walk on virtual eggshells around you. Except my possible reasons for emotional breakdown are rather different than what this cop might think.

***

When the news breaks that Theresa is dead, the house phone starts ringing off the hook. I answer a couple of the calls and then give up. I'm buried in a landfill of sympathy and questions. People have too many questions. How could such a thing happen? What a terrible tragedy. When the media catches wind, it's like the floodgates open. People show up at the apartment. They call all hours of the day. All these people coming out of the woodwork.

A woman named Rebecca who'd consoled Theresa after Sean's disappearance is the most recent visitor. She has to be in her fifties. Slightly overweight. Shoulder-length, graying hair cut in an unflattering bob. She looks like the type of woman who lives alone. Well, no—not completely alone. There is probably a house full of cats. Maybe some framed needlepoint.

"She always believed you'd come back to her. It was what kept her going all that time."

Why in the hell did I let her in the house? It's another one of those split-second, impulsive decisions I know I'll grow to regret. Not that it feels like I had much of a choice in the matter. She pushed her way through the door when I opened it. Now she's sitting next to me on the couch, trying to console me. Her hand squeezing my

179

arm. "I'm so, so sorry. I know you've had your troubles, but I know how much you two loved each other."

"It hasn't been easy," I admit, not that she knows why. "None of this feels real."

"No." Her eyes tear up and she's still squeezing my arm. "No, it doesn't. It must be overwhelming with all that you've been through."

"This is all very overwhelming."

"I know it is, Sweetheart. That's why I want to help. With funeral arrangements. We've started another fundraiser. I know you two have had your share of struggles over the years, like you just couldn't catch a break. But Theresa always believed things would get better. She was adamant that they would." She finally releases my arm from her grasp. "I thought maybe you and I could go down to the funeral home together. Make her final arrangements. I believe we've already got enough raised for a respectable service."

In other words, I can pawn all of the responsibility onto someone else.

"That would be…helpful. Thank you. I don't…I'm not sure how to handle this."

Her expression brightens some. Not because she's being helpful, but because she's being recognized for it. "Great! Now, I hope you don't think I'm too far ahead of myself, but I've already made an appointment with a funeral director. They're a family-run business, but I've heard they're very respectable." When I don't react, she lets a small, nervous laugh escape. "I figured if you were against it, we could always cancel."

"No. I trust your judgment. Theresa obviously had a lot of faith in you." And planning a funeral is the least of my worries now.

"It's going to be okay. I promise." She smiles and pats my knee. Probably sees my lack of emotion as grief, or maybe shock. It's funny how people see the things they want to see. How they make assumptions about intentions and motivations. This woman clearly sees a man in distress, a man who's been through a horrible ordeal and lost his wife in the process. The ultimate charity case.

And that's how I find myself sitting in a meeting, planning the funeral of a woman I'm supposed to love but killed.

Rebecca does all the talking. She does all the deciding. I simply nod my agreement in all the right places. I sign the paperwork—catching myself about to write *Katherine*, I quickly scribble *Sean* instead. Something so simple as a signature is automatic. We don't think about it. I'll have to be more careful. I only need to endure this charade a bit longer.

***

Sean only has one suit that I can find. It's ill-fitting and hardly appropriate for a funeral. Why on earth would Sean have a suit that's clearly meant for a much taller, larger man? Unless it isn't his. I slip on the coat, and I may as well be a child wearing an adult's clothes. The pants are about three inches too long. The waist, maybe more. They could be hemmed, but I don't know a thing about sewing. It seems like too much effort anyway. A belt would hold up the pants, but they'd end up looking ridiculous. Maybe shopping for a new one is the simplest option.

Not going to the funeral at all is also an option.

So is not caring one way or another.

What kind of man doesn't have at least one good suit?

I toss the oversized suit into a rumpled heap in the corner of the room. Perhaps a trash can would be a better home for it. Whether Theresa was keeping another man's clothing in her closet, or Sean raided the Salvation Army store when he needed formal clothes, or he used to be fatter and taller, I can't be sure. But if I'm to perpetuate this charade at least a little longer, an effort needs to be made.

I grab Theresa's car keys and five hundred dollars from the envelope I'd hidden away and set out to buy a new suit. That amount would only cover a fraction of the cost of one of Adam's suits. Except Sean isn't Adam. He isn't the type of person who bought high-end designer suits, and I have to keep reminding myself of that. Five hundred dollars would be more than adequate for a man like Sean. It's a constant battle between how I would do things versus how Sean lives. We come from two completely different backgrounds. I don't know how this half lives. I'm not even sure if I can fake it in a way that's convincing, but I have to try.

***

Two days later, I'm front row at Theresa's send-off, wearing a new two-hundred-dollar suit, not really listening to the words spoken. Not acknowledging the people who stop in front of me to offer condolences. I don't recognize more than one or two of them anyway. Damn Adam to hell for putting me in this situation.

I keep telling myself survival hinges on adaptability. Adaptability means blending in and analyzing the situation. Strategizing. Knowing when to act and when to play along. It's also knowing when to call it quits.

I can't do this anymore.

I'm fucking done.

Now that Theresa's gone, I can let go of the charade. Once the funeral is in the rearview mirror, I'll be able to fade from these people's lives. I can use grieving as an excuse to refuse visitors and phone calls and invitations. No more distractions.

And then finally I can get to Adam.

CHAPTER THIRTY

Had it been Adam who discovered my stash? Chloe? Thiago? I couldn't exactly ask. *Excuse me, could you please tell me what happened to the paraphernalia I'd been planning to use to kill myself? I'd really like it back.* Right. That was unlikely to happen. As unlikely as it would be for any of them to confront me with it. *What's this Katherine? Why do you have these hidden away in a drawer next to your bed?*

Both items disappeared without so much as a word. No lecture. No therapy sessions. But there were extra checks on my well-being. Thiago or Chloe lingering in the doorway after an exam. Never Adam. It might have been my imagination, but it seemed like Adam treated me differently. He was colder, more distant than usual. Like knowing what I'd been planning to do had changed how he viewed me.

I wasn't so strong, was I? It certainly didn't feel that way. Maybe I'd disappointed him.

"How are we doing this morning, Kat?" Chloe asked, armed with her shiny metal cart which held my liquid breakfast and whatever drugs they'd been pumping in me to keep me partially sedated. Most of the time I was awake and sort of alert, but with a heaviness that made damn sure I didn't find the motivation to try to move, let alone harm myself.

Although, it did numb some of the pain. And the caring. Like I was waiting to die. I didn't answer Chloe. She'd witnessed far more of my weakness than I was comfortable with. Nurse or not, it didn't sit well.

"Still not talking to me? Really, Kat. Everything that's been done has been for your benefit." She rummaged through the cart, pulling out her tools and organizing them on the tray. "Doctor Adam is prepping your host body today. The worst of all of this will be over soon. I promise."

That was a dangerous promise to make.

Chloe rested a needle and an empty vial on the tray. She took a rubber tourniquet and tied it right above my elbow. It was so tight, pins and needles immediately swarmed into my lower arm. Without needing to be asked, I made a fist. We had this routine down pat. I closed my eyes when she inserted the needle.

"We probably should've gotten some fluids into you first."

I glanced at the vial and the slow trickle of blood into it. "Maybe it's just that you've bled me dry already."

"As tempting as that would be, I'd like to save some for later." She winked. "Just in case."

"A slow, drawn out death it is, then."

"I'm glad to see you still have your morbid sense of humor."

"What else do I have left? I'm no better than a death row prisoner."

"Stop feeling sorry for yourself, Katherine." She capped the vial of blood and laid it on the tray. Released the tourniquet. Swiped the blood draw site with an alcohol pad, then pressed a bandage against it. "I'm sure it must feel that way, but I want you to know all of us—Adam, Thiago, me—we're all working together to make sure you have another chance. This is breakthrough medicine. Adam's been working overtime to plan every aspect of this surgery." She paused. Her expression was unreadable, and she wasn't looking at me—there was something infinitely more interesting to stare at on the bedspread—but no matter how imperceptible a change had been in her demeanor, it was enough that the hairs on my body stood on end. "You won't become another Emily."

There, out loud, was one of my greatest fears—that I would become another Emily, or something much worse. It didn't matter how many assurances I got. I couldn't shake the feeling that something wasn't quite right, that these three people so dedicated to keeping me alive and comfortable now, knew something I did not. They at least had the luxury of walking away from this unscathed no matter what the outcome. It was a huge leap of faith for me to put my trust in them, and nobody seemed to understand that. And they wouldn't ever. Their bodies were not the ones failing. They were not the ones taking a risk. Nobody knew what it was like to become a giant science experiment. What any of it felt like.

But I did.

I was living it. I'd never been on this side of things before. With it came a perspective I hadn't been expecting. All those people we'd taken in, believing we were going to help them, they'd had the course of their lives decided for them. Just like I was having my life decided for me. I felt heavier and heavier with the weight of all of the thoughts, the doubts. Pressure. Sinking me. Drowning me.

Stripping me of everything that made me a person.

"Kat?" Chloe squeezed my shoulder, but I barely felt it. She'd already hooked me up to an IV. Had she also added a drug to it? I was so wrapped up in my thoughts I wasn't paying attention, but the heaviness spread. Like my limbs were filled with lead. And my mind grew fuzzy. I was detached from my own body. Inhabiting it, but not really.

She wiped at my cheeks with a tissue. Were those tears? I hadn't even noticed. My body settled back into my bed, that now-familiar heaviness weighting my head. Making my muscles go limp. Consuming me. Yes, Chloe must've drugged me. The change was too abrupt. My eyelids slid down, leaving only tiny slits for openings. I was completely helpless. At her mercy. And I fought falling into unconsciousness with everything I had.

At anyone's mercy.

"How is she doing?" Adam sounded like he was talking through a tube. Or a tunnel. They both did.

"Worse, not better," Chloe said, agitated. Was it with him? Me? The situation? "We can't just keep her drugged all day long. It's not right."

"We do what we need to do to keep her from harming herself. One, maybe two days and we'll be ready. It'll only be a matter of time and she won't have to suffer any longer."

"Adam, she wants to die. I'm not just talking about finding pills hidden in her drawer, I can fucking see it in her eyes every time she's awake and coherent." Chloe was getting worked up.

I couldn't open my eyelids enough to see either one of them. What a strange feeling. Like one of those nightmares where you knew you were dreaming and kept telling yourself to wake up, but you couldn't. Through almost-closed lids, my eyes wouldn't focus, and everything beyond my lashes was a series of colorful blobs.

"How is any of this going to work if she doesn't even want to live? Do you think that's magically going to fix itself once she's in a new body?"

"Once she heals and realizes she can function normally again, she'll be fine." What I'd once seen as Adam's endless sense of optimism and faith in what I could accomplish, now had a darker twist. He wasn't being supportive. He was being willfully ignorant. Telling me what I was feeling rather than listening. But hadn't that been what he'd always done?

"I don't think it's so simple."

"Katherine is a strong woman. She will persevere no matter what is thrown in her direction. This little blip here is merely the result of being in a state of prolonged pain and discomfort. She will bounce back." That purported confidence in me felt like little more than a collection of meaningless words strung together. Lip service so devoid of emotion, I knew he was merely saying what he thought others wanted to hear. Like an apology that came after a public figure got caught doing something heinous. Were they remorseful or just sorry they got caught?

"And I think you're severely underestimating the mental impact this will have on her. The impact it would have on anyone. What she's feeling now is not suddenly going to go away. You could be creating a ticking timebomb." And there was Chloe, the unlikely superhero, swooping in to my defense. Saying all the things I probably should have been saying myself.

"I know my wife."

"Do you really? You keep saying that, yet you hardly spend time with her. You just keep her locked in this little room with no contact with the outside world."

"She's far too sick to go anywhere. It would only strain her body unnecessarily. She understands the gravity of her situation."

Oh, I understood the gravity of the situation all right, but not in the way *he* understood it. I knew there would be no free will in the equation. I was completely under Adam's control. Whatever he wanted was what would happen to me. I had to lie here and wait for it.

"I don't think—"

"I don't pay you to think."

Hearing their conversation was surreal, in a completely fly-on-the-wall kind of way. Odd that they didn't even seem to consider the possibility that I was still aware of my surroundings. Already talking about me like I wasn't there, or like I was nothing more than furniture.

"I…I realize that, Doctor. I do. And I mean no disrespect to you or what you're doing." Chloe must have known she wasn't getting anywhere with the argument. Adam was too stubborn. Caught in his own tunnel vision. Wearing blinders. "I just feel that we, as a group, have not spent enough time considering the mental health aspect of this process. I mean, are we trying to create a quality, long-term sustainable life? Or simply be able to say that we've successfully made a brain function inside a body other than its own?"

He wasn't going to listen to her, no matter how well she pled her case, no matter how much sense she made. No, he'd do what he always did with me. Say something that gave the illusion he was willing to consider her point of view to avoid further argument.

"Well, perhaps once the surgery is complete we can consider beginning a regimen of antidepressant medication." He paused. "If that seems like it will become an issue."

The lack of sincerity was obvious to me. Had Chloe also picked up on it?

"I'm glad to hear that." Chloe was back to all business. Put in her place. The passionate pleas on my behalf evaporated or were at least stuffed away into whatever box she kept them hidden inside. And I realized their voices sounded more muffled. Further away. I imagined myself walking down a long hallway, backward, away from them. It was brightly lit. I was alone.

***

Drip.

Drip.

Wetness hit my cheek. Warm. But quickly cooling as it rolled along my skin. Invisible tethers kept my eyelids closed and as I began to regain my senses, to join the waking world again, to become aware, I strained against them. The tethers snapped, but my lids were too heavy and too slow to rise.

Drip.

My eyelids fluttered. There was a sound kind of like wet, heavy breathing. Like saliva pushed through teeth and lips and then sucked back in again. Repeatedly. Whatever drugs they'd been forcing into me were hard to come back from. I was caught in cobwebs, wandering blindfolded and trying to find my way out. I imagined I was in that brightly lit hallway, running toward the door this time instead of away from it. Toward the sound.

And agitation gnawed at every footstep. Which turned to alarm and maybe a little panic because the door didn't seem to be getting any closer. Frustration. Was this a dream? Why wouldn't my eyes open?

Why won't my eyes open?

I heard my own heart pounding, a steady booming drumbeat. A war-march. Fast paced. Panic, panic, panic. Maybe this really was a dream. If it was, I needed to wake up.

Wet breathing.

Drip.

Drip.

Come on, wake up!

My eyelids fluttered again. Let in a few blips of light as well as a dark shadow in the middle. I forced them open. I was stuck in one of those panic-filled dreams where you tried desperately to do something you knew your life depended on, but you couldn't.

And then, I realized my eyes *were* open. Unfocused, but open. With the source of that horrible wet breathing maybe an inch or two from my face.

Emily.

Dear god, what was she doing in here? How did she get in here? I wanted to scream, but I was afraid to move or even breathe. As my eyes finally figured out how to focus, I noticed the blood. On her face. Smeared like war paint over her cheeks. Ringed around her mouth. Dripping from her chin.

From her chin onto my face.

Drip.

Did she realize I was waking? Did she understand? She was sniffing. More animal than human. Making that godawful slurping sound. I was transported back to that night Thiago and I found her in the animal lab, gnawing on a bloody rat corpse.

Blood dripping.

The blind rage that had overtaken her when she saw us.

I'd be fucked if that happened now. Must stay calm.

She was small, maybe five feet, a hundred pounds, but I didn't think I'd be able to fight her off if she attacked. Not now. I was so weak that getting out of bed was a chore, let alone being able to find enough strength to grasp onto her and throw her to the floor. I moved slightly, testing my limbs. They were weighted like bags of sand, and the muscles were shapeless piles of gelatin. My body was failing me yet again. If she attacked me, what would I do? I wouldn't be able to fight her off. It would be an enormous risk to do anything other than lie here and pretend I was asleep so as not to provoke her.

But what if she attacked anyway? I had no means of self-defense. Even if the drugs wore off a little more, I wouldn't have the strength. There was no call button or panic button in this room. Surely somebody would be in to check on me soon. I knew they were keeping a close watch on me. Hell, I wouldn't have been surprised if Thiago had wired this room with video surveillance.

But if that was the case, then where was he? Or Adam? Or even Chloe, for fuck's sake.

Why did Emily have blood on her face?

That was the real question. Where did the blood come from? Had she raided the animal lab again? I thought Adam secured the room after last time. No, they'd equipped the door with keycard access. I'd heard him discussing it with Thiago — the perks of being heavily sedated. People talked like you weren't even there.

That only left two alternatives. It was her own blood. Or she'd moved on to people. Maybe she'd attacked one of the other patients. Maybe there was a bloodied corpse lying in one of the rooms. What if I was about to become a bloodied corpse? I'd been thinking about dying a lot lately, but not in this way. It would be too long and drawn out, too painful. If I was going to die, it would be on my terms. Not with some half-human gnawing on my flesh. Not being eaten alive. Or bleeding to death.

How long it would take before someone noticed? My god, they'd been up my ass the past couple of weeks and when I needed someone, not a peep.

But it was the middle of the night, wasn't it?

Emily had somehow climbed onto my bed. She was on all fours, still sniffing me, but she'd turned so she was facing the other end. Almost like a dog or a cat, she crawled down by my feet, then curled up in a fetal ball and fell asleep. I stayed motionless, still afraid to move or make any sound that might trigger an attack. What was the story with this odd half-person Adam had created? What, if anything, was going through her mind? I hadn't seen any significant changes in her behavior or demeanor since the implant. Which led me to wonder whether it worked or if she was too far gone for it to be effective.

That was the most frightening thing about Emily. Not just the unpredictability of her behavior, but the constant wondering if she had any understanding of what she was doing. Either had the potential to be dangerous. Was there any thought process? What if some deep, dark, twisted narrative lurked inside her head? Something beyond our comprehension. Even if it was only on the level of a dog, or some other animal, there was something that drove her to do the things she did. Entering rooms. Attacking. How did she choose? Or was it simply random?

Why did she always seem to gravitate toward me?

There'd been such rage and hatred that time she'd attacked me. She'd zeroed in on me more than once. At times after the attack, that inclination still shone in her eyes. Hard to describe. Disdain, if such a creature was capable of feeling it. And why, out of all the rooms she could show up in, why mine?

Considering her past actions, there could be no coincidence. No random opening and closing of doors had occurred. Emily had made her attack then deliberately sought out my room. I felt that with a pronounced certainty. For now, I was safe, as the heavy, rasping breaths of sleep came from near my feet. But what if she woke? What if she was startled? The possibility that I'd have to fight off an attack in my weakened condition was truly frightening.

My stomach nearly leapt out of my throat at the sound of the door. Chloe opened her mouth to say something the minute she noticed my face. And the intruder resting at the foot of my bed. I widened my eyes at her and shook my head slowly. Thankfully she was intelligent enough and quick enough to keep her mouth shut. To understand that she alone would not be enough to restrain Emily if she woke and started to attack. Chloe offered a quick nod and backed out the door, holding it so it closed slow and gentle, and latched without making a sound.

I forced a slow, steadying breath and tried to calm my still-pounding heart. At least help would be on the way. Chloe wouldn't leave me hanging. She understood the potential danger. She was the one who'd tended to my neck wound after the *incident*. I had to lie still and hope for the best.

It sucked. There was no sugar-coating it. For a person who had prided herself on being independent, dying helpless was not something I was willing to swallow. A few excruciating minutes later, Chloe returned with Adam. His eyes glossed right over me and focused on Emily. Was I so repulsive? Invisible. *Insignificant.* You wouldn't know we were married. He treated me with the cold indifference of a stranger passing on the street. It hardly bothered me anymore.

Adam crossed the room and scooped *her* up into his arms, the gentle way one might pick up a small child so as not to wake them. Emily stirred, and began to open her eyes, but he hummed a soft tune under his breath and rocked her until her eyelids fluttered closed and her breathing evened out again.

"Shhh, it's okay."

She moaned softly in her sleep. Chloe held the door open and whispered something unintelligible to Adam. Once he was gone, she dropped the act and stalked to the adjoining bathroom. Water hit the tiles and she came back into the room to help me out of the bed. "Let's get you cleaned up."

Still slightly groggy from the drugs, and weak from lying in the bed for so long, I moved in shuffling steps toward the bathroom, with Chloe clutching my elbow for support. I shot a glance back to the bed. The rumpled blankets were spattered with blood. There was a trail on the floor, leading up to the bed. Halfway up the trail, in the middle of the floor, a clump of raw flesh. A bloody piece of meat.

A crime scene.

Chloe nudged me, urging me forward. "Don't look at it, Kat. We'll clean everything up and get you fresh sheets and blankets." She guided me into the bathroom where the shower was already running and running hot. Steam billowed out in great, misty clouds and collected right below the ceiling. Chloe helped pull the shirt over my head. I hated it. Felt like a child because of it. I just needed to push it out of my mind. Suck it up and allow it to happen, because I couldn't do it on my own.

She helped me into the shower seat. "Is the water too hot?"

"No." It was a little on the uncomfortably hot side, but I knew I had to scrub away what I'd witnessed, even if that meant taking a layer of skin with it. Not that it made any sense, but the discomfort somehow made me feel alive.

Chloe handed me a washcloth and a bar of soap. "Will you be all right by yourself for a few minutes? I need to take care of your room."

"I'll be fine." It was humiliating enough needing help to get into the shower. If I couldn't at least wash myself, while sitting, then all was lost. The water temperature had cooled slightly after running a few minutes but was still above comfortable. I didn't say anything to Chloe. I ignored the growing redness on my skin.

Chloe nodded. "I'll be back in a few minutes. Yell if you need anything. If you feel lightheaded or like you're going to pass out or —"

I held up a hand, irritated. "Enough. I can handle at least this. Please go do what you need to do."

She took one more cursory glance around the room. Was there anything I could hurt myself with? Probably what was running through her mind. I could almost see it in her facial expression. No, short of bashing my own head against the wall or somehow drowning myself, there were no objects that could be used for self-harm. "I'll be quick. Just yell if you need anything."

I waved her away, impatient to begin this one moment of freedom, even if it would only last a few minutes. That was precious to me. I was tired of being embarrassed by the constant fuss. Once she finally left, I closed my eyes and leaned my head back, so it rested against the shower wall. Let out a slow, calming breath. I hadn't realized how tense my body had become, but the heat from the water gave subtle permission for it to relax.

I gripped one of the handrails and pulled myself to a standing position, then set about scrubbing my face, lathering my body, and rinsing. Repeated it all until I was certain every drop of blood, no matter how microscopic, was gone. Only a few short moments later, Chloe was back.

"Kat? How we doing?"

"Fine."

"I've got a towel all set for when you're ready to get out. And a fresh set of clothes."

"Just give me another minute. I feel fine. I don't need any help." I wondered if she had any clue what she was signing up for when she'd first come to work for Adam. An RN wasn't usually expected to perform all the daily care routines like bathing patients or dressing them. There were usually others to perform those tasks. Did she mind? Or did she loathe it as much as I did? Maybe she resented having to do everything. Maybe she resented me.

Maybe.

I turned off the shower and braced my hands against the wall until a new wave of dizziness subsided. It was the vision-clouding kind that temporarily blacked you out and left you with millions of tiny particles swimming in the void. When it passed, I pulled the curtain aside, grateful for the small amount of privacy Chloe had afforded me, even though I knew she waited just outside the door — I felt her presence. I dried off and took my time dressing myself. When I opened the door, Chloe was waiting right outside as suspected. My room was already cleaned. New blankets and sheets. No sign of blood anywhere.

I allowed Chloe to take me by the elbow and lead me to my bed. "Why was she covered in blood?"

She didn't meet my eyes. "She got into the animal lab again."

"I thought Adam had locks installed."

"Somebody must have left the door unlatched." Something in the way she said it led me to believe that Chloe was lying. She didn't want me to know it was a person who'd been attacked. Had it been a patient? Or an employee?

"How careless." Her deception didn't deserve any acknowledgement. If I pressed her further, she'd continue to deny, so there wasn't really a point.

"Yep."

The dull, throbbing pain mixed with a burning, boiling molten lava churning inside my body, eroding the walls of my stomach. Creeping up my esophagus.

"Is it time for some more pain medication, Kat?" I couldn't even conceal my suffering anymore. When I didn't answer, she patted me on the back. "Don't try to be a hero."

What was the point of avoiding medication? Having a clear head wasn't going to get me anywhere, and it only made me constantly conscious of my predicament. And the pain bored a hole right through me. Sweat slicked my newly showered skin. The beginnings of a headache pulsed at my temples. Maybe it was time to give in.

I lay back on the bed. "Fine."

What else could I do?

CHAPTER THIRTY-ONE

Present

I've been half expecting his visit. People are so fucking predictable sometimes. This man—Billy—is transparent in his intentions. Theresa was like a daughter to him. Or so he claims. There's a creepy-old-man quality to his affection for her that I can't get past. An unrequited love that borders on stalking, but at the same time masquerades as something fatherly.

It probably isn't.

It definitely isn't.

He's been crying, obviously, and judges me because I haven't. Inserting myself into Sean's life has been a grave mistake. With people constantly reminding me how unlike Sean I'm acting, the defiant, almost arrogant part of my personality says *so what*. I'm *not* him.

This man is the worst of them. The former employer, the so-called friend of the family with the unusual fixation on Sean's wife. Has he harbored secret fantasies about her?

He smells of cheap liquor.

Cigarettes.

And it's obvious the moment I open the door, he has an axe to grind.

"What do you want, Billy?" I brace myself in the open doorway, arms folded.

"We need to have a little chat. About Theresa. I need to know what happened."

"I told you what happened. We argued, she took off, she never came back."

"I thought you'd take care of her."

In a matter of speaking I did take care of her, but I don't think he'd appreciate that sentiment.

"She took off. She was angry. There wasn't anything I could do."

He shakes his head, incredulous. "You coulda followed her."

I stare back at him, unmoved and still calm. "I could have, but I chose not to. I figured she needed time to cool off. By the time I realized something might be wrong and did go out to look for her, she was nowhere to be found."

"My god, she's right. You're a robot. No feelin' at all, it's like you're just recitin' a script."

"I walked that beach up and down calling for her."

"There really is somethin' wrong with you."

"You weren't there. You don't know what happened."

"I didn't have to be." He gets closer, in the puffed up, apelike way some men do when they were trying to intimidate.

"Billy, why don't you come inside before we disturb the neighbors."

There's nobody around. I haven't seen a sign of the downstairs neighbor in a couple of weeks, and the people directly next door tend to avoid us. Still, his eyes dart to the side, as if he's only just realized where he is, and that he's raised his voice. That he's all but threatening a grieving husband.

I step aside so he can pass, and he stumbles through the open doorway, toward the living room. Then I close and latch the door and follow him. The living room resembles a living room again. Now that Theresa is gone, I've started sleeping in the bedroom. After I washed all the sheets, blankets, and pillowcases of her scent.

"Why don't you have a seat, Billy?" It's hard to erase the condescending tone. This man is almost as pitiful as Sean and Theresa were. What they probably would've turned into if they'd gotten their acts together and lived long lives.

"I just don't understand it. What could've happened? Why her?" He starts sobbing.

Talk about not understanding. Grief. I don't get it. I can't remember the last time I've had a good cry or felt sorrow over losing someone. Locking my emotions away is something that was drilled into me from a very early age. I still vividly remember, at seven, when our family's German shepherd, Barnaby, had to be put down. He was old and suffered from severe arthritis. When my father saw me beginning to cry, he said simply, *all creatures that are born must also die. It is a fact of life. Your tears will not change that.* He'd shown such disdain, I vowed to never again cry in front of him. Or anyone. A pivotal moment in my childhood. My wake-up call, so to speak. When I realized that showing emotion made you weak. So, I'd stopped.

Charlotte.

No, I'm not going to soil her memory with this moment. I shake the thought away.

The atmosphere in the room, a compressed space between the two of us, grows more uncomfortable. I'm paralyzed by the weight of it. He's broken down completely, his body heaving heavy sobs between hitching breaths. I can only watch. Irritation simmering.

Why did I even let him in? Why should I be forced to face this unpleasantness repeatedly? It was bad enough having to endure Theresa's funeral. The appearance of her estranged family. Sean really hadn't been a saint. Good girl had run off with the bad boy, the loser. They'd had trouble off and on with drugs. Sean hadn't held a steady job for more than a few months at a time. They struggled with money. Why idealize that? As far as I'm concerned, I've put her out of her misery. Spared her a miserable future.

I go to the kitchen, find the vodka bottle Theresa had stashed under the sink, and return to the living room with it and two glasses. It doesn't seem convincing him to leave will be an option. Though booze won't shut him up either, it brings me back to the days of being a doctor's wife, entertaining guests. Inviting people I don't like into my home and playing nice. Pretending to care what they're talking about. Because really, it's all about appearances, and right now Sean—a.k.a. the grieving husband—needs to appear as the sympathetic character.

You don't need police up your ass, Katherine. Or that FBI agent. It would take away from the end goal.

I pour two glasses and set the bottle on the table. Billy downs his and pours another. I take a sip and put my glass down, cringing inwardly at the taste.

He doesn't say anything for a long while, downing two more glasses of vodka in great gulps.

"I don't buy this amnesia story. You're lying. About everything. What really happened to you when you were taken away? You're like a stranger." All that silence, and this is the best he can come up with?

"Sean died," I say, studying him for a reaction. Screw appearances. "And they put my brain in his body."

Billy shakes his head. Disbelief. Maybe a little disgust that I would even attempt to crack a joke, especially at a time like this. Perception is everything.

"That's why you don't recognize me. That's why Theresa didn't recognize me."

"Really. Then who are you?" He plays along reluctantly, but it's obvious by the heavy-lidded eyes and the slurred speech that he's quite drunk.

"I don't know anymore. The angel of death, perhaps?"

"I think they scrambled your brains." He laughs. A throaty, raspy, two-packs-a-day type of laugh, that's maybe at least one-part coughing. There are still tears in his eyes.

I stand, smiling. "Maybe they did. If you'll excuse me, nature calls."

This is dumb. I'm fucking dumb. *Appearances.* I snort under my breath and go into the bathroom. Run the tap and splash water on my face. Maybe it will clear away some of the thoughts I'm having. Didn't I make a deal with myself after the funeral, that the charade could be over? Because that man is a liability. An obstacle standing in the way of my end goal. He's suspicious of me. He knows I'm lying. I don't have any more fucking energy to play nice. What if he goes to the police with those suspicions? Or worse, what if he goes to the police with those suspicions *and* he's convincing?

Sean, are you in there? Do you see where I'm headed with this?

There's no answer. Obviously. What would I do if Sean answered back?

I stare at the reflection in the mirror. Sean's face is a mask. A permanent one. I have to wear it for the rest of my life, whether that ends up being hours or years. Those clear blue eyes stare back at me. Still, months after waking in that hospital, they taunt me. They're stranger's eyes. Challenging me. I hate the mirror because of it. When I'm not looking, it isn't as real. Those eyes are simply something to see with. And yet, now I own them.

Stop.

I open cabinet drawers, not searching for anything specific, but frantic all the same. Theresa must have had some weird obsession with lotions because there are a couple of dozen different bottles of varying scents and brands. And this drawer is a free-for-all. Like Theresa saved everything and dumped it all in here. Organization be damned. Spare toothbrushes and those mini dispensers of dental floss you get at a dentist visit. An unopened pregnancy test. Loose tampons. Three or four packs of shoelaces, the heavy-duty kind meant for work boots. Bandages, cotton swabs, tubes of antibiotic ointment. What a fucking mess.

I shut the drawer, but I've grabbed a pack of shoelaces and I'm already opening it without even thinking about it.

Billy has polished off most of the vodka while I was in the bathroom. Even when sitting he isn't steady. He's probably on the verge of passing out. From my angle, behind him, I can't see if his eyes are still open. At that moment, a picture of Adam appears, and his incessant talking *at* me, talking down to me, always giving the illusion he saw me as an equal when he really didn't.

You monstrous bastard.

And I, the stupid one, for going along with it for so many years. For allowing all of it to happen.

The shoelace is around Billy's neck before I have a chance to comprehend what I'm doing. The fact that he's drunk probably took some of the fight out of him. I pull so tight my hands shake from the exertion and the laces cut into my palm. He flails around and tries to pull at the lace, but I have it so tight, it sinks into his skin almost to the depth of the lace's thickness. A dry popping, ripping sound scrapes the back of his throat as he struggles for air.

It's over more quickly than it with Theresa. Maybe because he's drunk, or maybe because he's older, but loss of air is loss of air whether you're crushing someone's windpipe or shoving their head under the water. The result is the same.

When I finally release the tension and slip the shoelace away from his neck, Billy slumps forward, limp, his tongue protruding from his lips and his eyes wide and bulging. His bladder must have let go. There's a wet stain covering the crotch of his pants. I catch a whiff…perhaps his bowels as well. There's a curious lack of control that occurs within the body at death. All these functions the brain manages without any conscious thought that cease to exist when the body is fighting for survival. It's fighting so hard to stay alive that sometimes it forgets to do all the other things.

I let the shoelace fall to the floor. I'm now faced with having a body in my own home. Stupid, really. I should've taken him somewhere first, because now I have to get him down multiple flights of stairs and into a vehicle without anyone noticing.

Funny how, through all of this, the fact that I've taken another human life is the least of my worries. Maybe it truly does get easier with each one. I don't even know why I did it. There's been something lacking within me, and maybe this was a subconscious effort to find emotion, because I should be feeling *something*. Rage, anger, dissatisfaction, frustration. Anything. This man, he's been purely a victim of circumstance. Someone who happened to be in the wrong place at the wrong time. And as I stare at his corpse, wondering what I'm going to do with it, wondering how I'm going to dispose of it, I'm not even disturbed by this lack of emotion. No remorse, no sadness, no regret. Only the void. A blackness inside me that swallows any semblance of emotion.

Have I always been this way? So unfeeling, so uncaring? I don't think that's true, but lately, I find myself thinking less and less about life before inhabiting this body. While I still don't feel like I belong in it, the familiarity of my life before is also slipping away, and I'm caught somewhere in the middle, a living purgatory between two different worlds of hell.

I reach for the cell phone in my pocket. Thiago will be troubled by this, probably, but he's the only person I have to turn to. What other choice do I have?

Do I drag this man down the stairs by myself?

Do I put him in something?

Do I cut him up and take him out in garbage bags?

No, that seems far too messy. Thiago will be angry with me, but he'll at least know what to do and I'm not thinking clearly enough.

He picks up after only two rings. "Katherine." Almost like he's been expecting me. Does he have some kind of sixth sense?

"I need your help, Tee."

On the other end, a moment of silence. "Is everything okay?"

"I think…my sink might be clogged, and I don't want to trouble the landlord. Besides, you're the only one I trust to fix it."

There's another pause while he chooses his words. "I'll be over in a few minutes. Let me get my tools."

"Thank you. I really appreciate it."

He grunts. "It is not a problem." Then he hangs up, and I'm left standing there in silence. The phone still pressed to my ear. I shut it off and shove it in my pocket.

"How do I get myself into these situations?" My question is greeted with silence. Billy's slumped body taunts me like Theresa's had. I reach over and shove his head roughly, so he's leaning back. His vacant eyes stare out at nothing. Just as glassy and lifeless as Theresa's had been.

"Who knows," I say out loud. "Maybe you've gotten your wish. Maybe you're with her now and everything's just fucking fine and rosy."

I don't believe in an afterlife. I was raised on science. It's bred into me. My father was a biology professor and my mother was a high school math teacher. Then I went into medicine. Married into science and medicine, too. Logic has ruled every facet of my life. The idea of some mystical afterworld, or spirits living on after the physical body expires, borders on the absurd.

"Things just end, don't they, Billy?" He doesn't answer, not that I expect him to. "The light is snuffed out and then we rot. It's a pitiful ending for such a brief existence on this planet. All the work and the heartache, all the things we do every day to survive, they have no meaning in the end."

Billy stares back at me, neither agreeing nor disagreeing, just taking up space in the way that dead things do. Something oozes out of the corners of his mouth. He smells unpleasant. I'm thankful, at least, that the weather is no longer hot. This could be much, much worse. Perhaps all I need to do is crack a window.

***

Thiago stands, arms folded, in the entry way to the living room. "After the first time, it becomes far too easy." He looks up at me. "You cannot allow yourself to keep falling into this. You lose a bit of yourself each time."

"I've already lost everything. There's nothing that matters to me, except finding Adam and making sure he never touches a living human being again. Which, by the way, I expect to happen sooner rather than later."

"I told you to be patient. There are far too many searching for his whereabouts. You are being watched. It may not seem that way, but you are. Each of these transgressions is beyond risky. Just trust me when I say we need to wait until the time is right."

He's stalling. He doesn't want me to go and find Adam. Maybe he's hoping I'll change my mind or forget about it or something.

"How do I know I can trust you? How do I know you aren't running to Adam telling him every little thing that I'm doing?"

"I suppose you don't know for sure. Nobody can really know another person's true motives." Thiago and his too-cool demeanor must have become desensitized to death. And maybe I do trust him, although it's equal parts because he's trustworthy and because he's the only person I have to turn to. Sad, when you wake to the knowledge you don't have anyone.

"But I will tell you this, Katherine, and it is up to you whether you choose to believe. I have not spoken to Adam since he disappeared. His last words were to pretend I'd never met him. Or you. And I planned to take that to heart."

"I see." After what Adam did, I don't have any reason to believe he wants to look out for me. I don't really care about his lack of caring. It only fuels my need for hatred. Sadly, I can't even muster that. There's no room for sentimentality in my life. "And yet you still came to me when I asked for help."

"I always suspected that you would try to contact me, and I knew if that happened, I couldn't turn my back on you." He casts a glance at Billy. "Although this was hardly the scenario I envisioned."

"I'm not sure what's come over me. This certainly wasn't something I planned or looked for."

"I know."

"So, what do we do about…this one?" I jerk a thumb at Billy.

Thiago blows an exaggerated breath out of his nose. "We need to get him and his truck out of here. How did you do it?"

"With a shoelace."

His look borders on, *you've got to be fucking kidding me.*

"What? I didn't really think about what I was doing. I grabbed it. It was like suddenly I just got really angry, and I didn't know what to do with that, you know?"

"That sounds very unlike the Katherine I knew."

"Well obviously that has become the me now."

"The you now needs to show some restraint." Thiago sets his tool bag on the floor and opens it up. He hands me a pair of gloves. "Have you touched anything in or around his vehicle?"

"No. He came to the door."

"Good." He gestures to the gloves as he slips a pair onto his own hands. "Put those on."

I nod and slide them on.

"Get the shoelace."

"Why?"

"It's evidence. Just give it to me." Thiago picks up his tool bag with one hand, shoves the shoelace inside and zips it shut. "Once we get him taken care of, we'll need to come back and sweep for any other possible evidence."

Taken care of. I'm learning so much.

We each grab Billy under an armpit and hoist him between us. Maybe that way, we can play it off as if he's drunk and passed out, and we're getting him home safely. But it's late and not a soul seems to be around, and this is the type of neighborhood where everybody minds their own business and stays behind locked doors anyway.

We prop him up in the passenger seat and belt him in place. His head flops to the side and rests against the window. I climb into the driver's seat, reach over and unhook the keys from his belt loop, then start it up and follow Thiago's truck out of the city.

***

After about twenty minutes of driving, we pull into a new subdivision, one that, by the look of things, is still in the early stages of construction. There are piles of lumber bundled together next to naked concrete foundations. We park at the end of the loop. By the time I get out of the truck, Thiago approaches with a length of clothesline in his hands. With frightening speed, he fashions the end into a noose.

"It is wider than the shoelace, but maybe with his weight into it, this will make its own groove in his flesh. The longer it is before he's discovered, the better for us."

"Suicide."

He shrugs. "This man cared deeply for Theresa, no? It is conceivable that grief could push him over the edge." Thiago slips the noose around the corpse's neck, fitting the clothesline into the groove where I strangled him with the shoelace. Then he feeds the line through the handle above the door and ties it tight. He works with such care and precision. It's fascinating. Every detail accounted for. Once the seatbelt is released, Billy's lifeless body falls to the side, suspended by the clothesline around his neck. Will people truly believe it's suicide?

It looks convincing.

I want to but I can't tear my eyes away from the cab of Billy's pickup.

The weight of Thiago's hand presses on my shoulder. "Katherine, we cannot afford to be seen here."

"You're right, as always."

"Let's go."

We leave the darkened neighborhood in silence. It feels somehow inappropriate to carry on a normal conversation, or to laugh considering the weight of the situation. Of what I've done. I glance at Thiago. No, that's a *we* now. He's helped me dispose of two different *problems*. He's almost as guilty as I am.

"He expects you to look for him. He'll be waiting." There's caution in his words, but it's the first hint maybe Thiago is beginning to relent. That he's finally ready to lead me to Adam. "What do you hope to accomplish?"

"I want to see the life drain from his eyes. By my hands."

"You don't seem to understand. He is one step ahead of you, he has always been. It will not be easy to get to him."

"But he doesn't believe I can actually do it." I turn to him, irritated. "And that's why I need your help."

"You don't understand."

"What don't I understand?"

"Have you ever considered the possibility that his experiment—from putting you inside a male body to the way that you were wired—that all of it was engineered? The electrode implant has the capability to do far more than just regulate this body's immune system. You know this already. He'd tried it on Emily."

"It didn't do much of anything with Emily," I snap. "She only learned a couple words. She didn't act in any way that indicated intelligent thought. Adam peddled a ridiculous amount of hype for that."

"But what if it's working with you? Think about it. The disregard for human life. The violent fantasies. Maybe you were engineered for all of it."

"That's ridiculous. There's no way he could have the capability to do that."

"Katherine, there was a whole line of research Adam was working on that you were unaware of."

And here I am, running full speed with my head aimed toward a concrete wall. The impact splits me open and leaves me bombarded by all the things I haven't dared to consider. Things so far-fetched I stuffed them somewhere deep inside me, in a box labeled *impossible*. What if he *has* been controlling me this entire time? Clearly there's something wrong with me. Clearly Thiago knows what's going on. It's obvious secrets have been kept from me. That was clear the moment I woke in this body. And yet, the possibility Adam has also introduced this mind-altering technology inside of me, why hasn't that occurred to me?

Because I've been foolish. Smug in the belief that he wouldn't dare do any of those things. Like he never would have shoved me inside a man's body.

I reach over, grab the steering wheel, and jerk it toward me. We're on a back road and not going any more than thirty-five.

Thiago is quick to react. His foot slams against the brake, and he yanks the wheel hard in the opposite direction. The truck comes to an abrupt halt in the grass.

"Jesus, Katherine! What in the hell was that?" A flash of anger unlike anything I've ever seen from Thiago. Pure darkness, pure rage.

"Tell me everything you know."

"Here is not the time or the place. If you continue to be reckless, I refuse to help you any further." His voice indicates he is already beginning to calm down. The model of self-control.

"I'm sorry." It's as empty of meaning as it sounds. Thiago is unfazed.

"You need to try and reign in that thing inside of you, whatever that darkness is that causes you to lose control. It will be a liability, not an asset."

"How do you suggest I do that? Is there some sort of how-to manual?"

"That attitude doesn't suit you. The Katherine I knew was far more sophisticated and far more in control."

I lean back in the seat. "The Katherine you remember was found stuffed in an old freezer. To hell with what you know. I'm not even sure who I am anymore."

He stares out the driver's side window, drumming his fingers on the steering wheel. "When that man is found, I worry you will be placed under a microscope. It is far too coincidental that he has died right after Theresa. That it looks like a suicide may be enough to buy some time, but the mere fact that it happened, that both were connected to you, to Sean—it will raise suspicion. You need to be extremely cautious. That FBI agent is smart. And he is already watching you."

He's not fucking going to change the subject.

"I know my time is limited." And I do. It's possible the changes within me will lead to an early death. Not just possible, but probable. I'm anticipating it. And it has to be death, not prison. I sure as hell am not going to be locked up. I have to convince him before it's too late. "But if he's truly controlling me in some way, I need to know. That's no life. I need to stop it. I need to get to Adam now."

"Where he's staying, it is very remote. It's surrounded by acres of forest where the nearest neighbor is miles away. The house itself, as well as the driveway in, is monitored by an extensive security system. Video surveillance, motion sensors—there is literally no way to sneak in undetected." Thiago is still tapping the steering wheel and staring out the driver's side window. He bites his lip. Huffs a breath out his nose. What's going through his mind?

I persist. "Where is he?"

"North."

I'm not going to let him get away with more vague answers. "That doesn't help."

"I need to make some preparations first." He ignores my impatience as he always has. "But we will leave the day after tomorrow. You need to be ready."

"I've been ready since I woke in that hospital bed."

"There are still things you don't know. Things that you never expected." He backs up the truck and pulled onto the road.

"At this point, there's nothing that would surprise me."

"I believe he has Chloe with him."

My laughter is bitter and hollow. So predictable. He's always favored her. Treated her with more professional respect than he showed me. He took Chloe along and left me behind. In a strange body. Left to chance.

"And this is supposed to upset me? You think I'm going to go home and cry over a pint of chocolate ice cream? There's nothing that man could do to top what he's already done. Nothing more that could shock or anger me. It's yet another crime in a long, long list of them."

"Fair enough." Resignation. No more fight. No more trying to talk me out of it.

The tension between us is palpable. The remaining ride to the apartment is filled with excruciating silence. When he pulls into the driveway, he doesn't bother shutting the truck off. "What's your story? If someone starts poking around. Especially when they find him."

I shrug. "I'll come up with something."

"You'll have to."

"Don't worry, I will. Now, you tell me, what's the plan?"

"I will be by to pick you up the day after tomorrow. First thing in the morning. Be ready."

CHAPTER THIRTY-TWO

Past

The drugs wore off sometime in the middle of the night. I woke feeling agitated, my thoughts fixed on the previous day. Of Emily, covered in blood, invading my personal space. Of the cavalier way in which it was covered up. Anger was a great motivator. It provided energy where there wasn't any. Made you forget weakness and pain. Maybe it was time to take matters into my own hands.

They were lying to me.

They were keeping me prisoner here.

Drugged to the point of inaction.

Was my door locked? Somehow, I doubted it would be. I wasn't a threat. I was barely able to move, my body too weak to cause any trouble. They wouldn't have expected any trouble. People became lax when they didn't anticipate any problems. Would they be watching?

I glanced at the clock. 2:45 a.m. Probably not. They wouldn't have been watching me twenty-four hours a day.

They couldn't be

I slid the blankets off my body and forced myself to a sitting position. Waited for the dizziness to pass. Swung my legs around the side of the bed. Rested my bare feet on the floor.

I kept telling myself I'd just get up and check the door, to see if it was locked. To see if I truly was a prisoner. But I wasn't going to be satisfied with that. I wasn't going to stop there. I turned the knob, overcome by a profound sense of satisfaction when the latch clicked, and I was able to pull the door open. Nobody was going to keep me locked away like a criminal.

There were few things more dangerous than a woman who didn't care anymore. Didn't care whether she lived or died. A woman with an axe to grind who didn't care about consequences anymore was lethal.

No threat would have motivated me to stay put. I didn't consider what would have happened, how I would have reacted if the door had been locked. Just stepped into the empty hallway. How much strength would I be able to muster? It was little more than a passing thought. They've kept me here. Talked down to me. Treated me like I couldn't make decisions for myself. Treated me like a fucking child, incapable of doing anything. What about what I wanted? What if I didn't want to go through with the surgery? It only meant more misery. More days, weeks, even years bending to every one of Adam's whims. And that was assuming the surgery went through the way it was supposed to. What if I wasn't coherent? What if I became a fucking drooling monster?

I stood in front of Emily's door. Sometimes you needed to take matters into your own hands.

Tit for tat, Honey. You visited me and now I'm visiting you.

Sometimes you needed to do what you had to do because nobody else would.

She was curled in a little, round ball, hugging her knees to her chest, at the foot of the bed. Why was she more important than me? Why did Adam care more about this creature than his own wife? What would he do to me if I ended her life right there? How would he react? Would he withdraw my surgery as punishment? Allow me to die a horrible, painful death instead?

I wonder.

Or perhaps he was too obsessed with getting the surgery right. So obsessed that he was willing to sacrifice me and my future. *That* would not be my future. There was no fucking way.

I put my hands around her neck and began to squeeze. Her eyes snapped open, but instead of showing fear or any trace of emotion, she stared back at me. She didn't fight back. She didn't try to squirm away.

"Ma...ma." It was rasping and choked but unmistakable what she'd said. *Mama.*

I released my hands from her neck. Horrified. Adam and his stupid obsession with this creature was already abnormal, and now there she was calling me Mama. Rattling my cage. Forcing me to question my motives. Maybe she wasn't the monster I thought.

My body shook. Emily and I were eye to eye, and for the first time I saw something inside her. Something other than a collection of instinct and urges.

She caught my wrist and guided my fingers back to her neck. Was it my imagination? A world of pain and suffering lingered in those glassy pools. She was pleading with me. How had I not seen any of this before? Suddenly that determination to extinguish her life disappeared. We stared at each other a bit longer.

Her eyes grew moist. Her lower lip quivered. Her plea, no matter how silent, I recognized it. Was there a human consciousness in there? Maybe I imagined what I saw.

"Do you want to die?" I whispered.

A nod. The movement was slight and seemed to require considerable control on her part.

"Do you know what that means? All of this would end. The world would go dark." I paused. She listened to every word. Intent. Watching the movement as every syllable left my lips. "You would be free."

A thin strand of drool dribbled over the edge of her lip. I couldn't tell if she understood any of what I was saying. "Bu…bba."

A chill crawled across my skin. *Bubba.* It woke a memory. Many years ago, a tiny stuffed rabbit. Tan with little, black button eyes. Pretty basic as far as stuffed animals went, but Charlotte had loved him. She'd kept it right up until her death. Had Adam taken this charade a step further? Was he that desperate to have this creature mimic his own child? He was warped. Sick. Twisted. But not twisted enough for *that*…It wasn't possible, was it?

Suddenly my mind was racing. It made sense, why he was so attached. All the pieces were fitting together.

No, no, no. Not possible.

These little things I noticed, these similarities, they had to be coincidence. A situation manufactured by Adam as a product of his grief. Even all these years later, he was still affected by her death. They had been close. So close. Her death had been the breaking point of so many things. It was the beginning of the end of our marriage.

Sure, we were still technically married, but we were no longer close. We no longer acted like husband and wife. And that dynamic had shifted further south with my illness. Doctor, patient.

Charlotte…

I'd never seen the body of my daughter after her death. Adam had insisted it would be too traumatic for me. Always telling me how to feel. Always controlling what I did and saw. What if he had been hiding something? A terrible, horrible secret, one that stretched the furthest borders of what was ethical and what was wrong.

Why would that be so hard to believe?

I backed away from Emily. Just a couple of steps. She was still staring at me, and I at her. Did I dare say out loud what I suspected? I shook my head. Slowly. So wrapped up in my own thoughts I was reacting to them and not what was right in front of me.

"Charlotte." Her name came out in a single breath, and I hoped I was mistaken, that maybe I was a partly insane from the pain and the meds and constantly being stuck in Adam's damned building.

Her lips quivered again, and angry creases formed between her eyes. Her entire body went rigid. Shivering. Eyes bulging to the point they might pop. She was boiling to the point of explosion. When she finally opened her mouth, the scream was deafening. Blood curdling.

I backed away, until I couldn't anymore, until I felt arms around me. In gentle restraint. Pulling me backward, through the door. Chloe brushed around us, syringe in hand, and administered it to the shrieking Emily. My limbs no longer wanted to move, and I was sobbing. A complete mess.

"Come, Katherine. Back to your room." It was Thiago's calm voice soothing me, and his arms that held me close.

Emily had gone silent, and Chloe arranged her slack body on the bed and tucked a blanket around her. She approached us. "The doctor doesn't even need to know you were in here. It'll be our secret." She squeezed my shoulder and nodded at Thiago before leaving the room.

Once in my own room, I sat on the edge of my bed, hiccupping, my body still locked in the out-of-control spasms that followed a thorough crying jag.

Thiago watched on, silent, arms folded.

"I think I've finally lost it, Tee." My breath hitched. Another choked sob escaped. "I went in there to end her. Never in my life have I thought of harming another person, but I had such rage building up inside me, so much pain, maybe even jealousy for the attention he's paid to her. She seemed almost subhuman, like it wouldn't matter, like it wouldn't fucking count if I strangled the life out of her. Can you imagine?"

I might as well have been reciting a grocery list or an instruction manual, because he gave no visible reaction. "Sometimes, when we're under tremendous stress or pressure, we find ourselves thinking and sometimes doing things that are completely out of character. The point is, you didn't do it. You didn't cross that line. That's all that matters."

I laughed, a bitter ironic laugh, one that was coated with tears and filled with congestion. "Do you want to know the only reason I stopped? It was because when she looked at me, I started to think that my dead daughter was inside that fucking thing. I was convinced Adam had sewn my dead twelve-year-old daughter's brain inside the body of a sixteen-year-old, and all the coddling and overprotectiveness was because of that. My god, do you know the fucking worst part? She looked at me, the way she fucking looked at me, I could swear she wanted to die. I'm losing my mind. I think I'm hallucinating…or something…there's no way that's possible. I must be crazy, right?"

I broke down again, and Thiago sat next to me and stroked my hair. I pressed my face into his shoulder and sobbed. Thiago continued to comfort me, but he did nothing to alleviate my fears.

No, Katherine. It's not possible Adam could've done something so heinous.

Ha. Ironic for me to think using my own daughter as an experiment was wrong when we'd taken people without their consent for the very same thing. How brainwashed. So much tunnel vision. Adam had convinced me for years there was a greater good. All his work had a higher purpose to the medical and scientific community. To the world.

"You're not crazy," Thiago said. There was the reassurance I needed, although not presented in a such a way that it gave me confidence. He didn't deny the possibility Adam had used Charlotte's brain. He didn't say the idea was crazy. He just said I wasn't crazy, which could have been interpreted in any number of ways. Including me being right.

"Is it…is it Charlotte?" I needed him to deny it. I needed him to put my mind at ease.

"That is something you should ask Dr. Adam. It is not my place to say one way or another."

It is not my place to say.

Wasn't that the same as a yes? Once the possibility entered my mind, I couldn't shut it off. It was time for a little heart-to-heart with my husband. Whether he was going to be truthful with me or not remained to be seen.

This can't be happening.

"I need to lie down for a while."

I wasn't tired, I just didn't want to think about any of it. It was all too much. I clutched my stomach and winced. Exaggerated the pain. "Could you…get Chloe for me? I think I need something to take the edge off."

Thiago nodded. "Of course."

I sucked in a breath through my teeth. "I'm going to my room now."

"Do you need help?"

I shook my head. "No…just…"

"I'll get Chloe right away."

I walked back to my room and sat on the bed. Removed my shoes. Chloe arrived a couple of minutes later, medication in hand. I didn't need it for the pain.

I just wanted to mentally check out.

CHAPTER THIRTY-THREE

Present

Should I be preparing for my death? If I do come out of this alive, won't there be a jail cell waiting for me? Will I be okay with the finality of this? A constant sense of urgency claws at my nerves, pushing me along, keeping me running. I shove a couple of changes of clothes into an old, worn LL Bean backpack. I fought a terminal illness, was successfully integrated into a new body, and given a new chance at life—am I really going to throw that away?

In the end, I might not have a choice. Supposing I'm successful in my quest for revenge, and I take Adam off the playing field, so to speak, there won't be many options open to me. I will essentially have to disappear from society if I am going to live as a free person. Even if I am completely cleared of wrongdoing in both Theresa and Billy's deaths, I can't go back to masquerading as Sean Malone. There's no way I'm going to live out a life pretending for Sean and Theresa's friends and relatives. No way I'm working as a landscaper or some other bullshit manual labor type job. Sean has no degrees or training beyond high school. It would take considerable effort to reinvent that train-wreck of a life.

But I also don't want to die.

I don't want this long battle to simply end. It isn't fair after all I've been through.

The phone rings, and I let it go a few times while I go back and forth whether or not to answer.

What's the point?

I pick it up anyway. "Hello?"

"Sean? It's Pam. Have you seen Billy? He didn't come home last night, and he didn't call…"

At least he hasn't been found yet.

"Jeez, really? Shit. Yes…he was here last night. He stopped by around eight or nine, but he was only here for an hour or so before he left." I can only hope that sounds convincing. It's true. Mostly.

And he did leave after an hour or two, even if he wasn't alive at the time it happened.

"I…I see." Disappointment. Worry. I can't be the person to ease her mind. There was no late-night drunken crashing on the couch.

"Pam, if I hear from him, I'll be sure to let him know you were looking for him. He probably just visited another friend. Maybe had a couple drinks too many and decided to stay put."

"Maybe." Some hesitation creeps into her voice. Doubt. "But he would usually call."

"Who knows? Maybe his cell phone died and he didn't have a charger. Maybe he just forgot. Maybe he fell asleep before he had the chance."

"I guess that's possible. I just…he should've at least called by now. I'm worried. He wasn't acting like himself."

"Like I said, if I hear anything, I'll let him know you were worried. He was probably just sidetracked."

"Okay…thanks, Sean. I appreciate it."

It was inevitable that I'd get such a phone call, whether from Billy's wife or someone else, but I can't find it within myself to care. It probably shows. My lack of interest. Lack of empathy. Maybe they're right, and I have become a robot. Completely devoid of emotion. Lacking. Something is wrong with me.

There are two messages from Agent Nelson on my voicemail. He probably heard of Theresa's death, although there isn't so much as an offer of sympathy in either message. Only, *Sean, I have a few more things to discuss with you. Something came up in the investigation and I think you might be able to help. Worth a shot. Give me a call back.*

I won't be calling him back.

Instead, I lie in the bedroom, and the next thing I know…

I'm in that stark, white hallway again. Voices filter out through the ceiling. They're muffled, seeming far away, like my ears are blocked. This time, unlike the last, the lights flicker violently, creating a strobe effect. I'm not Katherine, the woman, anymore. I'm Katherine in Sean's body. Why am I standing here? What in the hell am I waiting for?

It stirs a vast and violent swirling storm of anger inside me. I take one step, vaguely aware of resistance. A loud clank. What I need is up there. My line of vision lands on that hole in the ceiling. Not to hear what's being said but to get to him. To get to Adam. The ladder is still there. The hole is still there. I take another laborious step.

Clank!

I am singular in my mission. To reach what's on the other side. Another step. The clang of metal hitting metal echoes through the hallway. Chains. How could I not have noticed? A heavy metal restraint. Cuffed tight around my ankle. The chain stretches all the way to the other end of the hallway, where it's attached to the floor. I am reaching the end of the slack. It will stop me in my tracks before I reach the ladder.

Who dares to keep me in here? Is it Adam? Does he know that I'm listening, that I am onto him? Maybe he's toying with me. Maybe he enjoys thinking he has the upper hand. That monster. Time for a jailbreak. Yeah, that's it.

Angry storms churn to rage. I stalk toward the end of the hallway. Grasp the chain, right where it attaches to the floor, and pull. Predictably, it doesn't budge. Somehow, I know I have to make it happen. I have to break free, or I'll be stuck here forever, and Adam will get away. He'll get away from me and get away with his crimes. There's no way in hell I'm letting him get away. Still, the chain won't move.

The cuff around my ankle is slightly loose. I can maybe fit a finger between it and my flesh. I sit on the floor, grasp the edge of the cuff, and slide it until it hits my heel. And I keep tugging. Gentle at first. Then, while pointing my toes and with more force. The metal digs into my skin. Cuts into it. The color in my foot darkens to a deep plum. I imagine my bones collapsing in on themselves. Folding into a neat compartment. Flesh and bone conforming to fit through a space screaming it's too small. But I don't care. I don't care.

I don't fucking care.

Something pops. Bones can be mended, but getting out of here…that's urgent. And that is now. Blood courses out of a fresh wound right at the base of my ankle. I strain at the shackle. Best to get my foot through before it begins to swell. Once that happens, there's no hope. I need hope now more than anything. The blood is slippery between the metal and my flesh. One more forceful tug and

I am free. I stand, shaky at first as the bones in my foot spread out and right themselves.

Freedom.

With a surge of energy, I whip around, rigid, adrenaline pumping through me, and begin to run. All that anger, all that rage, it explodes out of me in a deafening scream. Electricity surges throughout my body, extends into all my limbs. Numbing the searing, throbbing pain in my foot. A foot that doesn't want to hold the weight of this body. The hallway gets longer, the ladder further away. Then, a voice in my head—Adam's voice, smug and self-assured.

"Katherine, you'll never make it. You might as well give up."

I stop short of my goal, loud rumbling all around me, the floor vibrating beneath my feet. There's a trail of blood leading down the middle of the hallway. The floor begins to crack and pieces crumble away, falling into darkness.

He's not going to win. There's no way I am dying here and now.

"Katherine, wake up…"

My eyes snap open. I'm fully clothed, on the bed, the blankets tangled in my sweat-drenched body. Thiago. He's standing over me, hand firm on my shoulder. Shaking me. Swapping me from dream to awake as my brain rearranges pieces of reality.

"Tee?" My voice is still thick with sleep. Confusion. I know I'm in bed, that I've been dreaming, but it still feels real, still rattles my nerves.

"You must have been having a nightmare." He lets go of my shoulder, but he still watches me, arms folded. He's wearing a military-style outfit—utility pants, tight t-shirt, combat boots—but all black.

"How did you get in?"

"I helped myself to a spare key the last time I was here. Just in case."

I try to blink the sleep from my eyes. Clear the cobwebs. "I see. Why are you here?"

"It's time to leave."

"I thought the plan was for tomorrow." I sit and stretch my arms over my head. Yawn. Something doesn't feel right in my head. The fuzziness of sleep is taking too long to go away. I ignore it and push on.

"There has been a change of plans. We leave now."

My stomach jolts. "Did they find…?"

There's a ghost of a smile, just traces on his lips. "Relax, Katherine. Not yet. It is just that it's time to leave. Are you packed?"

I scratch my head through my hair. "I did last night." I point at the backpack sitting in the corner of the room.

"That's it?"

"How much could I possibly need? I don't imagine I'll be coming out of this alive."

He studies me. "You will not be dying on this trip."

I stare back, speechless. No smartass remarks lurk ready to aim and fire. I've simply assumed that I am doomed to become a casualty in this war. Even if I don't want to be. "What time is it, anyway?"

He glances at his watch. "A little past two."

"Where are we going?"

"You will see when we get there."

***

I sit in the passenger seat of the truck cab, shrouded in darkness, interrupted only by the occasional set of headlights. We're heading north on Route 495 going a steady seventy miles per hour. Thiago has always said the best way to remain inconspicuous is to travel within five miles of the speed limit. The cops, especially the staties, tend to turn a blind eye and instead pursue the ones that are really speeding. I can't remember when Thiago said this. Probably years ago, something in passing, but it makes me count how long he's been a part of our lives. Going on ten years. What exactly has earned that loyalty? It can't precisely be called a friendship.

I stare at him in the shadowy truck. One of those people who is ambiguous in age. I would guess somewhere in his thirties, although his hair is peppered with a few strands of silver. Possibly older.

He catches me looking, maybe senses it, even though his attention remains focused on the road. "Maybe you should try to get some sleep."

I move to watch the scenery whiz by. "I can't. Every time I close my eyes, I'm plagued by terrible visions."

"There is something else troubling you. Something besides Adam."

He's always been perceptive. Perhaps too much for his own good. But how much do I want to divulge? About my doubts. Or that I haven't been feeling quite right. "Why are you helping me? Why would you even want to get involved? Adam fleeing gives you the perfect opportunity to move on with your life."

"You find it hard to believe that I simply want to help?"

"Nobody helps with things like this out of the goodness of their heart."

"I couldn't turn my back on you, even if I wanted to." He breathes heavily through his nose. "Our lives are far too entwined at this point."

"Do you ever wish you'd taken a different path?" I stop short of asking if he wishes he never met us.

"I'm not sure what that would accomplish. The past is the past. I cannot change mistakes I've made or the things I have chosen."

"How does a person's path end up here?" I gesture openly at the inside of the truck, even though I mean not our physical state, but the entire situation.

"I was a troubled youth, Katherine. Reckless. I came to this country seeking something better, seeking opportunity, and instead I found things were not so easy. I worked long hours in jobs that I hated for shitty wages that barely paid the bills. I got into fights. I stole from rich clients and sold their belongings to seedy pawn shops. I was angry. But the one thing that kept me going, that kept me from completely falling into the dark side, was my love of technology."

He pauses his story, seemingly lost in a moment. I don't dare interrupt. I'll let him continue when he's ready, because this rare window into the life of a mysterious man is long overdue.

"I've always been good with computers. Back when I was seventeen, maybe eighteen, I hacked into the security system at one of the local banks in my hometown. When I showed my friends what I'd done, they hatched a plan to rob it. I could, after all, make sure they were never caught on camera. So, they did it, with my help, and they got away with it, but word began to spread of a young genius who could break into any surveillance system. Rumors grew out of control. I'd become somewhat of a legend. It was on the news. Authorities were on the hunt, but they never discovered who the culprit was. And I wanted to get away from it. So, I applied for a visa to come to the US. My sister and her husband already lived in Massachusetts. I moved in with them. I learned English. And I began my life here."

"Your past must have, in some way, followed you."

He laughs wistfully. One hand is on the steering wheel. His other arm rests beside him, relaxed. "I could not keep myself out of trouble, no."

"How did you meet Adam?"

"He caught me hacking into the hospital security system. I was working as a security guard at the time. There was an associate of mine who had access to the pharmaceutical stock. Just a few pills at a time. He sold them on the streets. Thousands of dollars' worth. And he gave me a cut of the profits for as long as I kept him in supply, so to speak."

"I'm sure it was a profitable venture."

"Without a doubt. When Adam confronted me, though, I thought my life was over. Instead, he offered me the opportunity to work for him."

"So, it was a little like blackmail."

"More like…he saw value in what I could do and recognized that I could be of use to him. This was when he was first getting ready to open his practice. He was already planning. He'd already known what he was going to do. I saw opportunity and the two of us came to an arrangement."

"And I suppose the rest is history." We've already covered quite a few miles and are nearing the New Hampshire border.

"I suppose." He adjusts his position in the seat. Switches hands on the wheel. He guides the truck off an exit before we reach the end of 495, where it merges onto I-95. "I want to avoid toll highways, to remain inconspicuous. So, we'll be taking a few smaller highways and back roads."

"I didn't say anything."

"You didn't have to."

I shake my head. "You didn't answer my question, you know. I've got this wonderful background history of you coming to America, and of securing employment with my husband, but I still don't understand why you would want to help me. If anything, I'd think you would be loyal to him."

"My relationship with Adam was one of mutual convenience. I was capable of doing things that he needed, and he compensated me well. It was less out of loyalty and more out of need. I am helping you because I want to."

"It's as simple as that? You just want to?"

"Free will is a valuable asset to possess." There he goes again, making vague statements in the form of life-altering advice. "What, you do not agree?"

I think about it. My own free will was taken out of the equation when my brain was inserted into a man's body. Now I'm pursuing my revenge. That's free will, isn't it? "Do you think it's wrong, what I'm doing?"

"I think it's…understandable, considering the circumstances," he hedges. We cross the border into New Hampshire, marked only by a small, unassuming sign.

"But probably not the right thing to do." I don't know what answer I'm pushing for precisely. Do I want him to talk me out of it? Do I want him to scold me? No. That isn't the case at all.

"I am hardly the person to be preaching morality, or right and wrong. I do know your personality and that you would not let this one go. You probably would not rest easy or be able to simply live your life."

"And yet you were trying to tell me to do that just a few days ago."

"Empty words. I needed to see what you were made of."

"There's no way I can just live out my life pretending to be Sean Malone. There's only so far claiming amnesia will take you. And then there's all the baggage, the people in his life…" I stop talking while I struggle to conceal my swirling thoughts. I've become a dangerous person. And I still can't fully trust Thiago with that. "I've already killed two of them. If I keep going through the motions, keep pretending to be this person I'm not, I know there will be more casualties."

"It's okay, Katherine." He reaches out and squeezes my shoulder and while it's a comfort, it feels odd and out-of-place in this male body. The way a man would treat a small child or a woman instead of another grown man.

I voice what has so often run through my mind since waking in that hospital. "I'm not sure who I'm supposed to be any more. I have memories and thoughts that don't match the body I'm in."

Thiago doesn't say anything for a long while. He concentrates on guiding the truck through the winding mountain roads. "Then maybe you need to stop focusing on what you see in the mirror and what you remember about your past. Maybe it is time to reinvent yourself."

That's far easier said than done. It's difficult to put into words what I'm going through mentally. While I can analyze my situation to death in my own mind, I've never really figured out a way to put a positive spin on it. In a way, I've already given up. I haven't seen a future. My mission to find Adam and exact my revenge doesn't include a plan for what will happen after. Can there really be a new life after Adam is gone? Part of me desperately wants that to happen. A bigger part can't picture it at all. Just a black void in my future.

***

I jolt awake, disoriented. Where are we? I don't remember falling asleep, or how much time has lapsed, but we're on a road lined with dense evergreen forest and the sky just above the treetops is tinted pink. The sun is coming up. I couldn't have been asleep for long.

I yawn and stare out the window. Aside from the occasional house, it's been nothing but forest since I opened my eyes. I need to urinate, but it's not that urgent yet. There's a steep, downward sloping embankment on either side of the road that would make pulling over nearly impossible anyway. Not that I want to stop.

The road ahead leads up an enormous hill. Once we reach the top, mountains come into view off in the distance, gray and shadowed in the low light of the early morning, but a solid reminder we're getting further from a place I once called home.

When we reach the bottom of the hill, Thiago slows the truck and turns right. He guides it onto a gravel road pockmarked with gigantic potholes. The bumpy ride wreaks havoc on my now aching bladder.

"It's an old logging road." It's the first thing either of us has said in over an hour. Maybe he's just making conversation, but I don't really care what this road is. Only where it leads and when we're going to get there. "All this is relatively new forest. Though you wouldn't know by looking at it."

I grunt an irritated response.

***

Forty-five minutes later, we take another turn down a long gravel driveway. At the end is a modest log cabin. This can't be where Adam is. There's no way we can just show up wherever he is. Not like he'll invite us over for coffee or dinner. Whatever Thiago has planned…

"I purchased this property not long after Adam and I first started moving things to his new place. He doesn't know about this." We get out of the truck, grab our bags, and head up the narrow path to the front door. He unlocks it and we go inside.

"Holy shit…" It's the last thing I expect. A complete contrast to what's on the outside. There's a wall of monitors, with computers and other electronic equipment below. It literally takes up half the room.

Thiago shoots me a sidelong glance. "I need to go down to the basement and turn the power on."

I nod, still in awe and with the overwhelming urge to use the toilet. "Where can I find the bathroom?"

"Down the hall and to the left."

"Thanks."

I finish up just as he comes back up the stairs. He crosses the room and flicks on a light switch, then goes over to the computers and powers them up.

The screens flicker and light up, revealing multiple angled views of what appears to be the same building. It must be Adam's place. How screwed up is this? Not that I am finally seeing where Adam is hiding—yes, that's disturbing on some level—but more the entire set up Thiago has puts me on edge.

Thiago has obviously been planning this for a long time. Whatever *this* is. A confrontation? Does he have his own revenge planned for Adam?

"Have a seat, Katherine. I'll put on a pot of coffee." He gestures to the sofa and I sit without giving a second thought.

Something doesn't feel right. My body aches, dull and throbbing in all the joints. Am I coming down with something? It's hard to tell if I'm feverish or not, but it's possible. Low grade at most, maybe ninety-nine or a hundred degrees. Just enough to make me feel a little under the weather.

"You're a little bit pale." He hands me a mug.

I shrug and take a sip. Cream no sugar. "I guess I'm just tired." No sense in worrying him. Or alerting him to potential weakness in the event I couldn't trust him. One could never be too careful.

"Well, we'll rest here for the night anyway." He quietly drinks his coffee and stares across the room toward the monitors.

I'm about halfway through the coffee when the symptoms worsen. One minute I'm okay, and the next, a skin-crawling, awful feeling being on fire. Like my body temperature is going haywire. I stand and stagger back a step and swipe a hand across my forehead. It's slick with sweat. Along with my neck and the sides of my face. But I have chills, and this overwhelming sense that I'm going to pass out.

"Tee…I don't…" My head is fuzzy. Did he drug me?

"Katherine? You don't look well at all." He doesn't sound concerned, but it could be my imagination. My vision blacks out. Briefly. Then it comes back, but my head is still fuzzy. I take a few steps before my vision blacks out again.

***

I'm lying in a bed, sheets and blankets tucked around me, wearing only a pair of underwear. A throbbing headache leaves me feeling detached and in a fog. What happened? Where am I?

The cabin. Thiago's bizarre little hideaway. It reminds me of something out of a movie—the home of some paranoid, tinfoil-hat-wearing shut-in. *Everybody's out to get me.* Did Thiago drug me? Maybe I'm the paranoid one.

"How are you feeling?" Thiago stands in the open doorway.

I frown. "I..." What do I want to ask him?

"You had a seizure." He looks concerned. I'm still too out of it to tell if it's genuine or not. There's a water bottle clutched in his hand.

Is that for me? The inside of my mouth is dry, making my tongue feel swollen.

"Have you been having them all along?" His expression is tough to read.

"No. I've never had one before." I squeeze my eyes shut for a moment. Every instinct hints at danger, that something is wrong. I can't shake that any more than the fog. "My head..."

He hands me the bottled water. "This is concerning. What if these are side effects from the surgery?"

I twist the cap between my fingers. The cap is still sealed, so he can't have put anything inside.

Jeez, talk about paranoid.

Thiago is watching me. I guzzle half the bottle in one motion and stop to take a breath. My parched tongue welcomes the wetness, so I tip the bottle to my lips and finish the rest. I close my eyes and will the pain in my head to disappear. In my mind, some of the fog has begun to clear. Some of the threads are reconnecting.

"Maybe this body is rejecting you. Or some of the connections have degraded. Or..."

"I've been fully healed for months." He's right that it could be a possibility. Organ rejection can happen at any time. Even months or years after a transplant. Is this my greatest fear coming true? "It's obviously possible that something was damaged slightly during surgery, something that would trigger a misfire inside. But it was one seizure. I'm not sure it's cause for alarm. Yet."

Maybe it's actually because he fucking drugged me.

"Katherine, I would tread carefully."

"This doesn't change anything. It could have been an anomaly. A one-time thing."

"It could be full blown epilepsy. It could even be the beginning sign of something much worse. Perhaps your body is beginning to break down." It could also be Thiago trying to convince me something is wrong when it really isn't.

"If that's the case, so what? What am I supposed to do about it? Just lie here? Whether it's a fluke thing or the sign of a bigger problem, my plans haven't changed. I need to get to Adam." I sit. The headache is already beginning to subside, but my mind is still a little fuzzy. "Where are my clothes?"

And why had he taken them off in the first place?

"You were sweating profusely, so I took them off." Maybe he can also read my mind. "Your bag is over here." Thiago lifts the backpack and sets it on the end of the bed.

"Thank you."

He shrugs. "Once you get dressed, I have something to show you."

After he leaves the room, I take my time getting dressed, still feeling a little lightheaded and out of sorts. Is this something I need to be worried about? Implanting a brain into a new host body is completely uncharted territory, so there's no way of knowing what sorts of long-term effects there might be.

What is or isn't normal.

I can't fix it right now anyway, so perhaps it's better to put it out of my mind.

I venture into the tiny living room, a room so overtaken by computer and surveillance equipment that it's astounding.

"You've put an extraordinary amount of effort into this."

He does not look up from the keyboard when I enter the room. At first, I think maybe he doesn't hear me. "It's something I've just felt compelled to do."

"Why?"

"Insurance. Preparation. Just waiting for the right opportunity."

"I'm not sure I understand." I think maybe I do understand, but I play dumb. Wait to hear from him directly.

"I may have worked for Adam a great many years, but I have never trusted him. This man needs to be stopped before he causes greater damage to the world."

"I agree." I pull up a chair next to him and sit. "Although, I do find it ironic for the two of us to be sitting here moralizing anything he's done, considering what *we* both have done."

"Sometimes there is a lesser evil and a greater evil. And Adam is a far greater evil than you or I. He doesn't see any wrong in what he's doing, yet he's damaged so many lives. Wronged so many families."

I study him, wondering how to frame my next question. Because what I see in Thiago's eyes nears pure hatred. "What did he do to you?"

"Ana Sophia. My niece. He stole her from me."

Now we're getting somewhere.

I scrounge my memory, trying to put two and two together, but I don't recognize the name.

"The one you know as *Emily.*"

"That hideous creation was your niece?"

He barks out an irritated laugh. "You have never been one for tact, Katherine."

"I wasn't aware tact was needed. Emily was brain dead when Adam took her. I'm sorry you lost your niece, but she was already a lost cause." Besides, it's my fucking *daughter* he put inside her.

"True. She was in a terrible car accident. The doctors said she would never wake. So, when Adam approached, saying he might be able to help, I wanted to believe. I convinced my brother and his wife to allow it. They agreed to place her under his care, not knowing what they were agreeing to. I had no idea what they were agreeing to. I had no idea the monster he would create..." Thiago is getting emotional. Kind of. His eyes get glossy and red, and his voice cracks. He inhales deeply, followed by a slow exhale before clearing his throat. "I had no idea."

Then he does break down and I'm at a loss as to what to do. So, I sit there, slightly uncomfortable. "She remained under his care for a number of years before that operation."

"He had convinced me early on that he might be able to help. That he was working on technologies related to the brain and healing. With weak promises that perhaps something could be done to reverse what had happened, to make her better. And I wanted to believe him."

"It's amazing to me how all of these things can be going on right under your nose and you can still be unaware they're happening. You probably think I'm foolish, or that there's no excuse, but I don't think I ever realized the depth of what Adam was doing. He kept me at a distance." What I did know and willingly participated in, however, makes me almost as guilty as him.

"I'm not sure anyone could truly know what's going on inside his head." Thiago's emotionless façade is back. "At any rate, I said there was something I wanted to show you."

We turn our attention back to the computer monitors. "Adam doesn't know about any of this?"

"No. I helped him set up the security system. He does not know that I am able to access it remotely. I gave the impression of handing over the keys, so to speak."

"And you think he believed that?"

"I told him to change the password every week for safety precautions. What he doesn't know is that passwords are useless. I can always bypass them."

The more I think about it, the more it makes sense. Adam, as intelligent as he is — brilliant really — has never been what one might call tech savvy. "So, what are we looking at?"

"There are two entryways. The main driveway, and a secret access tunnel that comes out about a quarter mile down the road. Both are highly visible to the surveillance cameras and would be impossible to infiltrate without Adam knowing." He gestures to the screens. The resolution is much higher than I would have expected for security cameras. "There are motion-sensor-activated cameras equipped throughout the surrounding property as well."

"You must know some way around. A way in where we can catch him by surprise."

"Only one." He taps the monitor that shows the front gate.

"What, we just walk right up to the gate and ring the bell?"

"No need. Every week, like clockwork, Chloe leaves the compound and drives to the nearest town." He shoots me a wry grin. "Adam has it set so that supplies are dropped off at regular intervals, but it seems the princess doesn't enjoy being cooped up."

"So, we could hitch a ride with *princess*." It isn't a bad plan, as far as plans go, and I am eager to get my hands onto Chloe. That bitch deserves everything that is coming to her.

"The vehicle is a black Escalade with tinted windows. Highly conspicuous in this neck of the woods, but plenty of room to hide."

"We'd have to do more than just hide. We'll have to take her hostage. Control her actions at knife or gunpoint."

"You're sounding a little too excited about that aspect. We do what we have to do, but our goal is not to hurt or kill anyone."

His goal maybe. Not mine.

"I'm serious, Katherine. Our number one purpose in this mission is to get to Adam. We need Chloe alive to do that."

"Did I say anything?"

He studies me for a moment, shaking his head, before turning back to the main computer screen. His fingers fly over the keyboard with impressive dexterity. A map appears. "The nearest town is here." He points to a spot on the screen and it highlights. Then he drags his finger along the screen, following the route. It too, highlights. "Almost twenty-five miles." He zooms in on the map.

"That's a long distance to try and keep her under control. What if she tries something foolish, like driving off the road and causing an accident?"

"I will drive, you will keep her under control."

"What if Adam sees she isn't the only one in the car?"

"He won't. The gate can be opened remotely from the vehicle itself. As I said before, its windows are tinted. And, it's been months since they've gone into hiding. People tend to get complacent once the immediate danger has passed. They're cautious, but not nearly at the level they once were. Neither one will be expecting us."

"How come you didn't go into hiding with them? Adam relied on you more than anyone."

"He did want me to at first. But I told him I would not be going. That I had family I needed to provide for, and that it would be more beneficial for him to have a contact on the outside that he could trust. It took some convincing, but eventually he agreed."

"How fortuitous."

"I have had to be one step ahead of him for a very long time."

"So, when is our little princess due for her weekly trip?"

"Tomorrow."

"Then it looks like we've got some planning to do."

CHAPTER THIRTY-FOUR

"You're much livelier today. What's the occasion?" Adam sat next to me, in my room. It was the first time we'd been alone together in a few weeks. He wore the mask of doctor. It wasn't so long ago I'd been struck by how much he'd aged, and once again I found myself contemplating why I'd insisted on staying by his side for as long as I had. It wasn't so much that he'd aged badly — he hadn't — as it was that he'd toppled off the pedestal I'd kept him on. Why had I held him in such high regard? He seemed so ordinary now. "Katherine? Are you feeling all right? You're grimacing."

He'd pulled the stethoscope away from my abdomen.

"I'm fine." Why had I stayed? The stark reality was, I had nothing else.

"I see." He seemed disinterested.

For years I'd had only the illusion of his support. I'd tolerated his calm indifference for so long, it was our normal. Why was I suddenly dissatisfied with that? Whatever rosy coating that had covered my vision was gone. No glow, no rainbows. What sat next to me was the *professional*. Not *husband*, that's *doctor* to you. And I wasn't going to let him avoid answering my questions.

"We haven't had the time to talk. And time is something I'm running out of."

"I'm not going to let you die, Katherine."

"Humor me, then."

He let out a heavy sigh, as though my simple request for conversation was burdensome. "If it's because I haven't been paying enough attention to you, I'm sorry. I've been so wrapped up in preparing for your surgery, making sure everything is right, that I haven't had much time to think about anything else."

Only a man who gave expensive jewelry to right a wrong would automatically assume I was starving for his attention. I wasn't going to let him off. "It's not that."

The way he looked at me, the blank confusion, maybe a touch of annoyance. I was a waste of time. The conversation was an inconvenience. *I don't have time for this*, was what that look said. "Then what?"

"Is having a conversation with your own wife really that distasteful?" My filter was gone, and I felt no remorse.

More impatience. A fleeting scowl he tried but failed to conceal. "You know that's not the case."

Of course it's the case, you bastard.

"If you're worried about the surgery—"

"Whose brain is inside Emily?"

There was an almost imperceptible widening of the eyes. "I've already told you it was a donor—"

"Or perhaps it's our daughter."

"Don't be absurd. How…how could it—" He was flustered. He stumbled over his words. I'd never confronted him directly on anything I thought might cause an argument. Always chosen my battles carefully. But now, what did I have to lose?

"Don't lie to me," I snapped. It was a harsh, loud, cold tone even I wasn't accustomed to hearing from my own lips. Forceful. Determined.

He flinched. "Kath—"

"Just because I haven't called you out on it doesn't mean I haven't noticed. The way you treat her, the way you talk to her, the relentless way you insist that she's going to get better. Did you know I visited her? I could see it in her. I fucking recognized her." I took a breath, but I was getting warmed up, and Adam was growing paler by the second. "To think that all this time would go by and I wouldn't notice, you are just a special kind of stupid. How *could* you? Why couldn't you just lay her to rest, let her suffering end? Instead, you've created this…this thing…"

"I couldn't let her die." Finally. An admission of guilt, but delivered in such a way that guilt was absent.

"She wants to die now!"

"She's confused. She still hasn't learned how to communicate effectively." And he continued to be in denial.

"She took my hands and placed them on her neck. I think that's fairly obvious what she meant." I omitted the part where I had gone in to strangle her myself. There were some things he didn't need to know. Unless he already did. Unless there was video surveillance set up in Emily's room. But no…he seemed genuinely surprised. So, if there was, he hadn't watched it. Or he hadn't noticed. "My god, Adam, how *could* you? And to lie to me about it…to keep it from me. She's my daughter too."

"I couldn't just let her die. To just stand by and do nothing, when I knew the technology was there, when I knew that I was able to fix it. I could make her better and give her another chance at life. Why wouldn't I take that opportunity? My own daughter?"

"*Our* daughter," I reminded him.

"Of course. *Our* daughter. Wouldn't you want the best for her? Wouldn't you want to give her every chance at life?" Talk about sinking lower than low. To somehow insinuate that I wouldn't have wanted those things, as if I was the one barrier that prevented our daughter from being saved. As if I didn't want it. Or didn't care. Was that what he thought? What a conniving piece of garbage. This was not my fault. He was not going to make it my fault.

Once again, I was struck by just how far removed from sane logic the man operated. He'd probably always been this way, though in the past I'd chosen to ignore it. Now it seemed repulsive and wrong.

I will not relent. I will not give in. He will never win.

I chanted over and over inside my head. A sort of battle cry. Because while my body was weak, my mind was not.

"This so-called life you've given her is *not* a life. Confined within the walls of this building. Trapped in a body that doesn't even function properly — we don't even know if she has full control over her mental faculties." At least I hoped she didn't have full control of her mental faculties. That somehow made it worse. To be aware of one's predicament but unable to do anything to make it better. Unable to force your body to do what you wanted it to. Completely aware of the limitations.

Not unlike myself. My situation.

I hoped she was unaware, but my latest interaction with her indicated a similar situation to my own. If that were true, then I wondered what her motivation had been when she attacked me. Was it anger? Or had she simply not realized what she was doing? Maybe there was a short circuit with some logic and reasoning, but at the same time, a basic understanding of her predicament. Maybe she at least knew how fucked up her life was.

"She's made progress." It frightened me how he accepted such a small measure of *progress* and yet he treated it like a major breakthrough.

"Please. She's never going to be any better than she is now." There had to have been some damage during the surgery. That was the only explanation.

"You can't know that."

"Can't I? I see what you refuse to. Something went wrong. You know it deep down, you must. And yet you continue to allow her to live in this miserable state. What kind of life is that? She won't ever be able to grow and become independent. No college, no job, no marriage, no children. No life outside these walls."

"Katherine—"

"No! You've doomed our daughter to the life of a lab rat freak, because let's face it, whatever went wrong with her, it can't be fixed. I wonder, Adam, what you have in store for me? If something goes wrong in my process, will I also be kept locked in a room? Because that isn't any kind of a life. I'd rather be dead than that."

"You won't be locked in a room." He was no longer facing at me. He stood and began to pace, seemingly deep in thought. Perhaps this was his way of avoiding my scrutiny. If he thought he was getting away from me, he was dead wrong.

"How am I supposed to know that? You're doing it now." By the look on his face, by his demeanor, the idea that I might not trust him hadn't crossed his mind. Yet.

"You're ill. Commuting would only put further strain on your body. Unnecessary strain. I keep you here to keep you safe and buy us enough time. I want to make sure everything is absolutely, without a doubt, ready. We can't afford to take any chances." He paused and let out a heavy breath that deflated his posture and his head bent toward the floor. "This time will be different, I swear it.

The surgery will be successful, and the three of us can be a family again. Don't you want that too?"

A family?

He was fucking batshit crazy. The haze had worn off and a sobering truth stared me right in the face. I didn't want any of those things. I didn't want him or to be a family. And yet, I couldn't bring myself to say it out loud.

Some deep instinct told me it was best to keep that truth to myself. It could provoke Adam or worse. No, it was time for some serious self-preservation. For the first time in a very long time, I needed to look out for myself.

I forced a smile. "Of course I do. I want that more than you could imagine."

The words came out sounding as empty and hollow as I felt, but I didn't think Adam noticed, because he seemed visibly relieved. His posture relaxed. My time of rebellion was over. He no longer needed to worry if I was going to be a problem. Just like that, his mind was eased. What a curious thing. He squeezed my shoulder and pulled me into a loose embrace. "Things are going to be different, Katherine. Better. Better than you can possibly imagine."

"I hope you're right."

CHAPTER THIRTY-FIVE

Present

Thiago and I drive to the little town where Chloe makes her frequent visits. As far as towns go this far north, it's good-sized. Not large like back in Massachusetts, not city large, but it's apparent this town is the only one for miles with a full-sized supermarket, multiple restaurants, a hardware store, auto parts shop, and a large motel. That means a lot more people. We'll be less conspicuous.

Nervous anticipation grips my gut. I have no idea if I will escape this confrontation unscathed, or if it's the ultimate suicide mission; I just know that it needs to happen. That whether I live for another thirty years or die tonight, I won't be at peace unless this happens.

We park at the grocery store, near the back of the lot. Thiago pulls out his laptop, plugs it into a port in his truck, and powers it up. He clicks on an icon that opens a surveillance program. It's on a much smaller scale than the setup back at his cabin, and yet here it is, a view of Adam's front driveway.

"So now what?"

He glances over at me. "Obviously, we wait." Thiago seems to have endless patience with my questions. Maybe he senses the significance of this confrontation. What am I thinking? He knows the significance. He's been building up for this for many years too. So much time harboring hatred and resentment toward Adam. Thiago, a small-time hacker, turned small-time criminal—the type of guy who operates in the shadows, far beneath the radar of the authorities. And yet, over the years he's become my greatest ally.

Or has he?

Somehow it feels too good to be true. This is the thought nagging at me, right now of all times, and it's inopportune. I have to trust him, don't I? He's taken me this far, gotten me this close. We're sitting in a goddamned truck in a town in the middle of East Bumfuck, Maine looking at surveillance videos of my husband's secret hideout. How can I not fucking trust that? But…that voice nags at me, an annoyance in the back of my mind. A mosquito buzzing around my ear. Maybe I need to have a backup plan.

Something to fall back on if Thiago turns out to be untrustworthy. What if this is all part of Adam's plan? That scenario is a possibility I need to prepare for if I plan to come out of this alive. That somehow all of this is a ruse. Thiago's story of betrayal could be a ploy to earn my sympathy and trust. Perhaps it isn't true at all. If that's the case, he's certainly leading me to my death or worse. Maybe Adam has a final experiment in store for me. Something big. Something dangerous.

"Katherine?" Thiago is staring at me. Can I really trust him? It's difficult to tell what's hiding behind those mysterious dark eyes. "Are you all right? You have this really…intense expression on your face."

"I guess I'm a little nervous when it comes down to this. I want this confrontation, but it's been building up for so long, it's a little hard to believe this is actually happening." It isn't precisely that I'm lying. More that I'm omitting parts of the truth. I know I should be a little nervous, no doubt, but maybe I should also be suspicious of Thiago's motives.

"You don't need to worry, Katherine. I won't let him harm you."

Can I really trust what's hiding behind those eyes? The more I think about it, the more I have my doubts. It hits me so suddenly and comes from out of nowhere, yet now I can't get rid of it.

"I know you won't." I try to erase the tightness in my voice. He's too smart. He knows me too well to believe that I am simply overcome by nerves. What if I've put a little too much trust in him? If it comes down to it, and Thiago really is working with Adam to trap me, I will have to kill them both. Because I am not prepared to die. Even if I have to live out my life in this body I hate, there is no reason why I should have to be the one to sacrifice everything. I've already sacrificed enough. I want to live and that means I have to be prepared for every possible scenario. To be one step ahead. "So, what's your plan? When Chloe shows up here, we can't just grab her in broad daylight. We obviously have to be discreet."

"We'll have to rely on the element of surprise."

"What if she makes a scene?"

"She won't."

"How do you know?" Is he lying to me? If he really is acting on some predetermined plan with Adam, then Chloe will be in on it too, won't she?

Thiago is still staring at me. Does he notice I have doubts? Is that suspicion in the slight wrinkle of his brow? "Are you feeling all right, Katherine? This doesn't have to happen today if you're not ready. I've waited years. A few more days or weeks won't make a difference."

I stare back. Unmoved. "No. I'm fine with today. There are no guarantees that either of us will even have a tomorrow, are there?" Inside my head a small war has started. A fantasy world where it's me against everyone else. Survival of the fittest. Except I don't have any weapons on me. Not even a pocket knife. How do I expect to defend myself if a problem arises?

"No there aren't any guarantees. For anything in life." He sets the laptop on the dash and reaches for a bag in the backseat. Without looking down, he unzips it, pulls out a large knife tucked in a leather holster, and hands it to me. "Maybe you will feel a little more at ease with some protection."

I take it from him. Suspicious. Slide the knife out of its holder and examine it. I know very little about knives, but this one appears to be for hunting or gutting large animals. The blade is about six inches long—straight along one edge, with a curve that comes to a sharp point on the other edge. The handle, a deep, polished wood. It's beautiful. Beautiful and dangerous.

"Thank you." Why has he given it to me? A show of trust? Or perhaps to give the illusion of trust and catch me off my guard. I'm leaning more toward the latter.

"I just hope you don't end up using it on me. But you're welcome." It's almost as if he read my mind. Maybe this is his way of letting me know that he knows where things stand. Maybe he recognizes my doubts and lack of trust. This is a peace offering. A show of faith. And once again he's pulled the rug out from under my feet. Or maybe I am going crazy.

"Why on earth would I use it on you?"

"You get this look about you every so often. A blackness rising in your soul. It's the face of a woman who isn't afraid to kill. A woman who even enjoys it a little. It's frightening."

"I don't look like a woman at all." I don't know how to react to that. He called me a woman, too. Probably the only person who'll ever think that again. The more he says it, the more he confuses the issue. I am doomed to live out a life with a confused identity. Male, female. Sean. *Katherine.* Certainly, I can't go through life being called Katherine when I'm physically a man. Who am I? If I survive and need to reinvent myself, who will I become?

"You know what I mean."

I suppose I do.

"She's leaving."

On the laptop screen, the camera facing the front entrance shows a black SUV inching slowly. It's almost time.

***

It's been quite a few months since I last saw her in person. Chloe doesn't look any different. I don't know what I expected, but considering she ran off with my husband, maybe I was hoping for some extra pounds or bags under her eyes. But there's perfect little Chloe with her shiny blonde hair pulled up into a high ponytail and one of those designer tracksuits that's more about style than function. She is woefully out of place in East Bumfuck, Maine. An outsider. A stuck-up bitch, but perhaps the townsfolk forgive that because she's pretty.

"Breathe, Katherine." Thiago grabs my shoulder, shaking. "We must keep a cool head, right?"

While watching Chloe, I'd pulled the knife from the sheath, and I grip it tight.

"At least I know you can act quick." He seems at least a little bit amused by this, or as much as Thiago can be amused by anything. "Can you control yourself?"

I sheath the knife. "Of course."

Chloe disappears into the store, and while we wait, Thiago packs up his laptop into its case and tucks it under the seat. We get out of

240

the truck, and I follow his lead. The knife rests in my front sweatshirt pocket. We loiter at the end of the store between a shopping cart corral and an ancient-looking ice machine.

She comes out thirty-six minutes later with a single, recyclable, cloth grocery bag hanging in the crook of her elbow, attention focused on the cell phone in her hand. Thiago and I make a beeline across the parking lot. We catch up with her before she even realizes we're there, Thiago on one side and me on the other.

"Don't make a scene." Thiago's voice is low, just above a whisper. "If you cooperate, nobody will get hurt."

I unsheathe the knife and hide it in my sleeve. Reveal enough that she can see it's there. She looks back and forth between us, her expression registering shock. Maybe a little disbelief. "You've got to be fucking kidding me," she mutters. Maybe even a little annoyance.

"How about we get in the vehicle?" Thiago nods at the SUV. He grips her upper arm. Tight enough to show he's serious. Loose enough so as not to arouse suspicion.

Chloe rolls her eyes. "Of course." She opens the passenger door without a fight and slides into the seat. I climb in the backseat and Thiago gets in behind the wheel. She leans around the seat to face me. "Nice meat suit, Kat. Have you taken it for a test drive? I've always wondered what it felt like to be a man."

I have the knife to her throat in an instant. Just slide my arm around the seat with reflexes faster than I realized I am capable of. One hand holds the knife. The other grasps her hair and pulls her head back. "I don't know, Chloe. I haven't yet had the chance to test the full scale of this body's capabilities. Would you care to help me?"

I should be able to smell the fear rolling off her. Instead, her posture is stiff.

"It was a joke, jeez, talk about an overreaction." She grits her teeth and the cords in her neck pop out.

"It wasn't fucking funny."

"Katherine, ease off. It's okay. What did we talk about earlier?"

"*We* didn't talk about anything. You talked *at* me. I just nodded my head and listened." I press the knife into her skin. Chloe doesn't flinch. What the hell is wrong with this woman? "*She* doesn't deserve the time of day, let alone to be allowed to breathe the same air I'm breathing."

"*Katherine.*" There's more warning this time. Enough to give me pause.

"It's all right, Thiago. She has every right to be angry. I would be furious if it was me." Chloe is still a little too calm for someone with a knife pressed to her throat. "And you being you, I suppose you didn't explain the entire situation, am I right?"

"There has not been time."

My body tenses. There's something going on, and I don't appreciate being left in the dark. "It took us almost six hours to drive up here. We had plenty of time for you to *explain*. What's going on?"

"Fair enough." He holds out both hands. Maybe it's in defeat. Maybe to show he isn't a threat. "But for now, please, just lower the knife and let's talk."

I settle back into my seat, arms folded, still gripping the knife. There was no way in hell I'm giving it up. "Fine. *Talk.*"

Chloe releases a low breath, the only sign she'd been distressed by my attack. Something was very fishy about this whole scenario.

"Well, first off, he was *not* supposed to bring you here." She exchanges glances with Thiago. Evidence of a shared understanding. Of a plan I'm not privy to. Yes, definitely fishy.

If ever there's a time to be on my guard, to be suspicious, it's now. And whatever these two are up to, no matter the motivation, it's obvious the only person I can trust is myself.

"I didn't plan to bring her here." What have they been planning that they want to avoid having me present? He turns to me. "Katherine, if you leave now, you will be able to move on with your own life. Craft a new identity. If you go through with this, I can't guarantee that."

"We've been through this already. I'm not going to live out my life wondering what could have been. What are you hiding? Why don't you want me to confront Adam?"

"I feel like no good will come from this. Call it a very strong gut feeling." Why did he relent and bring me along if he feels so strongly I shouldn't confront Adam? Thiago could have simply vanished, like a ghost, from my life. He could have abandoned me, and I would have had no way of knowing where to find Adam. Is it that he can't say no to me? Or is it more sinister?

Drugging me didn't create the desired effect. Of stopping me. Supposedly I had a seizure, but there's no way to know if that's true or not. The only thing certain is that I'd felt funny, then blacked out. When I regained consciousness, time had passed, and I was lying in a bed. The seizure was Thiago's story, but what's mine? What is real?

This is indeed where I need to tread carefully. Maybe he's leading me to a trap. Or maybe he isn't. He wants me to go or he doesn't. I can't be sure of anything, especially if he really did drug me. Because the other possibility is that he didn't drug me, and I am being paranoid.

No, something is going on, I just don't know what.

I will follow along as planned. Try not to allow Thiago or Chloe to see how little I trust them. I need them, because they know how to get where I want to go.

Maybe Adam has something waiting for me behind those fortress walls, something unpleasant. Is Thiago still under his employ? Is this his way of warning me, of giving me an out rather than voluntarily walking into it? I have to be prepared for anything. Including the possibility that Thiago might be betraying me. His entire story is so convenient. And while now they both play it off as though they're warning me away, something unsettling bubbles in my gut.

"The only thing that's obvious is that I've been lied to. Somebody needs to tell me what's going on. *Now.*"

The atmosphere in the vehicle grows heavy and crackles with electricity. It's a storm of my creation, but the emotions are all theirs. Somehow, I'm able to stay calm. Reigning in my emotions has always been one of my strong points. Self-control. But this is different. I know I should be angry, but I'm unable to get there. Like the fuse is snuffed out before it reaches the bomb. Or a door has slammed shut.

"Well, I guess you could say Thiago and I are on the same page. One of us needed to keep a close eye on Adam, and that someone ended up being me." She's holding back, and she looks to Thiago for support. "We didn't want to arouse suspicion with Adam. He expected his closest crew to follow him here. So, I volunteered to go with him and Thiago volunteered to stay on the outside. I'd keep him informed and vice versa."

"I was supposed to be the outside contact, and as I told you before, Adam was on board with this. It began with just being an ear to the outside world, or someone to procure items or services he could not himself. And then as things began to—"

But wait. Didn't Thiago tell me that Adam said not to contact him? To pretend they never met? Yet now he claims to be the outside contact. Which is it? They're lying, that much is obvious. I should be angry. Furious. What the hell is wrong with me? Am I completely dead inside?

"You're both babbling, but you're not really telling me anything. What the fuck is up with all this bullshit? *You* go with Adam"—I gesture impatiently at Chloe, then Thiago—"*you* stay posted on the outside. Blah blah blah. You do realize none of this makes any sense? You're trying to pass off this blatant, bullshit story as truth. Do you honestly think I'm that fucking dumb? Your reasoning is flimsy at best."

"Kat, I realize you're upset, but it's not so simple."

"Isn't it, though? You could have ended this at any time, *should have* ended it if you truly felt so strongly about it. And yet you just play along, dancing around the issues, acting like you're against him, but are you really?" I've raised my voice, mimicking the heated way of someone who is reaching their boiling point, even though I'm still not *feeling* anything. Neither one of them seems affected by my outburst.

"I told you we were buying time." Thiago is unnaturally calm, in a way that makes my skin crawl, but I am already too far into this to listen to that instinct.

"Buying time for *what*? Don't insult my intelligence. This is too convenient, all of it. If you truly didn't want me to be here, I wouldn't be here. There were so many ways you could've stopped it. So, the question is, am I here because you want it, because you want this confrontation? Or is it because Adam wants this?"

"You shouldn't get yourself so worked up." Again, Thiago, with the unnaturally calm attitude, telling me what to do. In a way that feels condescending. The funny part of it is that I'm not worked up. Something inside of me has to be broken, and I'm just now connecting the dots of its existence.

"Call it poetic justice. To have him destroyed by what he created." Chloe is watching me, intently. Does she know I don't trust them? "We had to wait for you to be ready."

"You do realize that sounds completely absurd. Ready for what?"

"I'm sorry, Katherine."

I catch movement out of the corner of my eye. Chloe's sneak attack. The needle has already pierced my skin before I can react. Before I can stop it.

"It's better this way." And as I rapidly succumb to the heaviness, as my conscious mind begins to drift, I think maybe I hear Chloe saying, *we need him to think we've captured you and brought you to him for this to work.* Followed by Thiago, apologizing again, *nobody is going to hurt you.*

But maybe I imagine all of it. Maybe my mind is playing tricks on me.

CHAPTER THIRTY-SIX

Past

Chloe shaved the last patch of hair from my head and switched off the electric clippers. Piles of thin, matted hair littered the floor around me. I remembered a time in my life when it would have been traumatizing. Back then, if someone had shaved my head, a heart attack would surely have been the result. Now? Not so much. I felt indifferent. I would either be dead soon or in another body. It was only hair.

Chloe picked up a mirror from her little supply cart and waggled her eyebrows, grinning, as she held it up. "Wanna see the new you?"

"Not particularly." But I looked anyway, and what greeted me was sadness, illness, and the dried-out husk of a woman I'd become. I looked odd and alien without any hair. One of those sci-fi gray men, minus the giant black eyes. My skin had such a weird hue under my bedroom lights. "Well, that's revolting."

"You could start a trend." She was still grinning, the evil little bitch. Perhaps enjoying it a bit too much.

"Fantastic. Shall I do yours next?" I grinned back, though on my face it must have looked positively sinister. Grotesque.

"I'm not sure I have the cheekbones to pull it off." She winked, un-fazed, and set the mirror back onto the cart. It could have been a jab. I doubted Chloe was that petty, but some of the things she said could be taken as cruel if you didn't know her. That said, it was very easy for her to brush it off. She wasn't in my position. Her own hair was platinum blonde, shiny, and bunched into a messy bun on top of her head. Untouched.

She busied herself with her act, pretending everything was fine, like that had been a normal haircut, and she fucking hummed while wiping the hair clippings from my bare neck. Then she pulled off the smock — purple with little rainbows printed all over, something I had not noticed earlier — and shook it over the floor.

"I'll clean this up and then we can get you showered."

I pretended not to hear what she said. Nothing she said mattered and I was tired of hearing her speak. Tired of the faux cheerfulness.

Tired of everything. The impending surgery weighed on me so much, I felt physically heavy. Maybe someone had filled my limbs with sand while I was sleeping. Surgery. Dying. It was all I thought about. In my mind I revolted against it, and yet I still allowed myself to be led toward it. It was a one-way street now, no turning back.

I pushed myself to stand, with the shaking limbs of a baby taking her first steps and walked to the bathroom. At the very least, I should have been able to wash myself. To have one last moment of dignity in a life that seemed full of indignities lately.

And Chloe came swooping in, ready to help. "Kat, hang on a sec, I'll help you, 'k?"

"No need. I think I can handle a shower on my own." It would be nice to be rid of the constant hovering. My god, I hoped that if the surgery was successful, more of this would not be in my future.

She opened her mouth to protest, then shrugged it off. "Suit yourself. Holler if you need anything. I'll be right here."

I'd expected more of a fight. I'd been bracing myself for it, but she already had her back to me and was sweeping hair off the floor. I pushed through the dizziness. Tried to enjoy a last sliver of freedom I'd been granted as I ran the shower and undressed. It was the second time in the past few weeks I was able to shower alone. Bliss.

But it was over too fast, and while I dried off, Chloe quietly slipped a pile of clean clothes onto the counter. My last change of clothes in this body. Last clothes, last rites. What was next? The death row inmate's last meal? There was something completely absurd, but also fitting, about that idea. Maybe I *was* going crazy, because suddenly that seemed funny and I succumbed to an uncontrollable fit of laughter. The kind where tears filled your eyes and your body shook in great spasms. It hurt. Felt like my insides were tearing apart, but I couldn't stop. I braced one arm against the wall and clutched my stomach with the other. At least I'd managed to get dressed first.

"Kat?" I hadn't heard Chloe enter the room and barely felt her touch on my back. Somewhere along the way my laughter had turned to uncontrollable sobbing. I was making up for a lifetime of hardly showing any emotion. Someday had arrived. That ambiguous, out-of-reach date somewhere off in the future was staring me in the face. It was *now*. And I was frightened. So frightened.

Chloe let it run its course without saying a word. By the time the tears dried, my eyes were swollen, and I couldn't breathe through my nose. My entire body shook from the exertion. I was near collapsing when Chloe placed an arm around me and guided me back to my room. Where a wheelchair was waiting. Ready to carry me to my uncertain future. Or my death. Maybe this was it. Maybe the clock was ticking toward the final seconds of my life. I'd close my eyes, and that would be the end of it. No more Katherine.

I'd been positive that ending things on my terms would be the way to go, but now, faced with the possibility, it didn't seem like such a rosy option. I wasn't ready to die.

But could I even entertain the idea of surviving this surgery?

"It's going to be okay," Chloe said. "I'm sure of it."

But I wasn't. That nagging, terrible gut feeling something was going to go wrong was unshakeable. "I've never been so terrified in my life."

"You don't need to be afraid." Her words seemed hollow. It could have been my imagination, but I sensed Chloe was also unsure about the operation. There were no overt outward signs, it was just another gut feeling.

Chloe wheeled me down the hall, and I felt every bit the death row inmate. On my way for that last injection. Except now it wasn't funny, and my gut twisted into tight knots, constricting the tumor inside. Or embracing it. Maybe they danced together in celebration. Somebody was going to come out the winner, but would it be me? Was it possible to cheat death?

We entered the operating room, where Adam waited, where my host body lay in what was essentially an ice box, with a sheet draped over it. Was I ready for this?

Adam. "Katherine. Are you ready to be a part of medical history?"

What a curious way to put it. Part of history. As in, the past. No words of comfort, still, even so close to the actual event. Then, it hit me. Another intrusive thought. Was this situation my fault? All those years of holding back emotions and creating this image of an invincible, untouchable woman—maybe people thought I didn't need reassuring. Maybe they thought nothing bothered me. The idea that I might be terrified hadn't even created a spark in Adam's imagination. He was all about innovation. Medical technology. Science. And he seemed to believe I shared this enthusiasm. As if I was so detached from my own life that I wasn't worried about what might happen.

"I don't suppose I have a choice at this point."

"I won't allow anything to go wrong. I've spent the past couple of months analyzing and re-analyzing all the data from Emily's surgery. I've isolated two separate issues." He paused to bring up images on the computer monitor. I expected him to go on and explain what those issues had been, but instead he continued his sales pitch, undeterred. "Not only that, but scans of your brain as well as your host body have been mapped in the computer. The software has been vastly improved. We have a guide for the entire surgery, right down to every nerve, every vein, and every tendon. Couple that with what we know went wrong in the first surgery. There will be no chance for error this time."

"I see."

At that point there was no fight left. I was on a collision course and it was time to force acceptance.

"You have nothing to worry about." Adam was so relaxed and confident.

So why wasn't I?

They positioned me on the operating table. Chloe prepped my arm where the IV would be administered. The one that would put me to sleep. There was no turning back. I had to lie back and let it take me. I barely felt the needle pierce my skin.

"We're just going to give you something to help you relax, okay?" Chloe's voice was the one constant, attempting to sooth. But I already knew the trick. *Something to make you relax* was actually the main event, and it caught you off guard as you drifted under. You didn't even know it was happening.

"When you wake, this'll all be better. A new chance. A new life."

My eyelids became heavier and I lost the struggle to keep them open. Didn't even realize it had happened until I was alone in the darkness. Caught in a world between sleep and waking. Maybe I was sitting in the middle of a dark room. Maybe I didn't know where I was anymore. But I heard voices. Adam and Chloe. And it wasn't all fine and rosy as it had been when they first laid me down.

"You can't! What are you thinking?" Chloe sounded alarmed. She was sounding the alarm. Upset. What was going on? I felt the particles in my mind scattering, making coherent thought near impossible.

"My hand was forced. You knew full well what happened to the other one. Maybe this is a blessing in disguise." The drugs should have rendered me completely unconscious, so why could I still hear? Why in god's name could I still hear?

His hand was forced? Nobody forced Adam to do anything he didn't want to.

"How could you think that? You have no idea what kind of effect this will have. There are so many factors."

"What other choice is there? This was biologically a better match, even than the first choice."

"I don't know...I mean, I don't know. What about compatibility?"

"I told you, that shouldn't be an issue. I've checked and rechecked the chemistry."

"But psychologically, there are so many unknowns."

Unknowns. So many unknowns. I didn't understand the context of the conversation, and soon they were just two angry-sounding, abstract voices. Not making any sense. Or I no longer had the capability of making sense out of it. Then, the voices seemed muted, like someone had inserted earplugs. Maybe I was inside of a vacuum. In the middle of a black hole. Getting sucked away into the nothingness of outer space. Was this how dying felt? A slow fade from reality, where the voices grew further and further away? And then my consciousness would be next. Once that light was snuffed out, there would be nothing left.

I fought desperately to keep it lit. Was this where everything ended for me? Maybe this really was death. Whatever unknown Adam was peddling, it was going to fail. I'd heard real, palpable fear in Chloe. But I was losing this battle. Sinking deeper and deeper into blackness.

CHAPTER THIRTY-SEVEN

Present

I wake, still groggy, my head pounding. I'm in a bed. In a room I don't recognize. That sparks a restless energy inside my head as some of the fog from a drug-induced sleep begins to lift. It only confirms my suspicion Thiago had drugged me at the cabin. At least I'm not crazy.

Motherfucker!

My arms and legs are held in place with heavy leather straps.

Look at me now.

Restrained. Cursing myself for being so stupid. For trusting someone I shouldn't have.

Why didn't I see any of this coming?

Anger surges inside me, an uncontrollable, mad rush of water set free from a dam and rocketing through waterways. It interferes with my thoughts. Sends the particles of logic and reason scattering. A dark storm cloud mixing up the signals. Nothing is rational or coherent or makes any kind of sense. I can't think of any sane reason to be this angry, to be so affected—this situation is awful and unexpected, but I don't really know *what* is going on yet. I should be mad, yes. Yet this is beyond mad. It's dark and violent and overpowering. I can't push it away. I can't think through it. I can't calm myself down.

"It's powerful, isn't it?" I hadn't noticed Thiago in the room. He appears through the fog and the shadows. "What you're feeling."

I rage against the restraints. Thrash about. The straps cut into my skin. My muscles strain, burning with exertion, but the pain hardly registers.

"Don't hurt yourself, Katherine." Thiago is eerily calm.

"Fuck...you!" Flying spittle, cords popping from my neck, jaw clenching tight. Pure rage.

"This is an incredible piece of technology." Thiago holds a tablet, his attention focused on the screen.

All at once, whatever intense rage that has me in its powerful grip, it lets go. Like I've just been wrung out, squeezed dry, and dropped back onto the bed. My muscles are limp and achy. My heart pounds. I struggle through deep breaths to relax myself. The tickle of newly formed sweat rolls across my bare skin.

"It does far more than Adam ever imagined. But then again, his creativity when it comes to technology has always been close to nil. He's what you might call old school."

Now Thiago's eyes are black and cold and distant. Miles away and devoid of heart or soul. This is not the man I thought he was. Something has changed drastically. I trusted him, even confided in him. I allowed him to lead me here, to this place, in the middle of nowhere. And here he is babbling nonsense about technology.

Instinct tells me to be cautious. It warns me to be suspicious. Yet somehow, I've been lulled into a false sense of security. Why is that?

My heartbeat has calmed some. "Where are we?"

"Exactly where I said I'd bring you. I *do* keep my promises, Katherine." He is still fixated on the tablet screen. "I see your heart rate has calmed nicely."

With sudden stark clarity, like a window has been opened and a bold-lettered billboard faces back at me, it hits. That tablet has a direct link to what is going on inside me.

The implant.

It has to be. All of it. Thiago mentioned it's capable of controlling me and influencing my emotions. But how far does that influence extend? When Adam implanted Emily, he attempted to trigger coherent speech. That was a failure. Or so I thought. For the implant to be affecting me, to the point someone else can control my emotions, is an outcome I never even considered.

"Where is he?" I try to focus. Change the subject back to what I want. To fight his influence. How am I supposed to battle against something so far beyond my control? Thiago is tapped into the implant in my head. He's manipulating me. I let that sink in, the gravity of this entire situation. It means I'm not in control. I hate not being in control. I have to fight it. With everything I have. "Where's Adam?"

"He is indisposed at the moment." Thiago sets the tablet onto the bureau by the door. Across the room. Away from where I can see it. Then he laughs. "Alive and unharmed. We have him kept in a different room."

"Why the restraints? Why drug me? Why the fuck do any of this?"

"Relax. All safety precautions, I assure you. Nothing personal."

"Don't pretend you care about my safety."

"I don't." He folds his arms. "I was referring to *my* safety."

"Is Adam restrained too?" The question comes out mocking. That someone else is imprisoning my husband triggers a possessive jealousy. Not in the sense that I care what happens to him, but because I want to be the one to inflict pain. I want to be the first one at him. Possibly even the one to end him. The point is, it should be my decision to make.

"No. He's sleeping."

"You mean you drugged him."

Thiago's expression suggests that he did. This, he accompanies by a slight shrug, but gives no verbal acknowledgement. "He has no idea what's going on. We took him by surprise. It will be quite some time before he regains consciousness."

"Why?" I repeat. Not that I expect to receive an honest answer. Thiago seems to enjoy toying with me. Whatever his plan is, he isn't about to give it away. He wants to drag this out. "Why are you doing this?"

He studies me. Silent. Too silent. Is this the look of a psychopath? Or am I the psychopath? Maybe we all are. "Get some rest, Katherine. We have a long day ahead of us tomorrow." He pauses for a moment. "You will be safe in here."

What an odd thing to say. I'll be safe in here, but I can't leave. Without further explanation, he turns away from me, collects the tablet, and flicks the lights off. Then he disappears from the room. I lie still, in complete darkness. Well, not completely still. Twisting my arms in the restraints. Twisting and turning. Searching for any chance the leather might give so I can loosen it somehow. Maybe get one hand free. One hand free means freedom — once I have one out, I can undo the others.

I strain against the straps, pushing upward and out with all my strength, lifting invisible weights. The leather digs into my skin. I don't care if I hurt myself, because I *will* get free.

Maybe it's my imagination, or wishful thinking, but the straps have become looser. My forearms move easier. Keep working, that's all I have to do. What else is there? Sleep isn't going to happen. I'm wired and wide awake. Unwilling to make myself any more vulnerable, which is a laugh, considering my current predicament.

I keep working for hours, although the darkness has long since distorted my sense of time and space. I might as well be frozen and locked in a tiny box. That and the complete silence. No white noise to break up the emptiness. Only the creaking and shifting of my body on the bed.

The restraints are loose enough now that I can slide my arms through them, up to my hands. I just have to force one of those hands through. Only one. A little like giving birth, isn't it? Perseverance and then the big payoff. Endure the pain and discomfort and you'll be rewarded. I keep working at it, bending my arms at the weird angle required to pull my hands through.

When it finally happens, and I force my right hand through, I lie still, listening to my own heartbeat, willing myself to calm down. What if Thiago is monitoring all my vital signs? What if he's sitting in the room next door watching all of this? Maybe there's a night vision camera hidden somewhere in this room and he's monitoring every move I make.

I hate this. The paranoia. But I can't discount any possibility. After all, someone I thought I could trust has turned out to be the enemy. Hell, I still don't know to what extent he's fucked me over, or how much he's capable of controlling with that little device. I know he needs to be stopped. That my survival depends on it. That my sanity depends on it. I cannot live out the rest of my life wondering if I'm acting on my own accord or if someone is influencing my emotions.

Keep calm, Katherine.

I force myself to take deep, even breaths. Not to rush into freeing myself. If fluctuations in my vital signs trigger an alarm, if Thiago thinks I'm doing anything other than sleeping, or lying here, it means the end of my chance. He'll catch me, then drug me again.

I have to be prepared for anything.

Ten, maybe twenty minutes pass, I can't be sure how long, and nothing happens. I reach over to my left arm and undo the strap. Then I sit and free my legs.

That was too easy.

It shouldn't be this easy. If this is a test, I need to be on my guard. I turn so my legs dangle over the side of the bed, with my feet hovering right above the floor. Too quiet, too still, too easy to free myself. *Is* this a test? Or has he simply underestimated me? These things circle the inside of my head on a loop.

At the very least, I need a plan. It's time to take Thiago out of the equation. But how? I'll have to find a weapon. Also have to figure out where he is. Is he sleeping? Waiting in another room monitoring me? I'm in an unfamiliar house, so I have no idea how many rooms there are, or where anything is, which poses an additional challenge. I'll have no way of knowing if any hazards lurk beyond this bedroom door until they're right upon me. But I have to try, don't I?

Sitting here, waiting for something to happen to me isn't going to work. I can hide by the door and catch Thiago or Chloe unaware as they enter the room. And then what? Hope that I can overpower them? What am I thinking? Of course I can, in this man's body. I have a better chance while wearing this body than I would have with my own. It boils down to confidence. I have to believe I can do it. Thiago isn't that big. If I catch him by surprise, I can probably take him.

But I don't want to wait for something to happen. That's the riskiest course of action. If I'm going to go down, it will be fighting all the way. I cross the room and rest my ear against the door. Searching for sounds, anything that might indicate someone is nearby. I place my hand on the doorknob, waiting. Nerves churn my insides.

I turn the knob, in slow motion, hoping against hope that it won't make a sound, though by this time, my heart hammers so hard I can't hear anything else. The latch clicks, and the door pushes outward. I freeze again. Half expecting someone to grab me, for someone to jump out of the darkness, and as I linger in the open doorway, my muscles tense in anticipation. Still nothing. I force a calming breath. This is far too easy. Something is off.

I step into the hallway, closing the door behind me, and pause to listen again. No signs of anything or anyone. With my back pressed against the wall—at least nobody can sneak up behind me that way—I slowly ease my way down the hallway. It ends at a large, open kitchen. I sneak a look in the direction I came from. There's nobody around. The kitchen is illuminated by a series of night-lights. They cast an eerie yellow glow across the room. A sickly hue emphasized by shadows lurking in all the corners and crevices.

It's similar to the kitchen in the house Adam and I had owned together. Expansive, with lots of windows, except this one also has two large skylights. There's an island in the middle of it all, with a set of stools on one side. On top of the counter, a butcher block with knives in it and a large ceramic jug filled with cooking utensils. I find it amusing that a man who spends so little time in the kitchen has one filled with so many *details*. Along the wall, a large stainless-steel refrigerator with the freezer on the bottom. Matching stove with a glass cooktop. A set of ceramic canisters on the counter next to that, the kind that might hold flour, sugar, or other dried goods.

I pull a knife from the butcher block and hold it at my side. Not too big, not too small, but capable of doing serious damage if I want it to. I cross the room, past a heavy wooden table. It's long enough for four chairs along either side. On the far wall, a glass sliding door that looks out into the backyard. I want to hate it, but I don't. It's very isolating, yes, but in a way it's also serene and peaceful.

"I didn't think that would hold you."

My stomach rockets up my throat. I didn't hear Thiago's approach. No creaking floorboards in this house. He moved with the stealth of a feline stalking prey. "And I thought that was a little too easy. What do you have planned?"

"It's not something I can explain right now. You must understand, Kat, there *is* a plan in place, and it *will* benefit you. You have a role to play, but it is not yet time."

He called me Kat. Chloe is the only one who does that. Thiago has always opted for the much more formal Katherine, just as Adam did. Just as everyone else always did. Is this an attempt to throw me off my guard? Faint nausea tickles the back of my throat, but it seems to be the result of nerves rather than the need to be physically ill. I still have my back to him. An uncomfortable tingle creeps across my skin and sprouts gooseflesh all over my body. I have to distract him. To keep him from attacking. "You drugged me and strapped me to a bed. I fail to see how that benefits me."

"We don't want you to do anything rash or impulsive."

None of this makes any sense. The contradicting statements. What is his angle? He's the enemy now. He has betrayed my trust. No matter how precarious it was to begin with, it had existed. I turned to him for help, feeling that he cared, that we shared a bond in the past. That he helped me before. I can't have misjudged him so severely, can I?

I sense rather than hear or feel that he's moved closer. Is there a syringe hidden in one of his hands? Maybe he plans to overpower me. Or is he simply hoping he can reason with me? I don't care. And I don't hesitate any longer. With speed and reflexes that surprise even me, I whip around and bury the knife in Thiago's abdomen. Even in the dim light of the room, the shock in his expression registers loud and clear. How could he not have anticipated that?

Rather than let go of the handle, with all my strength, I bury it deeper and slice upward, toward his ribcage. He doesn't scream or cry out, but he opens his mouth, and a strained, breathy sound comes out. Almost like the wind has been knocked out of him. He clamps both his hands over mine. His palms are cold and damp and lack the strength or coordination to stop my attack. He staggers backward into the table.

"What, you don't have anything else to say?" I cock my head to the side, stunned that watching him suffer brings no joy — no feeling whatsoever. It's almost like watching a movie where you don't connect with any of the characters. "See, the thing about me, Thiago, is I've never appreciated being toyed with. And while I might not always acknowledge them, I remember *every* slight. Every attempt to manipulate or undermine." I move closer to him.

"Katherine…" It comes out sounding strained and choked as he struggles to find his voice.

"Even the so-called little things. The sometimes-subtle things that we women learn to brush off. Such as other people assuming we aren't capable of something without even bothering to find out if we are or not. Do you know what that's like? How about when you're called a partner but instead you're treated like an intern?" I pull the knife from his stomach. But I'm not yet ready to give up my weapon. Thiago immediately reaches down and presses his hands into the wound. He sinks to his knees and wobbles like he might pass out. I grab a handful of his hair and hold his head upright.

"You know what I really hate, though? What I absolutely despise more than anything? Is being told how I'm supposed to feel or how I'm supposed to act. I have no desire to be the puppet for your little plan. I no longer care to find out what that plan is. I'm sick of doing what everybody else wants. I'm going to do what *I* want."

There's no remorse when I slam his head against the edge of the table. The impact is hard enough to knock him unconscious. I let his body slide to the floor and he falls, slumped over. He's still breathing. Moaning lightly. Will he bleed out and die before he ever regains consciousness? Or will he wake in excruciating pain? It doesn't matter to me. I crouch next to him. In the low light, it's difficult to judge how fast he's bleeding. It probably won't take long.

"I thought we were friends," I whisper. Then stand. Still without remorse. Maybe Thiago has shut off whatever it is in my brain that controls empathy. Or maybe the operation itself has turned me into a psychopath. It probably would have been smarter to preserve his life, so I could at least find out what controls what. There's always Chloe.

Speaking of Chloe…I have no idea where she is or what her role is.

I find a light switch and flip it on, figuring Thiago was the biggest threat and I've already taken him off the playing field, so why not be able to see what I'm doing. It really is a beautiful house. Maple floors and trim. Cream-colored walls. With all the windows, the lighting during the day must be phenomenal. Adam spared no expense with furniture or décor. Yet, despite its beauty, it doesn't have the feel of a home. It's a photo spread in an interior design magazine. A little too set up. Too perfect. Not lived in enough.

The plan, as I understood it originally, was for me to live here with him. Obviously, that hasn't happened. Lies and deception brought me to where I am now. The question is, where do I want to take it from here? I haven't really thought this through. I haven't thought much beyond finding Adam and confronting him. Now, supposedly, he's somewhere in this house. Incapacitated. Well, if Thiago is to be believed. Surprisingly, this isn't as thrilling a prospect as I once expected it to be. The thought of cornering Adam like a caged little rat and forcing a confession from him has lost some of its luster. He'll have to pay. But in a way that truly forces him to understand.

"Kat?" Chloe halts in her tracks at the end of the hallway. "Where…where's Thiago?" She glances at the knife still clutched in my hand. It's smeared with blood. Her attention darts between it and my face and the room behind me.

I stare back at her. Trying to decipher her intentions. Impossible to do as twisted up as I am right now.

"What's going on?" She backs up a step. Seems to shrink away from me. Cautious but calm. Maybe a little nervous.

"Why don't you tell me? Because to be honest, I'm a little ticked off right now. And I think it's about time somebody starts giving me answers."

"Where's Thiago?"

"Bleeding out on the dining room floor. And unless you want to join him, I suggest you let me ask the questions."

Chloe gets this pinched, panicked expression, and when she speaks, the words race out at a frenetic pace. "Fine. I will answer any and all questions you have, as honestly as I can. I promise you that. I owe you that. No, *we both* owe you that. But you need to let me help him first. Jesus, Kat, you can't leave him there to die." She pushes past me, and I'm once again confused and overwhelmed by conflicting emotions. Well, not precisely emotions that I *am* feeling. More like things I *should be* feeling. I remember back to all the times Chloe cared for me, particularly when I was sick and weak. Right near the end. How she defended me when Adam made questionable decisions. Had that all been an elaborate act? Because none of this makes any sense. I don't detect any hostility with Chloe—not even really with Thiago, although I did feel he was dangerous. Or potentially dangerous. What doesn't add up is motivation.

Nothing adds up. Not even my lack of feeling.

I follow her into the dining room. Thiago is semi-conscious now. His breathing shallow. His skin pale and moist. Chloe already has his t-shirt torn open and a dishtowel pressed against the wound.

"He'll probably die. The wound is deep. I think I may have pierced the liver, but I suppose time will tell. He's already lost a significant amount of blood. Can't you see he's in shock?"

"Not now, Kat," she snaps. "He cannot die. Hold this in place while I get some bandages." She pauses and looks at me with a heavy dose of disdain. Borderline hostility. "You can put the fucking knife down now, you know."

"No." She can try all she wants, but I will not be intimidated. I'm not ready to relinquish my weapon, either. I do, however, hold the cloth to Thiago's wound as she asked, fully aware of the irony of the situation, that I caused this injury and now I'm entrusted with helping to care for him. Knowing that he's probably going to die. Still, I do it. I obey her command without questioning why I'm doing it. Perhaps the aspiring doctor in me is still buried inside the psychopath. The doctor who can do no harm unto others. Ha.

Chloe hurries from the room. Thiago is unconscious again and bleeding heavily, and after a minute or so, the cloth is almost completely saturated. I feel the steady pulse of blood flowing out beneath my fingertips. At this rate, he isn't going to make it. Then Chloe returns clutching an armful of bandages and other medical supplies.

"Get out of the way." She shoves her way around me, then hovers over Thiago, her eyes tearing up, her voice with a softer lilt. "I'm going to stitch you up." Then she's working, with the same fervor and determination as any other ER professional. It is, after all, this precise section of the hospital Adam recruited her from.

She gets about halfway through stitching the wound when Thiago stirs, his eyelids fluttering to life, and a weak moan escapes his lips. "It's okay. You're going to be okay," she says.

Thiago's eyes are glassy and unfocused. His color ashen. He isn't one hundred percent with us. He isn't fully aware.

I watch with detached interest. Darkness growing within me. The seeds of mistrust have long been sewn, and this is the aftermath. I can't take any more chances.

These two, regardless of what they've done for me in the past—they're not people I can trust now. They aren't my friends. They'll never be my friends. If I allow this to go on, any of it, without taking the upper hand, I run the risk of falling into the same traps I've fallen into already. More people to control my life. Even without emotion, I know I'm sick of others dictating the course of my life. It's time to put a stop to this. All these thoughts swirl around, creating the perfect storm before it implants into the forefront of my mind.

It's time to control my own destiny.

Time to be free.

I react. To some primal instinct that lurks deep within. It isn't driven by emotion—it seems that well is dry. I reach around and slice across Chloe's throat. She stiffens and there's a delayed reaction, where she's confused and hasn't realized what I've done at first.

I meet Thiago's eyes just as she starts choking and clutching at her neck. He's awake and aware enough to know what I've done. Fear. Anguish. All these things materialize in his expression. He shakes his head from side to side, slowly, as if that will stop what I've done. As if it will undo any of this.

Chloe has stopped mid-stitch, and blood still seeps out of his open wound in a slow but steady flow. Hers gushes from beneath her fingers and drips down the front of her shirt, onto the floor, onto Thiago. It occurs to me, as I watch them die, that these two have a much stronger bond than I first gathered. I sense she cares for him deeply. Maybe even loves him. At the very least, years of working and possibly conspiring with each other have pulled them together. Where, then, do I fit in all this mess? Are they friend or enemy to me?

"Well, this is unexpected." His voice slices right through me. Halts time. Leaves me open, bleeding and vulnerable as the two on the floor in front of me. Maybe I'm hallucinating or listening though a filter. I expected a different reaction, to hearing his voice again. That I'd jump into action and attack, or at least hurl some witty one liner at him. Instead, I freeze. Let the chill of the moment crawl slowly over me. Let it consume me. Adam. Alive, in the flesh and unharmed, standing right before me. Not drugged and locked in a room. And seemingly in command of the entire situation.

He has the audacity to smile at me. "My, my, you've had quite the adventure, Katherine. So good to finally see you. And welcome home."

CHAPTER THIRTY-EIGHT

I would have every right to attack considering what he's done. I should. But I don't. Instead, I allow him to lead me back down the hallway and into what appears to be an exam room. He gestures toward a chair and I sit, just like a puppet This man, staring me in the face. This monster, staring at my *other* face. The face that is me but at the same time isn't me. And Adam, who is nothing more than the man who made this body mine. No longer my husband. Little more than a stranger, and yet I know him inside out. No feelings. Devoid of emotions like love or lust or comfort.

I am sitting in an exam room, on something that resembles a dentist's chair, while Adam circles me slowly. Poking and prodding. Shining a light in my eyes. Testing my reflexes. Blood pressure, heart rate, temperature. All the things your doctor usually tests during a routine exam. And I sit there and allow it to happen.

Funny, I imagined myself snuffing out his life. Of storming into this house like a soldier straight from hell, delivering a bloody valentine on the other end of a knife or an axe — heck, it didn't really matter how or with what. The point is, I held onto that. Clung to it. Fantasized about it. And now? Now that I'm faced with it, I'm frozen by indecision. I don't feel like it. What changed?

"Remarkable." He's said that word multiple times now. Like he can't believe his own experiment is a success. Or he can't believe I survived and I'm sitting here in front of him. Was he expecting me to self-destruct?

"Knock it off, Adam. This charade of yours is nauseating."

He chuckles, unaffected, and brushes me off like he always has. "There's no doubt my Katherine is in there."

"I'm not *your* anything."

"You will always be *mine*." These are not the words of one lover to another. They're a declaration of ownership. I am property. Or something that closely equates it.

Irritation ripples right beneath the surface of my consciousness. Dulled, somehow, and kept inert by an invisible barrier. Is this the result of Adam's control? Is he monitoring my emotions? Working to keep them under control. Because I want to be angry. I want to lash out like I did when Thiago first brought me here, when I was strapped in place and thrashing about like a captured wild animal. Whatever he tapped into at that time, it's out of reach, and I sit here, numb, frustrated—but not frustrated enough for action—watching him.

"I need answers, Adam."

His look in return is bland, and maybe a little soulless. "I'm not sure what you want from me. The host body you chose was compromised. I went with the optimal replacement."

"A fucking *man*."

"Mm, yes, that part wasn't ideal, but let's face it, Katherine, you and I—our entire marriage—was over long ago. Long before you became ill."

"What does our marriage have to do with anything? Just because our marriage may have been…troubled, it doesn't mean you get to decide, to just *decide* to put me in a man's body. That's not the same as choosing another host. There were three other women to choose from. Why a fucking man? I'm not a man. I'll never feel completely comfortable in this skin. You've made me a prisoner in this body." My words don't have the conviction I desire. Not enough of a fire to scorch him. Maybe he's flameproof. Maybe I am the equivalent of a wet match.

"Oh, come on. You were ready to die. What does it matter?"

Is he deliberately trying to bait me? Here he is, saying all these awful things to me, while I float in a void of no feeling. Knowing perfectly well I should be feeling something, that anger should be surging through me. Logically I know all these things too, yet the lack of emotion inside me keeps me detached. It may as well be happening to another person. "You're sick."

He studies me, silent. Adam has never been one for confrontation. If you push back hard enough, he always relents, in order to avoid conflict. Then when you aren't looking, he'll do whatever the hell he wants anyway. "All I've ever desired was to help you, Katherine."

He is never going to see my perspective. Empathy, putting himself in the other person's shoes, has never been a trait that belong to Adam. In other words, I'm not going to get him to feel any remorse. If he apologizes, it will be empty. Void of meaning. He'll simply do it to shut me up and get me off his case. So maybe I need to beat him at his own game. Placate him. Then, when *he* isn't expecting it, I'll go in for the kill.

I turn away from him. Arms folded. "Well. I guess it doesn't matter." I can almost feel the relief coming off him. That I'm not going to continue this confrontation. "What's happened has already happened. I can't change it."

Am I giving in too easy to be believable? I glance at him. No, I don't think so. Old Katherine would have done the same. I spent a great deal of our marriage projecting the illusion that I was giving in, much the same as Adam had. The only difference being I hold grudges. I don't forget perceived slights. Whereas Adam thinks nobody notices what he's doing. Right now, I might not be able to summon the emotion to react to my predicament, but logically I know right from wrong. I know what he's done is beyond unforgivable. That the cavalier way in which he brushes off my worries and fears like they mean nothing at all are signs of completely narcissistic behavior. None of which should be allowed to continue unchecked.

But for now, I will play along. Feign compliance.

"I'm glad you see it that way." I can't tell from his tone if he believes me or not. He doesn't sound skeptical. Still…one can't be too careful. I'll have to sneak in the occasional barb.

"What else can I do?" I want there to be an edge to my tone, but I can't produce it. Whatever he's controlling is also keeping me pacified. It's time to figure out what he is able to do with the implant. How far he can go with it. How precise. "That said, I do have questions. And I'd appreciate honest answers."

"That's reasonable to expect." He pulls a stool from underneath the counter and sits on it. "What is it you'd like to know?"

"About the implant, first and foremost. I need to know what you can do with it. I want to know how it works."

He shows signs of wanting to squirm, in the way that the body subconsciously moves away from things that make us uncomfortable or that we fear. It's little more than a twitch. But enough that I notice it. I'll have to be careful how I approach this.

"I'm just curious." I shrug. "When we first used it in Emily, you kind of glossed over the full range of capabilities. You introduced it as a way to stimulate brain activity. With the bonus of being able to monitor the immune system. Clearly there is more to it than that."

"True. You are correct. It has the capability of controlling a range of bodily functions. The technology has been adapted to deliver electric current to the targeted location in the brain, and they are able to communicate back and forth."

"So that energy current could control a range of emotions. Stimulate anger perhaps. Or dry up emotions altogether. What you've been doing with me, for example." His face flushes, and there's a sharp intake of breath as he opens his mouth to rebut. I brace myself for it, but he just sits there with his lips hanging open. Speechless? How he can be surprised that I've figured out this much, that I know he's been tweaking my emotions? That boggles the mind. Whether it's arrogance or that he's underestimated me, I'll probably never know for sure. I force a smile. It stretches uncomfortably and meets with resistance from all my facial muscles. "I understand. This is cutting edge technology. You said so yourself. It only makes sense that you would test all its capabilities. I would have done the same."

His posture relaxes. It is subtle in movement, but enough to signal his relief. I hope I can convince him I'm not angry he's been experimenting on me. Rather, I'm speaking to him as a colleague. An *understanding* colleague. "I'm glad you see it that way."

"I *am* a little bothered that you didn't include me more in the planning stages of this. You thrust it on me with Emily, but you never did show me how it worked. You always used to say we were partners and yet you completely cut me out of this line of research. Why is that?"

"It wasn't a deliberate thing—"

"Relax. I'm not trying to argue. I'm simply trying to appeal to your sensibilities. I have a proposition." He's so easy to manipulate. Even in this body, even with a lack of emotion, I still know which words to say to appeal to his ego. And his ego takes the bait every time.

"What sort of proposition?"

"My cooperation in exchange for information." It's much easier to lie without emotion interfering. I don't feel any guilt or remorse or even a hint of nervousness. "In other words, I will allow you to continue to conduct experiments. To use me toward your research. All I ask in return, is that you share your research. That you show me how all this works. It's the least you can do to make up for putting me in this body. I might even forgive you."

"That sounds…reasonable." He seems reluctant to agree. But he's also intelligent enough to know that I've backed him into a corner. He can force experimentation against my will, but the results will be too narrow. A cooperative test subject, on the other hand, has infinite possibilities.

"I'm glad you see it that way. I think we'll make great partners, Adam. But, obviously, as partners, we need to be on the same page first. Don't you agree?" I want so desperately to enjoy this, but however he's controlling me makes it impossible. "Starting with the device, of course. This nano-chip that's part of the implant. How does it work?"

"Well, essentially it has the ability to store information and then in turn relay that information to specific regions of the brain. The chip has a microscopic — for lack of a better word — antenna built into it."

I've already learned most of this from Thiago, but at least I've got him talking. "What is the range of physical space required to control it?"

"Not far. Similar, in fact, to the range of a Wi-Fi hotspot. That said, it is designed for practicality. In other words, a physician can pre-program what he wants the chip to control, and the device will continue to deliver that therapy until it is programmed to do something else."

"What did you program with me?"

There's a glossy sheen on his forehead. On his upper lip. Perspiration. His pupils have dilated. "I didn't know how you would react to your new…situation. And once I realized that I wasn't going to be there to monitor every little thing that happened after your awakening, I had to give you the optimal chance for survival. The safest way to do that was to tone down your emotional response. To keep stress levels at a minimum. To keep you from harming yourself. That tempered response allowed your body time to heal and adapt."

It also took away my ability to feel much of anything. There has been some anger, but not nearly as much as would be justified. Mostly I've been numb.

Hearing him admit this out loud is somewhat of a shock. Sort of how I imagine it to be when a spouse admits they've been cheating. A difference between suspecting and knowing because you're hearing the words with your own ears. It makes it real. Irrefutable. You can't hide from it anymore. And yet, without the interference from an emotional response, I'm able to formulate a clear picture of what's going on.

"Interesting. And I suppose it's still on the same setting? Except for when Thiago was fiddling with it. So much anger surged through me I thought I might explode."

"Actually, all he did was release your ability to process emotions again. Unfortunately, it wasn't done gradually, and it led to an overload. It was a side effect we hadn't anticipated." He seems more relaxed now. Smug, even. That same excitement over his research I'd once been attracted to now turns my stomach. It makes me want to resent him. If I could even feel such a thing anymore. I wonder how Adam would respond to having one of those little transmitters shoved into his brain. It's only fair, isn't it?

"It was quite…unpleasant." I don't elaborate because something else distracts me. Knowing what I want to do comes suddenly. Gnaws at the protective coating between emotion and no emotion. The thought sticks in a place where I can't forget it. But I have to set it aside. Store it in that compartment for later, because there's a natural order of things and I haven't yet arrived at that part of the script. "Now, please tell me that when the time comes, you're not going to strap me into that bed again."

"I know you might not believe it, but that was for your protection. I have no plans to restrain you again. As long as you remain reasonable."

What an odd choice of words. *Reasonable.* "Thiago said strapping me in had been for his protection not mine."

"He had been instructed to provoke you. To try and spark an emotional response and see how it worked. It was purely an act, by the way."

I'm not so sure. Maybe it was partially an act, but I sensed real hostility in him. Saw it in his eyes.

Thiago. In the short time Adam and I have been talking, I've already forgotten what I did to him. Had I been too impulsive in attacking him? Or Chloe? Remorse is still elusive. The product of emotion I don't have. And Adam is no better. We simply left the room. Left the two of them lying there, bleeding out on the floor.

"Speaking of, do you think he's dead yet?" There was a time when I would've shown a little more respect for human life, but those days are far behind me.

"If not yet, then soon. Although I do wish you'd shown some restraint. Thiago was an invaluable source of knowledge." So, the loss of knowledge is more important than the loss of life. He doesn't express any worry over this man who's been under his employ for years. Little more than indifference that I've snuffed out that flame without a second thought. He shrugs. "And Chloe, well, I suppose she's worn out her usefulness now that you're here."

"He was plotting against you, you know. Both of them were. I did you a favor." Or had that also been part of Adam's plan? Giving me the illusion Thiago and Chloe were on my side, that they were out to get him, when in reality, they were still very much under his influence.

"Indeed."

Maybe he's just humoring me.

Two can play at that game. "I suppose we should clean up the mess. Before it stains that beautiful hardwood floor."

***

While Adam retreats to the garage to find tarps and industrial cleaning supplies, I venture back to the dining room. Both Chloe and Thiago have succumbed to their injuries. The top half of her body rests on his, and he's pulled her into a loose embrace. Blood pools out around them in a wide puddle on the floor. Dark, crimson. Still I feel nothing.

Life is so fragile. So fleeting. We're all here, and we fight so hard just to survive, and yet all of it can be snuffed out in a single moment. Just like when I took the lives of Theresa and Billy.

There's something surreal and impersonal about the human body after death. Once the brain shuts off, and everything that makes us who we are ceases to exist, there is nothing left but inert flesh. Kind of like meat in a butcher shop.

But this is meat with a face. A face I should feel some attachment to. It's eerie; this silent stillness. Vacant eyes staring out at you, not seeing you or reacting. Part of me wants to turn away. The part I listen to wants something else.

Thiago, let's hope you can do me one last solid.

I shove Chloe's arm out of the way, lightning quick, so I don't have to feel her cooling flesh any longer than necessary, and grimace as I reach into Thiago's pocket. There's obviously no smell yet, but it doesn't stop the crawling sweat or the twinge of queasiness in my gut. My fingers close around the syringe, and I say a silent thank you to the corpse on the floor in front of me. It doesn't make any difference that he likely planned to use it on me. That despite the loss of life, I acted in self-defense. It doesn't make my crime any less despicable.

Still, as master of my own destiny from here on out, this find is necessary to my survival. A key part of my newly hatched plan. Incapacitating Adam will only be a start, but at least I won't need to search the house for his medical supplies. I stow it carefully in my pocket, casting a quick glance around the room the be sure Adam hasn't sneaked up on me, that he hasn't seen me take it. No guilt or nervousness to trip me up. My face, a mask. I know also, deep inside, that my plan is the best course of action. There will be no easy way out for Adam. He doesn't deserve to just end. He'll spend the rest of his natural life paying for it. The longer it's drawn out, the better.

When I do hear his approach, accompanied by the rustle of a plastic tarp and deep, clomping footsteps, I stand and face him. Secure that he is dropping his guard, little by little. I can't drop mine for even a single second.

"They've both expired." My hands are covered in blood, as are the bottoms of my bare feet. I'm still standing in the puddle of blood. It's squished up between my toes and become tacky. I feel like a child caught standing in the middle of a great mess. "I checked."

"Well, that will make things easier." He sets the items on the kitchen counter. "Help me move the table and chairs out of the way. We'll lie the tarp out and put them both on it. Since I only have one tarp."

"Well, then let's get started."

We move the table and chairs to the far corner of the room and spread the tarp on the floor. Then Adam picks up Thiago under the arms and I grab his ankles and we move him to the tarp. Followed by Chloe, then we tuck the tarp around them tight and roll them up in it. Adam hands me a roll of duct tape and I make several passes around the end to seal it up while he does the same on the other end, until it looks like a gigantic, blue plastic sausage. He opens the back door and helps me drag the bodies outside onto the back porch.

"We'll bury them in the backyard later. First, let's clean up the blood before it dries."

It takes the better part of the day to clean up the blood then dig a hole at the edge of the woods to bury them in. Adam and I work in relative silence. A tentative peace established between us. Not to be mistaken for trust. Not to be mistaken for husband and wife. Just two people covering up a crime. When it's done, he pats me on the shoulder like I'm an old friend, or a child.

"I'll show you where the shower is, so you can get cleaned up. I'm sure I have some clothes here that will fit you."

CHAPTER THIRTY-NINE

Adam has a theory. That emotion is the root cause of any conflict. A key motivator. If you keep it out of the equation, the subject is agreeable. Pliable. Perhaps that's why he welcomes me back into the fold so readily. All the while, unaware of what is going on inside me. Unaware of what I know to be the real, unfiltered truth. Which is that without the interference or the influence of certain emotions, the brain is capable of far more ruthless and calculating actions than he can imagine. Without remorse or empathy, those actions have no boundaries.

I keep these things to myself. Operate as an eager student, willing to catch up on everything I've missed. All the while allowing my body and mind to be subjected to countless tests. These I endure with an infinite well of patience. After all, I have time. Plenty of time.

Adam adjusts settings on the implant chip using the same tablet Thiago had used. "Here, I can select where I want to work. This one will affect how you process pain." He shows me the screen. On the top half is a topographical line drawing of the brain on a black background. He selects the appropriate region, and it zooms in to the graphic. On the bottom of the screen are wavelength frequencies, with each line appearing in a different color. Below that, a text field. "Once you've selected a specific region, a new dialog box will open. From there, you can adjust the levels, depending on the desired effect."

"And you can have multiple things programmed at once, obviously."

He looks at me, startled. "Well, yes. Of course. It would be dangerous to suddenly stop one therapy. Gradual adjustments are always the safest route. But yes, having multiple therapies going at the same time is possible."

"I see."

I remember back when I was ill and contemplating suicide, how they'd discovered my stash and it had conveniently disappeared. But now I have a cool head and I like to think I learned from my mistakes. I have to be one step ahead. Always thinking. So, I keep the syringe I took from Thiago's pocket with me at all times. He can't find out I have it. And I have to continue to earn Adam's trust. To make him believe I am devoted to his cause. Because the more I think about it, the more he needs to be taken out of the equation. He needs to lose everything and pay for what he's done. I'm the only one capable of that.

***

Lying in bed at night, wide awake and free of any distractions, I obsess about when I am going to carry out my plan. I'm not being impatient. Because impatience is a breeding ground for mistakes and I've been so careful thus far. On the other hand, waiting too long means more opportunity for things to go wrong. It's too easy to become complacent. I've been paying close attention to Adam's habits. Monitoring every little thing and filing it away in the back of my mind. The time is tonight. The time is now.

I climb out of bed, wary of creaking floorboards, or anything else that might alert Adam that I'm awake and out of my room. I ease down the hallway, with my back to the wall, taking slow, easy steps toward Adam's bedroom. What if he locked it? That would make this difficult. Plan B would mean catching him unaware at some point during the day. More opportunity for mistakes that way, more chance that he'll fight back. It's so much easier to take care of it while he's already sleeping.

The door is unlocked. I turn the knob in slow motion, pausing until I'm confident he hasn't woken. I recognize the long, drawn out breaths of sleep. And I step inside. Administer the dose without Adam so much as stirring. I wait a couple of minutes to be sure the drug has entered his bloodstream. Since he's already sleeping, it will be difficult to tell when it takes effect.

I drag him out of the bed, down the hallway, and into the fully equipped lab. There's no way a person would be able to sleep through this. I'm sweating from the exertion, but pleased with myself for getting this part right. My muscles burn. He's much heavier than Theresa had been — probably outweighs her by a good fifty or sixty pounds, and I can't quite lift him. Yet somehow, I manage to get him onto the operating table. The room has essentially the same setup as the old lab, but on a smaller scale.

There is much to prepare, but I have a very limited window of time before he comes to—maybe twenty-five minutes to a half-hour, so it's best to set up intravenously administered anesthesia first. Make sure he stays under. Adam—or perhaps Chloe—had kept a neat, organized system. Everything labelled. Everything one needs for say, a minor surgery, all within reach.

It has been quite some time since I've set up an IV or prepped a patient for surgery, and I certainly haven't done that in this body, with these fingers, but somehow, I don't miss a beat. I turn Adam on his side and shave his entire head. Not wasting any time, I clean off the remaining hair and set up the harness on his head. I know this surgery by heart. Performed it in tandem with Adam countless times.

He showed me where he keeps the case with all the transmitters. There are five of them left. All fitted with nanochips and easily programmable. The software Thiago designed is idiot proof. Each is encoded with its own serial number, so once it is activated, you can be sure you're adjusting the one you want.

The entire surgery, from drilling the hole in his skull to installing the electrode, and then testing to see if it's sending and receiving signals, takes just under four hours.

***

I keep Adam heavily sedated as he recovers from the surgery. After about a week, I finally ease him off the anesthesia, and he lies in the bed, in restraints, while I sit across the room waiting for him to regain consciousness. I've spent considerable time going through the programming and getting to know what each of the settings are. There are adjustments to be made. Tests to run. All in the name of science.

I want to enjoy this to the fullest, to prolong each second and savor the taste. Adam begins to stir. Followed by increased eye movement beneath closed lids, and eventually the struggle to open them. Then, when they do open, his eyes stare right through me. Maybe he can't quite focus yet. I recognize the confusion associated with coming out of an anesthesia-induced slumber — it's something I've felt countless times in the past. It takes a while for your mind to catch up with the world.

"Wakey, wakey, my love." I pull a chair up to the bed and sit beside him. This face needs to be the first thing he sees. This voice, the first thing he hears.

First comes recognition. Then, realization. Who I am and who has the upper hand in this situation.

"Katherine…what…what have you done?" Funny that he's already concluded that I've *done* something. His voice is groggy and still has the rasp of recent sleep. The network of lines in his forehead and between his eyes grows more pronounced. I can almost see the lights coming on inside him.

He tries to move. Writhes in his restraints. More realization.

"You really shouldn't strain yourself. You're still in recovery."

"What did you do?" His face turns red from the exertion of trying to free himself.

"Well, if you won't calm down on your own, maybe I'll have to take matters into my own hands." I pick up the tablet and wink at him. "Now, it's been quite some time since I've performed this procedure." I pause and stretch my lips into a mocking grimace. "I was a bit rusty at first, but once I got in there and really started tinkering around, well. It's a bit like riding a bicycle. You never really forget, do you? Now, to see if it worked or not."

"Katherine…"

I hold up a hand. "There's no need to thank me. This is medical technology at its finest, you said so yourself. I have to say, it was a little overwhelming at first, getting in here and seeing all these different settings. There are so many possible therapies. And you, dear husband, are in dire need of therapy."

Before he can respond, I make my first move. I enhance the sensitivity of his pain receptors. He immediately lets out a groan, and his entire body goes rigid, muscles contracted, teeth gritted, eyes squeezed shut in agony.

"Tell me, where does it hurt?"

"Every…where…" Sweat rolls across his skin. Spittle collects at the corners of his mouth. His expression freezes in a pain-induced rictus, and as I adjust the frequency of each new wave, each incrementally more intense than the one before it, his entire body spasms.

"Don't forget to breathe, Dear." I release him from the pain and he collapses into the bed.

"Why…would you do this?"

"The fact that you even need to ask is astonishing to me. But then again, you've never been the type of person to pick up on subtleties or emotional cues. You've always been so wrapped up in what you wanted to see and your end results, that you never really stopped to consider what your test subject might be feeling."

He is calm, no doubt drifting in the euphoric sea of no pain, that magical state your mind places you in when intense pain suddenly ends. I remember back to my old body, plagued by frequent migraines, and the feeling that overtook me once the medication finally kicked in.

"You've made your point, Katherine." He says this with closed eyes. Completely relaxed. But with the same familiar arrogance lurking behind his words. Some things never change. "Now please, just stop this nonsense and release me."

"You're not in any position to be making demands." What to try next…there are too many possibilities. An endless combination. But I land on fear as the next logical direction, and amplify it, just a few notches above normal. Adam's eyes snap open. There's a spike in his pulse. A hitch in his breath. I slam my fist down on the table next to us, and it rattles the tray of instruments. Adam startles, his entire body stiffening again, and his arms and legs want to flail out, except they're tied down. I turn up the amplification. He's shaking now. A dark stain spreads across his crotch. He's pissed himself.

"Please," he whimpers.

I tilt my head to the side. Even in my own dulled emotional state, there's something profoundly satisfying in watching him suffer. "It doesn't feel so great when somebody's fucking with your mind, does it?"

He whimpers again. Tears leak from the corners of his eyes.

"Honestly, it's not about revenge." I lean back in the chair and study the tablet screen. "It's about what's right. And since we're being honest here, I've never really felt what you're doing to be right. Cutting-edge science will always push boundaries of what some feel to be safe or ethical. I get that. Experimenting on defenseless animals, for example. Or kidnapping people from the streets and explaining it away, as if they've got nothing of value to live for or nobody to love them. But who are you or I to decide these things? We are not gods. We don't speak for everyone."

"What do you want?" He weeps freely now, fear tempered and mixed with despair.

Bless Thiago for mapping every possible human feeling and programming them into this little device. I'm in complete awe of it.

"Interesting you should ask that, Adam. Because in the entire time we've been together, I don't think you ever truly cared about what I wanted. It was all about what you *thought* I wanted, or what you thought I *should* want, but you never paid close enough attention to listen to what I actually wanted." I adjust the sliders marked fear and despair, swapping their intensity levels. "How does it feel now?"

Instead of answering in words, he lets out a deep, chest-heaving sob.

"It's bad, isn't it?" I shake my head in mock pity and examine him closer. I haven't done much to adjust my own levels—it is simple enough to switch between the two transmitters on this device, which Thiago made nearly idiot-proof too—but I have changed some. Considering how things have been for me, I feel *something* now. Satisfaction. Maybe some amusement. On a small scale. "Could you describe it for me? No wait—let me guess. Kind of like you lost your job, totaled your car, your wife left you, *and* your dog died all at the same time. Am I right?" I grin at him, but he is far too caught up in his own emotional state to respond. "I'm pretty sure there's a country song out there that sums it all up nicely. Perhaps I'll find it for you sometime."

"Please…make it…stop." He chokes this out between cries, and I feel a sense of disappointment that none of this is genuine. Fully aware that I've manufactured this reaction synthetically. Still. There is something about seeing him reduced to a blubbering infant—something mesmerizing.

"I fully cooperated with you, didn't I? Every little test you wanted to run, I just lay back and took it. When it was me in that bed, you had a bottomless well filled with patience. Where is it now, I wonder? I have a lot to catch up on, and I'm sorry, but it just isn't the same being on that side of the clipboard." I point at him, even though he isn't paying attention.

"What…do you…want?"

It's the second time he asks this. I don't have a real answer, because in truth, I don't know what I want. I just knew what I don't want. Death is too easy. He needs to suffer to truly pay for all he's done.

"Honestly, Adam, I'm still trying to figure it all out. I didn't choose this situation, and I'm still very upset with you about that. It's the hand I've been dealt, though, so now I need to figure out where I go from here." I pause and watch him. He's still sniffling and hiccupping. "But I suppose that wasn't really what you were asking, was it, Adam? What you wanted to know isn't what *I* want, but what I want with *you*. What I'm going to *do* with you. Isn't that right?"

He still isn't answering.

"I suppose I'm trying to figure all that out as well. I mean, you have to be stopped. Receive a dose of your own medicine. But death is not the answer to this problem. It's too easy. Too predictable. See, I've at least thought about it that far."

"I'll take you down with me. Whatever you have planned, you'll be just as guilty."

"You're so smug, so sure of yourself, even now. I've done some terrible things, yes. Some of them unforgivable. But one could argue I wasn't in my right mind the entire time. You see, there are degrees of guilt, Adam. And yours is much higher." I tap the screen on the tablet. "And I just want you to know that I'm willing to sacrifice myself if that's what it takes to bring you down. But I don't think that's going to be necessary."

I adjust his levels to a nice, docile, better-than-doped-up state.

"Who's the smug one now?" He laughs bitterly. "My god, I will never get used to hearing that voice, but it's still the same biting tone you've always taken."

"Get used to it? How do you think *I* feel? I'm the one who has to live with it. You, well... *You* created this, sure." I gesture at my body. "In a way, you're responsible for everything that's gone wrong with it. And maybe a little bit of what's gone right, too. It really is a medical marvel, when you stop to think about it. The fact that you've done something no other person alive has done, is quite remarkable. It's a shame the world will have to go on without ever knowing what you've done."

I know I've struck a nerve with him. His ego can't handle the bruises, even if his pride doesn't allow him to admit it. He clenches his jaw and presses his lips into a thin, tight line, but he doesn't argue with me.

"No recognition. No awards. No accolades. Instead you'll be remembered as a monster."

"Just get it over with already," he snaps.

I chuckle, ignore him, and continue. "You'll always hold a special place in my mind for what you've done, even if the rest of the world is unable to see your contribution. It's amazing how medical science has progressed, though, isn't it? Particularly with regards to the brain. Shock therapy, lobotomies. Those aren't so far in our rearview mirror, are they? This device here, it's the best of all those worlds. Infinite possibilities. Why, I could even replicate a lobotomy if I wanted to."

I notice the spike in his pulse, although he doesn't produce a visible reaction. I smile at him.

"You might as well make yourself comfortable." I pat his knee then lean in and kiss him on the forehead. "This is going to be a long night for you."

I happen to glance at the tablet screen and there's a tab at the top of the program display I hadn't noticed before. *Other transmitters within range.* I click on it. An active transmitter. Which means there is someone else alive. Somewhere in this house. Who could it be?

I already know.

CHAPTER FORTY

I find her in the basement, in a set of finished rooms. It has a bedroom, a bathroom, and a small living area. All nicely decorated and comfortable. Yet at the same time, isolated and underground. Candy wrappers litter the floor, and amongst them, a plate with what appears to be dried blood on it. What on earth has he been feeding her? It never occurred to me to look down here before now.

He kept her as a prisoner. Emily. Charlotte. What am I supposed to call her now? I assumed she had been a casualty of the lab being abandoned, but now that I think about it, she's the one thing he wouldn't have given up on. He wouldn't have ended her life.

But this? This is not really living.

We stand across the room from each other, no hostility, no anger, really no emotion at all. Staring. It's almost as if she expects me to be here. That there's some natural order to this meeting.

"Ma…ma," she says. There's dried blood on her chin and spatters on her t-shirt.

How does she know who I am? I doubt Adam sat her down and explained what he did. Perhaps she recognizes me inside this skin. On an instinctual level. Her hair has grown to just past her shoulders, now concealing the surgery scars and the bald spots where no hair will grow again. Aside from the blood, she resembles a regular teenage girl in that respect, even down to the jeans and t shirt. Chloe must have selected clothing for her. Adam certainly doesn't have an eye for such details. Except, the shirt is inside out and backwards, with the tag sticking out prominently just below her neck.

"Yes, Darling." I hold out my arms to her, suddenly aware that despite our difficult past, we now share a common bond. A common enemy. Her lower lip quivers, and tears spill from her eyes. She runs to me and throws her arms around me into a tight embrace. Perhaps I'd been too quick to write her off as a waste of life, as inhuman. "It's okay now. I'm going to make him pay for what he's done to us. From now on, *we* are the masters of our own destiny."

As she clings to me and weeps, I feel tendrils of anger puncturing the veil of no emotion. Perhaps there's something left inside me after all. One thing is certain. I am no longer going to be manipulated by anyone. And this child will no longer live as a prisoner. She is not the monster.

***

Maybe I've taken it a step too far. Watching him suffer is supposed to make me feel vindicated. It's supposed to right a wrong. But the reality is, nothing will ever change for me unless I make the changes. And Adam will never truly feel remorseful.

By the time I'm finished with him, Adam is barely coherent. Barely responding. The door creaks open, reminding me that I am not alone in this endeavor.

"It's okay, Em. You can come inside." She enters, a docile little creature, shuffling, her head bowed slightly, and stands next to me. Adam moans, but his glossy, vacant stare isn't fixed on anything. The noises coming from his throat never form into words. Emily flinches and cowers behind me. Funny how the dynamic between us has changed. How I once loathed her, but now I'm comforting her. Considering building a life with her by my side. Both of us, survivors.

"He can't hurt you anymore."

She grasps onto my shoulder with both hands, still standing behind me.

"See?" I say. "He can't hurt anyone. And we can make him do whatever we want." I snap my fingers next to his head. He turns, in slow motion, toward the sound and makes a whiny, whimpering sound, like a wounded pup.

I've thought long and hard about how to punish him, how we can atone for some of the things that have been done. I know how to handle it, but it requires a failsafe. There's no way I am going to allow myself to be implicated in any of Adam's crimes. As far as the world is concerned, Katherine Powers is dead. But Adam is the slippery, backstabbing type who would've found a way to implicate me as Sean. He's already claimed he would bring me down with him.

So, I have to prevent that.

And it seems, so far, that I've accomplished phase one of that plan. Keep him from being able to communicate effectively. No coherent speech. No ability to write or type. The trick is to destroy the pathways between thought and speech, to really scramble things up in there. I'll have to test it out a bit more before we move on to phase two, but for now I'm reasonably sure he's unable to communicate.

I've created a drooling monster. Be patient, monitor the situation, that's all I have to do. And so, we wait. It lasts a few days, because I have to be sure. Is he faking? There must be no doubt in my mind that he isn't.

When it's time, I dress Emily in a clean pair of clothes. Kneel before her and catch her chin in my hand. "How would you like to help me take Daddy for a ride? To a place he can never hurt you or me again. Would you like that?"

I can't be one hundred percent certain that she understands everything I just said to her, but she's listening and fully focused on what I'm saying. When I finish, the corners of her mouth turn up into an almost-smile and she nods. And I know, then, that she does. That we're on the same side.

About the Author

JL Strange writes unsettling psychological horror with a sci-fi twist. She was born and raised on Cape Cod, Massachusetts and studied animation at Rhode Island School of Design. Telling stories became an obsession, although she still creates art whenever the mood strikes. A single mother with a newly empty nest and lover of all things outdoors, she's currently pursuing life's next adventure.

Read more at https://www.authorjlstrange.com/.